THE SENATOR'S WIFE

to: arel
julia gabriel
2019

THE SENATOR'S WIFE

JULIA GABRIEL

SERIF BOOKS

THE SENATOR'S WIFE

Published by Serif Books

The Senator's Wife was originally published in two volumes as *Drawing Lessons* and *Chiaroscuro.*

THE SENATOR'S WIFE

PART ONE: DRAWING LESSONS

1

"Come to dinner tomorrow. And bring your wedding gown."

Marie Witherspoon creased her forehead in puzzlement. Of course, she'd go to her best friend Nishi's house for dinner but ...

"My wedding gown? Why?" She put her cell phone on speaker and set it next to the textbook she'd been reading.

"We're going to need it. Just trust me."

Marie trusted Nishi more than anyone. In fact, Nishi might be the only person Marie truly trusted anymore. But Nishi was—in addition to being one of the top public relations professionals in Washington, DC—a well-known evil genius. Those two things might be related.

"Normally, you just ask me to bring beer or something," she countered. "You've never even seen my wedding dress."

In the silence she could hear Nishi rolling her eyes. "Well, I'd like to see it tomorrow. And you can bring beer, too. It goes great with curry barbeque."

"You know I'm a sucker for Imran's curry barbeque."

"That's why it's on the menu, sweetie. See you tomorrow."

NISHI AND IMRAN BHAT lived in a spacious, four-bedroom home in Ashburn, Virginia, an outer suburb of DC known for its acres of cookie-cutter tract housing, excellent public schools, and traffic-choked roadways. Local officials were fond of bragging that the town—more a collection of fiercely competing subdivisions, really—was home to both the Washington Redskins and more than seventy percent of the world's internet traffic. At times, it seemed as though all of Loudoun County was a giant vacuum cleaner sucking people by the thousands out of the city and inner suburbs and plopping them down in lovely hardwood- and granite-filled homes. Indeed, when Marie herself was in need of a new living situation five months ago, she rented an apartment in Ashburn, Virginia.

So it was a short drive to Nishi's house for Marie, a six-pack of chilled microbrew on the floor of her Honda and a white pouf of silk and lace on the seat next to her. Despite repeated texts to Nishi all day long, she still had no idea why Nishi wanted to see her gown.

She pulled into the driveway and parked behind Nishi's gleaming BMW SUV. *I'm probably about to be sweet-talked into loaning the dress to a client of hers for a photo shoot.* She'd be okay with that, she decided, as she rang the doorbell, then let herself in. *It's not like I need the dress or anything.*

The smell of burning incense hit her as soon as she stepped inside, causing her to wrinkle her nose. She'd never known Nishi and Imran to burn incense.

"Marie!" Nishi skittered into the foyer. "Let me take that for you," she said, looking at the pile of white fabric in Marie's arms.

"There's beer under here somewhere," Marie said. She followed Nishi into the soaring, two-story family room where Nishi unceremoniously dumped the wedding gown on a sofa.

"What's with the incense?" Marie asked.

"Atmosphere."

Marie was about to ask "atmosphere for what?" when her eyes were drawn upward, transfixed by the white paper cutouts of ... something—she couldn't tell what—tied to the ceiling fan and spinning gently in its wake.

"What on earth are those?" She blinked her eyes. She could get dizzy watching that. Or maybe it was the incense that was fogging her brain.

"It's Chinese funeral paper," Nishi answered matter-of-factly.

"Who passed away?" She was almost afraid to ask. Nishi had a large and far-flung family.

"Your marriage passed away. Five months ago. And I've sat by and patiently watched you mourn yourself into a deep, dark funk over the loss of your dickhead ex-husband—pardon my French—Representative Richard A. Macintyre of Pennsylvania. But the mourning period is officially over."

Yeah, Nishi had never liked Richard Macintyre, even apart from his status as unfaithful partner to her best friend. A part of her wished she lived in his district in western Pennsylvania so she could vote him out of office next time. She'd met Marie and Richard when his office hired the public relations firm Nishi worked for to provide the two of them with media training during his campaign for the U.S. House of Representatives. Nishi took an instant dislike to him.

Marie, on the other hand, became a fast friend, the two of them bonding over the similarities in their families. Marie was the daughter of a former U.S. Senator, Nishi the daughter of an Indian diplomat. Both understood the odd pressures that came with country over family.

"See?" Nishi pointed to the spinning paper. "There's your Lexus. The house in Great Falls. Your engagement ring—"

Marie had to laugh at the sight of that. What Nishi was calling an engagement ring looked more like a giant baby pacifier.

"Yeah well, artistic pursuits are not my bailiwick," Nishi said. "And there's the Capitol. In a traditional Chinese funeral, the mourners burn paper reproductions of items the deceased's soul will need in the afterlife."

"So we're holding a mock funeral for my marriage tonight? And who here is Chinese?" Marie was mildly amused by the idea, especially as long as it involved Imran's curry barbeque.

"We're incorporating all the best elements from several cultures' funeral traditions. And it's not a mock funeral, dear. It's going to be a *real* funeral."

Marie laughed at the joke. "We're burying my wedding gown in your backyard?"

Nishi snorted. "I don't want that thing in my backyard. We're not burying it. We're cremating it."

Marie's breath caught in her throat. "We can't *burn* my wedding dress. It's a waste. I could donate it to Goodwill so someone else—"

"Did it ever even occur to you to donate it before, oh say, right now?"

"Well, no. But I could. I spent a fortune on it."

Nishi leaned over the back of the sofa and fingered the dress. "This is real silk. Good. It'll burn. Synthetic fabrics just melt. Not that watching an entire wedding dress melt wouldn't be fun, but we're going to want ashes."

"Nish! I'm not burning it. I'll give it away."

Imran appeared in the doorway of the family room just then. "I believe it's bad luck to get married in a wedding dress from a failed union." Imran gently pried the six-pack of beer from Marie's white-knuckled fingers.

"It's not my fault the marriage failed," Marie cried. Well, her parents held a different opinion on that matter, but it wasn't even

Marie who had wanted the divorce. She had wanted the two of them to go to counseling, to try and work things out, to get Richard to give up Maya. That was what Marie had wanted.

Nishi slung an arm around Marie's shoulder and began leading her toward the kitchen. "Marie, no one is saying it was your fault. What we're saying is that it's time to move on."

Marie looked around Nishi's bright and cheery kitchen with its yellow walls and cherry cabinets. She felt tears coming on. "This is what I wanted. A nice house and two point five kids, a golden retriever and some goldfish. Just a nice, normal life."

Nishi was kind enough not to point out that one couldn't really have a normal life married to a member of Congress. Marie's own childhood had been nice, but not that normal.

"That's all I wanted." Tears began to sluice down her cheeks. Imran discreetly made himself scarce, slipping through the door to the outside deck, platter of spiced and marinated chicken in hand. "See? You have the perfect husband."

A loud hoot was heard from out on the deck.

"Thanks, Marie," Nishi said dryly. "He's going to lord that over me for the next month, at least."

Marie couldn't imagine Imran lording anything over his wife. Imran *was* perfect, or pretty darn near it, as far as Marie could tell. He was tall, dark and handsome, for starters. He was graceful and athletic, with an easy smile and sharp-as-tacks brain. He worked in IT for a large accounting firm and coached youth soccer, even though he and Nishi didn't have any children yet. And he was proud of Nishi's career and her success. Nishi would never be pressured to quit *her* job.

If that wasn't perfect, Marie didn't know what was.

Nishi popped the caps off three beers and handed one to Marie. "I don't think you wanted enough, actually. But that's what tonight is about. We're saying goodbye to what is gone and done with to get you ready for something new."

TWO HOURS LATER, Marie was stuffed with curry barbequed chicken and beer. The evening sun was slipping down into an orange and purple sky, though the August heat remained behind. From around the neighborhood she heard the sounds of kids playing outside in the dwindling light, the thwat-thwat-thwat of sprinkler systems starting up and—in the distance—the faint vibrations of a summer concert. She slouched down in her deck chair, wanting nothing more than a nap and dearly hoping that Nishi had forgotten the whole burning her wedding dress idea.

No such luck. While Imran put a few fresh logs into the fire pit, Nishi went back into the house to retrieve the dress.

"You know, I had a military wedding so maybe we should have a twenty-one gun salute here," Marie suggested, tongue in cheek.

Nishi draped the dress over the back of another deck chair, then faked climbing over the deck railing. "We can do that. Just let me run down to Starbuck's and borrow somebody's gun."

Marie stared into the struggling flames in the fire pit. They grabbed at the logs, tiny fingers of orange and yellow trying to gain some purchase, a hold on existence. That was the way Marie had felt for the past two years, like she'd been struggling to ignite. Every time she thought she almost had it, a gust of wind came along, or a torrential downpour, or the logs just plain fell over and crushed her little flame.

Meanwhile, Nishi had lined up a pair of scissors and three lighters on the table, like they were surgical instruments, and three fresh beers.

"We need a eulogy first," she said. "Do you want to start?" She looked at Marie, who shook her head. "Okay, then I'll go. My earliest memories of the deceased are of a marriage entered into with the best of reasonably good intentions. It was a merger of two powerful families, the political Witherspoons and the storied

Macintyre military dynasty. It joined Marie Witherspoon—who possessed the talents to be a good political wife but not perhaps a great one—with the soon-to-be newly elected congressman Richard Macintyre."

"My turn," Imran cut in. "The honeymoon was spent on the campaign trail, shaking hands and kissing babies in the hills and valleys of western Pennsylvania," he intoned. "Now, as a Carnegie Mellon alum, I am rather fond of Pittsburgh. I need to be clear about that. Go Steelers-Pirates-Penguins."

Marie fought back a giggle. She wasn't supposed to have fun at this. Mourning her marriage was not funny. Imran took a long, theatrical swig of beer and gave her a look. She bit down on her lower lip to kill whatever crew of mirth was mutinying in her.

Imran continued. "But. It is not commonly regarded as a top honeymoon spot."

Marie snorted, then clapped her hand over her mouth and nose.

Nishi raised her hand. "Wait a minute." She gave Marie a stern look. "We need to decide. Is this going to be one of those funerals where everyone is sniffling and clutching their tissues or the kind where people tell bawdy stories over the casket and then someone faints?"

"I vote for bawdy fainting," Imran said. "Not to be confused with body painting."

"Oh god, guys," Marie laughed, finally giving in to it. "We aren't capable of being serious about this."

"Okay then. Bawdy fainting it is. Your turn, Marie." Nishi handed her a beer. "Here. You can drink while you do this. You're spending the night here anyway. I forgot to tell you."

Marie rolled her eyes in the darkness, and stood. "Campaigning on my honeymoon was not that bad," she said to the white dress on the chair. "It made me feel important, like a grownup. And I like Pittsburgh, too, by the way. But the marriage never got out of campaign mode. It lost the early straw poll, had a few meh debate performances, and then underperformed on primary night."

She took a long draw on her beer, and then another one. "I knew, going in, that Richard was more in love with my father than me." Her voice was quieter now. "Or maybe more in love with the idea of me, of being married to a senator's daughter. But I thought he'd grow to love me, eventually." She scratched at the beer label with her thumbnail. "Obviously, I thought wrong."

Marie sniffled and Nishi enfolded her in a tight, loving hug. She leaned into the hug, as she'd been leaning into Nishi for months now. Nishi didn't need a faux eulogy to know what had gone wrong in Marie's marriage. She'd been the shoulder Marie cried on throughout the whole sorry thing.

"I think Richard was the one guilty of wrong thinking," Imran said quietly.

"Dickhead!" Nishi shouted into the night. Someone in the dark shouted it back to them, like an echo. Nishi had the uncanny ability to go from respected—even feared, by some—professional woman to thirteen-year-old boy in the snap of a finger. Marie wasn't the only person who cherished her for that.

"All right, enough eulogy. We've been through all this before anyway. Let's fire this sucker up," Nishi said.

Imran poked at the logs with his long grill spatula, causing a brief flare of light in the darkness, while Nishi picked up the scissors and snipped away at the night.

"We're going to have to do this in pieces."

"Oh, let me." Marie relieved Nishi of the scissors and promptly cut a lace-covered sleeve off the gown. "Here, Imran, you do this piece." She cut the other sleeve off for Nishi, then sliced out the bodice for herself. If she was going to burn her wedding dress, she was going to start with the part that had covered her heart.

The three of them sat around the small stone fire pit and held their pieces of silk and lace to the flames. The silk burned slowly and periodically the fabric smothered the fire, forcing them to prod the logs and add paper to get it going again. Cremating a wedding gown was a two steps forward, one step back sort of process, it turned out. Just like a marriage, Marie thought. Although hers had been more like one step forward, two steps back.

The moon rose high in the sky and one by one the lights in the neighboring houses went dark. There were no more kids' shouts in the distance, only the occasional ambulance siren or jet roaring overhead on its final approach to Dulles. It took nearly two hours to burn the entire dress, yards of pristine white silk and lace, and it smelled like hair held too long in a curling iron. But at the end they had a nice little mound of black powdery ash.

Afterward, Imran stayed outside to watch the fire burn down.

THE NEXT MORNING, Marie made the short drive back to her apartment to shower and change before meeting Nishi on the bank of the Potomac River. The river was wide and calm this far west of the city, unlike a few miles east where white water churned and tumbled over prehistoric rocks. On the far shore stood nothing but trees, trees that were in the state of Maryland.

Already the day was hot and sticky. She pulled the cloth of her tee shirt away from her back and flapped it a few times in a vain effort to generate a breeze. Marie had arrived first. But then, there was nothing in her apartment to distract her and keep her from leaving. No hunky husband like Imran, say.

"Coming!" Nishi's voice came from behind her.

Marie turned to watch her friend jogging toward her, across the wooden walkway that bisected a preternaturally green golf course. Nishi's loose black linen shift billowed and flapped as she ran. She was wearing large, dark sunglasses and a bag strapped around her shoulders in such a way that it looked like the straps of a parachute. Marie half-expected her to take flight, to suddenly soar over her head, the wedding gown ashes trailing behind her. That would be so like Nishi, to fly.

Marie and Nishi's families were similar, but their childhoods couldn't have been more different. While Marie had been firmly rooted to Washington, Nishi's youth had been a bit more peripatetic. Her father had done diplomatic stints in so many countries, even Nishi had to stop and count how many when asked. She'd been educated at the finest schools in the world, a year or two at a time. And despite her exotic Bollywood actress looks, Nishi could make herself fit in anywhere. She could talk to anyone —from prince to pauper—often in their own language, even.

Marie longed for Nishi's ease in the world. That was one thing she had gained from her marriage to Richard. A place where she fit. A role to fill. She and Richard had quickly become the city's golden "it couple." They were young, attractive, smart. Two people who were going places, and everyone wanted to know them, invite them, show them off.

It was shallow, she realized that now, but it was the first time she'd actually had a starring role in her own life. As a child, she'd always been more of an accessory to her parents' lives. They loved her, she didn't doubt that, but she couldn't imagine how their lives would have been any different if she'd never been born. Just for once, she had wanted to change someone's life.

Beside her, her friend's ragged, post-running breathing had slowed back to normal.

"So I gather we are tossing the ashes into the river?" Marie said.

Nishi gave her a big smile. "Toss, sprinkle, hurl. However you want to get them out there. Imran confessed this morning that he contemplated pissing on them last night to get the fire to go out. But he was afraid a neighbor might see and report him to the HOA."

Marie wrinkled her nose at the thought. "Let's get this show on the road, then. If I'm moving on, I don't want to spend all day doing this."

"Yup, you are moving on. So this is your last chance to tell me anything about your marriage to Richard that you haven't told me already. Or forever hold your peace."

"I believe that comes from weddings, not a funeral."

Nishi gave her the no-shit-Sherlock look. "Last chance."

Marie thought for a moment. Was there *anything* she hadn't dumped on Nishi in the past three years? God, no wonder Nishi wanted to cremate her marriage. She had to be sick and tired of hearing about it.

In truth, Marie was sick and tired of thinking about it. She knew she needed to move on. But easier said than done, and all that.

"No last juicy tidbit before you go back to being Marie Witherspoon?" Nishi prodded.

Before I go back to being Marie Witherspoon.

Marie shook her head sadly. "Believe it or not, there is one thing. Remember when you congratulated me on keeping my maiden name, in the name of modernity or feminism or some such?"

"Prescient move now, huh?"

"The reason I kept my maiden name is because Richard didn't want me to take his." Tears sprung to her eyes. *This is the last time I cry over this man. The absolute last time.* "He wanted the Witherspoon name to always appear next to his. What was the point in marrying William Witherspoon's daughter if people didn't read the name everywhere?"

Marie felt Nishi's arms wrap around her as she broke down

into full-on sobbing. Nishi held her while she shook and hiccuped, letting all the tears drain out of her one last time. When it was all over, Marie stepped back and pulled up the hem of her tee shirt to wipe her eyes and nose. She gave Nishi a sheepish smile.

"The ridiculous thing is I wasn't even dying to take his name. It was just the fact that he didn't want me to." She wiped her nose again.

Nishi took Marie's face in her hands, palms to cheeks. "There is someone better out there for you, Marie. I know it. Somewhere is a guy just waiting for you to show up in his life. And when you do, you won't even remember who Richard Macintyre is."

"Can you promise me that?"

"Yes, I can," Nishi said.

"All right then. I am bucking up from here on out. Let's poison the water supply with these ashes."

Nishi shrugged off her canvas bag and pulled out the ashes, now securely packaged in a plastic kitchen container. Marie snapped off the red lid and walked to the water's edge. She held the container out to Nishi.

"No." Nishi shook her head. "You toss them all in. Or sprinkle or hurl, however you're going to do it. Just make sure they all go into the water so none of them remain in Virginia. Throw them all out of state."

Marie poured out a handful of ashes, closed her fingers around them in a fist, drew back her arm and then threw them into the river with as much force as she could muster. The black ashes scattered like an explosion and dropped silently over the water.

"Damn. You've got an arm on you!" Nishi said.

"I was always good at softball in gym class." She looked at the plastic container in her hand. She'd already thrown more than half the contents in just one handful. "My marriage didn't produce many ashes. I wonder what that says about it."

"I think it just says you wore a size four wedding dress."

Marie snorted. "I couldn't fit into this thing anymore anyway. I *starved* myself for that dress."

She kicked off her sandals, then waded knee deep into the state of Maryland. She held the plastic container aloft, then flipped it over, dumping the rest of the ashes into the Potomac. They lay on the surface, the water too still to carry them away, a black scum of dashed hopes and starry-eyed dreams. Marie stuck her hand in the warm river water and shooed them away.

Back on dry land, she wiped her hands on her tee shirt. Snot, saline and now fouled river water. She'd have to change again when she got home. She held out the plastic container to Nishi. "Don't know if you really want to wash this out and use it again."

"I'll trade you." Nishi took the container and thrust a folded piece of paper at Marie.

"What's this?" Marie unfolded the sheet, goldenrod yellow and eight-and-a-half by eleven. It was a printed certificate. "This entitles the bearer to three months of drawing lessons," she read out loud. Below that, in smaller type, a name, phone number and an address in Middleburg.

"You said you used to love to draw."

"I did." Marie had minored in studio art at Yale, the only thing that had made a major in poli-sci bearable.

"I was originally thinking champagne or expensive truffles made with fairy diamond dust imported from Saturn."

"Those are both fattening," Marie pointed out.

"Well, right. Not that you need to worry about that. But you consume those and they're gone. I wanted to give you something that would last."

"Thank you, Nish." She refolded the paper and gave her friend a quick squeeze. "This is perfect. I would love to take drawing lessons again."

2

Marie couldn't remember the last time she'd picked up a pencil for any reason, let alone to draw, and yet here she was turning her car off a country road in western Virginia and into the gently curving driveway of the home of Luc Marchand. Marie had never heard of Luc Marchand, though Nishi swore that he was famous. In certain circles, anyway. And he was French. That was all Marie knew about the man with whom she was about to begin three months of drawing lessons.

She braked her car to a stop in front of the house and stepped out into the August heat. She took a deep breath. Amazing how much cleaner the air was out here than just thirty miles back, in the smog-choked suburbs of Washington, DC. Out here, you could almost forget that Washington even existed.

Marie looked up at Luc Marchand's Middleburg home, an old Colonial-era Virginia farmhouse with weathered gray stone and meticulously-restored windows. Gracious old maples shaded the front lawn. Behind the house, miles of yellowing fields dropped away beneath a pale blue sky.

A tasteful wooden sign next to the front steps read, "Studio in back. Follow the red brick road." Ah yes, if she looked carefully, she could make out a trail of faded red bricks pressed into the lawn, a walkway as old as the house.

Behind the house was a newer building, its board and batten siding painted a fresh deep red. The building looked like a cross between a carriage house and a small barn, though it was far too close to the house to have ever been the latter. The place reeked of old, understated money, the kind of money her mother chased incessantly as a professional fundraiser.

She knocked lightly on the studio's door and heard what sounded like the scraping of wood against a floor, muffled footsteps that stopped for a moment and then began again. The door opened and a man stood before her, a man whom Marie would have pegged as French even if she hadn't known beforehand to expect it.

Marie knew that the French were a varied people. But still, she had in her mind what a French person should look like. Dark hair, always. Lively, tousled curls. A jaded, slightly annoyed expression.

Check. Check. Check.

A white shirt. Check. Luc Marchand was wearing an impossibly white tee shirt. Marie doubted one could buy a tee shirt that white and crisp in the U.S.

A scarf wrapped insouciantly around the neck. Check. Luc Marchand's was more of a paint rag than a scarf, but it had the same general effect.

Clever shoes. She glanced down at Luc Marchand's feet. Okay, well not so French there. His feet were bare.

"You must be Marie?" he asked, rolling the r in her name so that it sounded like ma-rhee and not muh-reee. "Marie Witherspoon?"

Marie was momentarily struck speechless. She'd never heard her name pronounced in a French accent.

"You are not Marie Witherspoon?"

"Yes. Yes, of course I am," Marie managed to squeak out. Her tongue felt useless in her mouth, like a limb that had fallen asleep.

"Of course you are," he said, an amused smile flitting across his lips. "Come in."

She followed him inside the carriage house. He took her purse, set it on an old wooden chair, then looked Marie up and down, assessing her, taking her measure. She flushed.

He laughed. "I am a man, and not an old man. So, yes, I will look over a woman." He nodded at her. "You are a pretty woman."

She tried to fix a look of injury to her face. The nerve! But part of her was flattered, nonetheless; after years of living in Richard's desert of indifference, being called pretty by a man—even an arrogant Frenchman Marie suspected she wasn't going to like—was a welcome mirage. Then she remembered the decidedly un-French attire she had chosen to wear that morning. Military green cargo pants, out of fashion for several years now, and whose cuffs were worn and fraying. A black cotton tee shirt, faded in the wash to a bluish tinge. No clever shoes. No scarf. The few times Marie had tried to tie a scarf, she'd ended up with something that looked more like a noose.

And she hadn't replaced the blowdryer that had died the morning after Richard served her with the divorce papers. Her hair was tied back in a limp, pathetic ponytail.

"Sorry," she apologized, looking down at her clothing. "I dressed for an art studio, I guess."

"Nothing to apologize for. I'm just French, that's all. I find, in the states, I can take all manner of liberties if I simply say afterward, 'I am French.'"

Marie's failed injury was replaced, at last, by a smile. "We expect bad behavior from you."

"Ah, she speaks. I will try not to behave too badly with you. But I cannot make any promises."

Marie was stunned into silence. She had assumed that Nishi

had picked Luc Marchand out of some community art center's directory of class listings. There was no shortage of people in the Virginia foothills who fancied themselves artists. She'd been expecting someone older, paunchy, balding.

Luc Marchand was none of that.

Marie wasn't sure exactly how old he was, but she guessed late thirtyish. He was over six feet and definitely not paunchy. Lanky, that's how Marie would have described him. Not skinny but not overly muscled either. His movements as he crossed the studio to a tiny kitchenette on the other side had an almost desperate carelessness to them, as if he were daring the floor to trip him or the ceiling to rain down on his head.

He held up a bottle of red wine. Marie frowned. At ten in the morning?

"Oh right," he said. "Too early for an American. Coffee then?"

He set about grinding and measuring and filling the coffee maker. He swung his arms and hips around the tiny space and yet he didn't once bump into the sharp corners of a countertop or allow a stray coffee bean to fall and bounce into the sink or behind the wastebasket. Despite the seeming unchecked carelessness of his limbs, there was a graceful economy to his movements, a purposefulness to each step and turn. He didn't seem like the kind of person who would go into a room and then forget what he came in for. Marie did that all the time, as though her days were constantly rebooting.

He looked up and frowned at her. He gestured toward a small metal cafe table and a set of those grey metal bistro chairs that had become all the rage in the furniture catalogs. "Sit down, please."

Marie sat and looked around his studio while the coffee sputtered and hissed into the pot. The studio looked like the studios she remembered from school. Messy. Canvases in various stages of completion, or inspiration, stood like sleeping sentries around the room. There were landscapes and horses and children and opulent interiors. From a glance, it was hard to say what Luc Marchand's artistic style was.

One particularly tall canvas held the rough outlines of a life-sized woman's head and torso, arms and shoulders. She looked like some spectral creature in the process of materializing. Or disappearing, Marie couldn't tell which.

Two mugs of coffee appeared on the table, along with a small white pitcher of cream and a matching bowl of sugar. Luc Marchand flipped a chair around and straddled it, leaning his chin on the chair back.

"We won't do much drawing today. A little, maybe. But we need to get acquainted with each other a bit first, so I can determine how best to teach you."

This close, Marie noticed the small scar on his forehead.

"I fell out of a tree when I was eleven," he answered her unasked question. He pushed the cream and sugar toward her. "So. Your friend signed you up for private drawing lessons. Have you drawn before?"

"In school." Marie's tongue remained uncooperative. She had to force each word from her mouth. "I took a few classes."

"And where was that?"

"Yale."

He lifted an eyebrow, tilted his head down slightly in a gesture of deference. "You must have been a good student."

Marie shrugged. "It wouldn't have mattered either way."

"And why was that?"

Marie hesitated. She wasn't expecting twenty questions out of a drawing lesson. Usually you just showed up, sat down behind an easel and began to draw. And she really didn't want to get into the whole complicated situation that was her family.

"I would tell you I don't bite, Marie, but sometimes I do."

Marie felt her face grow hot. Normally, she wouldn't recognize innuendo if it bit her on the ass, but Luc Marchand seemed entirely composed of the stuff. He made it hard to miss.

"My father was a senator."

"And he's not a senator now?"

"Lobbyist now. No one ever goes home after they leave Congress." She spit out a sharp laugh. "It would have taken wild horses to drag my mother back to Indiana."

"And your mother. What does she do?"

"She runs a fundraising firm."

Luc Marchand seemed to consider this, stroking his chin thoughtfully. "And are you married?"

"Separated."

"I almost hate to ask you what your husband does."

"My soon-to-be *ex*-husband is also a senator. From Pennsylvania."

He appeared amused by that piece of information. "Why are you divorcing?"

"It's a long story."

Luc looked down at his bare wrist. "We have time. Your friend paid for the entire morning."

"I'd rather not talk about it." Even as the words came out of her mouth, she knew Luc Marchand wasn't going to let her get away with that answer.

"Okay."

He surprised her, after all. She'd been certain he was going to pick and probe, make her rip off that particular bandage. Still, he made her uncomfortable. He was staring intently at her face, like maybe he recognized her. He could have seen her photograph in the paper or a magazine. That was entirely possible.

She looked away from his gaze, toward a nicked and stained work table along the studio's back window. Brushes and rags littered the tabletop. Beneath the table, the wooden floor was dusty and stippled with morning light. It was all too Vermeer. She hadn't been in a painting studio since college, but the smell of paint and old wood and dust was stirring up an old yearning in her. Nishi had been on the mark, as usual. Drawing lessons would be enjoyable—she glanced back at Luc Marchand—if Mr. Fancy French Artist could lighten up a little.

"Let's go outside," he suggested.

He collected two sketchpads and a fistful of pencils from the table Marie had been staring at. He turned to her.

"Come."

Outside, she followed him down the gentle slope of the back lawn, to a low stone wall that looked as if it had once seen Colonial militia running past, bounding over it, muskets under their arms. More old maples sheltered a wooden picnic table and benches. Beyond, the fields and rolling hills went on forever, it seemed, stopped only by the low dark mountains on the horizon.

Luc took a seat on the wall and patted the spot next to him. When she sat down, he handed her a sketchpad and pencil. She flipped over the cover to the first, empty page.

"Draw blue," he said.

"What?"

"Draw blue."

"You mean draw something that *is* blue?" Marie asked for clarification.

"No, I meant what I said. Draw blue."

She frowned. "Do you have that condition ... what is it called?" She tried to pull the word out of the depths of her brain.

"Synesthesia?"

She nodded.

"No, I do not."

He flipped open the sketchpad on his lap and Marie watched in wonder as his hand flew across the page. When he was finished, the center of the page was filled with a swirling tangle of lines.

The man was crazy. Marie began to doubt he was even a real artist.

"See? That's what blue looks like to me."

"Why is that blue and not red?" she asked.

He shrugged. "I don't know. That's what I see when I imagine blue."

"That doesn't make any sense to me. What are you thinking about when you do that?"

"I'm not thinking about anything. I'm simply seeing." He tapped her sketchpad. "Don't think. Just draw."

Marie stared at the ivory cotton paper in her lap and tried not to think. But thoughts intruded anyway. How quiet it was out here. How hot a late August breeze could be. How uncomfortable this man was making her feel. Whether the paint stains on the back of his hands were permanent. Why he hadn't put on shoes when they came outside.

"You're thinking, Marie. I can hear the gears turning."

She sighed. "I don't know what blue looks like. It's the color of the sky, or someone's eyes. Or water."

"Then choose another color. It doesn't matter so much which color. Let your mind go blank and allow your fingers to take over."

Marie took a deep breath and tried to do as he instructed. She let her pencil begin to move across the paper. It felt entirely random, at first, but after a few seconds her movements became more purposeful. It was maybe even enjoyable, she admitted to herself, just a little.

After a minute, she lifted her pencil from the page. Luc leaned into her to take a closer look, his arm pressing against her shoulder. "And what color is that?"

"Red," she declared confidently.

"Hmm. Doesn't look like red to me."

Her bubble of momentary confidence burst. "Yellow?"

Beside her, Luc Marchand's laughter jostled her shoulder. "We'll compromise and say orange."

Then before Marie knew what was happening, Luc's arm was on her back and pulling her body against his chest. She opened her mouth to object, but found her lips quickly sealed over with his. She tried to free her lips from the kiss, trying to speak, but the only sound that came out was more akin to loud humming than any meaningful protest. Pushing at his chest only made him tighten his arms around her more securely.

He lifted his mouth away from hers for a split second, just long enough to say, "Relax, Marie. It makes a kiss more enjoyable." Then he resumed the kiss, his hand now cradling the back of her head, pulling her lips further into his mouth.

The nerve of the man! She squirmed in his embrace, trying again to free herself. It was too hot outside to be doing this! Her skin felt like it was melting, all liquid-y and ... melting-like. He tasted like coffee and chocolate. Her mind tried to attach itself to that thought—chocolate this early in the morning?—but gained no purchase. Her thoughts were like liquid, too, the knowledge that she should resist him sliding right past a dawning awareness that this was a kiss unlike any she'd ever had bestowed upon her.

A kiss she suddenly—desperately—didn't want to end.

She let the pencil drop from her fingers and slid them into the hair at the nape of his neck. He groaned into her mouth and she opened her lips to him, inviting him in. His tongue twirled around hers, sending a shiver that she couldn't identify as either hot or cold down her spine.

"Marie." God, the way he said her name. The r's rolled and tumbled into her mouth, spilling into her chest before settling into her hips as a spreading pool of desire.

She wanted this man. She wanted his lips on more than just her mouth. Wanted his hands on her body. All over her body. She wanted to be flat on her back beneath Luc Marchand, his weight pressing her into the damp heat of summer grass ...

And then just like that, it was over. Luc pushed away from her, his breathing ragged, and the hot summer air resettled between them. There was a wild look in his eyes, but Marie barely saw it for all the spots and flashes of light shooting through her vitreous jelly. She tried to focus on his face, on his lips. The lips that had left hers bruised and tingling. But nothing settled in her vision. All she could see was light and color, the shapes of her desire.

"Marie?" The r's in her name were deeper now, huskier. Deprived of oxygen.

Breathe. Air into lungs. As the light show in her eyes faded, Luc Marchand's face began to come into focus again. No one had ever made her insides do that before ... just liquefy. She hadn't even known you could do that with something as innocent as a kiss. There was nothing innocent about this man. The months since the divorce filing had left Marie unsure of what exactly she knew anymore but this was a no brainer. Luc Marchand didn't have an innocent cell in his body.

He reached toward her and flipped over a clean sheet of paper on her sketchpad. "Now draw a color for me."

Now? Now he wanted her to draw? When the only thing she could think of was ripping off her shirt and begging him to touch her? How could she draw now?

"Any color," he prodded. "I don't care."

He leaned over and picked up her pencil, gently curled her fingers around it. How was it that he was touching her hand, yet she felt his hands everywhere?

She began to run the pencil across the page with as firm a touch as she could muster. Her hands were shaky, though, and her heart was still pounding with both fists against her chest. But she did her best, on the off chance he might kiss her again. Already she was craving another kiss like that. Just one more hit, that's all she needed. Please. Just one more.

When she was done, she tilted the pad up for him to see. The lines were spidery and delicate, outlining narrow shapes she had shaded in.

"And what color is that?" he asked.

She studied it for a minute, wanting so very much to get the answer right this time. "Grey," she declared finally.

He nodded. "Yes, I can see that. Grey. *Bon.*"

She wasn't sure she'd actually been seeing grey, but grey was what she was feeling. Indefinite, nebulous, cloudy. She felt all of those things right now. Everything in her life had been black and white. Her life had been on a track. She'd had a role to play, a purpose to fulfill. She'd had status. Then Richard filed for divorce. Kicked her to the curb.

Ever since, she'd been wandering across a field shrouded with fog. Not sure what she should be doing. Or what she wanted to be doing. Letting other people make decisions for her. And now she had stumbled into this man and his sexy r's rolling off his tongue, his kisses that had rendered her temporarily blind. Like she hadn't been blind enough already.

"Why did you kiss me?" she asked.

"I wanted to turn off your brain, so you could draw."

Oh.

"So that was all just a drawing lesson?"

"Yes, Marie, it was."

But his eyes said otherwise. She wasn't *that* blind. He ran his hand back through his hair, damp and curling from the heat. Instantly, she recalled the feel of it, the skin between her fingers sizzling to life.

"Do you kiss all your students?" she asked.

His face darkened. "Not normally, no."

Not normally. What did that mean?

He stood. "Let's go inside where it's cooler."

Cooler was a good idea. Something had just happened here and she wasn't sure what. Marie needed her normally cooler head to prevail. She was not in the habit of kissing sexy French men. Sexy French men were not in the habit of kissing her. She imagined Luc Marchand was going to regret this in the morning. Conceivably he was already regretting it.

She stood and followed him back up the hill. She was not noticing his very fine ass. No, she absolutely was not. Her imagination had gotten the best of her back there. Or maybe it had just been a simple lack of sex. That's what Nishi would say. *You just need to get laid. Take the edge off.*

Easy for Nishi to say. She was married to Imran. Imran was perfect. Luc Marchand was clearly not perfect, even if his ass was.

Luc held the door of his studio open for her. Compared to the sunny day outside, the studio was cool and dark. Marie blinked her eyes several times until they adjusted to the dimness.

"Water?" Luc asked.

"Please," she answered.

Inside, things were different. Like there'd never been a kiss outside, just minutes ago. Her internal organs were solid again, her skin no longer melted chocolate, the pool of desire in her hips leaking away. But her lips, those were still tender and kissed.

Luc set two glasses of ice water on the bistro table and motioned for her to join him.

"So, Marie, why are you here?" He took a long drink of water and studied her intently.

She nervously palmed her glass. "To take drawing lessons?"

"You don't sound so sure."

"I'm here to take drawing lessons," she said again, this time with more authority.

"But this wasn't your idea, was it? It was your friend's idea?"

Marie shrugged. "I drew in college. I used to draw all the time."

"But you stopped."

Marie really didn't want to get into this, the demands on her time as a young politician's even younger wife. Evening receptions, Kennedy Center openings, charity boards, her mother's neverending fundraising circuit, ribbon cuttings back "home" in Pittsburgh, interviews and photo shoots, organizing dinner parties at their home in Great Falls, hiring caterers, deciding seating arrangements, then reading up on everyone's pet legislation, and on and on and on. And then after the on and on, making it to the gym before it closed because heaven forbid she not look like the young, perfectly adorable wife.

There hadn't been time for drawing or knitting or gardening—not that she wanted to knit or garden, but if she had there hadn't been time for it.

"If you were really passionate about it, you would never have quit," Luc added.

She sighed and flicked her hand through the air, conceding the point. "Do you only take on passionate students?"

Luc Marchand flipped the chair around so he could lean back, away from the table. He crossed his arms across his chest as he studied her face. Marie dropped her eyes to stare at the paint rag tied around his neck. The paint rag couldn't stare back, or remind her of kissing.

"I prefer to, yes. I can only take on so many students at a time, so I want to make sure each one is serious about learning. I expect my students to put in the necessary amount of time to do this well. So I need to know whether this is something you want, or whether you're just here because your friend paid for the lessons."

"Most people don't care, as long as they get paid."

"But I do care, Marie. I don't want to invest the time in someone who doesn't know why she's here."

He tilted his chair back, letting the front legs lift off the floor. Marie could see the schoolyard condescension in the gesture.

"Are you looking for something fun to do on the weekends?" he asked.

Marie shrugged. "Have you ever been through a divorce, Mr. Marchand? It's not much fun."

"I've never been married, no. But fun is not what I teach. So tell me, would you be here if your friend hadn't paid for your lessons?"

She was stuck. The answer, of course, was no. She was back working at her mother's firm and due to begin evening classes for her MBA in a few days. She was saving money like a madwoman so she could move away—escape was the better word, really—from DC when she finished her degree. Drawing lessons were a frivolity she wouldn't have indulged. Nishi had known that.

That was the simple answer. The harder truth was that no, she hadn't even thought about picking up a charcoal pencil or paintbrush in years. The idea had not even been on her radar until Nishi had presented her with it.

But now that it was on her radar, yes, she did want to take drawing lessons. She just couldn't say why. It was something she felt, not something she knew.

Outside, a gust of wind swept up a small pile of leaves and twigs into a sudden cyclone, a swirl of green. Just as quickly, the wind lost its gumption and released them. Marie and Luc watched, together, as leaves hit the studio's large picture window and then were quickly whooshed away.

"So Marie?" Luc said. "No reason? No reason why you want to take up drawing again?"

She sought frantically for words, but none came.

"You have to go, then. I don't teach people who don't know why they want to learn. When you have a good reason for taking up my time, return."

Marie picked up her bag and slung it over her shoulder.

"Well. Okay. I mean, I don't think that's ..." *Just shut up already.* "Well then. Goodbye." She felt his eyes burning into her back as she walked toward the door. Outside, she hurried to her car, humiliated, her ears hot and buzzing. She slammed the car door shut, narrowly missing her own ankle. *Well, that went well.* She hoped Nishi could get her money back. Was he being serious when he said he only taught people who know why they want to learn? Whatever happened to the concept of learning for the sake of learning? Maybe that was out of fashion these days. Or out of fashion in France.

If she were Nishi, she'd march back in there and tell him exactly what she thought of his arrogant, pompous, French ... pomposity. She'd demand to be given her damn drawing lessons same as the next person who showed up with cold, hard filthy lucre.

Not to mention the way he had kissed her! Taken advantage of her. Made her feel things she hadn't come here to feel.

She leaned her forehead against the steering wheel. She wasn't Nishi. As Marie Witherspoon, dutiful daughter of a former senator and chameleon-like soon-to-be-ex-wife of Congressman Richard Macintyre, she was going to turn the ignition and carefully back up the winding driveway, hoping she didn't take out Luc Marchand's mailbox or any of his—probably heirloom—plantings. She would look both ways up and down the road before pulling out, and then she would drive the speed limit all the way back to her apartment, where she would eschew the handicapped and inexplicably "reserved" parking spots for the closest other available spot she could find. Later in the day, she would thaw some of Imran's curried barbeque chicken and have that for dinner. Then she would surf the internet for awhile before taking a shower and falling into bed.

That's what she was going to do. In her fog-shrouded field,

doing what she always did was the safest way to avoid injury. Doing something out of the ordinary, say driving to Middleburg for drawing lessons, could lead anywhere. Over a cliff. Into a ditch. Stuck in a dead end.

She inserted the key into the ignition and turned. As she backed up the driveway, a hard knot of irritation—at Luc Marchand, at Tricky Dick Macintyre, at herself, at the entire damn world—tightened in her chest.

At the top of the driveway, she looked away from the rearview mirror and down toward Luc Marchand's lawn and the stone wall. She remembered the coolness of the stone through the thin cloth of her pants, the liquidy thing her insides had done, and how *edible* Luc Marchand had tasted. She had wasted a perfectly good Saturday morning. And yet, as she drove the winding country roads leading back to suburbia, everything looked sharper—the rough bark of trees, the hard glint of cars, the splintered wood of fences—and more in focus than it had in years.

3

"You're kidding. He made you leave?" Nishi asked, incredulously.

Marie popped open her plastic clamshell container of salad. All around them, DC office workers were ordering sandwiches, salads and soup and rushing back out to busy K Street, on their way back to lunch at their desks. Marie and Nishi tried to get out of their respective offices and meet for an actual face-to-face lunch once a month.

"He said I could return when I had a good reason for taking up his time." She stabbed a patch of lettuce with her fork.

"The bastard! I paid for those lessons." Nishi uncapped her bottle of ginger iced tea. "Are you going back?"

"He said I could, when I figure out why I want to take drawing lessons."

"Tell him because your friend paid for them. Duh." In Nishi's crisp and perfectly unaccented voice, courtesy of a peripatetic diplomatic childhood, "duh" sounded like a withering putdown.

Nishi Bhat had been her best friend since the day Richard had hired Nishi's firm, the largest public relations agency in Washington, to provide him and Marie with media training. Nishi had taken an instant dislike to Senator Macintyre but felt an immediate kinship with his wife. The two of them had bonded over the similarities in their families. Nishi was the daughter of an Indian diplomat. Both Nishi and Marie understood the odd pressures that came with country over family.

Nishi and her husband Imran had been Marie's rock during the darkest hours of the past five months. Nishi had been the shoulder Marie cried on. She'd taken Marie in without hesitation when Richard changed the locks on the Great Falls house, which he wasn't supposed to do but who was going to challenge a member of Congress? Even her own parents had advised her to let it go.

Every twenty to thirty seconds the door to the deli opened and another blast of oppressive summer heat washed over their tiny square table. Perspiration trickled down Marie's spine and she could practically feel her linen dress and jacket wrinkling further by the minute. Nishi, of course, looked cool and collected in a white silk blouse and unwrinkled navy skirt. Her inky dark hair was still neatly slicked back into a ballerina-worthy bun.

"How do you do that?" Marie asked her.

"Do what?" Nishi took a bite of her wrap sandwich.

"Not sweat."

Nishi covered her mouth to keep from spitting out tuna and lettuce. "I'm sweating on the inside."

"Yeah well, I'm sweating on the inside *and* the outside. When I finish my MBA, I might move somewhere cooler. It wasn't this hot here when I was a kid."

"It's getting hotter everywhere."

They chowed down on lunch for awhile. Marie kept her head bowed to her salad. There were two kinds of people in DC. Those who had heard about her impending divorce, and those who hadn't. Today she wanted no one's pity or commiseration or clueless sucking up. She *got* it. Richard was the youngest person elected to the Senate since Joe Biden. That had made her the wife of the youngest person elected to the Senate since Joe Biden. They'd been the new Washington "it couple." And now they weren't anymore, and people were curious.

But she was just so *tired* of people expecting her to explain why she and Richard were divorcing. *Ask him* was always the answer on the tip of her tongue, the retort she had to bite back.

"So he didn't give you any kind of lesson at all?" Nishi asked after awhile.

Marie was glad it was hot. The heat hid the sudden flush to her face. She'd gotten a lesson all right, just not the kind Nishi had paid for. "We did a little drawing. He had me draw colors."

"Draw colors? Like scribble with crayons to see what color puce or midnight mountains majesty is?"

Marie would pay good money to see Nishi go mano a mano with Luc Marchand.

"No, he wanted me to draw what blue looks like to me. I had to just make it up."

Marie shared most everything with Nishi, but the last thing she wanted to talk about with Nishi was Luc Marchand. Nishi was like human truth serum; if you were hiding something, she could get it out of you. And Marie had spent the past four days trying to shove the memory of that kiss down so deep inside even she wouldn't know where it was hidden. She still wasn't sure what to make of it. He'd taken advantage of her, clearly. People often thought Marie was several years younger than her actual age of thirty, but she was old enough to know that kissing had nothing to do with drawing. She'd never seen a professor kiss a student before. Not in class, anyway.

But the kiss had worked. That was the most confusing thing of all. Not that Luc Marchand had taken advantage of a young woman alone in his studio—or that she had enjoyed it, which she couldn't deny she had—but that after the kiss she'd been able to draw his silly request. Draw a color.

"I'm sorry, Marie. I had no idea I was signing you up for psycho drawing lessons. I asked around the office for suggestions and he was the only artist who got more than two recommendations."

"Well, he's very French." Marie borrowed Luc's all-purpose excuse.

"Ooh la la. I lived in Paris for a year."

"Lucky you."

But Nishi didn't hear her. Marie watched in amusement as Nishi's expression grew distant, then waved her hand in front of her friend's face.

"Earth to Nishi?"

Nishi shook off whatever memories she was privately enjoying. "Sorry. First kiss in Paris."

Marie sat up straighter. This was something she'd never heard about. "With Imran?"

"Hah! No. I was fourteen. I didn't meet Imran until college."

"So ... cute French boy?"

"*Very* cute French boy. *Amazing* kisser."

Marie felt herself blushing.

"That's all we did, kiss," Nishi hurried to clarify. "I mean, we were fourteen. Babes. But ...." She shook her head and Marie could see her fading into memory again. "I might give up sex to be kissed like that again."

Marie clapped her hands over her ears. Too much information—she really *really* did not want to know that Imran was not the world's best kisser. Nishi and Imran's marriage was the only thing that sustained her faith in men anymore.

"Maybe you're just romanticizing a first kiss."

"Oh, Marie. It wasn't just the first kiss. It was the thousandth kiss, too. Then we moved to the states and the American boys," she sighed. "You can never tell whether they like you. They talk to you, then ignore you for a week. Call you on the phone, then at school pretend you've never met. With Olivier, I never had to wonder whether he liked me or not, you know? He seduced me, even though all we did was kiss. What woman doesn't want to be seduced?"

Wow. This was a side of Nishi that Marie had never seen. Uber-professional, ball-breaking Nishi, one of the top public relations professionals in Washington, DC, a woman who was paid to make people famous or keep them from becoming famous—depending on the circumstance—going all dewy-eyed over a fourteen-year-old boy? The woman who had helped her burn her wedding gown and dump the ashes in the Potomac?

Then Marie sighed too. *What woman doesn't want to be seduced?* Marie did. All through those long nights of the soul—otherwise known as her marriage—she had imagined a man who would want her just for herself, not for her family or her connections or her surname. Someone who would talk to her, eat with her, pick her up and carry her back to their bedroom ... all romantic crap, she knew. No one did that anymore. Hell, probably no one ever did. They were just stories made up to keep women in an everlasting state of hope.

Well, except for Imran. He probably picked up Nishi and carried her back to bed every night.

She looked at her best friend, who was at that very moment hoisting a now-empty bag of chips to peer inside, then shaking it. Of course, two more chips fell out. Nishi popped them into her mouth with gusto. Nishi could always pick up the world and shake it, and two more chips would fall out of what for anyone else would have been an empty bag.

"I swear they put fewer chips in every year. One day, we're going to open a bag of chips and there will be nothing inside.

Nothing but air," Nishi said, crumpling the foil bag in her fist. "So how are things at Witherspoon & Associates?"

Marie shrugged. "The same as before, I guess."

"I can get you hired at my office. Just say the word."

"It's easier to just work for my mother until I finish business school. You got to pick your battles. Plus, this way I can keep tabs on what my parents are up to."

"Please tell me they're not still jonesing for a reconciliation. Does your father need Richard that badly?"

"Well, it helps to have a family member on the Senate Armed Services Committee. That's why DefenseTech hired him in the first place. Not to mention Richard's Pentagon contacts, which dad would lose."

The Macintyres were military royalty, dating all the way back to the War of 1812. Someone in the family had fought in every war since. Marie's parents had introduced her to Richard and their marriage had been a political alliance from the start, though Marie had fancied herself in love with the dashing junior senator. Who wouldn't have? Richard had been the most eligible bachelor in Washington, bar none. Handsome, whip-smart, his career on a meteoric rise—and still in possession of his boot camp physique. It had been so easy to believe that Richard Macintyre was her birthright, that she'd been born to be a senator's wife like her mother.

Amazing how quickly one's entire life could fall apart.

Nishi was checking her phone for messages. "I've got to get back. Meeting at one. I think for Christmas I'm going to sign you up for a dating service. Since the drawing lessons aren't panning out."

Marie rolled her eyes. "I'm still married, technically. The divorce won't be final for a few more months, thanks to my parents' attorney dragging his feet on my financial statements. They are still waiting for Richard to change his mind."

"Legally, you're still married. But when your husband files for divorce because he wants to marry his mistress—who's a gossip blogger, hello—I'd consider you no longer *technically* married."

"Excuse me, I prefer to think of her as a society and style blogger," Marie said, using Maya Redfearn's own tagline, "given how often I show up in the damn thing." Richard's mistress was the "proprietor" of the J Street Chronicle, and not above taking thinly-veiled swipes at Marie in it. Marie had assumed these public jabs would end now that Maya had what she wanted—Marie's husband—but apparently not.

She waved off Nishi's legal hair-splitting. "I'm not ready for men yet."

THE CAB PULLED up to the curb, where Marie paid the driver and got out. She'd taken a cab to and from lunch with Nishi because, contrary to Hollywood filmmakers, metro went nowhere near Georgetown.

Witherspoon & Associates was housed in a narrow brick rowhouse with a tidy little flower-filled courtyard out front. Marie unlatched the iron gate, marched up to the front door and rang the doorbell, leaning over in front of the bay window so Maeve, the receptionist, could see her. Only her mother and Maeve had keys to the place.

The door buzzed harshly and the lock clicked open. Inside, the building was hushed and softly lit. Maeve was a well-groomed, motherly woman in her sixties. Eileen Witherspoon insisted on hiring older woman for the front desk and keeping them on until they retired. Less chance they'd be spotted dancing on tables somewhere.

Maeve looked up at her warmly. "Your mother is still at lunch. I expect her back around two."

Marie winked at Maeve. "I'm sure she'll find me if she needs me."

Maeve had never said a word about the divorce, simply picking up with Marie as though she had never left her mother's employ. Too bad that couldn't be said about all of her mother's staff.

She pushed open the door to her office, expecting to resume working on the report she'd been writing before lunch, only to find what looked like dozens of signs stacked against her desk, the wall, the filing cabinet. She sighed and dialed Maeve.

"Maeve, I think all these signs were delivered to the wrong office."

"No dear. Your mother was very clear that they be put in your office."

"Buzz me when she gets in, please Maeve?"

She flipped through the large, brightly-colored signs printed with candy canes, Christmas trees and presents. They were for her mother's fundraiser that weekend. Every Labor Day weekend for the past three years, her mother and Richard had held "Christmas in September" at Marie's old private school, an event that raised money for the school's scholarship fund and collected holiday toys for needy children. Marie begged off this year, citing the obvious.

She quickly read through the signs, scanning for typos and finding none. She restacked them against the wall and returned to the report she'd been working on before lunch. She was compiling a list of local technology millionaires, their estimated net worth, and the causes and campaigns they had supported in the past. You couldn't have money in the DC area and expect to escape the notice of Eileen Witherspoon. In some ways, the ways that mattered, she was more powerful than Marie's father. If you needed to shake the change from society's sofa, Eileen was the person you called.

At two o'clock sharp, Marie heard a light rap on her door.

"Mother." She stood quickly. "These signs—"

"Just drop them off at the school Saturday morning," Eileen directed. "Are they all there?"

Marie's head swung between the signs leaning against the wall and her mother, dressed in a tailored royal blue suit. "I guess. I didn't check ... I'm not going on Saturday," she finally managed to spit out.

"Of course you are, dear. You go every year. Your father will be there. You'll probably see some old classmates. It'll be fun."

She looked at her mother as though the woman had sprouted a second and third head. *Fun?*

"I thought Richard was going to be there."

Her mother waved her hand in the air, then leaned over Marie's desk, reading down the list of names on the computer screen. "Yes. He's in charge of the toy donation. As usual."

"I don't want to see him. I'd rather stab myself in the eye with a shrimp fork."

Her mother looked up from the computer screen and arched one perfectly penciled eyebrow at her.

"I don't think it's a good idea for the two of us to be there. The press will have a field day with this," Marie rephrased.

Eileen turned back to the computer. "I've spoken to all the reporters who have been invited. You're the marketing director here. People will expect you to be there, and I need someone who is familiar with the school as backup. Just be nice to Richard. Maybe he'll reconsider." She straightened and brushed past Marie as she headed for the door. "Nice work so far, dear. E-mail it to me when you're finished."

"You've got to be kidding." Marie was still back on "maybe he'll reconsider." "I don't want him back, not after everything he's done. And there will be other alumni there who know how to get to the kitchen and where all the bathrooms are. She dug her fingernails into her palms in frustration. The last thing she wanted was to be in the same room, even a very large room, with Richard.

In the doorway, Eileen turned back to face her. "Being a senator's wife is a privilege, Marie."

"A prison, don't you mean? Can you *try* and look at this from my perspective, mom?"

Her mother shot her a sharp look. "My marriage was never a prison. There was never a minute I didn't appreciate the blessings it gave me. What kind of life do you think you'd have if your father hadn't been a member of Congress?"

Marie couldn't take it any longer. Anger and exasperation churned inside her chest, then finally spilled over. "What kind of life do you think I had with Richard? Do you have *any* idea how many nights he never came home? I don't recall dad just not coming home at night. And all those times you nagged me about starting a family already? That wasn't *my* fault. *He's* the one who didn't want to. I tried to make things work, but it takes two to tango."

She shoved a stack of file folders across her desk. Her mother's face remained impassive, expressionless.

"So no, I really do not want to go to the fundraiser this year. It's not like you'll raise any less money if I'm not there."

"I need you to go, Marie, and that's all there is to it. Your absence will provoke more talk than your presence."

4

Marie's heels clicked crisply down the school corridor, past the clusters of men and women in business suits and expensive hair cuts chatting, pumping hands and exchanging cards. Whispers followed her down the hall—*he got the house ... he sold her car, did you hear? ... is he still ... mistressmistressmistress*—pushing her toward what waited for her at the entrance to the gym, the double fireproof doors thrown open to her mother's realm.

Everyone here would be poorer by the end of the evening. That was small consolation to Marie, though, for being the object of everyone's gossip.

With that in mind, she had dressed carefully. Slim navy sheath, yellow linen cardigan. Both colors set off the copper highlights in her hair. She had even splurged on a new hairdryer. Her hair hung in soft, loose waves around her shoulders. She needed to look professional, stable, pulled together. Not like a woman who'd been cheated on and then tossed aside.

She took a deep breath and pointed her chin forward, clutching the toy she was donating to her chest like a shield. Richard was standing like a sentry next to the entrance to the school's gymnasium, expertly decorated for the night by her mother's minions. As Eileen Witherspoon's daughter, Marie was one notch above minion status.

Richard's posture was ramrod straight beneath his black suit, red tie, polished-to-a-mirror shoes. His blond hair was cropped short, as usual. He smiled and shook hands with each new arrival, made a few seconds of small talk—Richard was a natural politician. But as Marie approached, the welcoming light in his blue eyes darkened to dull contempt.

"Ms. Witherspoon," Richard said.

"Senator Macintyre," she replied. She held out her hand to shake his, like all the other guests, but he ignored it. *Fine, whatever.*

"What did you bring?"

She let him pry the box away from her chest. It was the newest version of a popular video game console.

"Nice," he said, then added, "expensive."

She shrugged. How she spent her money was no longer any of his business.

"It looks like we're going to have a good turnout tonight," she said, subtly reminding him of her place in the solar system. She might be his scorned wife and their families might be continuing their alliance without her, but tonight she was here as Eileen Witherspoon's daughter and a trusted staff member of Witherspoon & Associates. For most of the guests, their loyalty lay with her mother, not Senator Macintyre.

She hurried away from him, her heels click-click-clicking against the polished wood gymnasium floor. Inside, she stopped for a moment to let her eyes adjust to the dimmer light. The ceiling and walls were draped and shrouded with long swaths of velvet and silk. Upholstered chairs and settees were grouped throughout the gym where a teenaged Marie had played basketball and volleyball, albeit not well. Attractive, twentyish waiters and waitresses in black pants and ties ferried trays of hors d'oeuvres from one small cluster of guests to another. Marie had to hand it to her mother; there were few people in this world who could transform an ordinary school gymnasium into a venue people would pay $500—plus a toy—to come to. Marie had not inherited that ability, that was for sure.

Just off from the center of the gym was a circle of tables manned by Marines in dress blues. Marie headed there first, dropped off the video game console, then went to the bar for a drink to salve her nerves. With a cool glass of sauvignon blanc firmly in hand, she made herself look busy by perusing the long tables along the back wall. There were four tables, each filled with bidding sheets for the silent auction. Apartments for a weekend in New York, San Francisco, Paris, London. Ski condos in Aspen, Killington, Tahoe. Limousine rentals, helicopter tours, spa days. Everything beyond Marie's budget, of course, but a girl could dream.

She sipped at her wine as she walked slowly down the line of tables, letting her eyes glide from clipboard to clipboard. Occasionally, a particularly large bid made her shake her head in wonder. She would never have the kind of money to bid thousands of dollars on a landscape architectural consultation or a family portrait painted by renowned French artist, Luc Marchand.

Marie stopped in her tracks. She read the bidding sheet again, to be sure her eyes weren't playing tricks on her. Luc Marchand had donated something to her mother's fundraiser?

"*Bonjour*, Marie," came a low voice, barely above a whisper, behind her.

A pair of hands settled on her shoulders, their warmth seeping right through the thin linen fabric that should have protected her.

"Making some bids?" he said.

She turned to look at him. Luc Marchand was sharply dressed

in a slim-cut black suit, white shirt and silvery gray tie. His dark hair had been combed into submission.

"What are you—how do you know my mother?" she asked.

He smiled a slow, lazy smile at her. "I don't. A friend of mine went to school here. She talked me into donating a painting. Said it would be good publicity for me."

"It will. Plenty of wealthy people here tonight."

"I was surprised to see you here. You look lovely, I might add."

Marie's face flamed. "Thank … thank you," she stuttered. She looked back at the bidding sheet. "Is that what you charge for a painting? Twenty-five thousand?" She looked down at the last of the twelve bids already listed.

"Mm-hmm."

"Impressive. What do you charge for drawing lessons?"

He leaned in close to her ear. "I believe your lessons were a gift, no?"

A lick of heat raced down her spine. What was it about a French accent, she wondered? There wasn't time to wonder long, however; just then, a tall thin woman with a riot of dark blonde curls appeared behind Luc.

"Sorry about that, darling," she said. "I had to go say hello to someone and when I turned around, you were gone."

Marie took what she hoped was a discreet step away from Luc. She hoped, too, that her cheeks had returned to their normal color. Of course, Luc Marchand wouldn't be here alone. Anyone who looked like he did—and with a French accent, to boot—was probably never alone.

"I came over here to check on the bidding," he said to the woman, "and I ran into Marie here. She is contemplating taking lessons with me."

So he hadn't forgotten about his ultimatum. *You can come back when you have a good reason for taking up my time.* Marie extended her hand to the woman. "Marie Witherspoon. Nice to meet you."

"Samantha Smith," the woman replied. "Your mother does a lovely job with this event every year."

Great. Luc Marchand's date knew her mother. Is there anyone who didn't know her mother?

"Yes, she does. Um, excuse me, I see my father over there." Marie was five hurried steps away when Luc touched her elbow from behind.

"Marie. Have you figured out why you want to take drawing lessons yet?"

She looked up at his dark eyes, the hard set of his jaw. She swallowed hard. The question had been on her mind almost constantly since last week, but she had come up with nothing more impressive than the simple desire to draw. That, and she wanted to be kissed again.

"No, I haven't, Mr. Marchand. I'm sorry. I'll try to give it some thought. I've been bus—"

Luc Marchand reached out and tucked a stray lock of hair behind her ear. "No need to apologize, Marie. I was just wondering."

As she walked away, she was pretty certain her hair was on fire where he touched it. It took every ounce of willpower not to peek back over her shoulder at him.

Her father didn't smile when she joined him at the toy table, a spot that guaranteed he'd see everyone who came by as they dropped off their donation. William Witherspoon was still a slender man, even in his sixties. Judicious use of Grecian formula kept his salt and pepper hair more pepper than salt.

"Dad," Marie said. She nodded toward his empty hand. "Can I go get you a drink?"

"Maybe later. Your mother was worried you weren't coming." His eyes toggled between her face and the room behind. When she was a teenager, this had bothered her to no end, her father's inability to focus solely on her for even a minute or two. Now, she merely accepted that this was who he was.

She sighed. "What's eating Richard tonight?"

"Oh, some businessman in Pennsylvania is putting together an exploratory committee. He's thinking of challenging Richard in the primary next year."

"That's less than a year away. Kinda' late to get in the game now," she said.

"Yeah. I wouldn't worry about it if I were him. Who was that you were talking to over by the auction tables?"

Marie looked toward the auction tables but Luc Marchand and his date had disappeared. "Some artist. I happened to be looking at his auction."

"Some nice donations your mother secured for the auction this year. Speaking of your mother, she just motioned to us. I believe she wants to speak to you."

Marie squinted to spot her mother in the crowd. She fought the urge to roll her eyes. Her mother was engrossed in conversation with another woman. Her father was just trying to get rid of her, and not even attempting to be smooth about it. Well fine, Marie didn't want to hang out at the donation table anyway. Sooner or later, Richard would claim it as his turf.

She was twenty feet away from her mother when a flash of silver passed through her peripheral vision. She turned to look, only to see Maya Redfearn staring directly at her, a look of barely-disguised glee on her face. Marie raked her eyes up and down the other woman's body. Typical Maya. Always dressed for attention. Tonight, a slinky silver dress snaked over her voluptuous figure and stopped just above matching silver stilettos.

I can't believe he brought her tonight. Her parents were here!

When her mother finished her conversation, Marie approached. "I thought you vetted all the press for tonight," she hissed.

Her mother's gaze followed hers to the silvery vision that was Maya.

"She wasn't invited. Not by me, anyway." Eileen Witherspoon frowned.

"So much for dressing up and being nice to Richard. This is what I get in return. Public humiliation."

"You're being a little dramatic, Marie."

"How is this not humiliating for me? He's parading his mistress right beneath my nose. At my own mother's event! Aren't you embarrassed by it?"

"Maya Redfearn is not important enough to be embarrassed by. And I seriously doubt that Richard will ever marry her. Mistresses rarely become wives."

MARIE WITHERSPOON PASSED within mere inches of him, so close he could have reached out a hand and grasped her sleeve. Or better yet, grabbed her by the waist and pulled her into the crowd with him. Why had he given her that stupid ultimatum? *I only take on passionate students.* In my dreams, he thought as he watched her disappear into the throng of people.

He'd wanted to get rid of her, get rid of the temptation to kiss her again. But the minute she was gone, he regretted his impulsive decision. He wanted the temptation. Wanted it bad.

He took his beer and stationed himself by the silent auction tables. He'd been abandoned by Samantha again for one of her gallery's patrons. Sam was here to do business, not raise money for her alma mater. Luc was supposed to be here for the same reason, though his heart wasn't in it tonight. He'd rather be home painting or, failing that, drinking. But Sam persisted in dragging him to these functions.

Samantha Smith was a classmate of Luc's from their grad

school days at the University of Virginia. Sam had married well and now divided her time between raising her daughter and running a local art gallery in Leesburg, Virginia, on the outer fringes of the DC suburbs. Her gallery was the only place Luc's paintings sold these days—and even those weren't the sort of paintings he really wanted to do. Sam's clientele had an almost insatiable appetite for still lifes and local landscapes. There were places in Virginia Luc could practically paint with his eyes closed by now.

They, along with his commissions, paid the bills so he tried not to resent it, but it was increasingly a struggle. He was thirty-seven now. This wasn't how his life was supposed to play out. A failed middle-aged artist and disgraced professor, the grandson of a beloved artist. Living in virtual exile and obscurity in the country, alone.

Back when he was a Ph.D. student, he'd envisioned a life of teaching in the fall and spring, painting in the summer, a wife and houseful of children. Even in his most hopeful moments—and they were few and far between now—he saw none of that. Stretched ahead of him as far as the eye could see was simply more of the same. Painting rich people. Letting Sam fix him up with newly divorced women.

He looked around for Sam and spotted her over by the bar now, muscling her way through a thicket of people. It was hard to miss Sam's mass of amber ringlets in a crowd. He sent her a text asking for another beer.

"Monsieur Marchand?"

He turned in the direction of his name. A petite—almost childlike—woman with stiff, messy blonde hair was smiling hopefully at him. In her hands she held the clear lucite clipboard for the family portrait he had donated to the silent auction.

"Yes?" he replied, mustering a small, polite smile.

Her hands were positively skeletal, he thought. He didn't

understand the desire of women of a certain age to starve themselves into the bodies of thirteen-year-old boys.

"A friend of mine, Amanda-Lynn Trevor? She's a client of yours? I'm looking for someone to paint a portrait of my children and she recommended you?"

Her penchant for speaking in questions grated on his nerves.

"Yes, Amanda-Lynn." He'd painted Amanda, her beloved children, her beloved horses and her husband's beloved Lamborghini.

The woman waved the clipboard in the air between them. "I bid but, you know, I never win these things? So if I don't, what does your schedule look like? Amanda said you're pretty busy?"

Luc pulled his phone from his suit pocket and swiped open the calendar. "How many children and how old?"

"Three. Ages four, six and twelve."

He swiped through several months. "It would have to be after Christmas."

Her face fell. He was expecting that. People like Christmas portraits, but the idea never occurs to them until the weather begins to cool.

"But if you wait until spring, an outdoor portrait is always nice. Or we can fake a Christmas scene inside and you'll have it for next year," he suggested.

The idea of a fake Christmas portrait seemed to cheer her a bit. He handed her a business card. "Call me if you don't win."

The woman continued to stand in front of him, inspecting the card, both front and back, as if it were potentially counterfeit or held some secret message. He hoped she wasn't planning to stay and chat him up further. The women at these events were never his kind. Too forward. Everything you needed to know about them was right there on the surface. They had no hidden depths. Luc liked hidden depths in people, those dark caves where they lived their true lives.

Of course, some people fall into their caves and never come

back out. Grace had done that, blonde, delicate Grace with the voice like church bells. Luc had been the cave that opened up beneath her feet and swallowed her whole.

"Here. Sorry I was gone so long." Sam was back at his side with a fresh bottle of beer for him. She glanced at the woman studying Luc's business card. The woman took the hint and left.

"I see you emerged from your shell long enough to drum up some business." Sam handed him the beer.

"She wants a portrait of her children done."

"Children are tough."

"Easier than horses. And more interesting than cars."

He took a long draw from his beer, watching across the gymnasium where Marie Witherspoon was either arguing or intensely conferring with her mother. Marie looked like a younger, prettier version of her mom.

"Poor kid," Sam said. "If I were her, I'd be hiding in the ladies room right about now looking for a window to crawl out of."

"Why?"

Marie Witherspoon had nice legs, he noted.

"Both her estranged husband and his mistress are here tonight."

"Ouch."

Lovely hair, too. Long and silky, a melange of red and brown. He hadn't noticed that so much when she was in his studio. She had worn it pulled back in a ponytail that day.

"Ouch is right. Plus, her parents are here of course. Her father is a former senator and a powerful lobbyist in the defense industry. Her mother has a direct line into half the wallets in DC." Sam's gaze searched the room. "Her husband is over there, next to her father. And the mistress is behind him and to the left."

Luc eyed the woman. She was not as pretty as Marie Witherspoon, although he could see why she appealed to some men. But to Luc, she could have stepped straight out of a comic book, with her exaggerated and unnatural curves, the overly wide-eyed look that made men believe she was hanging on their every word. And of course, there was a segment of the male population that had eyes only for blondes, even though any discerning pair of eyes could see that she really wasn't.

"Why would she come then?" he asked, looking back at Sam. He blinked to erase the image of the other woman from his vision.

"I doubt she had a choice. She works for her mother. Though she doesn't seem as cut out for it as her mother is."

"Ah." Marie Witherspoon had seemed upset last weekend when he asked about her family.

"They practically arranged her marriage to Senator Macintyre. That didn't take either, obviously." Sam shook her head sadly. "Poor kid," she said again.

Luc watched Marie as her conversation with her mother ended. He could practically see the energy rushing out of her body. She looked like a poor kid tonight, her shoulders slumped beneath her sweater, her eyes dull and defeated, her husband's mistress circling her like a shark.

But the Marie Witherspoon he kissed last weekend behind his studio had been no kid. He was not in the habit of kissing students. But Marie Witherspoon appealed to him in a way no woman since Grace had. If she hadn't kissed him back, if her indignation had gotten the better of her, he would have stopped.

But she did kiss him back. She'd been soft and pliant in his arms, her lips warm and sweet, her struggle to breathe pushing her breasts against his chest. The memory had sustained him all week.

5

She wasn't looking for Luc Marchand. Really she wasn't.

She mingled. Chatted up her mother's big donors. Introduced herself to new faces. Said hello to the school's headmistress. Smiled at people whose conversations dropped off a cliff when she approached. Pretended that her husband's mistress was invisible.

But her gaze found him over and over again. He was too easy to spot, in his sharp black suit. And something about him made him stand out in the crowd. She couldn't quite put her finger on it. Maybe it was just that he was European. It was always easy to tell which tourists were European and which were American. The clothing was always just a little bit different, and the men wore shoes that no self-respecting American man would ever don.

Luc's date kept leaving him alone, which was unwise, Marie thought. Every time she left, another woman approached to fill the vacuum, though Luc Marchand was never more than merely polite. From the expression on his face, he looked like he was answering questions he'd answered a million times already.

Marie was disappointed that he had a girlfriend. Now when she replayed that kiss in her mind, an image of his beautiful girlfriend was going to pop up. She didn't want to be the other woman, even in her dreams. She'd spent enough time on the other end of that situation herself.

But the gnawing sensation in the pit of her stomach wasn't a bad reaction to the wine. She was a tiny bit jealous. She sighed. This was the last thing she needed right now. An unrequited infatuation. Why had he kissed her when he was seeing a woman who looked like that? Sure, it could have been part of his teaching technique, as he'd claimed, but he could have given her a lesser sort of kiss. A polite buss on the lips. That would have sufficed. There'd been no need to practically devour her, to ... to arouse her.

Yes, that's what he'd been trying to do. She had tried to avoid that conclusion all week long, but there it was. That kiss had been intended to turn her on. But why? And the more important question: could she pay him to do it again? Just one more time? Then she could die happy. Maybe whatever Nishi had paid for the lessons would be enough to purchase a kiss. If he wasn't going to give her the lessons anyway, on account of her insufficient motivation ...

She shook her head to clear her internal ramblings, shake herself back into the present moment. Buying a kiss? That was desperate.

At nine o'clock, her mother announced the winners of the silent auctions. She watched as the winner of Luc's portrait—one of her mother's midlist donors—pressed her body into his for the photographer. There was the sour gnawing in her stomach again. How could his girlfriend just stand by so casually, watching and smiling happily, when Marie was fighting back the knowledge that she could look up where the auction winner lived in her mother's database, then go burn down her house or something?

"Bid on anything?"

Maya had sidled up to her, and was now standing way too close for Marie's comfort. Marie leaned away, plastering an obviously fake smile on her face. Anyone watching would forgive her that.

"I was going to bid on my husband, but ..."

Maya cut her off, her own fake smile never wavering. "Don't be a bitch, Marie darling. He was always too much man for you."

"Heard he's being challenged for his seat already," Marie countered. "Will you still want him when he's on K Street?"

"I love him. It doesn't matter to me whether he's in Congress."

"Well, K Street does pay better," Marie said in a louder voice than was strictly necessary. She tipped the rest of her sauvignon blanc down her throat and walked away. Two could play at this game. After all, she was the wronged party here.

Still, the gossip hurt and Maya knew that, went out of her way to fuel it whenever it began to subside. Marie's mother was right: mistresses never become wives. That truism was behind the gossipy speculation that followed Marie around. Why wasn't Richard just keeping her as a wife? There must be extenuating circumstances causing him to buck tradition and divorce her. She couldn't have children, people said. She was in the closet. She was frigid. She was a harpy. She drank too much, used pills, had multiple DUIs. Her father and Richard weren't getting along.

All false, of course. But it stung, nonetheless.

At nine-thirty, she said goodbye to the handful of people who would be offended if she left without doing so. She spotted Luc Marchand holding court across the gym. He caught her eye and smiled. She gave him a tiny wave—all that she could manage before her heart stuttered dangerously out of rhythm. Unless she could come up with an acceptable reason for taking drawing lessons, she'd likely never see him again.

Look on the bright side. At least now she knew that kind of kisser existed. It wasn't just a cruel hoax perpetrated on women by Hollywood.

Outside, the school parking lot was dark. She walked past row after row of luxury sedans and SUVs, looking for where she had parked her Honda. She was halfway down the aisle to her car when she heard quickening footsteps behind her. *Damn him.* Richard was following her. She picked up her pace and pressed the key in her hand. She saw the lights flash and the comforting beep-beep as the car unlocked. She could make it. Her car was just ahead, six cars away. Five. Four. Three. Two … she whirled around, in a rage.

It was Luc Marchand.

"Marie." He smiled at the anger on her face. "Expecting someone else, I hope."

She fell back against her car. "I thought it was my—"

"Your ex-husband? I have to say, I wouldn't want to meet him in a dark parking lot either."

She looked at him, confused. How would he know who Richard was? She'd never taken Richard's last name. Richard hadn't wanted her to. It was her name he had married, after all.

He cocked his head toward the school. "My friend Sam pointed him out."

Marie looked around. "Where is she?"

"She left in her own car."

"You came in a separate car from your date?"

Luc laughed. "Sam? I'll have to tell her that one. Even if she weren't already married, she wouldn't date me with a ten-foot pole."

"So … you're not …?"

"No. Sam is a friend of mine from university." He shook his head. "I may be French, but even a Frenchman wouldn't leave his date to follow another woman out to her car."

"You followed me?"

"I've been following you all night with my eyes."

Oh my. She looked down at the macadam, away from his heated gaze. Even in the dim light of the parking light, Luc Marchand's eyes glittered with something Marie wasn't sure she could handle.

"I'm sorry," she mumbled, all the nerve and pluck of her encounter with Maya vanished into the night. "I haven't figured out yet why I want to take drawing lessons. I'll work on that this week. Maybe tomorrow. Tomorrow is Sunday ..."

She was rambling but powerless to stop. He was following her with his eyes? She couldn't look up at him. How much she wanted to kiss him again was written all over her face, she was certain. He took a step toward her and touched her shoulder lightly. A shiver ran through her body, even though it was early September and still summer in the Washington area. "I thought I might offer up a few suggestions," he said. He pressed a finger to her chin and lifted her face.

Her eyes widened. "Oh, you don't have to do that. I'm sure I'll think of something. I've been busy—"

His thumb gently closed her mouth, and it was all she could do not to suck it in between her lips. The inch of space between them sizzled with energy.

"But a parking lot isn't the place to discuss them. Is there somewhere nearby we can go? For coffee or a drink?"

Marie thought for a moment, unable to take her eyes off his lips, unable to move her eyes up to meet his. "Someplace quiet," he added.

She had lived in the Washington area her entire life and now she was drawing a blank on where there might be a restaurant or coffee shop. It was a struggle to think with him standing this close to her. That was the problem. If she leaned forward even just a hair, her breasts would touch his chest.

She wanted her breasts to touch his chest. And other parts of her body, too.

"There's a 24-hour pancake place on route seven," she managed to spit out, finally. "It's not fancy, but it probably won't be busy at this hour."

"Bon. I don't care whether it's fancy or not." He took her hand and began to lead her back the way he'd come.

"Wait." She pulled her arm back. "I have to take my car."

He looked at her skeptically.

"If my parents come out later and see my car here, there will be an all points bulletin out for me."

He nodded, looking disappointed, but he took her hand again and walked her back to her car. He tugged open the driver's side door. Marie climbed in quickly, bumping her knee sharply against the bottom of the steering column. She winced at the pain. He would think better of this once he got on the road. She was going to find herself sitting alone in her car, like an absolute idiot, in the parking lot of a strip mall. She just knew it. Sexy French artists were not interested in women like her.

"Marie."

Regardless, she would remember forever the way her name sounded on his lips. She turned and was surprised to find him leaning into the car, his face just inches from hers. In an instant, he closed that tiny distance with a hot devouring kiss, his tongue pushing at her lips. She opened her mouth and let him in, let him push her head against the seat and grind his lips against hers. She dug her fingers into his hair and kissed him back, tasting his lips, enjoying the spikes of heat that were driving through her body. Kissing him felt just so damn good.

Then, like someone had flipped on a light suddenly, she remembered her parents and Richard. And Maya. Most of all, Maya. She could be walking through the parking lot right this very minute. She would see Marie with this man's tongue down her throat. She would see the frenzied look on Marie's face, desire and craven weakness. She would take a picture of it.

She pushed Luc away. "I'll meet you there."

6

"Why did you kiss me back there?"

They were seated in a rear booth at the Pancake Palace. "Palace" was perhaps overstating things. But it was quiet and mostly empty, a few bleary-eyed truckers at the counter and some slightly drunk teenagers crammed into a booth at the front, where the manager could keep an eye on them.

"To make sure you'd show up here," Luc replied.

She looked at him incredulously. "I didn't think *you'd* show up."

"I asked you to come. Why wouldn't I show up?"

The lone waitress set down two cups of black coffee between them. Marie pulled hers across the formica and wrapped her hands around it. She shrugged her shoulders.

"You're you and," she gestured at herself, "I'm me."

"What does that mean?"

She shrugged again and he bit back the impulse to reach across the table and hold those shoulders still. But if he touched her ... if she hadn't pushed him away back in the parking lot, he would have climbed into the car with her.

"You're a senator's wife, yes? A senator's daughter. And you hang out with people who have more money than God. What are you doing here, Marie? Sitting with a man you barely know—" he looked around the garishly decorated restaurant. "In Pancake Hell."

What was *he* doing here? Sitting with a woman who was still technically married, according to Sam, and who seemed to belong to fairly powerful people connected to the U.S. government. Luc had acquired his citizenship a few years back, but he imagined that dallying with a senator's wife—even an estranged one—might be grounds for revocation.

"Um, I ... you said you had some suggestions," she said nervously. "For why I could take drawing lessons. Other than that my friend paid for them."

The way she sunk back into the orange vinyl of the booth, clearly regretting her last words, concerned him. He leaned forward, his elbows shoving their way across the table, trying to bridge the distance between them.

"Are you afraid of me, Marie?"

"No. Yes. No." She shook her head and closed her eyes. "No."

"Three no's and one yes. So some of the time, you're afraid of me."

When she opened her eyes, there was a dull weariness in them. She waved a hand off to the side. "Some of the time, I'm afraid of everyone." She picked up her coffee and stared into the dark liquid before taking a sip.

"Did your husband mistreat you?"

Her hands jerked in surprise, causing her coffee to slosh over the side in a thin trickle. She carefully set it down on the table and wiped up the small spill with a napkin. Then she shrugged. Again.

"Depends on your definition of 'mistreat,' I suppose."

"Did he ever hit you?"

"No."

She had hesitated a beat too long.

"But there were times I thought he was going to."

The waitress returned to top off their coffee.

"I don't really want to talk about this," Marie said. "I thought we were going to discuss my lessons."

"*D'accord.* But in order to teach you, I need to know what makes you tick. I need to know something about your life."

"But you haven't decided that you're going to teach me yet."

He regarded her porcelain skin, her pink lips—the taste of them still fresh in his memory. Truth be told, teaching was the last thing he wanted to do with Marie Witherspoon. He wanted to push that pretty yellow sweater off her shoulders and unzip that slim dress. Roll her stockings down over her hips and thighs, peel them off her lovely toned calves ... he felt a tightening in his groin.

What was going on here? She appealed to him in a way no other woman had since Grace. But why? She was beautiful, yes. But she came with more baggage than a 747. Not only an estranged husband, but one who was a member of Congress. He had issued that ultimatum last week to send her away, to get the temptation of her lips—and the way she had pressed her breasts into him—as far away from him as possible.

And he had regretted it all week. Who was he kidding? He wasn't about to send her away again. He was too weak a man. He wanted her, and he would give in until he found out why.

She was looking at him expectantly. But her guard was up, too. She was waiting for him to turn her down. She wanted him, too. That had been plainly evident in the kiss. Both of them. She might not really want drawing lessons, but she definitely wanted him.

"Why did your friend give you the lessons?" he asked, stalling for time. He had racked his brain on the way here for these suggestions he had promised, but come up with nothing. He was always shooting off his mouth like that. It was how he had ended up in the United States in the first place. He'd said unforgivable things, things that had neatly excised him from his own family when he was younger. It was how he had lost Grace. Unforgivable things.

"She remembered that I took some studio art classes in college. She thought it might cheer me up."

"You were depressed over your marriage ending?"

She shrugged yet again. "I was more surprised, I guess. I guess I thought he would stop seeing her after awhile. No one marries their mistress." She laughed bitterly. "Or that's what my mother keeps telling me."

"You would have stayed with him then, if he'd given her up?"

Another shrug. He was going to have to teach her not to do that.

"Probably," she admitted.

He pulled a pen from his inside pocket and slid it across the table toward her, then followed it with a napkin. "Draw yourself, please."

She lifted an eyebrow. "Now?"

"Yes. Just a quick sketch."

He sipped at his cooling coffee while she slowly drew. When she finished, he pulled it from beneath her fingers and looked at it. "Not bad," he allowed. He held out his hand for the pen, then made his own sketch of her on a fresh napkin.

"How do you do that?" She shook her head in amazement. "I thought mine was pretty good but compared to yours, it doesn't look anything like me."

"You have some skill, Marie, but you don't *see*."

"You're talented. I'm not. I just *like* to draw."

"My family would tell you that I am an untalented hack. That may be true. But I was taught to *see* the way an artist sees. My *grandpère* taught me."

Suddenly Marie's eyes lit up. "Can you teach me that? To see like an artist?"

Something inside Luc swelled near to bursting. Hope or dismay. One of the two, he couldn't tell. But she had a reason now and he would get to see her again. She would come back to his studio and he would teach her. He would resist her appeal. Or not.

He reached across the table and pulled her small, soft hand into his. He circled his thumb over the pulsing vein beneath the skin of her wrist. His dark eyes met her lighter ones. Maybe that was it. There was about her a quality of—not innocence, exactly—but uncertainty, a sense of someone beginning to try her wings for the first time. Grace had been that way, and he had crushed her wings.

He sucked in his breath as her fingers gently curled around his. Her skin was so soft, the bones of her fingers so delicate. So fragile. So breakable. He should run and tell her to run, too. Eventually, he would do something unforgivable.

But he was a weak man.

"*Oui*. I can teach you that, Marie."

7

The following Saturday, Marie arrived at Luc Marchand's studio promptly at nine in the morning, as he had requested. The door was ajar. She knocked lightly on the frame.

"Mr. Marchand?"

"Come in," came the reply.

When Marie stepped into the studio, darker today because of the cloudy sky outside, Luc Marchand was sitting at the large half-finished canvas she'd seen the previous weekend.

"Or should I call you Monsieur Marchand?"

"You should call me Luc." He turned around with a welcoming smile. "But also feel free to call me bastard, asshole or son of a bitch as the occasion arises." None of which sounded all that terrible undergirded by a French accent, Marie thought.

He took her overnight bag and placed it in the corner of the studio. "You can stay until tomorrow?" he asked. When Marie nodded, he added, "Bon. Immersion is the best technique for learning a language, and the same is true for drawing. Plus, you'll be drinking. It won't be safe for you to drive home."

Today Luc Marchand was wearing paint-spattered khakis, the

cuffs rolled up to reveal bare ankles, and a worn chambray shirt faded almost to white. He looked over Marie's outfit—her best-fitting slim jeans and a pale yellow silk blouse that didn't entirely hide the lacy bra beneath. Dark coral polish on her toes peeked out from her wedge sandals. She had tried on four other pairs of shoes before finally settling on these.

"Come," he said, picking up a thermos and a backpack and heading for the door. "We'll start outside."

Marie followed him to the low stone wall where they had drawn the last time. And where he had kissed her. She felt a bud of heat begin to unfurl in her chest. Would he kiss her today?

She sat next to him on the wall while he unzipped the backpack, pulled out two coffee mugs and proceeded to fill them with coffee from the thermos. Marie gratefully accepted the mug he offered, wrapping her fingers around its welcome warmth. Beneath the clouds, the morning air was laced with a damp chill. Her blouse was not warm enough and a shiver convulsed her body.

"It's not this cold back in Loudoun," she said.

"I think there's a cold front coming in. We're supposed to get rain later today. Take a deep breath," Luc suggested. "Relax into it. It's only cold because you've been conditioned to think it is."

Marie gave him a skeptical look but did as he asked. She filled her lungs with the cool air, then let it all whoosh out.

"Better?"

"Not really," Marie replied.

"Good thing we have all weekend, then. If you want to see things for yourself, you have to start with what's all around you. So the air is a little chilly. But how uncomfortable is it, really? It's not outright painful, yes?"

He stretched out his legs in front of him and Marie noted that he hadn't put on a jacket or sweater himself before coming outside. He was wearing just his khakis and that thin, worn shirt.

"Relax your arms. Let yourself feel the air on your hands.

Through your blouse. Let yourself enjoy the way it feels. Find pleasure in it."

Marie tried to do as he said, but it was hard to stop her mind from thinking it was cold. The skin on her arms pulled up tight into gooseflesh.

He nodded at her coffee mug. "Drink."

When the hot liquid hit her taste buds, she nearly spit it back out.

He smiled and said, "Take another sip. Hold it in your mouth for a minute."

"You've got to be kidding. This stuff is sludge."

"Humor me."

Marie imagined lots of women had humored him over the years, but she did as she was told and filled her mouth with bitter coffee. She tried not to focus on how terrible it tasted.

"Okay, you can swallow."

Marie shuddered from the scorched aftertaste.

"How was your week?"

"Fine," she replied.

"What did you do?"

"Work. And I started school this week, in the evenings."

He gazed up at the heavy grey clouds speeding past. "School for what?"

"Business school. I started on my MBA years ago. Then I got married and had to stop."

"Do you have children, Marie? I never asked." Luc pulled a sketchpad and some pencils from the backpack.

She shook her head sadly. "No. That was supposed to be the reason behind my quitting school and work. We were going to start a family right away. But then Richard met Maya."

"Ah. I see. So now you're picking up where you left off?"

"Trying to. My parents are still hoping for a reconciliation. They don't think my husband having a mistress is that big a deal."

"A lot of politicians have them."

"Well, Richard decided he wanted to marry his." She stared off at the mountains in the distance.

"Your husband made the wrong choice." Luc reached over and turned her face toward him, his thumb lightly stroking her cheekbone. "She is nowhere near as beautiful as you are, Marie."

She looked at him, surprised and embarrassed by this unexpected display of tenderness. Disappointed a little, too. Part of her had been expecting—hoping—that he would rush her the minute she arrived and kiss her passionately. Instead, he was acting as though they had never kissed. Not here two weekends ago, not in her car in the parking lot. Maybe he'd forgotten. A man like Luc Marchand probably kissed so many women, they were all a blur after awhile. Or maybe he regretted it and was hoping she wouldn't bring it up.

He let his palm fall away from her face, leaving her cheek suddenly naked and bereft. "Here. I'll trade you," he said. He handed her the pad and pencil and took back her coffee mug.

She was glad to be rid of the foul stuff he called coffee.

"Do I get to draw now?" she asked flipping open the cover of the sketchpad to a pristine sheet of paper.

"Draw away."

"Anything in particular?"

"Whatever you want. I just want to see what you can do, as a baseline."

Marie spent the rest of the morning and afternoon sketching. A cluster of buildings on a neighboring farm. The sky as geese flapped against it. The rounded stones of an old crumbling foundation. Inside Luc's studio, she drew carafes and baskets of fruit, paintbrushes standing in a jar like cut flowers, the crusty sandwiches he fixed for their lunch.

Through it all, he said nothing about anything she drew. Often he wandered away from her entirely, leaving her by herself to stare hard into the heart of an object, trying to will its lines and planes to flow through her fingers and onto the paper. She was making peace with the idea that he wasn't going to kiss her again, although every time she looked at him her body ached with the need to touch him.

That was okay, she told herself. She was here for drawing lessons. It was unreasonable to expect romance too.

She needed drawing lessons, that was for sure, she thought as she flipped through her pathetic attempts at art. Her geese looked more like unmanned drones, paintbrushes like spindly weeds. Maybe Nishi should have given her cooking lessons, instead. That would have some practical application, at least. She was ready to stuff the sketchpad deep into her overnight bag and sneak out the door to her car, never to return, when Luc appeared next to her and gently tugged it from her clutches.

"Come. Help me with dinner."

Marie nearly melted. *Help me with dinner.* How did he manage to make those four words into the sexiest thing she'd ever heard fall out of a man's mouth?

An hour later, the old farmhouse table in Luc's home was set with a large serving bowl of pasta, dressed simply in garlic, olive oil and freshly-grated parmesan; a platter of hot fragrant bread and a second bottle of merlot.

"How did it go today?" he asked as he refilled her wine glass.

Marie contemplated the burgundy liquid in her glass, and the flicker of golden candlelight reflecting through it. "You might be wasting your time with me."

"*Non*, Marie. You have the skill. You have good instincts. But you draw from your mind, from how you think something should look. I will teach you how to draw what you see, not what you think."

He scooped pasta onto her plate. "But first, we eat. I will show you after dinner."

When the second bottle was empty, Luc cleared the table and brought back the sketchpad and pencil.

"I'm not sure I can draw right now," she protested. "I've had too much to drink."

"Actually, you've had just the right amount to drink." He blew out the candle on one of the candlesticks. "Enough to shut off your brain for awhile and let your other senses take over."

"No, I'm pretty certain I'm too drunk to even draw a straight line." Marie drew her finger in a wiggly line across the table. "Am I slurring my words?"

Luc covered her hand with his, stopping it in its path. "If you're drawing lots of straight lines, you're not seeing properly anyway." Then he leaned over her and covered her mouth with his. His lips were warm, his breath spicy with wine and garlic, and Marie froze, unable to move or even breathe. Had her heart stopped entirely or was it simply beating too fast for her to feel? She couldn't tell.

His lips teased hers open so he could suck gently on her lower lip. A mellow warmth began to spread through her body, her arms and thighs prickling with tiny fingers of heat. When she felt his tongue brush against her lip, she tensed in the chair. He placed his hands on her shoulders, leaning into her.

"Am I slurring your thoughts, Marie?" He breathed the words, hot and low, into her mouth.

She had just enough consciousness left to nod.

"Good. You don't need to think anymore tonight. And you definitely won't need to speak."

"But—"

He resumed the kiss, harder and more insistent this time. "You are not to speak again tonight until I say you may. Or the lesson ends."

Just as Marie began to allow herself to kiss him back, he

groaned and lifted his lips from hers, breaking the kiss. The look in his eyes was dark and wild.

"For the rest of the evening, you'll need only two senses, Marie. Seeing and touching."

Marie bit down on her lower lip, pulling it into her mouth—not to stop the flow of words swirling in her brain—but to keep the taste of Luc Marchand from evaporating off her skin. He had done that on purpose, she was certain. Commanded her to use only two senses, but made it impossible to ignore a third.

"Close your eyes, Marie."

Luc stood behind her chair. She closed her eyes, then gasped in surprise as a velvet blindfold was tied around her head. She opened her mouth to speak, but Luc cut her off.

"Shh. No words, remember?"

A shiver of fear raced down her spine. She was to use only two senses tonight, and now he was cutting off one of the two. Maybe Nishi should have run a background check on the guy. Maybe Marie should have done that herself before agreeing to come back here. She could see the headlines now: Congressman's ex-wife found dead in artist's studio.

She felt something cold and heavy placed in her hands.

"Here." Luc's voice was soft now, less commanding. "Hold this. Touch it."

Marie held the object in one hand while her other hand roved over it. It was long and slender, cool to the touch. She tapped her fingernails against it. It was made of some sort of metal.

"Oh, it's—"

"Shh. I know what it is. Just feel it."

Her hands continued their exploration. She was holding a candlestick, but not one of the candlesticks that had been on the table while they ate. Those had been sleek and glass. This one was cast from an intricate mold. Her fingers glided over its curves, stopping to explore when they came to sharp points or shallow ridges. Her thumb dipped into the hole at one end. She scraped away a sliver of old wax with her nail.

Just as suddenly as she had been blindfolded, the candlestick was gone from her hands. Luc untied the blindfold and laid it on the table, next to the sketchpad.

"Now draw what you just held."

Marie looked around for the candlestick.

"It's not here. Draw it from memory, from the way it felt in your hands."

She picked up the pencil and began to sketch in the candlestick's curves and points as best she could recall them. Quickly, though, she realized she couldn't remember which end of the candlestick had been the top and which had been the bottom. Luc sat opposite her and watched intently as she worked.

When she finished—or gave up—she set down the pencil and pushed away the pad. Luc went into the next room for a moment. When he returned, he set the candlestick down next to her drawing. Marie groaned and closed her eyes. She wasn't even close.

"It's okay, Marie," came Luc's voice, soft and understanding. "This is where most people start, blind. You just need practice."

Her eyelids felt like lead weights and she was unable to contain a sudden yawn. Too much wine and too little sleep last night.

"It's late. Why don't I show you to your room?"

Silently, Marie followed Luc to his guest room. Her weekend bag sat on a wooden luggage stand, the bed's covers had been turned back to reveal fluffy white pillows, and a grey cashmere robe hung from a hook next to the room.

"This is—"

"Shh." Luc closed the window blinds. "We'll talk at breakfast."

When he left, Marie let out a quiet, controlled exhale. Was this how he conducted all his lessons? It was odd. She'd had some weird birds for art professors in college, but Luc Marchand took the cake. No talking. Blindfolds. Kissing. DWI, drawing while intoxicated. She giggled, until her mind wandered off to pursue other questions. What would it be like to kiss Luc Marchand while blindfolded? Whom else had he tied a blindfold around?

Stop it. You cannot be jealous.

But she was.

Outside, the storm that had been brewing all day on the horizon arrived with a rolling shudder of thunder. Rain slapped against the windows of the room. She sucked in her lower lip, searching for any lingering trace of garlic and wine, any last faint taste of his kiss, and thought unkind thoughts about every other, unnamed, faceless student who had been kissed by Luc Marchand.

"DID YOU SLEEP WELL LAST NIGHT?" Luc asked as he cleared away the breakfast dishes. He looked well-rested, clean-shaven and with none of the dark shadows that marred Marie's eyes. His navy linen shirt was pressed and tucked neatly into unwrinkled khakis. Marie thought of the sweat-soaked pajamas stuffed into her weekend bag.

"Yes, I did," she answered. She hadn't, of course, and offered up a silent prayer that he wouldn't call her on the lie. The last thing she wanted to do was explain the dream she'd had, the one that had left her unable to go back to sleep.

In the dream she had been not a student, but a model. A model like the ones she had drawn in her college drawing classes. She sat on a wooden stool in the middle of a studio, her blouse and bra and jeans in a heap on the floor. But instead of modeling for a class full of undergraduates, she'd been modeling for just one person. Luc Marchand.

Normally, Marie wasn't one to remember dreams in vivid detail. When the sun rose, the contours of her dreams faded into the light and usually she was thankful for that. But this morning, she couldn't seem to shake the details of last night's dream. Nor was she sure she wanted to. It had been nighttime in the dream, the windows of the studio black against the darkness outside. From overhead, a pool of yellow light illuminated her. She'd had to squint to see Luc behind his easel, his eyes shifting between her and his sketchpad as he drew. No one said a word. The only sound had been the thunderstorm washing over the valley.

Marie had never worked as an artist's model before, nor ever had the desire to. In fact, she'd always felt vaguely sorry for the classroom models with their gooseflesh and muscles quivering from the strain of holding still. In her dream, though, it had been the most arousing thing she'd ever done, sitting there perfectly still while Luc Marchand drew her breasts.

"Marie?" Luc's voice broke into her reverie. "Is that your phone?" The smirk on his face and the carefully-lifted eyebrow said *well, are you going to answer that?*

Marie shook off the last of the dream. Yes, that was her phone trilling from the bottom of her purse. She dug it out.

"Hello?"

It was her mother, asking her to come into the office today.

"I can come in later ... late afternoon, mother ... I'm sorry ... not before then ... I'm not at home ..." *Where was she?* "In Middleburg. I'm shopping with friends ... no, we can't leave yet ... I'm sorry ... I'm helping her look for ... a wedding gown ... there is now ... I'll see you later this afternoon."

She ended the call and dropped the phone back into her bag. Then she pulled it back out and silenced it.

"Bon," Luc said.

She turned to face him. He was sitting at the table.

"There's a line between apologizing and groveling. I think you just crossed it," he said.

She shrugged.

He did an exaggerated imitation of shrugging. “What’s this? You do this all the time.”

“It means I don’t know.”

“I think it means you don’t want to talk about it.”

Marie stood awkwardly, her arms hanging by her side, at loose ends—the way she was so often these days. She crossed her arms over her chest. She knew the protective gesture was ridiculous even as she did it. She hadn’t really exposed her breasts to this man. A dream didn’t count.

“So you’re helping a friend shop for a wedding gown right now?” Luc sipped from what surely must be cold coffee by now, an amused smile playing around his lips.

She shrugged again, which made him laugh and say something in French that she couldn’t understand.

Marie sat down in the chair, scooting it away from Luc a few inches. He hooked his feet around the chair’s front legs and pulled it back.

“You can’t tell your mother that you’re here?”

She looked at him incredulously. “That I’m at a man’s house this early in the morning? Not unless you want a few uninvited guests with badges and guns.”

“You could have said you were taking a class somewhere else. Isn’t that a reasonable weekend activity?”

“Then I would have had to tell her where. And run the risk that she knows someone there, and will talk to them later, and then my lie would be found out.”

“You’re really afraid of your parents, aren’t you? That’s why you pushed me away in your car.”

“I don’t have ordinary parents. And unfortunately, my life doesn’t operate separate from them. I’m just a teeny-tiny little planet in their orbit.”

Luc leaned forward and placed his palms on her knees. “Do you want to leave? I don’t want to cause trouble for you.”

"No, I don't want to go," she said at last, lifting her gaze from where his hands were burning a hole through her jeans. His body was so close to hers, distractingly close, that it was hard to think. "I just have to keep certain parts of my life private from them. Even if I didn't, I don't know that I would tell them. This is something I want to do for myself."

"It will be challenging. I don't let my students slack off."

"I understand that."

"I will push you, Marie. I will push you to push yourself, because that is the only way to learn anything that is worth knowing."

When she nodded in agreement, he lifted his palms from her knees and flattened one against the table, splaying his long, charcoal-stained fingers. "Close your eyes and touch my hand."

"No blindfold this time?" she asked.

"I have to be able to trust you, Marie. If I tell you not to look, I have to trust that you won't."

She closed her eyes tight, then began tracing the outline of his hand with her fingers. Her touch was tentative, feathery.

"Harder, Marie. You won't break me."

She pressed harder, feeling the soft veins just beneath his skin, the bony knobs of his knuckles. When she ran the tip of her finger gently along the curve of his cuticle, she heard him draw in his breath sharply. She waited for him to ask her to stop. When he didn't, she continued, flattening her palm over his hand, taking in the heat of his skin. How does one draw heat, she wondered. That was probably something Luc would expect of her. She flipped her hand over and ran the back of her hand over his, concentrating on the texture of his skin. It was softer and smoother than she would have guessed. She'd never really paid attention to a man's hand before. When Richard had held her hand, it had been to keep her next to him, to keep her in line. It had never been a romantic gesture.

She turned her hand palm down again, and began to slide her fingers between his, slowly, stopping at the knuckles, trying to picture the way the lines grew wider at each one. By the time her fingertips reached the soft skin at the base of his fingers, his breathing beside her was shallow and deliberate. Marie was suddenly aware that their arms were resting against each other on the table's edge. Luc's skin was hot. It took every ounce of willpower not to open her eyes and look him in the face.

But she kept them closed. Without saying a word, she lifted her hand from his and reached for the sketchpad. She turned away before opening her eyes so as not to catch a glimpse of his hand. She began rapidly drawing in the lines of his fingers. She had to do it fast before the memory of how his hand felt faded from her mind. When she was finished, she set down the pencil and looked at her work.

It was awful.

She began to tear off the sheet so she could crumple it up and throw it away. Luc stopped her.

"It's terrible," she protested.

"It's a start. To be good at anything it has to be your obsession. You have to be so obsessed with drawing that you begin to look at everything in terms of lines and planes, light and shadow."

"But how can I look at lines and planes if my eyes are closed?"

"Not all seeing is done with the eyes, Marie."

He took her hand and placed it on the table, closed his eyes. He had long lashes, like a child's, she saw. She watched as he ran his fingers, all of them, lightly over her skin. His touch was registering in parts of her body where his fingers had no business being. She could feel them on her scalp, tugging through her hair. They were leisurely tracing her spine, vertebra by vertabra. They were tweaking her nipples into hard little peaks.

She glanced over at him to see whether his eyes were still

closed. He had to know what this was doing to her. She could hear that her breathing had gotten louder, unsteady.

"You chew your thumbnail," he said.

"I do it when I get nervous. It's a bad habit, I know. I should try to stop."

"I'm not passing judgment, Marie. I'm simply observing. That's important if you want to draw well. Seeing without judging."

He continued his exploration of her hand. His index finger traced a spot just below her third knuckle. "You have a scar here."

Marie frowned and leaned over her hand to look. "Oh, that. How can you feel that? It's tiny."

"The texture of the skin is different."

"Or you noticed it earlier, when your eyes were open. Isn't that what palm readers do? They watch people before they sit down, figure them out ahead of time."

"I'm going to pretend I didn't just hear you accuse me of being a charlatan, Marie."

When she turned her head to look at him, his jaw was tight, his nostrils flared. She'd angered him.

"How did you burn yourself?" he continued.

"I was at a barbeque at a friend's house."

"You were helping to cook?" He continued to finger her scar.

"Yes."

"You're lying." He pressed more firmly on her hand.

"How do you know that?" she challenged him.

"You started to pull your hand away as you said that."

She sighed. "We were burning my wedding dress. A spark flew up and landed on my hand. Satisfied?"

He was silent for a minute, continuing to touch her hand. "*Putain*," he said at long last. His fingers stopped, resting—finally—on her skin. He seemed to be momentarily at a loss for words.

"You really burned your wedding dress?" Out of the corner of her eye, she saw him—long-lashed eyes still closed—shake his head.

Victory swelled inside Marie. She had Luc Marchand flummoxed. Surely that didn't happen often. He said something in French she didn't understand, then his fingers began roving again. They stopped at a bruise she'd forgotten she had, his thumb pressing tenderly into the slight swelling there. She closed her own eyes now and let herself sink into the sensation.

"Burning your dress, that's rather extreme, isn't it? You must really hate him."

Did she hate Richard? She considered the idea. She had at times, yes. Those nights he didn't come home. The day she discovered the letters from Maya in his closet. The morning she'd opened the divorce papers—she could have killed him at that moment, if he'd been standing there. But did she hate him now? Right this minute?

No, she didn't think she did. It was more that she just wanted to be rid of him. She no longer wanted him—or Maya—in her life anymore.

"It wasn't my idea," she said to Luc. "Burning the dress was a friend's idea." She giggled. "It was kind of fun, actually. A relief, you know?"

"And this friend, was it the one who gave you these lessons with me?" Luc was no longer touching her hand. He had covered it with his palm, just resting there.

"Yes," she answered.

"I think your friend knows you better than you perhaps know yourself."

"She knows everyone better than they know themselves."

"It's good to have a friend like that. Sam—the woman who was with me at your mother's event—is that person for me."

Wait … is Luc Marchand … confiding in me? The room felt perfectly still to her all of a sudden, and quiet. The only thing she was aware of was the feeling of his hand covering hers, firm and warm.

"And do you listen to everything she says?" she asked.

Luc chuckled, and slid his hand slowly off of hers. The sensation was so exquisite, it was almost painful. "Eventually. Sometimes she has to, you know, whack me over the head a few times first."

He flipped over a new sheet of paper on her sketchpad and began to methodically draw. The moment, whatever it had been, was over now. Marie watched as a perfect reproduction of her hand appeared, with its ragged thumbnail and scar, the pale shading of her bruise.

"I'll never be able to do that," she said when he set his pencil down.

"I think you will," he said, "if you want to. Art won't simply bestow itself upon you, Marie. You have to beg and plead for it to visit you. Then, when it turns on its heel and walks away, you have to throw yourself at its feet and weep."

What would it take to get him to bestow another kiss on her? Begging? Pleading? Whatever it was, she was prepared to offer it. Marie had never done anything harder than smoke a cigarette at high school parties, but she was beginning to understand the nature of addiction. She would throw herself at his feet and weep. Yes, she would do even that.

8

"My leg is falling asleep, Uncle Luc." Ellie Smith fidgeted impatiently on the stool in Luc's studio, tugging at her black velvet dress, then the pearl choker clinging to her neck.

"Just another minute, *chérie,* and you can rest," Luc said soothingly. He daubed ochre paint onto the canvas, then swiftly blended it with his brush.

"He's almost done with the hair, sweetie," Sam chimed in.

"God, mom, do not call me sweetie. At least not in public. Please!"

"I'm pretty sure my studio doesn't count as 'in public,'" Luc said, smiling into his canvas.

Ellie was Sam's twelve-year-old daughter. He leaned in toward the canvas and brushed in highlights on the hair. Ellie was a miniature version of her mother, graceful and composed beyond her years. If Luc ever had a daughter, he'd want her to be like Ellie. If Grace hadn't … he choked on the thought.

A snippet of piano sonata pierced the air. "Is that mine?" Ellie called over to her mother, who was sunk deep into the faded upholstery of Luc's most comfortable chair.

Samantha shook her head as she answered her own phone. Luc smiled in amusement at Ellie's disappointment. She was a popular girl, according to her mom and dad.

He painted for a minute more, capturing the thick dark blonde hair that Ellie had inherited from her mother. "There. Got it. You can rest now, Ellie."

Ellie slid down from the stool on which she'd been perched and grimaced as she stretched her stiff arms and back.

"Mom, can I have my phone?" she asked before heading into the tiny studio bathroom.

"Are you doing any other Christmas portraits this year?" Sam asked.

Ellie's portrait was to be a gift for Sam's parents.

"Did a few over the summer. But no more on the horizon at this point," he replied. An image of Marie Witherspoon in a black velvet dress, posed perfectly still for him, flashed through his mind.

"Are you working on anything new?"

"Yes."

"Good." Sam was silent for a minute. "I'm going out on a limb here for you, opening a new gallery with a one-man show for you."

He nodded and squeezed out more paint. "I know that, Sam. I appreciate it. I'll have new work for you. I promise."

Sam looked around the studio, her eyes slowly scanning the room. "It's just that I don't see anything in progress."

"I'm still in the study phase."

She looked at him skeptically. "I need a whole show's worth."

"I'll have it for you. I promise."

Sam walked over to the bathroom door, rapped sharply on the wood. "Ellie? Luc is waiting."

When she returned to her seat next to Luc, she asked, "The Witherspoon girl? Did she decide to take lessons with you after all?"

Luc was surprised Sam remembered.

"Yes." Luc rubbed his aching fingers, then lined up his brushes. "She did."

Sam watched him fuss with the easel, silently debate one brush versus another, and unroll and re-roll his sleeves. Then she spoke.

"Keep that professional, Luc."

"You've already told me who she is."

"I know. I'm just escalating the threat level. It's an ugly situation all around, from what I hear. Her parents were shocked by the divorce, apparently. Totally gobsmacked. Rumor always had it that they practically arranged the marriage to begin with."

"I didn't realize people still did that these days." Luc pretended to look closely at the canvas.

"You don't want to get mixed up in that, is all I'm saying. I have a new corporate client who's interested in art lessons. She's divorced. Not too bad looking. Has her own money."

"No offense, Sam, but I'm French. I need a little mystique, a woman who understands the fine art of seduction. These rich women you send me are about as seductive as the suburban tanks they all drive."

"Ah, you want a Citroen kind of woman. Quirky but elegant."

"Yes, I do. A Citroen DS." He chuckled. "I want a *déesse.* A quirky, elegant goddess."

"Don't know if I can find you one of those around here."

Sam and Luc looked in unison toward the bathroom, where Ellie had just emerged.

"Ellie, dear? Do you think you can manage another fifteen or twenty minutes? Enough for Luc to get started on the arms and shoulders?" Sam asked.

As Luc painted, Ellie's face wavered between boredom and barely-restrained giggles. His child would have been eleven this year. Every time he thought of it, the crack in his heart widened a little further.

After Sam and Ellie left, he tidied up the studio and returned to the house, where he opened a bottle of burgundy. He slumped into a chair at the dining table and stared into the glass of wine. Sam was right to be worried. He had no new work of his own, work that wasn't commissioned by clients, underway—and he was running out of time to meet Sam's deadline. For a while there, her permits and other paperwork had been mired in city bureaucracy. But they'd been sprung free and things were moving again.

He needed some ideas, that was all.

He fiddled with the edge of a sheet of sketch paper lying on the table, folding a corner back and forth until it tore off. He flipped the sheet over. It was a drawing of Marie Witherspoon. He'd made it after last weekend's lesson with her, two days of almost unbearable awkwardness. She had wanted him to kiss her. It had been written all over her face. And he had, once, after dinner. But that had been to help her draw, not for her pleasure or his own.

Not that it hadn't been pleasurable. It most certainly had been. So pleasurable that he had wanted to kiss her over and over, then take her back to his bed and fuck into the wee hours of the morning.

But that probably wasn't a good idea, fucking Marie Witherspoon. For all the reasons Sam had enumerated, plus several more. He owed this woman three months of drawing instruction. Sleeping with her could endlessly complicate those three months, months when he needed to finish a lot of work for Sam.

But god he wanted to.

He held his empty wine glass up to the light. He needed to behave himself around Marie Witherspoon. It sounded as though her entire life had been mapped out for her and she'd just been following the GPS, until her marriage took a wrong exit. He wanted to help her draw—she had some talent, actually, unlike the wealthy housewives Sam sent his way—but that was as far as he should take it.

He refilled his glass and took a long slug, letting the wine's heavy spiciness work its way into his veins, then leaned back in the chair and regarded the sketch some more. Despite being drawn in a matter of minutes, he liked it. With only her shoulders, breasts and part of her torso, it reminded him of a broken piece of ancient statuary. Venus. Aphrodite. Déesse.

9

Luc was standing on the endlessly-climbing Dupont Circle metro escalator, slowly ascending up into the sunshine as if being reborn from the maw of hell. Washington's subway system was particularly charmless, as far as public transportation systems went, though Luc supposed it did accurately capture the side of Washington that was dark, underground, its very blandness designed to divert attention.

Above ground, Luc rather liked Washington, DC. Parts of it felt very European to him, the classically-inspired buildings, the understated scale of the skyline. There were no skyscrapers in Washington, forbidden by an act of Congress. He imagined that lots of Americans would be horrified by the anti-capitalist heavy handedness of such a decree—if they were aware of it, which of course they were not—but Luc was glad of it for himself. He could never imagine himself living in New York, say, in those deep canyons of glass and concrete, or in San Francisco with its endless hills of sun-bleached buildings.

It made sense to him that Washington had been designed by a Frenchman.

He zipped up his leather jacket as he strolled the blocks from Metro to Q and 21st Streets. The October sunshine was deceiving. The air was much chillier than it looked, almost as chilly as Luc's disposition. He'd been painting like a fiend since Sunday, determined not to let Sam down. She'd forgiven him many things, but wrecking the opening of her new gallery wouldn't likely be one of them.

But he needed a few hours break, a respite from the pressures of his studio. The Phillips Collection, tucked away just a few blocks from the busy-ness and traffic of Connecticut Avenue, had long been Luc's favorite museum in the U.S. It reminded him of his grandfather's home in Paris with its gracious old rooms and walls hung with impressionist and early modernist paintings. Luc paid the admission fee and bounded up the winding staircase to the third floor, the special exhibitions gallery.

He peered inside the white-walled room. *Alistair Smith & Elizabeth Calhoun: A Model Revealed.* He glanced around. Large portraits. He'd never heard of either Alistair Smith or Elizabeth Calhoun. That was all the recommendation he needed. He felt the need to see something unfamiliar and fresh, something that might prove to be the lightning bolt of inspiration he needed for Sam's show.

He strolled the perimeter of the room, casually taking in the paintings. He ignored the framed, handwritten letters paired with each. The canvases varied in size. Some were small and square, no more than twelve inches on each side. Others were large, nearly life size. All of them depicted a female model but in none of them was her face visible. In the large portraits, her head was turned away from the artist or her face obscured by a large hat or a scarf blowing in the wind. Many of the smaller paintings were partial nudes, a ribbed torso or softly-curving hip or the elegantly muscled slope of a calf. There was a coy secrecy about all of them that was appealing to him.

He headed back to the beginning of the exhibit. He liked to look at the works before reading a curator's explanation. He wanted his own impression to be his first.

"Alistair Smith was a relatively unknown American artist living in New York in the 1940s when he met Elizabeth Calhoun, the wife of U.S. Senator Teddy Calhoun. For decades, the identity of the woman in Smith's paintings was a mystery and the artist himself refused to say who she was, taking the secret to his grave. Finally, when Elizabeth Calhoun passed away in 2001 and her children discovered boxes of correspondence between Elizabeth and Alistair Smith, the mystery woman was unmasked. For nearly fifteen years, Elizabeth had been Alistair's lover, muse and mystery model. Last year, the estates of Calhoun and Smith generously gave their correspondence and his paintings to the Phillips Collection. This exhibit marks the first time that the letters and paintings have been publicly shown together."

Luc returned to the paintings. This time he leaned in to read the letters, some of which were penned in a thin, spidery script and others in a blockier, more masculine hand.

Dear A, I am drowning in the dullness that is Washington. Nothing here interests me now, not since meeting you. I mark off every hour as it passes, for it is one less hour until I see you again. Who was the genius who decided that there should be twenty-four tedious hours in every day? Will you paint me when we meet? You were hesitant when I broached the idea before. Please reconsider ... your loving E.

The letter was hung next to a pencil study, a quickly-drawn sketch that showed Elizabeth Calhoun walking toward the viewer, her face fully visible. He stepped back to look up at the tall painting. Elizabeth was dressed in a simple brown skirt that skimmed her calves, low-heeled oxfords, and an ivory blouse that draped suggestively over her breasts. A yellow scarf covered her hair. Unlike the study, however, the painting showed her looking back over her shoulder, her long neck stretching away from prying eyes.

My dear, sweet El -- It is not that I do not wish to paint you -- please never think that -- there is nothing I do more than contemplate painting those stormy grey eyes -- your rose-flush cheeks -- when I am done with that, I have but mere minutes left in my day -- no, sweet El -- it is exposing you I fear -- for me, I worry nothing -- I am no one -- a failed artist, merely -- I am ever your A.

Ah well. Luc saw the compromise. Alistair would paint Elizabeth, but never show her face. A doomed love affair. Sam had suggested to him once that that was what Grace had wanted. Not a love affair, but a doomed love affair.

He skipped over several other large portraits in favor of the smaller, partial nudes. He stopped in front of six grouped together on the wall. Long, slender fingers cupped around an apple. The small of a back. Hair cascading over a shoulder. The point of a hipbone. The curve of a delicate ear and the swoop of a jawline. The lush, ripe swell of breasts.

He had painted Grace many times; she had begged him to, just as Elizabeth Calhoun had apparently begged Alistair Smith. Most of those paintings were gone, sold by Sam to people who collected such things. Luc was a coward in that regard. He couldn't bear to keep them but neither could he bear to burn them, as he should have. Instead, they now belonged to other people, a circumstance Sam was certain Grace would have been thrilled with.

He frowned at the small paintings on the wall. Is this what Elizabeth Calhoun would have wanted, her hips and breasts hanging on the wall of a museum? He turned away, to return to one of the larger, clothed portraits. But the nudes drew him back again. He had drawn Grace's breasts over and over. She had wanted it, of course, but it had given him great pleasure too. Elizabeth Calhoun's breasts were nothing like Grace's, of course. Grace had been small and thin, all planes and angles, her breasts the tiny buds of an angel.

Elizabeth Calhoun's breasts were full, plush, ripe like a wanton fruit whose juices would spill over one's lips and chin if one were rash enough to take a bite.

My dearest E, the letter next to the paintings read, *man has not invented pillows so soft as yours -- when may I again rest my weary head on them?*

Luc was struck by a sudden vision of Marie Witherspoon's breasts in the moment before he settled his cheek against them. Or what he imagined to be Marie Witherspoon's breasts, for he hadn't seen them of course. Even so, he knew that Marie's shape was closer to Elizabeth Calhoun than Grace had been. He drew in a sharp breath, and the memory of Marie's perfume came back to him. He hadn't realized he'd even noticed her perfume.

He tore himself away from Elizabeth Calhoun's body, hurrying down the stairs to the bottom floor cafe. He curtly—rudely—ordered an espresso from the young man behind the counter and took it out onto the terrace, where he collapsed into a cold metal chair.

His brain was crowded with Marie Witherspoon. Suddenly everything reminded him of her. The leaves on that tree over there, the same rusty copper shade of her hair. The espresso, with the same burnt aftertaste of her kiss. It had been three days since he'd seen her last, and he didn't think he'd make it until Saturday and her next lesson with him.

Fuck it. He pulled out his phone and tapped her name on his contact list.

10

Marie was typing thank you letters to the silent auction donors and wondering when she would get to Luc Marchand's name, when her mother barged into her office.

"Marie dear, I need to cancel lunch today. I'm sorry. I have a last minute appointment in Potomac. Maybe tomorrow?"

Marie nodded. "Tomorrow is fine. Who's the meeting with?"

"The Hadley School. I've been trying to get in there all year."

"Well, good luck then."

Her mother tilted her perfectly-coiffed head to one side and frowned. "How are you doing these days? I feel like you slip in and out of here. I barely see you some weeks."

"Mother. We talk every day."

"About business, yes. But not about your life."

Marie's inner child was rolling her eyes. "No, I haven't heard from Richard lately. Nor do I expect to. You and dad need to let go of that idea."

Eileen sighed. "It's not too late for the two of you to call off the divorce."

"You're speaking to the wrong person about that. I wasn't the one who initiated the divorce." Marie turned toward her computer, a hint to her mother.

"But you could call him once in awhile. Keep the door open."

Marie fumed as she listened to her mother's heels click down the hall, then down the staircase to the front door. It was a good thing she cancelled lunch if that was what she had wanted to talk about. Marie seriously doubted that Richard would welcome the occasional phone call from her. The subject of their marriage was closed, as far as Marie was concerned. She had closed that door, flipped the deadbolt, and wedged a chair beneath the doorknob.

She sent the next batch of letters to the printer down the hall and was leaving to retrieve them when her cell phone rang. She turned back toward her desk and glanced at the caller ID.

Luc Marchand.

She snatched up the phone and answered. "Hello, this is Marie."

"Bonjour, Marie."

Why was it that when he said her name, all manner of things began to vibrate deep inside her body? She should have let the call roll over to voice mail so she could listen to him say her name whenever she wanted.

"Mr. Marchand. If you need to cancel our lesson this weekend, that's perfectly okay—"

"That's not why I'm calling, Marie. I'm over at the Phillips Collection right now. Do you know it?"

"Yes. Of course."

"Could you meet me for lunch here tomorrow?"

Luc Marchand was inviting her to lunch? For a moment, her office began to sway and she leaned on her desk to steady herself.

"Marie? Are you there?"

"Yes. Yes. I'm here. Actually, I could meet you today." Why wait until tomorrow? Tomorrow she might be stuck having lunch with her mother, deflecting questions about Richard. "If you're there right now, I mean."

"I'll be in the third floor gallery."

MARIE STOPPED in the doorway to the gallery, not bothering to even look at the exhibition title. Despite her love of art, she couldn't care less about it today. Luc Marchand was the art she was here to see.

She peered into the white-walled room. The gallery was empty, save for a lone figure standing in front of a large painting, his back to her. Faded jeans stretched from his rather fine backside down to short, distressed boots. A black leather jacket hung from his broad shoulders. She spent a moment just taking him in. *Seriously, frame him and hang him on the wall.*

He turned, as if sensing her hot stare, and smiled. She joined him next to the painting, then glanced around at the rest of the gallery. A mix of large and small paintings hung on the walls, along with many smaller sketches and handwritten pages.

"What show is this?" she asked. "I didn't look when I came in." She turned back to the painting Luc had been studying when she arrived. It was a portrait of a woman sitting in an upholstered armchair, a blanket wrapped around her shoulders and body. Clearly, the viewer was meant to assume that she wore nothing beneath the blanket. Her bare feet peeked out from the bottom, small and delicate. Her chin was tucked into her chest, hiding her face. The whole pose was so vulnerable, so real, it made Marie want to lean in and try to look up at the woman's face.

"This is Elizabeth Calhoun," Luc said, "painted by her lover, Alistair Smith."

Luc moved behind her, settling his hands onto her shoulders.

"Do you think they are good?" she asked. Conversation might help her resist the overwhelming urge to lean back into Luc's body.

"Good is relative. What do *you* think, Marie?"

She studied the painting for awhile. "She doesn't want to be seen. They were lovers, you said?"

"Yes."

"She doesn't want anyone to know that."

Luc followed her as she went from painting to painting, carefully inspecting each. She read Elizabeth's entreaties to Alistair, begging him to paint her, and yet in none of the paintings did she show her face. Who was she? Why did she not trust her lover to see all of her?

Marie was four paintings from the end when she gave in to her curiosity and strode over to the curator's introduction. Disappointment washed over her as the words sunk in. Wife. Senator. Mystery woman. Unmasked. This was why Luc had wanted her to come to the museum. The parallels were so obvious they were like a slap in the face.

And yet ... there was something very *hot* about them all. She returned to the small partial nudes, Elizabeth Calhoun's hip, her calf, her hand over her breast. Despite their small size and scope, looking at them felt like being let in on a secret, like peeking through a keyhole into someone else's very private life.

It reminded Marie of her dream, the one in which she modeled for Luc Marchand in a dimly-lit studio. Just the two of them. It wasn't a dream that came to her every night, but it haunted her daydreams every day.

She turned to look back at Luc. He was standing ten feet away, watching her with a wary expression on his face. He knew he had taken a risk inviting her here and yet he'd done it anyway. Marie aimed a forgiving smile at him.

"I wish I could afford to have you paint me," she said. She gestured toward the walls of the gallery. "Not that it would be the same ..." She rushed to qualify her wish as she realized the comparison she was making.

"I would pay to paint you." Luc's voice was low, more a rumble vibrating across the air than words spoken out loud.

She laughed nervously and turned back toward him just in time to see his chest right in front of her face. The next thing she knew she was in Luc Marchand's arms and his lips were brushing her ear.

"I'm serious, Marie. Name a figure."

A wave of heat spread across her cheeks and then downward through her body as she thought of the dream. It was completely a figment of her nighttime imagination and yet it had been so real ... and so arousing. More arousing than anything she'd ever experienced in real life.

"Would you model for me?"

She felt as though his words passed straight from his chest into hers. She nodded her head against the leather of his jacket. "Yes," she said so quietly she could barely hear her own voice. "I would like to do that."

"Have you modeled before?"

Her heart dropped. Great. He needed her to have experience?

"No. Not really."

"Not really?"

"Well ... I dreamed I modeled once. More than once."

"You modeled more than once or you had the dream more than once?"

She could hear the amusement in his voice.

"I had the dream more than once."

"And for whom were you modeling?"

She hesitated. She feared he would laugh but already he was threading his hands through her hair, cupping the back of her head, making it clear that there was no way out of answering.

"You," she whispered into his chest. "I was modeling for you."

"Only me?" His hands tugged on the back of her head, pulling her face up to look him in the eyes.

"And did you like it? Modeling for me?"

She nodded.

"Why, Marie?"

"You'll laugh at me."

"I promise I won't."

"It turned me on," she said quietly. Her eyes flicked away from his face.

"What were you wearing?"

His hand stroked her cheek and she leaned into it, closing her eyes. "Nothing."

"You were completely nude?"

She heard the note of surprise in his voice. She nodded.

"Did I touch you in this dream?"

"No. All you did was look at me ... and draw."

She was suddenly aware of a growing hardness against her stomach. Luc Marchand was aroused by her dream. "But I wanted you to touch me." There. It was out. "I wanted you to desire me."

"I'll make you a trade, Marie."

His lips were lowering, getting so close she could taste his breath.

"If l kiss you, will you agree to model for me this weekend?" His breath caressed her lips.

That was it? No begging or pleading needed? No weeping? She stretched up to close the minute amount of space between her lips and his. "Yes."

She felt his hand on her lower back, pressing her body tighter against his. There was no mistaking his hardness now. She was dizzy from that knowledge, dizzy with anticipation.

But when he kissed her, his lips were disappointingly light on hers and for a moment she feared this would be merely a chaste peck on the lips. That was not what she wanted. Every nerve ending in her body was screaming in protest, craving his touch.

"Kiss me." The words, with their unmistakable note of begging, were out of her mouth and into his before she could stop them. Her body quivered in his arms. This was torture, being so close to what she needed and yet not being allowed to have it. He was going to make her beg for it, after all, like a junkie on the street.

Well, she would beg. She was desperate enough to do it.

"Please."

Just when she was about to beg again, he pulled her tighter against his chest and kissed her. Hard. She felt her body melt into his, every nerve ending sighing as the sweet relief of his kiss spread through her veins. She kissed him back, trying to get more of him, more of his taste and scent into her blood. His groan vibrated against her breasts.

"So you think about me when we're not having lessons?" He trailed kisses down to the collar of her coat.

"Sometimes." *All the time.*

"I think about you too, Marie." He unwound her scarf to get more access to her neck and collarbone. "From the day you walked into my studio, I've been thinking about you."

"But ... you sent me away." His lips on her skin and his breath skittering beneath the front of her blouse made it harder and harder to think straight.

"Ah, chérie, I was trying to send you away for your own good."

Luc buried his face in the curve of her neck, and Marie wanted this moment to last forever. Just Luc Marchand's lips against her skin, his body pressed into hers. As soon as he moved away, her body would ache with desire again. Only this time it would be even more painful.

She had never *needed* another person's touch the way her body craved Luc Marchand. Even at the beginning of her marriage to

Richard, it had never been this intense. Never touch-me-or-I'm-going-to-die intense.

"I am a disaster where women are concerned," Luc said, kissing his way back up to her jaw, her chin, her lips. "But you won't leave my thoughts alone, Marie. Every time I try to push you out of my head, you slip back in. You're tormenting me."

No one had ever been tormented by thoughts of her before, though Marie was familiar with the sensation. Luc was tormenting her thoughts, too.

From across the gallery someone cleared a throat and Luc took a step back. She felt the reluctance in his parting. Out of the corner of her eye, she saw a black-suited security guard glaring at them. Her face flushed furiously with embarrassment.

"I have to get back to work," she said. She began to wrap her scarf around her neck, to hide her just-kissed skin, to keep the feel of his lips from evaporating into the air.

Luc tugged the ends of the scarf from her fingers and tied it for her. He gently squeezed her chin between his thumb and finger. "Practice your modeling for Saturday, oui?"

Oh, oui.

BACK IN THE OFFICE, Marie printed the rest of the thank you letters with their matching envelopes and signed her mother's name to each—except for the one addressed to Luc Marchand. She signed that one simply "Marie." Then she carefully folded each letter into thirds, slid them into the envelopes and affixed stamps to them. No impersonal metered postage for her mother. At Witherspoon & Associates, every piece of correspondence was handled by an actual person.

Marie, generally.

Eight years out of college and she was still doing an entry-level job. Oh, her business cards read "director of marketing" but she didn't have the authority to do anything without her mother's say so. Nishi was a senior vice president already. Her mother didn't take the idea of a career for her seriously. First, because she had been waiting for her to marry Richard and have children. Now, because she was waiting for Marie to reconcile with Richard and have children. Return to the career she was born to: politician's wife.

Marie's plans and her mother's did not mesh, obviously. In a year, she would be finished with her MBA and able to start an actual career. One of her own choosing.

She took the stack of letters down to Maeve. "I haven't missed the mailman yet, have I?"

Maeve looked up from her computer screen, smiling. She was always happy to see Marie. "No, dear. I expect him in ten or fifteen minutes so you're good. Also, your mother phoned. She won't be back to the office this afternoon."

"So I can sneak out early?" Marie joked. There would be no sneaking out. Marie needed a job at the moment and she wouldn't put it past her mother to fire her. Her employment at Witherspoon & Associates had been terminated, without question, when she married Richard. "Ah, I've got plenty to do to keep me busy."

Starting with daydreaming about Luc Marchand some more. Every time he kissed her, it was like she'd never been kissed before. Three times now. That's how many times she'd been kissed by Luc. She was definitely keeping count.

He had wanted her at the museum. Sure, probably it was just an involuntary reaction. He was a man. There had been a woman in his arms, ergo he was turned on. She didn't care, as long as he kissed her again—with any luck as soon as this weekend. She didn't need him to care about her or—heaven forbid—love her. She just needed to feel the things her body did around him, the way everything inside her swirled around and around when he looked at her.

But there were two more days to get through until she could see him again—two and a half, if you counted the rest of today—so she put him out of her mind as best she could. She had been procrastinating all week on finishing the report for her mother on the fundraiser's press coverage. The *Post* had taken the easy way out: *Eileen Witherspoon and Sen. Richard Macintyre joined forces again to ...* The local television evening news shows had run clips of her mother's major donors enjoying themselves; Maya had managed to insert herself into two of those.

The local business journal was the only outlet that had bothered to clarify the new relationship between her mother and Richard: *Witherspoon & Associates CEO Eileen Witherspoon and her soon-to-be former son-in-law Richard Macintyre, senator from Pennsylvania.* Marie glanced at the byline. The reporter was relatively new and, based on his fresh-faced photo, not long out of college.

And then, of course, there was the J Street Chronicle. Maya had written a lengthy post about the evening, name-checking as many people as she could and posting multiple photographs of herself and Richard. Marie scrolled through the photos, beginning to hope that she had escaped Maya's lens. But no. There she was. Standing by herself, her wine glass tipped to her lips. The very picture of boozy loneliness.

Lovely. She had spent so much time at the event schmoozing, which had been her sole purpose for being there, and Maya managed to get a photo of her alone. Looking eminently pathetic. The jilted wife drowning her sorrows in alcohol while the victorious mistress is happy and beloved by everyone.

She took a screen shot of her photo and pasted that into the report, as well. Not that her mother would care. Marie was supposed to just suck it up and smile.

She scrolled through the rest of the photos. Her eyes stopped on one of Luc and Samantha Smith, deep in conversation. Maya's caption noted that Samantha Smith was adding a Dupont Circle location to her successful S. Smith Fine Arts Gallery in Leesburg. Luc wasn't mentioned.

Right beneath Luc and Samantha Smith's photo was another one of Maya and Richard. Richard looked even less relaxed than usual, gripping Maya's hand tightly but with several inches of daylight separating their bodies. She was leaning toward him. His posture was perfectly straight.

"He isn't going to marry her, Marie," her mother kept saying. "He may think so now but eventually the folly of that will become apparent to him. You just have to wait him out."

But Marie wasn't interested in waiting him out. Getting dumped by your husband for a floozy like Maya Redfearn was humiliating. It had been on the front page of the *Post.* "Sen. Richard Macintyre and Wife to Divorce." Below the fold, but still. The front page! For months, every mention of him in the press included, "Senator Macintyre, who recently separated from his wife of five years, Marie Witherspoon ..."

And of course, Maya gloated to no end on her blog. Every photo of the two of them together was captioned, "Senator Richard Macintyre and his fiancee, Maya Redfearn ..."

It just sucked. Privately, of course, some people were aghast at Maya's brazen behavior. Some people would have the grace not to flaunt their homewrecking prowess all over town, but not her.

She e-mailed Nishi a link to the blog. *She knows I have to tabulate all the press coverage for my mother.*

Of course she does. Let it go, dear.

Easy for Nishi to say, of course. She didn't have someone making her look like a fool week in and week out. Not that anyone would be able to make Nishi Bhat look like a fool.

She sent Nishi another e-mail. *Check out guy in photo with Samantha Smith. That's the artist you gave me lessons with.*

Nishi's reply came an instant later. *No. Freaking. Way. You get to spend time with him? She's stuck with Sen. Dickhead. (Dick is a diminutive of Richard, right?)*

Marie smiled. Nishi was her ballast, her metronome. She steadied her when she wobbled, gently pushed her back on course when necessary. She leaned in toward her computer screen and stared hard at the photo of Luc and his friend. Would she rather be with Richard or Luc Marchand? No contest there.

She finished up the report and e-mailed it to her mother, so she could get around to what she normally did at this time of day. Look busy and pull up her memories of that dream.

I would pay to paint you.

A dream she would get to act out this weekend.

11

When Marie arrived at Luc's studio Saturday morning, she found him arranging and rearranging groupings of flowers and fruit, a bottle of wine and a tiny china tea cup. He fiddled with a white cloth napkin, trying to get the folds and creases just so.

She dropped her weekend bag on the floor. He turned around.

"Marie! Good morning." He strode over to her, barefoot, and dropped a kiss onto the top of her head.

He wore grey, paint-spattered sweatpants that hung off his narrow hips and a loose tee shirt, an outfit he managed to make unbelievably sexy in Marie's eyes. Or maybe that was just because she'd spent the rest of the week obsessing over him. He could wear a burlap sack and she wouldn't care at this point.

"I thought we'd do some still lifes today," he went on. "Do you feel up to that?"

Her heart dropped. What happened to the modeling? That's really what she wanted to do today, not draw.

Was it possible that he had forgotten? Or reconsidered? Maybe that whole scene in the museum had been a dream, too.

"Sure," she replied.

She looked around his studio. There were two new canvases up since last weekend, with paintings in progress. Paper sketches were tacked up to the walls. Coffee mugs and wine glasses littered his work table. She looked back at Luc, who was rubbing his jaw as he looked at her sketchbook. He hadn't shaved that morning. He looked distracted and his studio looked as though he'd been busy this week.

"I'll make us coffee while you get started," he said.

He had definitely forgotten. She sighed inwardly and pulled her sketchbook and pencil from her bag. Oh well. She could live on the memory of that kiss from the museum, dream or no, for awhile.

But I wanted to model for you.

She stared at the flowers, trying to isolate their lines and shadows. Flowers were hard, and Marie wasn't sure she was up to hard this morning. She leaned in and ran her finger down one of the stalks. Luc was right; touching things helped her see them better. But how did he draw things he couldn't touch? She was half afraid to ask.

Instead she busied herself drawing. Occasionally Luc would wander over and add some new object to the tableau. A spoon, a glass of water, some scattered coffee beans, spilled sugar. She rubbed the sugar between her fingers. *Impossible.* How could she touch sugar and understand how to draw it? He was fucking with her now.

At noon, someone rapped on the door. She turned her head to see Luc carrying a white pizza box into the studio's kitchenette.

"Hungry?" He smiled at her.

She was, she realized.

"You're looking at me like I've just grown a second head," he added.

"I never pictured you and pizza together."

"Why not?" He uncorked a bottle of wine and poured two glasses.

She shrugged.

"Marie." How was it that he could infuse her name with so much impatience and exasperation? "Shrugging is not answering the question. Come, sit down."

She pulled out a chair at the small table in the kitchen. "I don't know. It seems too normal for you."

He laughed as he set two plates on the table, then the glasses of wine.

"Believe it or not, I consider myself to be perfectly normal."

They ate in silence for several minutes, then Luc reached over and took her hand. He rubbed her aching knuckles. She winced.

"You need a break, don't you?" he said.

She nodded.

"Are you still willing to model for me?"

She looked at him and was surprised to see a wary hopefulness on his face. Maybe he hadn't brought it up earlier because he wasn't sure she still wanted to.

She was dying to, of course.

"I would like to draw you, Marie. But only if you want to."

"I do," she replied.

He sipped his wine, watching her. Marie felt her body grow warm under his gaze.

"And you were naked in your dream?" he probed.

A wave of heat spread over her face and neck but she nodded assent. She had worn only his gaze.

"It was like an ordinary figure drawing class," she started to explain. "Only you were the only student."

"And are you okay with that? Posing nude for me?"

"I *want* to be okay with it."

"But you're not sure."

She hesitated before answering. In her dream it had been so

liberating to openly sit there and let him look at her body. Of course, the dream began with her already naked and sitting on the stool. It conveniently skipped over the part where she had to actually take off her clothes in front of him. And that was the part that gave her pause now. Could she pull her sweater off, her bra, her jeans? Could she really do that in front of him?

They had kissed. She had felt his erection against her stomach. She had confessed that she wanted him to touch her. But she'd never been naked in front of him. It was an arousing idea, modeling nude for Luc, but she wasn't sure it was a good idea.

She hid behind her glass of wine, letting the dark red liquid trickle down her throat. The wine was cold compared to the heat raging in her chest. She could barely stand the intensity of his gaze now—what would it be like while she modeled?

"I don't want to do it if you're not a hundred percent certain, Marie."

"Ninety-nine percent?"

He shook his head. "I don't want you to do something you're going to regret later." He stood and whisked away their plates. When he returned, he held out his hand and pulled her up from the chair. "What if I go first? Would that make you more comfortable?"

He didn't wait for an answer. She watched as he rooted through a sizable collection of chairs and stools in the far corner of his studio, all jammed together like commuters on Metro. After some minutes of consideration, he pulled out an old wingchair upholstered in a fabric so faded and threadbare the original pattern was no longer discernible. He carried it to the center of the studio and set it down.

When he pulled his tee shirt over his head and dropped it on the floor, Marie's heart nearly stopped. He pushed his sweat pants down over his hips and calves, stepping out of them. He kicked them aside.

"You're going to draw me." He hooked his thumb beneath the waistband of his black boxer briefs. "On or off?"

Marie's eyes widened. "On." Not that she didn't want to see him nude. In fact, she'd spent way too much time in the past several days imagining just that state of affairs. Her face grew warm at the thought.

He shot her a disappointed look.

"I'm not sure I'm ready for figure drawing yet." She gestured toward the flowers and other objects she'd spent the morning staring at. "There's a big difference between still life and figure drawing."

Luc chuckled and took a seat on the chair, leaning back into the upholstery and stretching his legs out in front of him. "Hmm. This is rather comfortable." He slapped the arms of the chair lightly. "I don't think I've ever used this chair. Get your sketchbook. Go."

"This is going to be terrible, I'm warning you." She pulled a chair over and balanced the sketchpad on her knees.

"Closer, Marie. You can barely see me from over there."

"I can see you fine." But she scooted the chair a few inches closer.

He rolled his eyes. "Another foot or so, please."

She was way too close to him now. She could barely see straight. She certainly couldn't think straight, though that probably had something to do with her holding her breath. That he had left his briefs on really made little difference. There was still so much of him on display.

She'd drawn from live models in college, but they had tended toward the skinny, pale, ill-fed look.

Luc Marchand didn't look like that.

Non.

Not at all.

One, two, three, four, five, six. Yep, six, Marie counted. She'd never actually seen that particular body phenomenon live and in the flesh. Only in pictures and movies. Luc Marchand was a little more *built* than she had expected. In clothing he looked tall and lean, but now she could see that he was, in fact, well muscled.

"Marie? Are you going to draw?"

Luc's words brought her back to the present. She closed her mouth, which had somehow fallen open. Yes, she was gaping open-mouthed at him. That probably accounted for the little half smile on his face.

She readied her pencil. Where to begin? Definitely not the face. Had she noticed that he wasn't clean-shaven today? And there were dark circles beneath his eyes. He looked like a man who had spent all night … an image of Luc lying in bed, his bare shoulders gleaming in the dark, crept into her mind.

Not that it was any of her business how he spent his nights.

She forced her attention back to her drawing. She would start with the shoulders. He had pretty clean lines there, with that ledge of muscle extending from the back of his neck to the nice, rounded point where his arms met his shoulders. That was easy enough to draw. The curve of his bicep. Yes, she could handle that. The smattering of dark hair on his forearms. Totally manageable.

She spent the next thirty minutes carefully, painstakingly, recreating his torso and abdomen on paper. Shading, then erasing, then trying again. It was easier to draw pale, skinny and ill-fed than a veritable map of the male musculature. The sketchpad began to blur beneath her.

"Breathe, Marie. Art requires oxygen."

Had she really been holding her breath again? Yes, she realized as she inhaled and filled her lungs with air, she was. She closed her eyes for a moment, to clear her brain, then glanced over at him. He was smiling a lazy, sexy smile at her. God, all she wanted was to sit here and rest her eyes on him. Screw drawing. She'd never be able to capture his likeness on paper anyway. If she could just memorize the way he looked right now, that would be enough. To have this picture in her head.

"Carry on, Marie."

Her eyes dropped back to the paper. Could she skip over his hips and … that part, and just move on to his legs? He had very nice legs, lean and finely-muscled but not vein-poppingly big like body builders. Marie didn't like legs like that. She considered her drawing for awhile, trying to calculate how much blank space to leave if she were to skip to his legs.

But he'd make fun of her if she did. Merciless fun. She was going to have to just plow through the next part. She took a deep breath and looked back up at Luc, only to see—to her horror—the fabric of his boxer briefs pushing upward.

"Do you, um, need a break?" she asked.

"No. Do you?"

"Maybe. Yes. I can't draw—that."

He glanced down at himself, amused. "I have to say this is very arousing, modeling for you. I had no idea. Was your dream like this?"

A deep red flush engulfed her cheeks and neck. There was no way to hide it but she looked down at her feet anyway.

Luc sat up, leaning his elbows on his knees. "Why are you embarrassed by that? I don't mind if you have dreams about me. I just want to know what they are."

"I'm not comfortable doing this," she said, looking at her unfinished drawing with the gap where Luc's hips should be.

"I'm trying to make you a little uncomfortable, Marie. Not in a mean way, though. A little disorientation often makes people see what's around them in a different way. That's art, isn't it? Seeing things the way no one else does."

In her peripheral vision, she saw him pick up his sweatpants from the floor and pull them back on.

"Let me see what you've done."

"It's not finished."

"That's okay. You have to start somewhere."

She reluctantly handed over her drawing, trying not to think about the fact that the unfinished portion was now hovering just inches from her face. She should never have let him kiss her again at the museum. Not that she hadn't wanted it—or enjoyed it immensely—but now all these *feelings* had been unleashed in her. There was a chemistry between them, and she'd had little experience with chemistry. Certainly there hadn't been any between her and Richard.

It wasn't that she minded the way it made her feel, the prickly sensation on her skin whenever she thought of Luc, like a thunderstorm was about to roll in. It made the hours spent in her mother's employ far more bearable than they otherwise would be. Of course, she felt chemistry with Luc Marchand. What woman wouldn't? Luc could stroll down the street and leave a swath of distracted, chemical devastation in his wake.

But in his presence she couldn't keep her thoughts straight. His energy was distracting. She wanted to improve her drawing skills, truly she did, but how could she focus on that when every nerve ending in her body was screaming to be kissed?

Luc was still studying her drawing, silently. It was awful. No question about that. She should leave. That would be the best thing for today. She couldn't focus on drawing right now. Perhaps she would come back next weekend, if the chemistry had cleared by then and she could sit next to Luc Marchand without him short-circuiting her brain.

Luc nearly dropped the sketchpad as Marie brushed past him, hurrying toward the bathroom. Any faster and she'd be flat out running. Her drawing was terrible. Her still lifes from the morning had been much better. When she could touch and feel something, she was able to capture its essence on paper.

But with this drawing, she'd been working from her head again, too worried about whether she *should* be doing this, too distracted by her feelings. He needed to get her to *see* and not think.

He glanced toward the bathroom door, then quickly retrieved a mat and a blanket from a box beneath the work table. He had just enough time to spread them on the floor, strip off his sweatpants and boxers, and lie down before he heard the bathroom door unlatch with a dull click and swing open.

"Ahh!"

Her startled gasp wasn't followed by footsteps so he knew she was still standing just outside the bathroom. He resisted the urge to sit up and look at her.

"Are you okay, Marie?"

"Yes ... I suppose. What are you ... doing?"

"Waiting for you."

"You couldn't wait with your clothes on?"

"You've seen most of this already, Marie."

"You want me to draw you again?" she asked.

"Yes. But you need to *see* me first."

"Well okay, I think I've seen you now."

"Not with your eyes. With your hands, Marie."

"You want me to touch you ... without any clothes on?"

"Yes." He heard her sigh. "Come here, Marie. Please." Her shadow fell over his body. He smiled up at her. "Your drawing ... you were trying so hard not to *look* at me that you weren't able to *see* me. You wanted to rely on your memory of anatomy to fill in the blanks so you wouldn't have to look at my body. True?"

She shrugged and he chuckled. "At first, I thought this," he shrugged his shoulders against the mat, "meant you didn't know. Now I realize you're actually saying 'yes' when you do that."

"I don't know, Mr. Marchand—"

"Luc. That's part of the problem right there. You can't possibly *really* see me if you're thinking of me as 'mister.'"

He held her gaze as she stared down at him. Doubt and desire were fighting it out on her lovely face. He closed his eyes to give her some privacy, some space to think it through.

"Don't leave, Marie," he said quietly, eyes still shut. "Trust me on this. When you draw me afterward, it will be so much better. I would like the chance to see that better drawing."

He opened his eyes in time to catch her gaze flick down to his groin and then back to the general vicinity of his face.

"Do you model for all of your students?" she asked.

Ah. She was jealous. He liked the idea of that. "No. I told you. I've never modeled for students. When I teach figure drawing, I hire experienced models."

"So why not do that now?"

He glanced around the studio, as if looking for someone. "Because I'm improvising. I was planning to draw you today, but I think we need to do this first."

Her eyes lit up, just a little, but it was there. He might still be able to pull her back in.

"Are you embarrassed by seeing me this way?"

She nodded, her eyes fixed on the mat beneath his shoulders.

"Why?" She opened her mouth to answer but he cut her off. "Take the time to think about it, Marie. I don't want some glib reason. I want the truth."

She closed her eyes for several moments. Her eyelids were shadowed with makeup and he felt an urge to march her back to the bathroom and wash her off. She was so used to standing behind other people, letting other people speak for her, think for her, decide for her. All things that got in the way of art and friendship and ... other things he didn't want to contemplate at the moment. Things he knew he shouldn't want from this woman, this estranged wife of a senator.

Her eyes opened. "Mr.—Luc. I'm confused. You confuse me." She hesitated, watching him closely, but he was careful not to give away any reaction. She went on. "Sometimes I see in your eyes things I don't understand. That I can't interpret. Or maybe that I don't want to interpret. And there's no way—no way at all—that I can touch you here, like this, without trying to figure out what's going on in your eyes. You would have to get me drunk again and then you'd just have a sloppy drunk mauling you."

An image of Marie mauling his body arose in his mind. He fought down the urge to smile.

"Over there is the blindfold we used the first weekend." He pointed to the work table. "Bring that to me, please."

She retrieved it and began tying it around her eyes.

"Non, Marie." He stretched his hand toward her. "The blindfold is for me."

A look of surprise flickered over her face. He took the velvet cloth and tied it around his own eyes.

"Now you can't see what I'm thinking." He waited to see what she would do. He sensed her continued indecision. "Please trust me on this, Marie. Try it and if my body turns out to be too distasteful for you, we can stop."

He heard her tiny amused snort.

"Laughing at me is a good start."

"I don't mean to laugh—"

"I want you to laugh at me. This is pretty ridiculous, no? A man—a not unattractive man, can we agree on that?—is lying here naked and blindfolded and all but begging you to touch him. Carpe diem, Marie."

Long minutes passed until finally she spoke. "So what am I supposed to do?"

"Touch me. Start with my hair."

He held his breath while she worried a small lock of his hair between her fingers. He rolled his eyes beneath the blindfold.

"Sit here, Marie." He patted his chest.

"On you?" Her voice cracked.

"Yes, on me. You won't crush me."

He felt her gingerly straddle his chest, careful not to settle her weight fully on him.

"Ah!" she cried out when he slid his hands down her thighs and pushed out on her knees, causing her to land on his chest with a gentle thud.

"That's better," he said. "Now let's try this again." He found her hands and plunged them deep into the roots of his hair. He bit back a groan and pressed his hips down into the mat. Already it was torture not seeing her face.

"What does that feel like?" he tried to hold his voice steady. "Try to think how that might look on paper."

She worked her fingers through his thick hair. Each gentle tug on the roots was like a finger running lightly down his spine. She traced the wave in his hair with her palm. Her thighs relaxed a little against his chest as she wriggled her fingers through his hair some more.

"Now try my face." Her fingers slid out of his hair and gently grazed his face. He had to resist the urge to kiss her palm as it brushed his lips.

Then her hand disappeared.

"I feel like I'm groping you," she said.

"Don't feel. *See.* Think of it as seeing with your skin."

12

Think of it as seeing with your skin.

Marie took a deep breath and tried again. She ran her index finger along the ridge of Luc's fine, straight nose. She looked at the velvet cloth covering his eyes.

"Are your eyes closed under there?" she asked.

"Yes. Why?"

"Just wondering."

"It's good to wonder."

His face relaxed into a smile for an instant. Marie let the pad of her fingertip touch the deep groove between his nose and lips.

"That's called the philtrum," Luc said. "It means love potion in Latin."

"Really," she murmured. "That's an odd fact to have right on the tip of one's tongue."

"One learns a lot about human anatomy by learning to draw."

Marie touched each point of his cupid's bow, feeling for the first time how firm the line between lip and skin actually was. Then she ran her thumb over the tiny stalks of stubble on his jawline, trying to feel each hair as it scraped against her skin.

Luc's nostrils flared as she drew her thumb firmly across his lower lip. She found herself taking a deeper breath, too, trying to pull more oxygen into her lungs, and what had been the gentle warmth of her body against his was now a more insistent, probing heat working its way through her inner thighs and up into her hips.

She was shocked at the effect just touching his face was having on her entire body. Her skin was seeing him in places she wasn't even touching him with.

"Are you okay, Marie?"

She hesitated. *You've just died and gone to heaven* is what Nishi would say in a situation like this. But then Nishi had always been more of a carpe diem person. "Depends on how you define okay, I suppose," she said at last.

"I think you get to define okay for yourself, Marie. For me, having a beautiful woman touch me anywhere she pleases is a good definition."

He thinks I'm beautiful? She gazed down at his face, a face that would certainly meet anyone's definition of beautiful, and considered the idea. She couldn't read this man, not that she was particularly good at reading anyone, but she couldn't tell when Luc Marchand was being a teacher and when he was being a man. Which was it right now? Was he telling her she was beautiful because he wanted her to feel good as a student? Or did he really think that?

He flattened his palms against her thighs and gently pushed her hips off his ribs and onto his stomach. She gasped when she collided with his jutting penis.

"Maybe we should stop," she said.

"Only if you want to." He refolded his hands beneath his head.

Marie tried to control her breathing as she weighed the obvious wisdom of stopping against the singing of every nerve ending in her skin. Her body certainly didn't want to stop. What her body wanted was to rip off every last stitch of clothing she had on and beg Luc Marchand to make love to her.

"I'm not sure this is appropriate," she said.

"Appropriateness is just a value judgment."

"You have an answer for everything, don't you?"

"No." He sighed. "There are many things I don't have an answer for. Many, many things, Marie. But I know how to draw and I know you have to be willing to look at things. Until you are willing to *see*, you won't be able to draw the way you want to. Can you honestly say that you don't want to sit here and look at a naked man?"

Of course, she couldn't honestly say that. Any woman would want the opportunity to ogle a man like Luc Marchand. Marie could honestly say she'd never been this close to a nude body this perfect before. This openly sensual. He was a Greek god, a French Greek god.

"Hmm, Marie? Can you say that?"

"Yes, I want to look at you. But just because one wants to do something doesn't mean one should."

"Why not? Who's getting hurt here?"

Me probably. Already she wanted more than just to look at him. And *more* wasn't going to happen. When she finished touching him, then it would be on to drawing him again. Only this time she'd be trying to draw while sitting in a haze of sexual frustration.

"You are free to leave anytime you want, Marie. But step out of yourself for a moment and look at this situation. I am blindfolded, completely naked and there's a person sitting on top of me. You are the one in control here. Don't you see that, Marie? I can't force you to see things for yourself and I can't force you to take control of the moment you're living in. You have to do that for yourself."

"What do you want me to do?"

"What I want is plain to see, Marie. If you're willing to let yourself see it."

She didn't want to leave, she knew that. She wanted to stay, spend the entire weekend here with this confusing man who made her feel beautiful and crazed with desire and two inches small all at the same time. She wanted to drink in the sight of his body spread out on the mat for her like a sumptuous, decadent Roman banquet.

She reached down and rolled one of Luc's nipples beneath her thumb, then rolled it beneath her flattened palm. She closed her eyes and concentrated on how the small nub of flesh felt against the sensitive skin of her palm. In her mind, she could see a drawing of his chest begin to take shape. She ran her hands down his chest, feeling the bony ridge of each rib, forcing herself to ignore the primal urges screaming for attention, forcing herself to focus just on how his body felt beneath her hands.

And her body—it felt more alive than it ever had. She was beginning to understand what Luc meant by seeing with her skin.

"Do you feel in control now, Marie?"

She *was* feeling in control, she realized. Not because a man was blindfolded and pinned down by her weight, but because the man was aroused by the situation, by her. The tip of Luc's erection was pressed against the base of her spine. She shifted her hips and she felt a soft moan rumble beneath her. This was proving difficult for him, too.

She had never felt in control with Richard. She had simply been there to do what he wanted, to be posed and placed and displayed in whatever light best suited his life. It pained her heart to see that now.

She stood up suddenly, only to feel Luc's hands grab onto her ankles, holding her fast.

"Where are you going?" he asked.

"Just turning around, Luc. I want to look at ... the rest of you. Is that okay?"

"Of course." He let go of her ankles. "Though if you aren't comfortable saying penis, you can say throbbing member."

"I'm going to look at your throbbing—" She tried to suppress a giggle, and failed.

"Member, Marie. My throbbing member."

Luc's flat, taut stomach was bouncing with laughter as Marie straddled his chest again, this time facing his feet.

"It's a joy to hear you laugh," he said.

Marie glanced back at him over her shoulder.

"Cheater!" she cried. The blindfold no longer covered his eyes.

He smiled and shrugged. "I'm only a man, Marie. You have a lovely derriere and this is probably my only chance to see it this close."

Her neck and face grew hot. "Also you're French," she added.

"*Oui.* So I get a pass when it comes to admiring a woman's shapely behind. But proceed." He made a shooing gesture with his hand.

"Are you going to put it back on?" she asked.

"If you want." He grimaced. "But it will be easier for me if I don't. Lying here and thinking of England is not working so well. It might be more effective if I stare at the ceiling and count cobwebs."

She turned back to his throbbing member. "I'm just going to look."

"You may do whatever you like."

Marie's breath caught in her throat, as she considered what she might like. She felt his stomach muscles clench in anticipation beneath her thighs, then she reached out cautiously and traced—with as feathery a touch as she could manage—the swollen vein that ran along his length. The tiny moan she'd heard a moment earlier was now an agonized, full-throated moan.

She needed to stop before this went too far. He was turned on. She was turned on. If they kept going ... she couldn't bear to think of how he would look at her afterward. She stood up, intending to go get the sketchpad so she could begin a new drawing. But quicker than she thought any human could move, Luc's arms shot out and pulled her back down. In a flash, she was lying on top of him, her breasts pressed against his chest.

"Where are you going?" he asked, his eyes darker than she'd ever seen them.

"To get my sketchpad. I think I'm ready to draw you again."

"Fuck the drawing, Marie."

His chest was rising and falling beneath her. Her nipples ached. Her pulse had concentrated itself entirely between her legs.

"What are you seeing right now?" he asked.

She saw eyes dark with desire. Nostrils flaring with each exhale of patience. And lips ... how was it that she could feel his lips on every inch of her skin, just by looking at him?

"I see a man I want to kiss."

"So kiss him, Marie."

She brushed her lips lightly against his and was pulling her head away, when he plunged his hands into her hair and crushed her lips hard against his. His breath was hot and sweet as he parted her lips, exploring, tasting.

"Now you take over," he murmured against her panting mouth.

But her kiss was tentative again.

"Has any man ever just given you pleasure, Marie?"

Marie pulled away from Luc, surprised by his question. "What do you mean?"

"Your husband, I get the impression that he is more of a taker than a giver."

She shrugged.

"Today, you're the taker, Marie. Take what you want from my body."

"I don't want—"

He pressed his erection into her hips. At her tiny cry of pleasure, a low growl hummed in Luc's throat. "Marie." He pulled her cheek, then her ear, against his mouth. He nibbled lightly on her earlobe, making her hips move involuntarily against his. "Art requires honesty. You can't expect to draw well if you're denying what's right in front of you. Your body wants something right now. I'm offering it, but you have to take it."

Marie hesitated. This was one of those fork-in-the-road moments. One of those moments when you made a last-ditch sprint to catch the train—or watched it pull out of the station and disappear around the bend. How many times would she have the opportunity to have sex with a sexy-as-hell Frenchman? She shouldn't be getting this chance, even.

"Start with simple, Marie. Undress." He pulled the blindfold back over his eyes. "I won't watch."

She took a long, deep breath and then slowly stood up and pulled off her boots.

"And Marie? Let down your hair."

"You can't help being bossy, can you?" She pulled her cashmere sweater over her head and dropped it on the floor.

Luc smiled. "Maybe not."

She unzipped her jeans. "Keep the blindfold on. See? I can be bossy, too."

"Hmm. I rather like bossy Marie. Even if she apparently has on seven layers of clothing." He drummed his fingers impatiently against his stomach.

Marie tossed her bra onto his chest. He picked it up and slid the lace through his fingers. "I do want to look at this later."

She glanced at her purse, slung over the back of a chair. She hadn't thought to bring a condom. "Um, I don't have ..."

"In my wallet. My jacket's over there." He jerked his head toward the back corner of the studio.

She tore open the packet and unrolled the condom on him. Then she sat back and looked at him. He would have to keep the blindfold on. She could only do this as long as he couldn't see her.

"Are you sure you don't want to be on—" she asked, hesitantly.

"Yes, I'm sure I don't want to be on top. I am going to lie here and let you do whatever you want to do."

She stared at his body lying on the mat. A lazy smile played around his lips. She imagined the skin around his eyes crinkling beneath the blindfold. *Whatever you want to do.* She knew exactly what she wanted. She wanted him to fix the ache that was pounding deep within her hips. She wanted him to eviscerate the ache, demolish it, douse it with gasoline and throw a match.

"Marie? I'm getting cold down here."

"Sorry. Just ... thinking."

Luc's stomach vibrated with laughter. "Thinking about what? Normally, this is the part where people stop thinking."

"I'm thinking about what to do."

"May I offer a suggestion?"

"Please."

"Bon. Lie here," he patted his chest, "and kiss me."

Okay, she could do that. She lowered herself onto the length of his body, warm and firm beneath hers. She closed her eyes and allowed herself to enjoy the feel of skin against skin.

"Kiss me, Marie."

She opened her eyes. His lips were parted, waiting for her. She lowered her mouth to his, then pushed her tongue inside. Her fingers delved into his thick hair and she pulled his mouth harder into hers. His hips shifted beneath her, the rumble of his groan pulsed against her breasts.

Still, she kissed him deeper, consumed by the need to be swallowed up by Luc Marchand, to disappear inside him. When she needed air, she drew back to his lips, tasting them, devouring them, her hunger for a man finally unleashed. Luc's hips were rolling, the muscles of his thighs tight as he tried to remain still and let her do what she pleased.

He wanted her. That was all that mattered right now. Luc desired her. Maybe he wouldn't tomorrow, but she would settle for today.

She let her lips peel off his, taking one last nip. His lips were dark and slack from her kisses.

"Marie, I am about two seconds from begging you to just fuck me."

The thought of Luc Marchand begging her set her spine afire. She reached below and took him in her hand, guiding him into her. All she could think of was filling herself with Luc over and over, his rough breathing and her gasps of surprise spilling into the air around them. She was chasing the ache of desire. The faster she moved on his body, the faster it ran ahead of her until—just when she thought she couldn't move any faster—she caught up to it and slammed it to the ground, shocked at the way the impact spread, shuddering through her body. Luc's hands settled on her hips, pressing himself deeper into her, holding her there, just holding her.

"Now draw me," Luc said.

Marie groaned into his chest. The two of them were sprawled, spent, on the studio floor. The light spilling in through the window had mellowed into a late afternoon glow.

"Now is the time, *ma chérie*. When all of this is fresh in your vision." He gently grasped her bottom and lifted her off his softening, satiated erection.

"You have to keep this on, though." Marie tugged at the edge of the blindfold.

"Whatever you wish."

"I don't want to see what you're thinking while I'm drawing."

"Bon. That might be a distraction, given what I intend to think about."

Marie rolled her eyes, then stood and went in search of her sketch pad. As she walked across the studio, she was conscious of her nakedness but for the first time in her life, not bothered by it.

"Marie," Luc called out behind her. "Get a towel from that cabinet by the window. For you to sit on."

"Thank you."

She unrolled the towel onto the floor, flipped over a fresh page on the sketchpad and began to draw. Luc's hands were once again folded beneath his head. His legs were stretched out, his hips splayed open. He looked altogether languid, serene even.

"You were right, of course," Marie said as she began to pencil in lines and shading.

"I am right about many things, Marie. But about what, specifically, this time?"

"No one has ever just given me pleasure before. I was a pleasure virgin."

"And I was just giving you what little you were taking."

"That wasn't a little."

"Oh, Marie, you were merely sipping at the well of pleasure. I could bathe you in it, if you were to let me."

Marie's pencil stopped in its tracks above the paper, as she contemplated the idea that what she had just experienced could be somehow more.

"Where did you feel it?" Luc asked. "In your hips, right? In your ... throbbing member?"

She smiled at the memory. "Yes."

He shook his head. "You should feel an orgasm everywhere,

Marie. It should feel as though your entire body is disintegrating into individual particles of matter."

Marie considered that while she continued to draw Luc. Given that she had just experienced the best orgasm of her life, it was hard to imagine how one could be better. But she was beginning to think she should give Luc Marchand the benefit of the doubt. After all, the drawing she was currently doing was markedly better than the morning's.

"What was that little smile for, hmm?" Luc asked, pushing the blindfold up over his forehead.

She looked up from the sketchpad. If there was a sexier man on the planet right now, she couldn't envision it.

"I was just thinking that your teaching methods, unorthodox as they are, seem to be working," she said.

"Oui? Show me."

She turned the sketchpad around for him to see.

He studied it for a moment. "Bon. You are making progress. You can trust me, you know, Marie. I would never ask you to do something that would hurt you. Understand?"

Marie was about to draw some more when Luc's stomach rumbled loudly.

"I don't know about you, but sex always makes me hungry," he said. "Let's go out to dinner to celebrate your progress."

13

Marie looked up at the old weathered stone on the Red Fox Inn and Tavern, the crisp white trim, the green roof. "This looks like one of those 'George Washington slept here' places," she observed.

"Apparently that was the case," Luc replied as he held open the door for her. "Along with Jackie Kennedy and Elizabeth Taylor."

Inside, heavy wooden beams crossed the ceiling from white-washed wall to whitewashed wall. A fire was lit in the giant stone fireplace. It was cozy and warm, and Marie half expected to hear horses thundering by outside.

Female heads turned right and left as she followed Luc through the dining room to a table in the back. Steak, wine, dessert. None of it was a match for Luc in dark jeans and black cashmere. She allowed herself a little jolt of triumph. She had seen today what all these women were merely imagining.

The waitress arrived with menus and two glasses of red wine.

"A toast, Marie, to your progress." Luc raised his glass to her. "Seeing is always better than not seeing."

Marie felt her face warm.

"Although not seeing wasn't so bad for me today," he added. His eyes twinkled beneath his still shower-damp hair.

"You did seem to enjoy yourself," she said, immediately taking a sip of wine to cover up her boldness.

A smile played around Luc's eyes. "It's been a while since I've enjoyed myself quite like that."

Marie buried her face in the menu. She had no illusions about what had transpired between them earlier. It had been amazing sex, the best she'd ever had, but it was still just sex.

"Earth to Marie?" came Luc's voice, gently.

She looked up to see him watching her over the top edge of his menu. "Sorry. I was lost in thought there for a minute."

"Thoughts about us?"

She shrugged and looked back down at the menu. He chuckled.

"I'll take that as a yes."

Of course, she was thinking about *us.* She'd be thinking about this day for weeks. Correction, years.

When the waitress returned, Luc ordered the filet mignon and Marie the pumpkin ravioli.

"Marie, do you know what my favorite part of today was?" Luc passed the bread basket across the table to her. "When you were laughing. You don't smile nearly enough. You're so serious all the time."

"You're rather an intense person. Plus, I'm always afraid you'll say I'm not taking your lessons seriously. And I am."

"I know you are, Marie. And I don't mean for you to get discouraged. I'm just trying to push you out of that comfort zone you've been so comfortably entrenched in."

"Yes, well, I think you did that today," she said dryly.

"And was it all that terrible?"

She blushed again, and shook her head. "I think I've blushed more today than I have in all the years of my life combined."

"I like it when you blush, Marie. I like to see those freckles disappear and then slowly reappear."

She covered her cheeks with her fingers. He leaned across the small table and pried them off, then curled his hands softly around them.

"Thanks to that damn blindfold," he said in a low, husky voice, "I didn't get to see whether you have freckles in other places."

Her face was fully on fire now. "You do this on purpose, don't you?"

"Oui." He smiled a slow, sexy grin. "But it's not that hard to do, really. I don't think you're used to having men flirt with you. Did your husband never flirt with you?"

She thought back to the early days with Richard, when they were dating, before he'd met Maya. She shook her head. No, even back then Richard had never been flirtatious or tried to make her laugh or blush. He had seemed to know that Marie wouldn't have a choice in whether to marry him or not. She was a done deal from the beginning.

"He didn't know what he was missing." Luc let go of her hands and leaned back into his seat just as the waitress approached. "Well, lucky for me, eh?"

The waitress set their plates on the table. Marie took a deep inhale of the spicy sweet steam coming off her pumpkin ravioli. She suddenly realized how famished she was. A lot had happened since they'd had lunch. *A lot.*

"After all, if American politicians were smarter, I wouldn't be sitting here with a beautiful woman, looking forward to the rest of the evening."

"You say outrageous things like that and I don't know what to say back."

Luc's fork stopped in mid-air. "What's outrageous about any of that? You are very beautiful, Marie—yes, you are. I hope you are looking forward to the rest of the evening as much as I am. And we are allowed to make as much fun of politicians as we like. Yes?" He popped the steak in his mouth.

Marie focused on her dinner for awhile, trying to ignore the flurry of questions in her brain—and trying just as hard to ignore the lingering feel of Luc in her body. She wanted to look forward to the rest of the evening, but part of her was afraid to. It just seemed so improbable that a man like Luc would be interested in her. He'd get bored with her quickly—it hadn't taken Richard long to lose interest—and then where would that leave her? Where would that leave her heart? As much as she might like to be the sort of woman who could sleep with a man and walk away, she wasn't sure that she could.

She had to ask the question. "Do you teach all of your students like this?"

A look of surprise crossed his face. He took a sip of wine. "Of course not."

"Then why me?"

He raked his hand through his hair. "Isn't it obvious? It's because I'm attracted to you, Marie. Because I can't stop thinking about you. Because I want to teach you what you want to learn."

She gestured toward him, then pressed her hand to her throat. "I just don't see why you ..." Her voice trailed away.

"Why I am attracted to you?"

She nodded. It was impossible to miss the dark, hungry look in his eyes.

"Do you still want to model for me?" he asked.

She nodded.

"If you let me paint you, I will show you what I see when I look at you."

"Painting takes a long time, though, doesn't it? I'm sure Nishi didn't pay you for that."

His tilted his head and looked at her for a long moment. "You could do me a huge favor, actually. My friend Sam is opening a new gallery in December and she wants me to be the first show there. But I need new work to give her. Would you let me paint you for the show?"

"Like Alistair Smith and Elizabeth Calhoun?"

He shrugged. "If you wish. We could do it that way. I could obscure your face."

She thought about it. Elizabeth Calhoun had spent a lifetime denying her love, denying herself a chance to fully enjoy her desires, her pleasures.

Do I want to hide that way?

Granted, Elizabeth Calhoun had remained a senator's wife until she died. She'd had good reason to hide her affair. But Marie was released from those bonds when Richard filed for divorce.

I have nothing to hide.

Richard was openly flaunting a mistress.

If he can cheat on his wife, surely I can have my portrait painted. Those aren't even the same order of magnitude.

"No," she said. "I want you to paint all of me."

LUC UNLOCKED the studio and held open the door for Marie. "I'll make coffee," he said, heading into the kitchenette. He'd drunk too much wine at dinner, on top of the intoxication of having Marie pleasure herself on him this afternoon. He needed a cup of strong black coffee to clear his head if he was going to draw her tonight.

When the coffee was brewed, he handed her a mug and asked, "So tell me about this dream you keep having."

She took a sip of coffee. "Oh, you don't have to draw me that way. That's okay."

"I think it would be a good place to start, don't you? That way we can take a look at the differences between your dream and how *I* see you."

"This sounds like a lesson."

"Well, yes, I hope it will be enlightening to you. Discovering how someone else sees you should help the way you see things. We're doing each other a mutual favor here, Marie. I'm helping you see more clearly and you're helping me create new work for my show."

She was quiet for several moments. Watching her mull this over only stoked his excitement further. Painting Marie was going to be so rewarding, her hesitation, her shyness, the battle between desire and fear that was waging inside her. Occasionally, women came to him for "boudoir" portraits, gifts for a husband or lover. They were the least interesting portraits to paint, everything out there on the surface, nothing hidden, nothing held back to surprise later.

Marie held nearly everything back. He wanted to peel back some of that reserve in his paintings, get her to reveal herself to him. There was a passionate women underneath that composed exterior, a quirky déesse trapped and waiting for rescue. He, Luc Marchand, wanted to be the man to lure her out.

"We were here, in your studio," she began to speak again. "But it was dark."

He laughed. "And I was painting you in the dark? Ah, Marie, I am not that talented."

"No, no," she said quickly. "There was a light just over me. So I couldn't really see you behind your easel."

"So like a spotlight?"

"Yes."

He looked up at the ceiling of the studio. The bulbs in the track lighting couldn't be individually turned on or off, short of unscrewing them. He peered around the room. Ah! Over there.

He strode over to an old floor lamp and disentangled it from the mess of chairs and side tables he used as props.

"Will this work?" he asked. He trailed the plug over to an outlet, then turned off the overhead track lighting. The lamp gave off a soft, diffuse glow.

Marie nodded.

"And what were you sitting on?"

"Just a stool."

He dragged the stool over to the lamp.

"What were you wearing?"

"Just ..." She tugged at the waistband of her jeans.

"Just your jeans?" Luc was liking this dream already.

She shook her head, leaning down to remove her boots. She kicked them aside, then slowly unzipped the jeans and stepped out. Luc was dying to say a million things — *god you're beautiful I will paint you worship you make love to you whatever you want* — but he bit his tongue because now Marie was pulling her cashmere sweater up and over her head. Her dream was that he had painted her wearing just her bra and panties? Yes, Marie Witherspoon was holding back some very interesting sides to herself.

His breath caught in his throat as she reached behind her back and unhooked her lacy yellow bra, then slid the matching lace panties down her legs. She crossed her arms over her chest, a sight that pained him—he didn't want her to hide any part of her body from him—and turned toward him.

"I painted you like that? Wearing nothing?"

She nodded, not willing to look him in the eye. He walked over to her and tipped her chin up. "Are you embarrassed by the dream?"

She shrugged. "A little, I guess."

"Never be ashamed of your dreams, Marie." He ran his thumb along her cheekbone, then over her lips, which parted readily for him. The memory of Marie lying sprawled on his chest—her cheeks flushed a soft pink, her lips open as she tried to recover her breath, her heat wrapped around him—filled his brain. He watched her now, her face still flushed from the wine at dinner. She had washed off her makeup in the shower, revealing a trail of light freckles across her cheekbones. He was overcome with the urge to kiss each one. The shape of her face, her bones, the curve of her lips—even now, when she was clearly unsure whether she should smile or not—she had such classically beautiful proportions. She would be both easy and challenging to capture on canvas.

He touched a light kiss to her forehead. "You are beautiful," he murmured against her skin.

"Don't you need a sketchbook?" she replied, deflecting his compliment.

"I believe that's the least of the things I need right now, but ..."

He dragged his easel closer and propped a sketchbook on it. When he looked up, Marie was sitting on the stool, crossing her legs this way and that, finally settling on just resting her feet on the stool's rung.

"What should I do with my arms?" she asked.

"How did you have them in the dream?"

"I can't remember, that's the thing. I ..." She struggled to get the words out. "What I remember most is how I ... felt."

He looked at her slender figure perched on the paint-spattered stool, trying to take in the lines, the shadows—which were considerable in the lamplight—the mood of the scene. She looked like a character from an Edward Hopper painting, vulnerable and stoic at the same time. As if she were lost, but would keep trudging down the road by herself anyway. He shifted his chair and easel a few inches to the left. From this angle, the lamp illuminated her spine, knob by knob, and cast her face in shadow.

"Keep your arms crossed, I think," he said.

He began sketching in her form. That was easy. He'd spent

more than one night lying in bed drawing an outline of her form, just his hand and fingers against a blank canvas of air. It felt appropriate for this first painting to be all shadow and light, chiaroscuro, the simultaneous sadness and courage of nudity. She had come to him, wanting to draw but blind to what was around her. Wanting pleasure, but unwilling to admit it.

It took only twenty minutes to get a good study he was happy with. The week ahead would be a joy, every day in his studio translating this pencil sketch into a full-blown painting. He stood and carried it over to Marie, held it out for her to see. She was quiet for a long while, just staring at herself on the paper.

When she swiped a hand against her cheek, he dropped the book and pulled her up off the stool. Her eyes were wet, her lower lip quivering.

"What's the matter?" he asked.

"Is that the way you see me?" The pained expression in her eyes nearly slayed him. "It's so ... depressing."

Shit. This wasn't supposed to be her reaction, though he could see now that it wasn't an unreasonable one.

She tried to turn away to hide the tears that were now spilling down her cheeks. He pulled her to his chest, let his shirt absorb the tears. "*Non, non.* Not depressing. But you are sad, Marie. I do see that in you. Except for this afternoon, when you were laughing at me."

This afternoon, she had wanted him.

Right now, he wanted her.

He cupped the back of her head, threading his fingers deep into her hair. "I want to paint all the ways I see you, Marie. But you will have to trust me. Trust that I will be honest."

He ran his hand along the bare skin of her spine, pressing her body harder into his. "And you will have to be honest with me."

She tilted her head back to look him in the face. Then she surprised him by pulling his mouth down to hers and kissing him with a reckless abandon he hadn't seen in her before. Her kiss was hungry, desperate.

"Luc," she murmured against his lips.

He parted his lips for her. Tentatively, her tongue began to explore his lips. It was torture, and even more so when she dug her fingers into his hair and pulled herself into his mouth. He endured the exquisite torture as long as he could, then wrapped his tongue around hers and kissed her as deeply as he could. He felt her knees buckle.

He picked her up and carried her over to the mat and blanket they had christened that afternoon. He gently laid her down, then slowly undressed for her, pulling his sweater over his head, unzipping his jeans. Her face was dark with desire, her eyes hooded.

"Marie, you are beautiful," he said, joining her on the mat. "Extraordinarily beautiful. That's one thing that never changes about the way I see you." He caressed her face, then smiled slyly. "You've never had any medical emergencies, have you?"

The sight of her amused smile back at him sent a wave of heat through his body. "I'm not sure I can promise not to have one tonight," she replied.

"Just remember to breath, Marie, and you should be okay."

Her deep inhale drew his attention down to her breasts. He drank in the sight of her creamy skin. "Here is where we learn whether I have any medical emergencies."

He leaned down and pressed his lips to her soft curves, buried his face between her breasts and inhaled the scent of his own soap on her skin. It was unexpected, and intoxicating. Her skin glowed in the dim light and he took a moment to just admire her beauty.

"When I was blindfolded this afternoon, I tried to imagine how you would look beneath me." He smiled wryly, shaking his head. "My imagination is pathetic. Utterly lacking."

"I thought great artists could see everything. That's what I've been told."

"Oh, I'm going to see everything, Marie. And one day I am going to paint you like this, in the moment before I make love to you." He ran his thumbs over her eyelashes, trying to isolate the feathery touch of each one. "I want to capture this look in your eyes. Desire and disbelief."

He bent his head over her breasts, and she shivered as his breath caressed her skin. "Trust me?" he asked.

"Yes," she whispered in reply. She did trust him, oddly enough, certainly more than she had ever trusted Richard. "I trust you."

When his lips brushed her nipple, a rush of heat surged through her, every solid part of her body melting into hot, liquid need. He took her nipple between his soft lips, teasing it up into a hard peak, then his mouth began to explore every inch of the skin around it. As his breath warmed her skin, she arched her back, pushing her breasts toward him. She wanted more. She *needed* more, in a way she had never needed more from any man.

"Patience, Marie," he murmured against her skin.

He ran his tongue along the underside of her breast, then traced a hot line back up to her nipple where his own patience seemed to run out. He closed his mouth over her dark rosy nipple and began to suck, devouring her, pulling every pinprick of desire up to the surface of her skin. Marie felt her hips loosen and open. She ran her hands along his back, pulled his hips down toward her own. She wanted him inside her. She wanted to be filled with as much of Luc Marchand as she could take.

His moan of pleasure vibrated hot against her breast. She felt the tip of his tongue roll her nipple.

"Luc," she whispered.

"Patience, ma chérie," he said, lifting his head from her breast. "You have two of these, you know."

"You don't have to touch every—" The words disappeared from her brain at the sight of Luc's lips closing around her other breast.

"Yes," he murmured. "I do have to touch every inch of you."

"Luc ... please. It's too soon ... you're going to make me—"

He slipped his hand between her legs. "That's the whole point of this, Marie."

She gasped, her mind nothing but swirling darkness and light, teetering on the knife's edge of fear and want. What Luc was doing to her body, no one had ever done before and she wanted it more than anything she'd ever wanted. He was taking her with him into a wilderness of pleasure and she was going—willingly—even as she knew she might never find her way back out.

"Marie, let go," Luc commanded, his voice cracking. "Take this from me."

She rocked her hips against him, harder and faster, until her body fell apart beneath him, her need shattered into a million tiny pieces, fragile and glistening.

He kissed his way up her sternum and into the curve of her neck until his mouth settled over her lips. She couldn't move, her limbs collapsed, spent, on the mat.

"How was that, ma chérie?"

She smiled blissfully against his lips. "Good."

"Hmm. You shouldn't be able to speak after. I think I can do better."

"I don't need better than that."

"I'm going to give you better."

Marie closed her eyes, enjoying the sensation of her body floating back down to earth. Luc's lips disappeared from hers, only to reappear on her stomach. His tongue traced a slow, lazy circle around her navel.

"You have to promise me not to forget to breathe, Marie," he said.

"Mmm."

"Promise me, Marie."

"Promise ..." Luc had been right. There was a kind of orgasm that could make one's body feel like it had just disintegrated, and she'd just had it. If she died right now, she'd die happy.

Luc's thumbs were working circles over the points of her hips, around and around, but she was barely aware of it. It wasn't until he pushed her legs open, that her mind began to re-engage. She tried to close her legs but he held them open.

"We're not finished, Marie."

"You can ..." Marie struggled to form words.

"I can what?"

"Make love to me."

"That's what I'm doing." He chuckled, deep and sexy.

She felt his hair brush her hips as his head moved lower. "No," she protested and tried to close her legs again.

In an instant, Luc's head was hovering above hers, his hands caressing her cheeks. "No what, Marie? You don't want me to make love to you anymore?"

She opened her eyes to see confusion darkening his face. "I don't want you to look at me ... there."

His eyebrows lifted, just for a moment, then lowered. "Why not?"

She shrugged. "It's ..." her words trailed away.

He ran his thumb gently over her well-kissed lower lip, then frowned. "Please don't tell me that no one has ever looked at your body."

"Not ... not that close."

Luc closed his eyes, and took a deep breath, trying to control the anger he felt swelling like a hot bubble in his chest. He wasn't angry with Marie. But the men in her life, that was a different matter.

He opened his eyes and looked intently at her. "So no one, not even your husband—" he ground out the word like it was a bad taste in his mouth, "has ever made love to you with his mouth? Never kissed you intimately?" He rubbed his erection against her pubic bone. "Here?" He could see the shyness, the reticence, clouding her eyes again.

"No," she whispered, closing her eyes against his gaze.

"Ah, Marie." His kisses were soft against her eyelids. "You have not been giving yourself to men who deserve you. Not that I deserve you either, but I would be honored if you were to allow me to be the first man to see all of you."

She said nothing.

"When I paint you, Marie, I will show you how I see you. But I am only half of the tableau here. You have to allow yourself to be seen. Trust me, Marie. Trust my eyes."

He felt her legs part beneath him, just an inch or two at first, then she allowed them to fall open completely. He brushed his mouth against her ear. "*Merci,* Marie. Merci."

He lowered his head and parted her flesh again. He ran his tongue flat and hard against her, flicking the tip of his tongue against the swollen bud of her clitoris, her body bucking against his mouth. He felt a low throaty moan roll down into her hips as she pushed herself into his mouth. He kissed her, slowly, patiently pulling more and more of her desire down into this one, concentrated spot. Marie whimpered helplessly, her hips now rocking back and forth against his mouth.

"Come for me, Marie. Show me what your orgasm looks like."

He felt her tremble beneath his hands, then a softly rolling shudder began to take over her body until she cried out and her back arched off the floor. He kissed every quake and exhausted, sated sigh from her. He had wanted to make love to this woman since the very first morning she knocked on his studio door, and here he was making love to her twice in one day.

He drank in the sight of her body stretched out before him as he rolled on a condom. Her hair was fanned out around her lovely face, her eyes closed, her lips curved in sweet contentment. He laid a gentle kiss on the tip of her nose.

"Marie, have you fallen asleep on me?"

Her eyes fluttered open and she looked unabashedly into his.

"What are you seeing, Marie?" he asked. He brushed a lock of hair from her cheek.

"A man," she said quietly.

He traced her eyebrow with his thumb. "You can do better than that."

Her eyes shone dark with desire. He felt a delicate ankle hook over his calf. "I see a man who wants me," she whispered.

"Bon," Luc replied as his lips hungrily covered hers. The abandon with which she kissed him back split open the last shell protecting his desire. The first time they'd made love, he had allowed her to take from him—and she had taken only a small measure of what he could offer. Now he wanted to give Marie all the pleasure, all the ecstasy, he was capable of—more than she would ever willingly take for herself. He ran his hand along the length of her body, then cupped it around her bottom, tilting her hips open.

"Marie," he breathed against her lips, "I need to feel you closer." He felt her hands settle lightly, then more firmly, on his lower back. She pulled him into her and he went, letting himself sink helplessly into her warmth. He inhaled sharply as every ounce of desire he'd ever felt pooled deep in his groin, then he kissed her fiercely, trying to say with his lips all that he was afraid to say with words.

There had been dozens of women before Marie, but none he had wanted as much, none who had inspired him quite the way his déesse did. He moved slowly inside her and he could imagine nothing more beautiful. No sun-kissed landscape, no delicate wash of watercolor, no porcelain-veined marble. Together, he and his goddess were heading toward the very edge of beauty, that place where light disappeared, where consciousness fell colorless and notes were heard without sound.

He was close to it now, and he pushed harder, sweeping her desire up into his. He felt his lips moving around her name—*marie marie marie chérie chérie déesse*—until there was everything and nothing and their bodies came apart, atoms swirling in gasps of breath like pointillist dots of color pulsing, shimmering, glistening.

14

Marie floated through the week, her feet completely unacquainted with the ground. Nothing rattled her. Not her mother, even after the tenth or eleventh oh-so-casual mention of Richard. Not the marketing professor who dropped a surprise quiz on the class. And how was she supposed to study, anyhow, when she had other things on her mind?

Not even getting caught in a sudden downpour on Connecticut Avenue without an umbrella and no available cab in sight—just as Maya Redfearn happened to drive by. Sometimes Marie wondered whether Maya was tracking the GPS on her phone, so uncanny it was how she always managed to be in the right place at the right time. So she had ended up looking like a drowned rat in Wednesday's J Street Chronicle? Who gave a rat's ass, really?

Nishi was right. Maya was sleeping with Richard. She, Marie Witherspoon, was sleeping with Luc Marchand. Definitely a step up. She smiled. Maya had no idea what she was missing.

"Marie, dear?" Eileen Witherspoon interrupted Marie's

Thursday afternoon reverie, striding into her office without knocking.

Marie attempted to put a thoughtful look on her face and began shuffling through files on her desk—even as she wondered why she bothered. If her mother wanted her to be busier, she'd give her more projects to manage. The truth was, of course, that her mother didn't particularly want Marie working there at all. In her mind, it was just a way for Marie to pay the rent until she and Richard reconciled.

A small white envelope dropped flat onto her desk. She flipped it over and saw the Kennedy Center's logo.

"What's this?" she asked, looking up at her mother. Had her mother been wearing that outfit this morning? She hadn't noticed, so lost she was in thoughts of Luc. "Is that a new suit?" Her mother was wearing a royal blue St. John skirt and jacket, practically a uniform for power women in Washington.

Eileen nodded toward the envelope. "The Cantons can't use these tickets for tomorrow night. Would you like them?"

"You and dad don't want them?"

"You know your father detests the ballet. He falls asleep during the Nutcracker every year. Take Nishi or one of your classmates."

Surprised she's not suggesting you-know-who.

"Well, thanks. I'll send Mrs. Canton a note." But Eileen Witherspoon was already halfway out the door, on to more important matters than her daughter and disposing of an important donor's cultural largesse.

Marie flipped open the envelope and slid the tickets out. Box seats for American Ballet Theatre, Friday night. Her eyes widened as she counted the tickets. She had the entire box. She rang up Nishi.

"Do you and Imran want to go to the ballet with me tomorrow night? My mother just gave me the Cantons' box seats. It's ABT."

"Imran would strangle himself with a toe shoe ribbon before going to the ballet. And I've been working late all week. I owe him a night."

"Oh. Do you have any clients who could use them? I've got four tickets."

"Why don't you ask your artist friend?"

Marie was silent for a minute. She hadn't thought of that, asking Luc. But that would involve seeing him outside of his studio. She wasn't sure their "friendship" extended that far. Sex, sure—he was a man after all. But he might not want to make a habit of seeing her outside "office" hours. First the Phillips, now the Kennedy Center? She suspected that might be a step too far for Luc Marchand.

"I'm wink-winking on my end," Nishi added.

"I don't know. What if someone saw us?"

"Exactly! What a poke in the eye to Maya and Richard if someone sees you at the Kennedy Center with a hunk of a man like that. In fact, take a selfie and send it to me. I'll put it out there. We'll scoop the J Street Chronicle. That'll really chap her ass."

Marie covered her mouth to prevent her laughter from spilling out into the hallway. The idea of scooping Maya was tempting, if unwise.

"Seriously, Marie. It would serve the two of them right. You don't have to hide away from them. All I ask is that you wear something fabulous so no one mistakes you for his assistant or something."

"Or an usher."

"Or one of those women who used to take ballet when they were little and all but wear a tutu to the performance. Don't do that. Gotta go, dear. Call him. I'm daring you."

Marie stared at the tickets on her desk, ignoring the chirping of her email piling up. Nishi was right, as usual. *Why do I have to keep a low profile when I'm not the one who created this situation?*

What was the worst that could happen? He said no and never slept with her again. He probably wasn't going to sleep with her again anyway, now that she had "seen" him—and he had satisfied his masculine curiosity. On the other hand, if he said yes and someone saw them together and it got back to Richard and Maya ... well, score one for Marie Witherspoon.

She scrolled through her contacts, took a deep breath, took another deep breath and tapped Luc's name. He probably wasn't home anyway.

"Bonjour."

"Mr. Marchand!" she blurted out, surprised to actually hear his voice on the other end. *Stupid! Mister? You slept with the man.*

"Please call me Luc, Marie."

"Sorry. I wasn't thinking."

"You don't have to be nervous around me."

I do when you can read my mind from forty miles away.

"To what do I owe the pleasure of this call?"

"I have some tickets to the Kennedy Center for tomorrow night." *Be generic about it.* "I was hoping you might care to accompany me."

Her heart dropped at the silence on the other end.

"Are you asking me out on a date, Marie?"

"Well, um. Not really. It's just the ballet. Someone gave me free tickets. But they're box seats and I have all the seats in the box so it would be very private. No one would see you—"

She heard his deep, throaty chuckle on the other end.

"I don't care whether someone sees me at the ballet or not, Marie. But I'll only go if you admit that you're asking me out on a date."

Her heart was pounding now, her throat dry as paper. She took a deep breath to clear her head and ensure that she didn't keel over from oxygen deprivation. She knew it had been a mistake to ask him. He was going to extort things from her, some odd drawing lesson or humiliating personal admission.

"Are you inviting me on a date, yes or no, Marie?"

"Um, yes?"

"Um yes or yes?"

"Yes."

"Then I accept. What time?"

MARIE LIED to her mother on Friday afternoon and told her she was meeting Nishi at the Kennedy Center. Then Maeve called a cab for her. In the cab, she pulled off her sweater, transforming the sweet navy skirt she had worn all day at the office into a sexy halter dress that clung to her curves on top and swirled around her bare legs. The neckline plunged in a deep vee between her breasts, revealing a wide swath of creamy skin. She couldn't wait to see Luc's face when he saw it. He had never seen her in anything but business attire or jeans. Or, well, nothing at all. She smiled to herself as she rolled up the sweater and stuffed it into her purse, followed by her workday pumps. She pulled out a pair of silver, heeled sandals with straps that wound beguilingly around her slender ankles.

She unclasped her hair from its barrette and fluffed it out around her shoulders. The deep indigo shade of the dress set off her hair nicely. She wouldn't mind if Luc were to run his hands through her hair tonight. A chill skittered down her spine, just thinking about it. Then she applied just the faintest swipe of lipstick. Enough to give her lips some color but not enough to discourage a man from kissing her. She definitely wanted to be kissed again by Luc Marchand. Her heart raced with impatience as the cab slowly made its way down Wisconsin Avenue, into the heart of Georgetown. Traffic was Friday night heavy with employees trying to get out of the city and suburbanites coming in to the bars and restaurants. Georgetown on the weekend attracted a diverse crowd—college students from all over, tourists, young singles, the well-heeled—but it wasn't Marie's favorite neighborhood. Too noisy, too crowded and no parking.

She glanced at her watch every twenty seconds or so. There was plenty of time before the curtain rose, but what if Luc didn't wait? He struck her as a man for whom punctuality was of the utmost importance.

When the cab finally pulled up to the Kennedy Center, she thrust the fare at the driver and bolted from the back seat. People of all ages were already streaming into the long white building. American Ballet Theatre was a perennial favorite on the ballet schedule. It was a must-see event for every young would-be ballerina in the area. Marie's own childhood ballet lessons had been short-lived due to a general lack of flexibility and toes that just wouldn't point that hard.

She scanned the terrace in front of the building, expecting to see Luc leaning against one of the narrow bronze-colored columns as if he hadn't a care in the world. But no leaners resembled him. She hurried through the front entrance and into the Hall of States, ignoring the fluttering flags above her. She peered into the gift shop and box office, but no Luc there either. She stopped at the coat check where she pulled from her purse a smaller clutch holding her wallet and keys, then checked the larger bag.

The Grand Foyer was packed with people buying candy and sipping cocktails. She took a deep breath, trying to will calm into her system, as she threaded her way through the crowd. Maybe he hadn't come. Maybe he forgot, immersed in a painting, or gotten stuck in traffic. Middleburg was a bit of a drive from the city.

Another, even more unwelcome, idea popped into her head. What if she found him and he was talking to someone else? A man like Luc Marchand wouldn't go long without a woman trying to pick him up. What were her options then? Sidle up to them and hope he'd notice her? March over and stake her claim? Or quietly retreat, enjoying her box seats by herself?

Don't think about that. Find him first. She took another deep breath.

After searching the entire length of the Grand Foyer, she finally found Luc standing outside on the river terrace. She stopped just outside the door to watch him for a moment. He was wearing grey flannel pants and a pale lavender shirt, cuffs rolled up to reveal the muscles of his forearms. He was watching Georgetown's crew teams glide by on the Potomac River below. A young woman in a tight red bandage dress and impossibly high heels walked up to him, said something. Marie was too far away to read her lips. Luc shook his head, not even turning to glance at the woman. She teetered away. Marie didn't blame her for trying.

That said, however, if she didn't get over there more women would surely try. Better not to push her luck.

When she reached him, she placed a hand lightly on the small of his back. Even through the shirt, his back muscles were tight and hard and Marie was flooded with memories of last weekend. Not that those memories had been far from her mind all week. Quite possibly, they weren't even lodged in the memory part of her brain yet. After all, her skin still felt just-touched, just-caressed, just-kissed.

"Bonjour," she said, trying to mimic Luc's accent. Unfortunately, it sounded decidedly less sexy coming from her mouth.

He turned and looked at her with an expression of such pure pleasure, her heart nearly stopped. His eyes were big and soft, his white teeth bright in the gloaming. She'd never had a man smile at her that way, a smile that glowed from deep within his eyes. All her fears rose up and floated away like smoke from an extinguished candle. This wasn't superficial, polite pleasure she was seeing on his face. Even she could recognize genuine delight. It crossed her mind to toss the tickets into the river right then and there and simply go home with him.

"Bonjour, Marie." He leaned in and kissed her gently on the lips. But not too gently—there was a promise of something more in the kiss, something reserved for later. He leaned back and took in her dress, pausing at the exposed skin between her breasts. "You take my breath away."

"Thank you." She looked away, embarrassed.

"You're not used to people paying you compliments, are you?" Luc took her hand in his, threaded his fingers through hers.

"Not from men, I guess."

"Well, it's been awhile since I've been on a date," he said, "but from what I recall, I'm supposed to be a gentleman."

Suddenly it hit her with an intensity she hadn't allowed herself to feel all day. She was on a date with Luc Marchand. She, Marie Witherspoon, who just thirty seconds ago was still feeling a little like she was playing dress up in someone else's sexy dress and heels, was on an actual, honest-to-god date with the hottest man on the planet.

Please don't be a gentleman ran through her brain. Already he was scrambling her thoughts and words she had no control over were falling from her lips. "It's okay if you don't want it to be a date. I mean, I know what happened last weekend ... you're trying to teach me and I get that. You don't have to worry, though, that I'm fal—attracted to you. I *am* but—"

He ran a finger lightly along her shoulder then slipped it briefly beneath the fabric of her dress, right where it began to wind around her neck. Her words evaporated into the dusky air around them.

"Maybe my intentions weren't clear enough, Marie, but I'm trying to make you fall for me." He kissed her, and it was no gentle, reserved kiss this time.

All around her was a rush of silk and diamonds, suits and ties, as people sipped their dirty martinis and chardonnay and watched the planes gracefully bank the curves of the river on their final descent to the airport. If someone recognized her, now would be the perfect moment to snap a photo—her in Luc Marchand's arm, his gaze serious and intense, hers stunned and disbelieving.

"You wouldn't have to try that hard."

"On the contrary, it's proving rather harder than I thought it would be."

"I just didn't want to assume."

"Marie, when a man makes love to you twice in one day there's not much left to assume. I know I make *seeing* seem like some mysterious talent. But sometimes it's just a matter of seeing what's right in front of you." He tugged gently at the knot of fabric holding up her dress, then brushed his lips against her ear. "And when I untie this later, what happened last weekend is going to happen this weekend, too."

Inside the Opera House, Marie peered down at the orchestra level seating, where resigned men in dark suits followed women in sequins and furs down the aisle. Normally, that's where she would be seated, too. Richard liked to be seen as a man of the people. No box seats for him. He liked it when random strangers snapped pictures of them with their cellphones. Marie had hated it.

Up here in the box tier, no one would be gauche enough to photograph other patrons—or even make eye contact, really. That was a good thing, too, because she was still stunned from the words he'd spoken out on the terrace. He was trying to make her fall for him. He was planning to make love to her again this weekend.

Had she fallen for him? *More like thrown herself out of a cargo plane at thirty thousand feet without a parachute.*

She could still feel the path his finger had traced along her skin.

From the corner of her eye, she saw Luc scanning the theater, taking it in as though he were trying to memorize every line and shadow. He did that often, she'd noticed.

He caught her watching him. "This is my first time to the Opera House. I've only been to one of the other, smaller theaters here," he explained. "It's very red."

Marie's laugh was lost in the sound of the orchestra beginning its warmup. "Yes, it is very red," she agreed. The Opera House had red seating, red walls, red carpeting, red ceiling. It was thoroughly and unrelentingly red.

An awkwardness had settled in around them, now that they were inside. *Or maybe it's just my awkwardness.* She was too used to feeling on display in places like the Kennedy Center, like she was an accessory meant to be quiet and merely admired, and she couldn't shake the feeling now.

She let her eyes be drawn up to the gigantic, sprawling chandelier on the ceiling. Luc followed her gaze, cocking his head thoughtfully for a moment. She wondered how he was going to separate the lines and shadows of *that.* Best to just take a picture or try for an image more impressionist than real.

"That reminds me of an old Japanese painting, don't you think?" he asked her. "Like tiny white flowers against a red backdrop."

Marie had looked up at that chandelier dozens of times in her life but never saw what Luc was seeing. It did look like a Japanese painting, now that he had pointed it out, even if the chandelier had been a gift from Austria.

"I'll never be able to see things the way you do."

"Of course you will. It just takes a certain practiced innocence."

"You don't seem that innocent to me."

"I *practice* innocence, Marie. I try to look at things through my eyes, not my brain."

The orchestra was settling in now and that delicious air of anticipation was hovering over the audience. Just as the lights dimmed, Luc's hand cupped her jaw and chin and turned her face toward him. His eyes glittered in the darkness, hot and intense.

"Someone as jaded as you are," he whispered, "is not that innocent, either."

The curtain rose just then, revealing dozens of dancers posed onstage. Marie was breathless, both from the beauty of the dancers and from Luc's insinuations. She agreed with him. She *was* jaded. It was hard to grow up in Washington and not be jaded about a lot of things.

She looked over at him from the corner of her eye, as discreetly as she could. He appeared to be mesmerized by the swirl of music and movement and lights onstage. Did he even like the ballet? He never did say, and she'd forgotten to ask. Without acknowledging her gaze, he reached over and took her hand in his. A soft warmth bloomed in her chest and spread down her back.

Maybe he's not here for the ballet. He had said as much, hadn't he? But she didn't know him that well, and she knew she had to be careful not to let physical intimacy fool her into thinking she did. So he wanted to make her fall for him. But he hadn't said that he was falling for her. He might be just a player. A French player, but a player all the same.

She tried to push all these questions out of her mind, questions that couldn't be answered in the Opera House anyway, and tried to focus on the stage. Normally, she loved the ballet and especially ABT, despite her own failed attempts at the art. But the insistent warmth in her chest and the feel of his hand wrapped around hers were distracting in the extreme.

Her college boyfriends had held her hand, and Richard once in awhile—mostly when he was trying to keep her right next to him. But the feel of Luc holding her hand was ... different. Not merely friendly or possessive, but ... intimate. He wasn't squeezing her hand, or clutching it. His hand was *embracing* hers, gently, loosely, as though he was confident she wouldn't break his clasp. She wasn't planning to, either. A man like Luc could be confident in that way.

The ballet was into Act II, the lead dancers locked in a wrenching pas de deux, when Luc's fingers brushed against her lips. He pushed something small into her mouth, which immediately melted into rich, dark chocolate. She swallowed a tortured groan. A moment later, another piece of chocolate was slipped into her mouth ... and then another. He spent the next five minutes feeding her chocolate in the dark while the ballet continued beneath them.

Marie's taste buds were just becoming numb to the sweetness when a smaller, harder piece of candy crossed her lips. It was faintly sweet at first—more purely sugar than the chocolate—then it dissolved into a spicy fieriness. A red hot. One by one, he slipped the tiny pieces of fire between her lips. By the time the curtain fell at intermission, Marie's mouth was aflame, her tongue and lips feeling burned and acutely sensitive from the cinnamon.

As applause swelled and filled the opera house, Luc leaned into her and pressed his lips softly to hers. "Don't look at *us* with your brain, Marie. Just let yourself *see.*"

Before she had time to ponder that statement, his tongue slipped into her mouth and curled around hers, caressing, then drawing it toward him. She felt the sting of each gentle stroke blaze down her spine and splay across her lower back and hips like a pair of strong hands. He had primed her mouth for this with the candy. The sweet then sharp tastes had overwhelmed the nerve endings in her lips and mouth. Now his soft velvet tongue was both soothing her mouth and pushing the fire into the rest of her body.

He was no innocent, no matter what he said. Diabolical, perhaps, but not innocent.

Marie gave into his kiss. There was no point in resisting it anyway, even if she wanted to. He was the conductor here, playing her body, plucking notes from it, teasing her with the crescendo she knew lay in wait for her later.

15

Marie awakened the next morning to stripes of pale yellow sunlight laddered across her chest, and an empty space in the bed next to her. Quite possibly that had all been merely a dream last night, the ballet, the candy, his tongue doing things it surely hadn't been designed to do. She began to sit up, only to be stopped by Luc's insistent voice.

"No no no. Don't move. Just another minute or two."

Luc was sitting on the foot of the bed, his drawing pad propped on his bare knee, strategically hiding his groin.

"You were drawing me sleeping?"

"Oui. It's going to make a gorgeous painting." He waved his pencil at the window. "The light on your hair, the eiderdown next to your skin ... you should see it." He smiled.

"So these paintings are going to be for sale? It's that kind of a show, right?" She tried to picture herself on a gallery wall, her bare shoulders exposed, her hair tangled from sleep.

"Yes. That's the general idea." He continued drawing.

She was quiet, imagining last weekend's drawing hanging on a wall, too. Luc had spent all week painting from it and had been eager to show it to her last night, even though it was late by the time they got back from the ballet.

A large canvas was quite different from a drawing the size of a sketchpad. Her breasts were larger, for one thing, and somehow more bare. Paint was more lifelike than charcoal. Her face looked lonelier and sadder in color, too. Yeah, she got the whole Edward Hopper thing but still ... it wasn't as flattering as she had hoped a portrait by Luc would be.

At the sight of her chewing her lip, he stopped drawing. "Are you worried about people you know seeing them?"

She shrugged, a look of uncertainty on her face.

"I wouldn't worry about it, Marie. Washington's not an art town. Sam says most of her buyers at the Dupont Circle location will be tourists from overseas."

"I guess it seemed more abstract to me until I saw the ones you have finished."

Luc set down his sketchbook and crawled over the bed to reach her. He straddled her body over the covers, stroking her cheeks with his hands. "Marie, love, the paintings will be beautiful. I promise you that. You saw them last night. I don't paint like —" he wracked his brain for the names he was thinking of—"Eric Fischl. Or Phillip Pearlstein. Sour light and rolls of flesh. I am not like that. I am more ..."

He rubbed his noise against hers, a simple gesture that Marie felt far beyond her nose.

"Romantic?" she whispered hopefully, finishing his sentence for him.

"Oui. Anyone who sees my paintings will think your husband was out of his mind to let you go. And they won't all be nudes."

"But nudes probably sell better," she pointed out.

"Marie, that's not for you to worry about."

"I don't want to make your show unsuccessful."

"When paintings don't sell, it's generally not the model's fault." He tweaked her shoulder. "Come. Take a shower with me."

Luc's house was centuries old but some previous owner had remodeled the bath enough to squeeze in a narrow, grey-tiled shower next to the clawfoot tub. Marie stepped beneath the hot water and closed her eyes. The heat felt good seeping into her muscles. She was getting rather more exercise than she was accustomed to since meeting Luc. Who would have guessed that learning to draw would burn so many calories? It was better than a gym membership.

When she opened her eyes, Luc was still standing outside the shower, just staring at her. *Uh oh.* She knew where this was going. Instead of joining her, he returned to the bedroom to retrieve his sketchbook and pencil.

"Wash yourself," he said.

She lathered her hands with the bar of soap and ran them over her arms and neck while Luc's hand flew over the paper. *They won't all be nudes.* But some of them will. She worried that thought in her mind for a few minutes. Did she even want Nishi to see the paintings? Actually, it was the idea of people she knew looking at them that bothered her more than complete strangers. Her classmates might see them, or her professors. Her mother's donors or people Marie had grown up with. Old neighbors.

Oh screw it, she thought, as she added more lather to her hands. If people don't like the paintings, so what? It's not like she was stepping out on her husband. Divorce proceedings were already well underway. That was common knowledge, thanks to the *Washington Post* and Maya.

"Stop. Hold that position."

Luc's command jolted her out of her thoughts and she looked down at her soapy hands. They were resting on her breasts. She hadn't been paying much attention to what she was doing with the soap.

"Don't look up. Hold it just like that." His hand flew furiously over the page.

She stared at the water running into the drain until he set aside the sketchbook at last and joined her in the shower. He lathered up his hands and proceeded to wash her shoulders, then her breasts, patiently working his way down over her abdomen and onto her hips. *They were going to have sex in the shower.* That was going to be another first for her, like the oral sex had been last weekend.

Luc poured shampoo onto her head and massaged it in, working the bubbles through her hair with his fingers. It felt so amazing, her toes curled against the tile floor. Just like they had when his mouth was on her, between her legs ... the things he could do with his tongue.

"What's that little smile for, hmm?" he asked.

Her face turned hot and she was grateful for the heat and steam of the shower. "This might be better than sex," she fibbed. Nothing was better than sex with Luc.

"Turn around so I can rinse you."

Rinse me. Kiss me. Fuck me. Whatever he wanted to do to her, she would let him. *Even paint me.* She wasn't going to stop that and she knew it. She enjoyed modeling for Luc, enjoyed being the object of his attention ... of his art. She felt wanted when he was drawing her. Desired. She wasn't sure he was really *seeing* her, not in the way he thought he was or wanted to. But he was looking at her, and she would settle for that.

She closed her eyes and let the shower spray chase the suds from her hair. Luc's fingers wiped stray bubbles from her cheeks and nose. She grabbed his hand and pressed it to her lips, licking his palm. When she opened her eyes a second later, she was greeted with the sight of a wet Luc Marchand in front of her. A wet, *hard* Luc Marchand.

His words from last night came back to her. *Sometimes it's just a matter of seeing what's right in front of you.* Luc wanted her, however improbable that might seem to an outsider. But between them there was undeniable chemistry. She reached out and wrapped her hand around him. His groan was deep and lusty, pained almost. His warm hand covered hers, then slid her hand off.

"Just watch," he said.

He stroked himself up and down, up and down, never taking his eyes off her. His gaze bore into her face, her breasts, her hips—hot and dark and barely in control.

"I could look at you all day, Marie. I can never see enough of you."

"Do you see me when I'm not here?"

Still his eyes bore into her. "Yes," he rasped. "I've come more in the past week than in ..." His words trailed away, washing into the drain. His breathing was becoming shorter and shallower. His nostrils flared.

"You don't save yourself for me?" Her own breathing was labored now, too.

"Marie," he gasped. "Don't ... come ... let ... me ..."

He wanted her to save herself for him. But she wasn't sure she could. She was so consumed by watching Luc that she hadn't noticed her own hips beginning to rock back and forth. But he had. He was touching himself and yet she felt touched, too. The only thing in contact with her, though, was the water running down her back.

How is this possible? Just watching him ...

By the time Luc came, she was close to the edge herself. She took a deep breath to stop it, to give him a moment to gather himself. He leaned into her, one hand on the wall behind her, his chest heaving against her collarbone. After a minute, he slipped his other hand between her legs. She topped it with her own and stopped him.

"It's your time to watch me," she said.

He took a step back as she began to rock her hips, her hand sliding through her own flesh. Luc dropped to his knees, his eyes fixed to that hand.

The water ran over his head, through his hair, in rivulets down his back. She dug her fingers into his wet hair to balance herself as she swam closer to a climax. Her legs began to wobble, her thighs quivering. It was right there, almost in reach. Luc was staring intently at her, mesmerized, and through a haze of pleasure she recognized what he was doing. He was committing every little detail to memory. The lines and planes and shadows. His face blurred as she burst through the orgasm, water coursing over her face, her breasts, her hips.

In the tiny spot of her brain still functioning, she felt Luc's hands grasp her thighs and hold her steady.

THEY SPENT the rest of the morning outside, Luc drawing Marie while Marie attempted to capture on paper the acres of landscape beyond his property. Marie sat on the low stone wall where Luc had first kissed her and tried to maintain a straight face as he popped in and out of her peripheral vision, chewing on his pencil, the very picture of seriousness.

She preferred modeling for him over having him draw her while she was trying to do something else. It was hard to monitor her smiles and scowls minute by minute when she was focused on other things. Not to mention, formally posing for him turned her on. To have him intently staring at her—and only her—was heady stuff, intoxicating. But Luc flitting around her like an insect was distracting, not sexy. And she wanted sexy Luc all the time now.

At lunch, he drew her while she ate the dandelion salad he'd prepared for them. She drank more of his great burgundy, letting the wine warm up her veins.

"Is this what the paparazzi did back before cameras were invented?" she asked lazily. "Scurry around with paper and pencil drawing people?"

Luc smiled without looking up from his drawing. "That might be who I was in a past life, primitive paparazzi."

"Do you believe in past lives?" The wine and the sudden surfeit of sex had loosened up Marie's tongue.

"I believe in present lives."

"So you don't believe that what we do in this life affects where we end up in the next one?" She swirled the last spiky dandelion leaf through the mustardy vinaigrette.

"No, I don't, Marie. If that's the case, then I'm royally fucked for my next life."

She frowned. "Why would you say that?"

"As is your husband, I might add," he replied, ignoring her question.

"Oh I don't know. I wouldn't be here right now if it weren't for the fact that he's getting royally fucked by Maya Redfearn in this life."

"Well, in that case, I am glad for his misfortune."

He stood to clear away their lunch dishes. Marie followed him to the studio's kitchenette, worried that her questions, which she had intended to be innocent and throwaway, had made him crabby.

"What's on the agenda for this afternoon?" she asked, recorking the bottle of wine. "Are you going to draw me some more?"

"What would you like to do?"

"I'd like to try drawing you again, if you don't mind. But maybe not all of you. I think I should start small."

"You want to draw the smallest part of me? Well, that would

be my brain."

He grabbed his head and pretended to screw the top of his skull off. She laughed at his clownish behavior. Whatever crabbiness had been brewing was gone now.

"I meant like those small drawings at the museum. That focus on just one body part."

"Ah." He rotated slowly for her, like a product on display. "Which part of me are you considering?"

She knew she should do something like his bicep or calf, something prosaic. Easy. But in her heart, she knew that wasn't what she really wanted to draw. She tugged his shirt hem from the waistband of his old, soft khakis.

"May I?" she asked.

He pulled the shirt over his head and flung it aside. She unbuttoned and unzipped his pants. He let them drop to the floor and kicked them away.

"On or off?" He snapped the waistband of his boxer briefs.

The glint in his eye told her that he too was remembering the first time she tried to draw him. She was braver now—and she had already seen what was underneath.

"Off, of course," she answered, watching closely as the rest of him emerged.

You are beautiful. And mine. For now, for today, and that was all she would ask for. Just one day at a time. She would not let herself hope for anything more than that.

She found a mat and a blanket, and carefully spread them out on the floor. Luc lay on his back, one knee bent, posing as if for some cheesy calendar.

"You should be holding a paintbrush between your teeth or something," she joked. "Like it's a flower."

He rolled his eyes at her suggestion and instead made a show of arranging his penis just so. He was trying to be funny, but watching him touch himself made her want him. Made her want to touch him with her own hands. She pushed that thought from her mind. She really did want to draw him again. As great as the sex was, she wanted her lessons, too.

"You're being rather too optimistic about my abilities there," she said. "That's a little above my pay grade."

"I have more faith in your talent than you do."

She knelt down and pushed him over onto his stomach.

"The back of my knees, Marie?" he joked. "I have cellulite there, you know."

She lightly pinched the taut skin behind his knees. "Too bad. That rules that out."

She ran her nails across his shoulders, leaving a pink trail in her wake. "Looks like you have scars from thousands of women's nails up here."

"I do not," he said with mock indignation.

"So I can't draw your shoulders."

She brushed away the hair from the nape of his neck, then leaned in close, close enough for her breath to warm his skin.

"Hmm. Your pores are rather big here."

Luc snorted and she had to bite her lip to hold back her own laughter.

She moved down to his legs and pretended to consider his thighs and calves, lightly tapping her fingers over the well-formed muscles. "It would take forever to draw all these little hairs."

"I'd be happy to lie here forever for you."

"Yes, but I've got things to do."

Luc's shoulders bounced with silent laughter. She ran the flat of her palm over his ass. "No hair here." She dipped her head and dropped a kiss on the indentation at the small of his back. "Pores look okay." She lightly scraped her nails along the curve of his backside. "Hmm. Some evidence of ass-kissing but it doesn't look recent." She cupped his very fine ass in her hands and concluded, "I think maybe this is the part I should draw."

As she leaned back and picked up her sketchpad, Luc twisted his hips, slightly adjusting his position on the blanket.

"If there's one thing you have helped me see, Marie, it's that modeling is very ... rewarding. I'm beginning to think I've wasted my life on the wrong side of the easel."

"Glad to know there's something I was able to teach you, Mr. Marchand."

"Ah, you are teaching me many things, Ms. Witherspoon. But draw quickly. I have things I want to do, too, and all of them involve you."

16

Marie walked at a leisurely pace back to her mother's office. It was a sunny day with temperatures practically balmy for early November. The branches of the street trees in Georgetown were nude, the last leaves already fallen prey to autumn's changing moods.

She unbuttoned her wool coat so she wouldn't be overheated by the time she arrived at the office. She had a long afternoon of inputting data ahead of her. That, and her mother wanted her to brainstorm message ideas for the firm's holiday card. In the past, she had dreaded that task, with its requirement that one be both cheerful and clever. But she was looking forward to the upcoming holidays more than she had in recent years, even allowing herself to imagine spending Christmas Eve in Middleburg with Luc. Dinner and wine by candlelight ... opening gifts by the fire.

Yes, Marie thought she might have both cheerful and clever in her this year.

She'd just come from a longer than usual lunch with Nishi. Nishi had treated her to an expensive French restaurant tucked away on a cobblestoned side street in Georgetown in honor of

Marie, in Nishi's words, "getting laid." She was even beginning to think that this thing with Luc was more than just getting laid. She was leery of getting her hopes up but everywhere she looked, it seemed, little hopes were flitting about.

She smiled at Maeve as she passed the front desk.

"Marie—" Maeve began, then stopped. "Good afternoon."

Marie paused to ask Maeve what was wrong, but the older woman had picked up her phone and begun to dial. She made a mental note to ask on her way out at the end of the day. Maeve was widowed, her children and grandchildren living in the midwest and Texas. Maybe she was down about the holidays.

Mother should invite her to Thanksgiving.

Upstairs, she was surprised to see the door to her office closed. It was never closed, unless she was meeting with someone. Which she wasn't doing at the moment, obviously. She turned the knob and pushed it open.

"God damn, Marie, you must have been on a three-martini lunch. Or six, maybe."

Marie froze. Richard was sitting behind her desk, his expensive leather shoes propped up on a stack of file folders. Her computer monitor was cocked at an unusual angle. So this explained Maeve's stiff behavior downstairs.

"What are you doing?" she asked, quietly closing the door behind her. "Does my mother know you're here?"

"Of course she does. I stopped in to say hello to her first."

"Does she know you've been going through my computer?"

He rolled his eyes. "I can do whatever I damn well please where your mother is concerned and you know it."

"You still haven't answered my question. What are you doing here? And let me have my chair."

"I'm comfortable here, thank you."

He made her want to scream and stamp her feet and tear out her hair all at the same time.

"I've called off the divorce."

Just like that—with five measly words—everything went into slow motion around her, the shit-eating grin on his face, the goose-like honking of car horns on the street below, the white noise of the ventilation system, a conversation leaking through the wall of the office next to hers. There was suddenly not enough oxygen in the room.

"No," was all she could say when she regained the power of speech.

"Yes."

"*Why?*" This couldn't be happening to her. She must have tripped on the sidewalk outside and knocked herself out cold, or stepped off the curb and been hit by a cab. Any minute now she was going to come to and Richard would be gone.

"On the advice of my staff."

Marie vaguely remembered her father saying something about a challenger for Richard's seat in next year's election. She hadn't given it much thought since then. It wasn't her problem.

"You don't want to call this off. Your campaign manager does."

"Same thing to you."

"What does Maya think?"

"She understands. *She* wants what's best for me."

"Well, I want what's best for me and that does not involve being married to you."

Richard casually lifted his feet from her desk, then slammed them down on the floor. Marie jumped.

"Too bad, sweetheart. You *are* married to me. And will be until I decide otherwise."

"I'm not doing it."

"What happened to 'Richard! Let's try marriage counseling! We can work this out!'" He coldly mocked her. "Well, I've been counseled by my campaign manager to patch things up with you. We've had a change of heart and all that nonsense."

"You know, I've been seeing other men. Actually, I've been sleeping with other men."

"That will have to stop, obviously."

"Are you stopping with Maya?"

The sneer on his face was answer enough. "You really don't have any say in this."

"Yes. Yes, I do. I'll file for divorce."

He laughed. "You can't afford to file. I'll drag it out 'til you run out of money. Your parents won't pay for it either. Your father has millions of dollars in DefenseTech contracts he wants put into the budget. I can hold that up with the rest of the Armed Services Committee." He stood. "You can have your seat back. We'll be seeing each other around." He leaned in to kiss her but Marie snapped her face away just in time. His lips smooshed her cheek and she had to suppress a chilly shiver.

His footsteps were still echoing down the hall as she pulled up Google. Sure enough, one Samuel Varner, a Pittsburgh restaurant magnate, had thrown his hat into the ring for next year's primary. And he was making hay with the notion of Richard as an adulterer who abandoned his wife for a mistress. *Well, at least someone is on my side.*

She barged into her mother's office without knocking. Her mother looked up, startled, then hung up the phone. Eileen Witherspoon did not look surprised to see her.

"Richard was just here."

"I know, dear. I told you he'd come around. He needs you more than you need him."

She looked at her mother, dumbfounded, unable to believe her mother had just said that.

"You're right. I don't need him and this isn't happening, so wipe that idea out of your head right now."

"Nonsense. This is the best thing for you, Marie. You can go back to your normal life, have children—"

"I don't want children right now. And certainly not with him!" An image of Luc chasing a dark-headed toddler down his lawn flashed through her head. "Anyway, I've fallen in love with someone else." There. She'd said it. Admitted it. She was in love with Luc Marchand. Not just getting laid. Not just having an unserious fling.

"Oh seriously, Marie. You can't be in love with someone else this soon. Richard says you can finish your MBA, as long as it doesn't interfere with campaign events. I got him to agree to that." Eileen Witherspoon looked inordinately pleased with herself.

"Wait—you were negotiating this with him?" Marie could hardly believe her ears. "Can't he just marry Maya and be done with it? It's not like she's going away."

"Apparently, the bloom is off that rose. At least as far as marriage is concerned."

"And you believed that? If he needs a wife, she'll do just fine."

"It's not that he needs a wife. It's that he doesn't need an ex-wife."

"Well, when you file for divorce you generally end up with an ex-wife. Isn't that the whole point?"

"I believe he has seen the error of his ways." Her mother turned back to her leather-bound daily planner.

"If you believe that, I have all sorts of bridges and shit to sell you."

Her mother shot her a stern look but Marie no longer cared. She stomped out of her mother's office and back to her own. The first call she made was to Nishi.

"Richard's being primaried," she said by way of greeting.

"That's great news! Why the glum voice?" Nishi replied.

"He's called off the divorce."

There was dead silence on the other end.

"So you file."

"I don't have the money. And he's threatening to kill funding for my father's contracts in committee."

Marie closed her eyes and rubbed at her temples. Now that the initial shock of adrenaline was subsiding, a monster headache was building, wrapping its tentacles around her scalp.

"Well, then, you have to make him *want* to refile the divorce papers."

"How do I do that? Short of flying out to Pittsburgh and offing his opponent?" She sighed. "I'm actually thinking of emailing Maya, just to be a snide bitch. But I know I shouldn't be that kind of person."

Nishi snorted on the other end. "So let me. I'll send her a fake press release announcing that Sen. Richard Macintyre and his wife are reconciling in advance of his re-election campaign."

"Won't that get you in trouble at work?"

"Gah. No one likes her, Marie. Only Richard. And apparently not that much anymore."

17

Her mother's office door was open when Marie strode down the hall, coat on, bookbag slung over her shoulder. It was three o'clock and she was leaving early, daring her mother to stop her. But Eileen Witherspoon did not so much as look up from her desk as Marie passed.

"See you tomorrow, Maeve."

"You're leaving, dear?" The receptionist looked up from her phones.

"Yes. I've got a killer headache." A killer headache named Richard Macintyre.

"Well, take an aspirin, dear, and get some rest. Some hot tea. That always works for me."

Maeve put Eileen Witherspoon to shame in the motherhood department. *I can't believe she was negotiating with him. The nerve!*

She jogged around the corner to where she had parked her car that morning. There was a parking ticket stuck beneath the windshield wiper. Well, that certainly fit with the general direction in which her day was headed. She tugged it out and tossed it into the back seat. Maybe Richard could take care of that for her, hmm?

She had to get something out of the deal. She laughed out loud as she turned the key in the ignition. Or perhaps that was the way to get him to refile for divorce. She could run up unpaid parking tickets all over the city. That would be ridiculously easy. DC's city government was famously efficient when it came to parking enforcement. Maya would happily—no, gleefully—have a field day with that. *Are senator's wives exempt from the law? Then why does Marie Witherspoon owe thousands of dollars in parking fines to the city? No one should be above the law!*

Some hot tea did sound nice, she thought as she settled into the passenger seat and turned the key. And a hot bath. Maybe a shot of whiskey, she mentally added, even though hard liquor had never been her thing. Maybe if she put the shot of whiskey into the hot tea ... Richard could drive anyone to drink.

She made her way through the streets of Georgetown, down to M Street and then over the Key Bridge into Virginia. She picked up route 66 to the Dulles Toll Road, the late afternoon sun bright in her eyes. Toll road traffic was heavy but tolerable.

She wished upon Richard a lifetime of heavy traffic. Soul-sucking traffic.

"Damn it!" she shouted, followed by a few other choice words, the verbal equivalent of a voodoo doll in Richard's likeness. Then she took a deep breath. *Calm down.* A pinpoint of pain was poking at the back of her skull. No point in leaving work early if she made herself too sick to enjoy it.

How long before her mother began crowing to her friends—who were numerous—about their reconciliation? It had probably already started. And she had joked with Nishi about it but Maya was going to be majorly pissed about this. Suddenly she was no longer Senator Macintyre's fiancée? This was going to be World War III, Operation Bridezilla, scorched earth edition.

She had to tell Luc about this before it hit the grapevine. He didn't seem to pay much attention to DC gossip, or even read the papers much, but Samantha Smith was plugged in. The last thing Marie wanted was for him to hear it from someone else.

The cars ahead of her braked to a stop as they approached Reston. She leaned her forehead on the steering wheel to give her eyes a rest from the sun, then reached over into her purse for her phone. She plugged it into the dash and scrolled through her music, but nothing fit her mood.

At route 28, Marie normally steered north to get to her apartment complex in Ashburn. Today, she went south toward route 50. Route 50 would take her to Middleburg—and Luc's house.

Could nothing in her life be simple, she pondered as the highway miles fell away behind her. What had she done to piss off the universe?

Oh stop the pity party.

Richard couldn't make her reconcile with him. Nor could her mother. What could they do if she simply dug in her heels and refused? She would wait him out. Eventually he would tire of waiting—or Maya would, more likely—and he would file the papers again. Maya was not a patient woman, nor one accustomed to not getting her way. How long could it take?

Yes, Operation Heel Digging was commencing.

She let her car glide onto the exit ramp and made her way through Middleburg to Luc's road. She should have called first, it occurred to her, as she pulled into his driveway. What if he wasn't home? What if he had a client there ... or another student? He would have mentioned if he had another student, wouldn't he?

Maybe not. They rarely discussed their lives when they were together. Sex and drawing, that's all they talked about.

Damn it. The windows in his house were dark. She put the car in park and jumped out, then walked around back to the studio. There she breathed a sigh of relief. The studio was lit, the door even ajar. She stuck her head in and saw Luc sitting at an easel, his back to her. He was painting. His grey tee shirt clung to his shoulder muscles, which flexed with each stroke of his paintbrush. He was wearing those faded, worn jeans she loved. And his feet were bare. She loved that, too.

She rapped on the door frame. No response.

"Luc?" she said quietly. She didn't want to startle him while he was painting.

Still no reaction. Maybe he'd fallen into a coma from the paint fumes. She quietly stepped into the studio and walked toward him. She was two feet away when he turned, smiling, his face open and happy.

"Marie." He held open his arms. "I am so happy to see you."

She sank into his waiting kiss. His hands opened her coat, brushed her hips, then swept down along her thighs. This was simple, she thought. It had seemed complicated at first, but it wasn't. Luc wanted her. She wanted him. It didn't have to be any more complicated than that.

And she felt safe with him. Here in his studio, it was just the two of them, in their own little world. No one could touch her here. In here, she didn't have a power-hungry mother or a philandering husband whose motives were governed by poll numbers. Here, she just had him.

He pushed her coat off her shoulders and tugged gently at the hem of her suit jacket. "To what do I owe the pleasure of this visit?" he murmured against her lips.

She let him kiss her again before answering. "I left work early ..." He was kissing her jaw now, heading for her throat. Her brain was beginning to shut down, but enough consciousness was left to tell her that now wasn't the right time to explain about Richard. "... and my car had a mind of its own. It just sort of drove itself here."

She felt him smile against her neck.

"Hmm. I programmed your car to do that. So all your roads lead to me."

He pulled her so tight against him she could barely breathe. His hands were running over her back, then her arms, frustrated by the layers of fabric beneath them, her jacket, her blouse, her skirt.

Over his shoulder she saw the painting he'd been working on. It was the one of her sleeping, the covers of his bed pulled up almost to her shoulders. She looked ... peaceful. Not lonely or sad, not Hopper-esque.

Luc pulled away from her throat, sensing her inattention. When he saw where her gaze had gone, he spun the two of them around to face the painting head on. Marie was now sitting on his lap.

"I've never seen myself sleeping before."

"It's a lovely sight. You sleeping in my bed, right where you belong."

A thought was forming in the back of Marie's mind.

"And this one will go in the show?"

An idea.

"Mm-hmm. Though I was thinking about keeping it instead. Actually, I want to keep all of them but Sam tells me she can't invite people to look at empty walls."

A painting of me asleep in Luc's bed ... a painting of Richard's wife asleep in another man's bed ...

A strategy.

"I could always pose for this one again, sometime." She fired a smile of pure, unadulterated wickedness at Luc. She leaned in and licked the curve of his ear. "If you invite me to spend the night again, that is."

"You have a standing invitation, ma chérie. Anytime you want."

... Senator Macintyre's wife sleeping in the bed of artist Luc Marchand.

What do you do when you find out your spouse is sleeping with someone else?

Divorce them.

She had told Richard she was sleeping with "other men." That hadn't fazed him, even with her exaggeration. But if other people knew that she was sleeping with someone else, now *that* might faze him. If he were being openly cuckolded—and the evidence was in a gallery in Dupont Circle where anyone could walk in off the street and take a look—that might force a change of heart.

This was perfect. Richard would have to refile the papers when Luc's show opened. There was no way his campaign manager would want her around after that. An ex-wife couldn't be half as bad for his campaign as a wife who allowed herself to be painted nude by her lover.

Richard will be livid.

She kissed Luc long and deep, then looked at him while she held his face tenderly in her hands. She noticed for the first time the stubble shadowing his jaw and the dark circles beneath his eyes. Her eyes flicked up to his hair, which evidently had not seen a comb that day and sported random streaks of paint.

His stomach rumbled, making her laugh. "Luc, have you been painting since you got up this morning?"

He smiled sheepishly. "More or less."

She quirked an eyebrow at him.

"Okay, yes. Pretty much non-stop since eight or nine this morning."

She ran her thumbs over his whiskers. "You must be starving. Come. I'll fix you something to eat."

She stood and tugged him up, too.

"Uh, yeah, I don't know how much I have in the kitchen."

"Let's go look. I'm hungry, too." Lunch seemed like eons ago now, way back before Richard tried to blow up her world. *Hah.*

Well, she had her own little bomb to detonate on his ass—and the timer was ticking.

Luc closed up the studio and they walked hand in hand back to the house. In the kitchen, Marie opened and closed Luc's fridge and cupboards. He had milk, eggs, bread, cheese and wine. She could work with that.

"Omelettes?" she asked as she tied on a black, paint-spattered apron she found hanging on a hook in the pantry.

He laughed from the small kitchen table, leaning back in his chair. "That's really your only option, isn't it?"

She waved a spatula at him. "Wait 'til you see dessert."

His face went dark and hungry, and he obviously wasn't thinking about omelettes. "Can't we have dessert first? It's an old French tradition."

She gathered up a bowl, whisk, skillet. "Well, if you had bothered to eat earlier, we could have had dessert first. But not now. I don't want you passing out on me."

He pouted at her for a moment, but she was unmoved. "We're eating first."

"I like this take-charge Marie. You leave work early, barge into my studio and proceed to cook for me. I'm going to get this down on paper." He squeezed by her in the kitchen as she cracked eggs into a bowl. From a drawer he pulled out a small sketchpad and a pencil.

She looked at him incredulously. "Do you keep drawing supplies in every room of the house?"

He kissed her cheek as he made his way back to the table. "As a matter of fact, I do. One never knows when inspiration will strike."

She watched him from the corner of her eye as she mixed the eggs and poured them into the skillet. He was serious. He was actually drawing her puttering around the kitchen. The look of intense concentration on his face was way sexier than it ought to be, too. She turned back to the omelette. If she kept watching Luc, they *would* end up having dessert first.

She flipped the omelette, then slid it onto a plate. She uncorked the pinot gris.

"Don't wait for me. Eat," she ordered.

He frowned at the drawing.

"What's wrong?" she asked.

"It would work better if you weren't wearing a business suit under the apron. The lines are too similar."

"What should I be wearing then?" she asked as she set to work on a second omelette.

"Nothing."

She looked over at him and shook her head. "You have a one-track mind. Eat."

He dug into the omelette like a man starving, washing every other bite down with a gulp of wine. When she joined him at the table with her own plate, he had made a second sketch. He spun it around for her to see. In this one, she was nude beneath the apron. He had made the apron shorter, too, so that it barely grazed the top of her thighs.

"See?" He retraced the path of his pencil with a finger. "The lines are just better in this one."

"You're not going to put that one in the show, are you?"

"Why not?" He smiled wickedly at her. "Worried that it shows too domestic a side of you?"

She rolled her eyes. "Somehow I don't think 'domestic' is what people will take away from that."

He cocked his head, pretending to consider the drawing further. "Ah, you're right. Plus, your ex-husband might identify too much with this one."

Marie stared down at her omelette, hoping Luc couldn't see her discomfort. *After dinner. I'll tell him then.*

"Thank you for dinner, Marie. I probably would have fainted from hunger at some point if you hadn't come along."

She glanced over at his plate, now completely empty. He'd practically inhaled the food. "Do you work like that often?"

He got up and refilled his wine, poured a little more into her glass. "Actually, I haven't worked like this in years. Well, I haven't had a show in years. I haven't deserved a show."

She popped the last bite of omelette into her mouth. "It doesn't seem healthy, working without eating or resting." She looked pointedly at his whiskered face.

Her fingers were itching to touch him. She imagined those rough hairs brushing against her cheek, her breasts, her inner thigh.

He rubbed his jaw, smiling. "Or shaving. No, it feels good to give myself over to it again. It's what I love." His eyes dropped to her now-empty plate. "I believe I was promised dessert."

His eyes weren't smiling anymore. They were dark and fiery at the same time, and Marie felt the familiar tug of desire in her hips, low and heavy.

"Come." He stood and held out his hand.

"Where are we going?"

"My bed."

"Won't we get crumbs in the sheets, if we have dessert in bed?"

He pulled her to him, reached around to tug on the apron string. The apron fell to the floor, just before he crushed her to his chest. "Fuck the crumbs. After I devour you, I'll eat them too."

In the bedroom, Luc turned on a floor lamp in the corner of the room, casting a soft glow over the bed. He gently removed her suit jacket and carefully draped it over the back of a chair.

"I don't think I've ever undressed a woman in a business suit," he said.

She looked at him skeptically as she stepped out of her pumps.

"I think you attribute more experience to me than I actually have."

She laughed. "Luc, I can tell how much experience you have and it's a ton."

He nuzzled her neck while he reached around and unzipped her skirt, letting it fall to the floor. "Maybe I just have *good* experience."

She began to unbutton her blouse but his hands stilled hers. "I'll do it."

He kneeled in front of her and began unrolling her stockings. Marie moaned as his hands caressed her legs on the way down. The back of her thighs. The dip behind her knees. The curve of her calves. By the time his fingers danced over the instep of her foot, she was quivering with need.

He tugged her panties off next, then began work on her blouse. As his fingers popped each button through, Marie found it harder and harder to breathe. His smell swirled around her, wine and paint and ... Luc. If she could bottle his scent and wear it all day ... she smiled to herself. She'd be in a highly agitated state twenty-four hours a day.

When the last button was undone, he carefully slid the silk down her arms and added it to the jacket on the chair. Her bra was the only thing left and he made short work of that, too.

He looked over her, appraisingly. Marie wished she knew what he was thinking.

"You are stunning. That's what I'm thinking." He smiled, then added, "Sometimes you're not that hard to read." He plucked her blouse from the chair and swung it over her shoulders.

"Put this back on."

"Why?" But she did as he asked.

His eyes raked over her body as he quickly shed his jeans and tee shirt. "I like the silk against your skin. There's just the tiniest difference in texture and color."

"You see everything as a picture."

He cupped her face in his hands, tilted it up. "I can't help it. When I see beauty, I want to capture it, make it permanent."

"But some things are beautiful because they're not permanent. If they were, we'd get tired of them."

"I could never be tired of you, Marie."

His lips touched hers, soft and gentle, and the most beautiful warmth wrapped around her body. Where was sexy Luc, arrogant Luc, bossy Luc? She was ready to shove him onto the bed and have her way with him, yet he was taking things slow. It was like he had morphed into ...

The kiss wandered, roamed like an explorer over her jaw, her ear, her eyelids. When had her temple become an erogenous zone? He pulled her hips into his, and she gasped at how hard he was. His lips wandered back to hers. "Are you in love with me, Marie?"

... loving Luc.

Of course, she was in love with him. *You had me at bonjour.*

"Yes."

"Bon. Because I am in love with you."

Luc was in love with her! Marie's heart soared, then plummeted back to earth. *I can't tell him about Richard now. Not tonight.* She couldn't ruin his wonderful mood.

"So we agree on something, finally," she said with a smile.

He scooped her up in his arms and carried her over to the bed. She sighed as her body sunk into the fluffy eiderdown.

"I thought we agreed on lots of things. We both like this, right?" His mouth closed over her nipple, his tongue circling it until it was a hard peak.

She sucked in her breath. "You like that. But I *love* it. So no, we don't agree there."

Luc lifted his head from her breast long enough to look her in the eye and pick up the gauntlet she'd just thrown down. He kissed his way down her stomach, then circled his tongue around her navel.

"Hmm. You know, I think I prefer an outie and you're an innie," he said.

"Afraid you're out of luck there."

"Oh, I don't know. Maybe I could reverse it."

He dipped his tongue into her navel, then covered it with his mouth and began to suck. Marie's hips bucked off the bed and she tried to push Luc's head away.

"Stop ..." She twisted her hips in an attempt to escape his mouth.

"Ah. You're ticklish, Marie."

"Am ... not."

His hands skipped up her sides, tickling her waist, then beneath her arms. He chuckled at her protestations.

"Well, this seems to be another thing we disagree on," he said.

He ran a finger down to her hip, where he traced unseen lines on her skin. "You would look good with a tattoo right about here." He dropped a kiss on her hip.

"You don't mean that."

"Why not? I'm thinking a heart with my name inside would be lovely. I would have to be the one to draw it, of course."

Marie pushed herself up on her elbows to look down at Luc, whose head was now bouncing up and down with laughter.

She hadn't seen him this lighthearted, this carefree since ... well, since never. This was an entirely new side to Luc.

"You're always so serious," she murmured.

He slid up her body until they were face to face again. "I don't want to be serious all the time. Not with you." He kissed her. "I'm happy when I'm around you."

She felt her hips open with desire. She hooked an ankle around Luc's calf. He reached between them and slipped a finger into her wetness, groaning.

"Your body seems to agree with me on something. You want me." He pushed in deeper.

Yes, I want you. Wanted his skin covering hers, wanted his lips on every inch of her body, wanted him deep inside her. But she wanted more than that, even.

She wanted *him.*

She wanted serious Luc.

Sexy Luc.

Arrogant Luc.

Angsty Luc.

And now she wanted this new Luc, too—sweet and happy Luc.

She wanted all of them.

He was looking at her, one eyebrow lifted slightly in expectation. He was waiting for her. Waiting for the go ahead. He always waited for her permission when they made love, she realized with some surprise. As demanding and arrogant as he could be when he was trying to teach her to draw, he was never that way in bed.

She was seeing him, *really* seeing him, for the first time. She reached up and traced her fingers over the planes of his cheekbones, along the ridge of his brow, down his fine straight nose. She heard him suck in his breath, as his hips ground gently—but insistently—into hers.

"Is it terrible that I want to draw you right now?" she whispered.

He let out a tiny groan. "A little terrible, yes." He grimaced. "As a teacher, I appreciate the sentiment. But as a man ..."

She shifted her body beneath him, pulling him into her. He closed his eyes as he sank into her soft heat.

Not all seeing is done with the eyes.

Their bodies rocked together, his strokes sure and steady inside her, until they both were panting and clutching at shoulders, at hips ... at release. His quiet moan—*Marie*— sent her into a spiraling free fall she wasn't sure would ever end.

He locked eyes with her as he came, shuddering into her, and she felt laid bare to him. Everything she was feeling at the moment —lust, happiness, love, *trust*—was drawn on her face. She had never wanted that before, to be completely exposed to another person. Hadn't really understood why anyone *would* want it. But now she knew. And she wanted it with Luc. She wanted him to see every part of her, inside and out.

He kissed her, his chest still heaving against hers, then he regarded her face. "Is it terrible that I want to paint you right now?"

She gave his shoulder a light swat.

"I will paint you like this some day. With your skin flushed." He caressed her cheek with his palm. "Your lips open like this." His thumb rubbed across her lower lip. "Your eyes ... wanting more."

She tried to imagine such a painting. *Richard would be thoroughly humiliated.*

"Paint me now."

He grinned. "I've created a monster, I see."

No. But I'm married to one.

Her face gave away her disappointment.

"I promise you, ma chérie, I will make that painting one day."

"But not now?"

He shook his head. "I wouldn't want to rush it. I want to do it right." He smoothed her hair back from her face, touched her cheek. "See? This look fades so quickly. I would have to stop painting every few minutes to recreate it." His voice dropped a register, his eyes dark again. "We will need days just to ourselves to work on such a painting." He kissed her. "But don't worry. We will find the time. I promise you."

18

Marie's business ethics class was sidetracked on some matter of social media business netiquette that she'd lost interest in five minutes ago. While she waited for the professor to end the detour, she doodled. Well, it had started out as doodling but now she was trying to draw Luc's face as she had seen him the last time they made love.

That was last week, and the separation was killing Marie. Speaking to him on the phone and getting his sexy texts throughout the day were nice, but not enough. He was painting like a madman to get everything finished in time for the show. Apparently, his just-in-time business philosophy was making Samantha Smith more nervous than a stage mom.

Marie hadn't had much spare time either, between papers due for class and her mother's new interest in keeping her busy every minute of the day. Not that Marie's sudden essentialness to Witherspoon & Associates had anything to do with her mother's desire for her to reconcile with Richard. Of course not. But if it kept Marie too busy to see her new love, well that was just a convenient unintended consequence.

She scratched out her first attempt at his face and tried again. It would be much easier if he were modeling for her. She suppressed a little smile at that thought. She was so happy when she left Luc's that next morning. She had floated on air into the office. Late because her commute had begun in Middleburg, not Ashburn, but who cared?

Her mother had cared, unfortunately. But Marie just had to hang on until Luc's show, and everything would be solved. No way would Richard want her back when he found out about the paintings. He would have to deal with his re-election campaign on his own, maybe by making his constituents happy enough with his work that they no longer cared about his marriage. Now there was an idea.

She scratched out her second attempt, too. *Maybe next time I'll just take a photograph.* That would suit her purposes. She just wanted something to look at—okay, to daydream over—when they were apart. She wanted to tape his picture inside her notebook, sleep with it under her pillow, pull it out occasionally and kiss his paper lips while imagining it was really him. It was like being a teenager again, and that thrilling feeling when you liked someone and they liked you back. When you walked around all day in a fog of hormones and with a silly smile plastered on your face. When you jumped every time the phone rang and got to class late because you had lingered at your locker for just one more kiss.

When class ended, she buttoned up her coat and slung her bookbag over her shoulder for the short walk to Metro. Her stomach rumbled, but she'd eat at home. She leaned her shoulder into the wind and began walking.

"Marie."

Richard. Shit.

"How was class?"

"Fine."

She kept walking, determined to make it to the subway before he said whatever it was he was here to say. It wasn't a complete surprise to find Richard waiting for her. He'd been lurking around lately, calling her at the office, taking her and her mother out to lunch at see-and-be-seen restaurants.

"Can you slow down a minute? Please."

Saying "please" and "thank you" wasn't going to change her mind.

"It's late," she replied without slowing. "I want to get home."

"I'll drive you home. I want us to grab some dinner."

Oh who gives a fuck what you want.

"My car's at Metro."

"I'll drive you to the station, then." He sighed, quickly tiring of the conversation evidently.

"I'm too tired for this tonight, Richard. I'm too tired to go out and have my picture taken and talk to people—"

"We'll go somewhere quiet."

He grabbed her arm and hailed a cab at the same time. Before she knew it, she was in the back seat of a taxi and they were headed over the Key Bridge and onto route 50. He had given the driver the name of a shopping center in Falls Church. Wherever they were going, it would be hole-in-the-wall quiet. At least he hadn't been lying about that.

The cab pulled right up to the curb and a small storefront with a neon sign that blinked OPEN in the window. Café Saigon.

Inside, Richard draped an arm around the young, impossibly petite hostess, whispered something to her and nodded toward the back of the restaurant. The hostess—all dark hair and big eyes, bright pink blouse—returned his nod and picked up two menus.

"Right this way, sir. Ma'am." She nodded at Marie, too.

Marie trudged along behind them, unhappy at the way he had completely hijacked her evening. She truly was tired. She wasn't making that up. She slid into the booth opposite Richard and shrugged out of her coat.

"So? Quiet enough?"

He looked around at the dimly-lit restaurant, nearly empty on a weeknight. A young girl and boy, the owner's children probably, were seated in a booth near the front. Their dark heads bowed, they pored over schoolwork.

Richard ordered hot tea for her and a beer for himself. She quelled the anger she felt at not being asked what she'd like to drink. It wasn't the right battle. Not tonight. She would have ordered hot tea anyway. Part of the anger was directed at that knowledge. He knew exactly what she was going to order.

She no longer wanted him to know her. She no longer wanted to know him. They had no children. There was no logical reason why the two of them couldn't simply be excised from each other's life. Neatly, surgically. She looked across the booth and noticed, for the first time, that he wasn't wearing a suit like usual. Instead, he was wearing jeans and a shetland sweater. It was no secret where he must have changed after work. Maya's apartment was on Capitol Hill.

When the waitress came for their orders, Marie blurted out hers—a summer roll and lemongrass chicken—before Richard could speak. He looked a little pissed at her outburst, but calmly ordered his own summer roll and ginger shrimp.

"So how is Maya these days?" She wanted to go ahead and provoke whatever reason Richard had for this dinner, this night.

"Don't know. I'm not seeing her anymore."

"Yeah, right."

"Your mother asked me to stop seeing her, so I have."

"So that's all it took? My mother asking nicely?"

He shrugged. "I respect your mother."

You've never respected me.

"So if you're not seeing Maya anymore, why is she still talking trash about me on her blog?"

"She's upset. You won, Marie. She lost."

"Funny, I don't feel like some big winner here."

"Plenty of people think you are." He leaned back to make room for the summer rolls the waitress was setting down in the middle of the table. "In any case, we're not here to talk about Maya. We're here to talk about your boyfriend. Specifically, about whether you've dumped him yet."

"No, and I have no plans to." Marie nonchalantly—more nonchalantly than she felt inside—cut her summer roll in two and proceeded to swirl one half in the dipping sauce.

"It's not negotiable."

"Everything is negotiable. Isn't that what they say?" She bit into the roll. At least the food was delicious so far, even if that couldn't be said for the company. "And honestly? I don't believe you've stopped seeing Maya."

The smirk on his face disappeared in less than an instant, but she saw it. He was playing her mother. Her father needed Richard on the Armed Services Committee. In the end, her mother was not going to jeopardize that—and Richard knew it. He held most of the cards here.

Oh but there are some cards you don't know about yet.

"I'm not doing this, Richard. Sorry. Just not happening. A mistress wasn't a sticking point for your constituents the first time around."

"Things have changed since then."

"Yup. They sure have. I've met someone else. So you're on your own now."

He leaned in over the table, pushed aside the white rectangular appetizer dish. "You. Have. No. Choice." He punctuated each syllable with a sharp rap of his finger on the laminate table. "What. Part. Don't. You. Under. Stand."

"The part where you think you can just order me around. What are you going to do? Kidnap me every time you have a campaign event? Stick a wig on Maya and pretend she's me."

He was about to slam his fist on the table when the waitress showed up with their entrees.

"Can we get these to go?" he asked her. "And the check, please."

When the waitress left, he resumed glaring at her. As scary as his stare could be, it felt good to push back at him. And she wasn't scared this time anyway. *What part of "your wife is fucking an artist and he is painting her" don't* you *understand?*

19

The lettering in the window read "Luc Marchand. Déesse: New Work."

"Déesse?" Nishi said in perfectly accented French. "Is that referring to you? Goddess? Tell Richard to take that and stuff it where the sun don't shine. You don't get to be a goddess married to a Congressman."

Marie stared at the clean white letters, trying to tamp down the stew of nerves bubbling in her chest. It had been a hectic month, with Luc frantically (and sometimes crankily) painting to get everything done in time. And now the day was here. Luc's show was opening at Samantha Smith's new Dupont Circle gallery. She was nervous. Hopeful. Terrified. She'd brought Nishi as moral support and also, she had to admit, as someone to hide behind. It was one thing to pose nude for an artist, quite another to stand around while strangers eyeballed the paintings. She was nervous for Luc, too. If the show got panned or sales were dismal, she would feel responsible. Flattered as she was—and even though she needed Richard to be embarrassed by the show—she already worried that Luc should have spent the past two months painting more worthy subjects.

Nishi was peering through the window. "Good crowd."

The toxic brew in her stomach was at full boil now.

"Come on." Nishi took her arm. "Let's get a drink and then you can show me what I've been paying for all these months." She smiled warmly at her friend. "Drawing lessons, my ass. You were the one who was supposed to be drawing."

Marie had tried to prepare Nishi for the content of the show but, in the end, embarrassment won out. For all Nishi's bluster and bravado, she led a pretty straitlaced life. She lived with Imran in a perfectly ordinary suburban neighborhood, not even as nice a neighborhood as the two of them could afford. Nishi would never pose nude, she was certain of that.

Inside, the gallery buzzed with conversation and occasional bursts of polite laughter. The paintings were framed and artfully arranged on the walls, but it was too much for Marie to take in all at once. Her eyes skittered from one to the next, and then at the people milling about, cocktails and beers in hand. It was a well-dressed crowd, in tailored suits and dresses in shades of black and grey and navy, a mix of ages. Some looked far too young to buy art.

Ahead of her, Nishi casually took in the paintings, saying nothing. Marie was dying to know what her friend was thinking.

Nishi tugged at her arm, leading her toward the bar in the farthest room. Marie hadn't even spotted the bar through the clusters of people milling about, but Nishi always knew where to go and how to get there. It was one of the qualities Marie most envied in her. It was impossible to imagine Nishi lost or tongue-tied. No one pushed her around.

When they made it to the bar, Nishi turned to her and said, "Oh my god, this is your golden ticket right here." She nodded her head back the way they'd come. "You didn't tell me he was painting you—" she lowered her voice, "—nude. Richard will have to refile for divorce after this." She bounced up and down on the balls of her feet. "This is perfect."

That thought was the only thing that had sustained Marie during the past several weeks. Weeks of her mother's badgering (when are you moving back into the house), weeks of Richard showing up unannounced at her office to take her to lunch, weeks of Maya's snide jabs at her online. Weeks of hiding it all from Luc. She never had told him. He'd been working so intensely on the paintings for the show, Marie didn't have the heart to break the news. *Oh by the way dear, my husband wants me back.*

"Bonjour, ladies."

He took her breath away. It was just that simple. He was wearing a black suit, cut close to his body, and a pale yellow shirt open at the collar. No tie. His hair was its usual barely restrained bedhead. And yes, clever shoes.

She was wearing her favorite dress from her "it girl" days. A pale grey low-cut sheath covered with silvery beaded passementerie. It was sexy but sophisticated, and it always stood out in a sea of Washington neutrals.

She was no shrinking violet tonight.

Luc gave the dress a frankly admiring look, then leaned in and kissed her. He turned to Nishi and lifted her hand to his lips. "I am forever in your debt," he said to her. "If it weren't for your gift, I never would have met Marie. And this show would be filled with paintings of sappy landscapes."

Nishi launched into a torrent of French and even Marie had to smile at the surprised look on Luc's face. Nishi spoke a dozen languages, thanks to the dozen countries she'd lived in as a diplomat's child. Luc recovered well, and Marie thought what a pleasure it was to watch him converse in his native language. He grimaced, smiled, rolled his eyes. He was more animated in French than in

English, and she wished for the first time that she spoke French, too.

"But we are being rude." Nishi switched back to English, smiling at Marie. "I'm satisfied that I got my money's worth."

Marie heard Luc's phone buzz in his jacket pocket. He frowned. "Sam is paging me. I keep trying to disappear into the crowd and she keeps finding me." He leaned in to kiss Marie once more. "Don't leave without me."

Nishi fanned the air in front of her neck when he was gone, swallowed whole by the crowd. "Please tell me he's good in the sack."

Marie blushed, her body already tingling from just those few minutes with him.

"Okay, that's my answer. Let's go have a look at these paintings."

Luc surveyed the room. It was different seeing all of the paintings hanging together. He and Sam had decided upon a mostly chronological hanging. Not that most people would notice what Luc saw, the changes in Marie—and in how he saw her—from the first canvas to the last, but it was the way that felt most right to him.

He watched the crowd, taking note of which paintings people were spending the most time with, which ones seemed to generate the most discussion. He was disappointed that the most popular painting was the first one he'd done, Marie sitting on the stool as if she were an art school model. Her dream. Out of all of them, it was the most impersonal pose and the one she liked the least.

Luc's favorite was of Marie asleep in his bed, her head on his pillow, her body beneath his sheets. Just remembering it sent a frisson of pleasure down his spine. Spending the night with someone required a tremendous amount of trust, it had always seemed to Luc. Lying next to someone while you were essentially unconscious. Trusting that they wouldn't hurt you. Trusting that they would still be there when you woke. He half hoped no one would buy that one. He'd prefer it hang in his own bedroom. Of course, he could always paint another like it but it wouldn't be the same. He could never go back to the way he saw her that morning.

Most of all, though, he watched her.

He was dying to be with her, but kept his distance so he wouldn't draw attention to her. Even so, people whispered as they glanced between her and the paintings. He admired her courage in letting him do this. Sam thought they both were crazy. *And maybe we are. Crazy in love.* Luc hadn't been in love since Grace, and that was over a decade ago now. Sam had arranged dates for him with countless women, but nothing had ever taken hold with any of them.

"I know it's damned inconvenient," he'd said to Sam when he showed her the first few canvases. "I get that. But the heart wants what it wants. Mine wants a senator's wife."

Why Marie Witherspoon? So many women, so many years—and his heart had remained dead. Now it was alive again and he didn't care why. He was loathe to examine his heart too closely. That way madness lies.

"You think you can rescue her," Sam had said.

Perhaps. Perhaps he had that subconscious need. But a woman who would allow herself to be exposed to the world the way Marie was tonight hardly needed rescuing. She was learning to let herself be seen, and it had opened his own eyes too. For all his blather about practiced innocence, he'd been shut down for years. Emotionally. Physically. Artistically.

Painting rich people's lives had conveniently allowed him to keep his own eyes shut. You don't have to see much in order to paint a car or a yacht. They don't change. Everyone's Maserati looks the same. But every weekend, the Marie who showed up at his studio door was a slightly different woman. Every weekend, he'd been forced to see her in a new light, to look at her more closely, to look *into* her.

And when Sam's gallery closed in a few hours, he intended to look at her again.

THE BUTTERFLIES CAROMING around her stomach could have been from nerves, from the knowledge that Luc was in the same building tonight, or from the uncertainty she felt about her best friend seeing the show. Nishi hadn't said a word about any of the paintings so far.

"So what do you think?" she asked warily.

"They're beautiful, Marie. I mean, I have no idea how he got you to do this." Nishi gave a little laugh and shook her head.

"It was my idea, actually."

The surprised look on Nishi's face was priceless. "He's been good for you, hasn't he? You were always so gloomy with Richard. When you came into the office that first time, I don't think you said ten words. You seem—" Nishi waved her hand gracefully through the air—"freer now. More relaxed."

"I don't know what he sees in me though."

"Are you kidding? What he sees in you is all over the walls here." She looked at the painting they were standing next to, the one of Marie sleeping. "Anyone can tell that the artist painted his lover here. When I look at Imran sleeping, I see those luscious black eyelashes and how adorable his hair is, sticking out every which way. When I look at his twin brother sleeping, I see someone with sleep apnea who's drooling and badly in need of a haircut." She shook her head. "You know, before tonight, I would have said that I know you better than anyone. But I'm conceding that crown to him. He's unearthed a side of Marie Witherspoon I would never have guessed existed."

"I'm counting on a certain someone not liking this side of me."

"Oh, I don't think he will. Not at all."

Nishi pulled out her phone and began furiously texting.

"You're not inviting Imran, are you?" That would be weird, Nishi's husband seeing the paintings.

"No, no. I'm inviting some reporters. They need to get their asses down here asap."

"I thought you said the arts reporters were unlikely to cover a local gallery show."

Nishi chuffed. "I'm not texting them. I'm getting the political beat. They'll be beside themselves at this. Let's see who gets here first."

Nishi looked up from her phone. "Are you getting nervous?"

"Getting?"

"Relax. This is *it.* Richard will drop you like the proverbial hot potato after this."

Marie kept reminding herself of that throughout the evening. In a few days, she'd be free of Richard forever. She took another sip of wine, hiding behind the wine glass as best she could. She felt intensely watched. People eyed her curiously. Several asked if she was the model.

But no one seemed to know who she was, or mentioned Richard or her parents. She took a another long sip of wine, trying to calm her still fluttering nerves. She needed Richard to find out about Luc's show. It was her only way out. At the same time, she dreaded it happening. It would not be pretty. Nothing with Richard ever was.

She caught Samantha Smith staring at her, and not in a friendly way. The woman was unsmiling, her jaw set, her eyes cold and appraising. Marie's heart dropped into her feet when Samantha began walking toward her.

"Marie? May I speak with you for a moment?"

Samantha Smith looked even more imposing up close. Her black suit was immaculately tailored and her heels gave her a considerable height advantage over Marie. She didn't wait for Marie's reply. She took her arm and said, "Come back to my office with me," then to Nishi a quick "Excuse us."

Samantha Smith's office was small, with art books stacked everywhere. On her desk, on a side table, on the floor. Canvases wrapped in brown paper leaned against the walls. She herself seemed to take up ninety percent of the space. Marie had to fight the urge to shrink back against the wall.

"Good turnout tonight," Marie said.

"You had better not hurt Luc. He's been hurt by a woman before."

Marie tried to protest that hurting Luc was the last thing she intended, but Sam cut her off.

"I'll be honest with you. I didn't like the idea of this show. These paintings won't be hard for me to sell but you know as well as I do that there may be some ... fallout, shall we call it? I haven't mentioned to him that you and your husband are reconciling because the last thing I wanted to do was distract him before the show. Fortunately, he doesn't pay any attention to Washington gossip."

"I'm not getting back together with my husband. That's not happening."

"According to your mother, it is."

"Last I checked, I was an adult. My mother doesn't run my life."

Sam cocked an eyebrow at her.

"Would my mother have allowed me to do this? Pose nude for an artist? She doesn't even know about this yet."

Sam shrugged, conceding the point. "I won't see him hurt

again, Marie. It has taken him all these years to get over it. He deserves a woman who's going to stick around."

Marie followed Sam out of her office. The other woman quickly disappeared into the crowd, as if being absorbed by it. Marie realized she was shaking.

What woman had hurt Luc? And why had it taken years to get over? Had he been married before? If she were Nishi, she would have had the presence of mind to ask Samantha Smith these questions. But she wasn't Nishi, of course. And so she'd simply let Luc's friend run the conversation, say her piece and then end it without waiting for Marie to respond.

And don't you ruin his show, Marie wanted to retort to Samantha Smith. But of course she couldn't. Samantha and Luc were friends. She had a longer history with him than Marie did. *She knows him better than you do.*

I know Luc, too. I do. In ways Samantha Smith never will.

But doubts were wiggling their way into her chest. And these weren't butterflies, either—delicate, paper-thin wings flitting in and around her thoughts. These were house flies, sturdy and buzzing, coming back every time she swatted one away.

No. She'd just had nearly a month of utter happiness with Luc. Bliss, she would even call it. Yes, she would call it sheer, unadulterated bliss. They knew each other, *got* each other. Saw each other. Whatever his friend was insinuating was nonsense.

She was just jealous, that's all. *I bet she wanted Luc, too, all those years ago and couldn't have him. He didn't want her that way and she's never gotten over it.*

She threaded her way back through the gallery rooms, in search of Nishi. Maybe she'd heard back from some of the reporters. Media coverage, no matter how small, was essential here. Obviously, she couldn't just call up Richard and tell him about the show. He'd shut it down somehow, get Samantha's business license revoked or something. No, he had to hear it from a third party, as evidence that other people already knew about it. A few well-placed articles would speed up that process considerably.

Her spirits were rising again at the thought that she might be rid of Richard within a week. Sweet, glorious freedom!

She found Nishi standing in front of a group of small charcoal drawings. Marie's feet sticking out from beneath the eiderdown. Her chin and mouth, a mug of coffee kissing her lips. Her hair fanned out over her shoulders. They were intimate portraits, not so much of her but of moments in time, moments between them. She remembered each one with perfect clarity.

Nishi pointed to the last one, her laugh lilting and refined beneath her breath. The drawing was of Marie's abdomen, water sluicing down her skin, wet hair, hand between her legs.

Nishi laid her arm across Marie's shoulder. "Yup. Your ticket out."

20

Samantha Smith's beach house was all weathered grey siding, wrap-around decks and giant windows overlooking the Atlantic Ocean. It was Friday evening, six days before Thanksgiving, and Luc and Marie had arrived to spend the weekend together. The sun had set behind them, its orange-purple glow in the rearview mirrors. In the near distance, the ocean churned noisily beneath a dark, cloud-spotted sky.

"It's nice of her to let us stay here," Marie said as Luc pulled the car into the driveway. "I don't think she was too happy with me the other night."

"Sam worries about me. But the show is selling well, so I think she's over it." Luc beamed a big smile at her.

I won't see him hurt again. It has taken him all these years to get over it.

Marie wasn't so sure Samantha Smith would get over it. She was dying to ask Luc about his friend's cryptic comments but he was so happy, whistling-while-he-drove-happy. So Marie tried to be happy too for his sake. All had been quiet on the press front since the show on Wednesday; Nishi had cautioned patience. But

Marie was antsy. Whatever was going to happen with Richard, she wanted to get it over with. The anticipation was always worse.

Even worse, of course, would be for nothing to happen, for Richard to remain blissfully unaware of the nude paintings of his wife hanging in the heart of Washington. Marie had no backup plan to force his hand.

Luc cut the ignition, then reached over and covered her hand with his, warm and protective. "Your mother hasn't called?"

Marie had called in sick yesterday and today, just in case. "I told her I thought I should rest up so I was well for Thanksgiving. She and my father always have a lot of people over. My presence on Thanksgiving is more important to her than having me at work." Even less so now that her mother was expecting her to reconcile with Richard. Marie wondered how long it would be before her mother laid her off again.

She knew she had to tell Luc about Richard but how? And when? His feet had barely touched the ground since the show. He was in an expansive mood and looking forward to a romantic weekend a deux, just the two of them holed up in Sam's waterfront home. She didn't have the heart to spoil it.

He handed her a set of keys. "Why don't you unlock the house while I bring in dinner and the groceries?" They had stopped at a local restaurant to pick up two of their famed calzones, on Sam's recommendation.

Inside, Marie looked around Sam's house with awe. The kitchen sported stainless steel chef-style appliances and an island roughly the size of Maui. She ran her hand over the smooth, cool granite, the color of which—a melange of ivory, beige and gold—reminded her of seashells. When she set her purse on top, she heard her phone vibrate inside. She pulled it out to find a text from Nishi. *Story has broken.*

"Hope you brought an appetite." Luc was suddenly in the kitchen, sliding the restaurant's carryout bag and another canvas bag of provisions across the island. "Be right back. Just have to retrieve the wine. Don't want to forget that." He winked at her.

Marie shoved the phone back in her purse. She doubted she would have much of an appetite this weekend. She strolled over to the floor-to-ceiling windows that ran along the back of the house. Less than a hundred yards away, the ocean churned furiously, the dunes and sand deserted. She felt Luc's hands brush aside her hair, then his lips found her neck.

"What is wrong, ma chérie? Something is troubling you today."

She shook her head.

"I know you better than that, Marie." He took her hand and led her back to the kitchen. "Choose a bottle of wine for us."

While she inspected the labels—all French, all meaningless to her—Luc picked up a remote and pointed it at the small television in the kitchen. The Weather Channel filled the screen as she uncorked a bottle of burgundy, then went in search of glasses in Sam's giant kitchen.

"In the cabinet on the end," Luc said.

The weekend was expected to be mostly sunny, high temps in the fifties, nice enough for a walk along the beach. Luc watched the forecast through twice as he plated their calzones. Marie poured two glasses of wine while he began to scroll through channels.

"Nude paintings of a senator's wife are causing a bit of a scandal on Capitol Hill this week," a serious-looking blonde newscaster opined on CNN.

Marie held her breath as Luc's trigger finger sped past the channel. She carefully set a glass of wine next to his plate on the island.

He clicked back a channel. There on the screen was Samantha Smith's gallery, people walking past on the street, then a cut to the inside of the gallery. Marie held her breath as the camera panned the walls. Several of the paintings were blurred inside their frames. *"Due to the graphic nature of the show, we cannot show you all of the portraits."* There was Sam describing Luc as an important artist—Luc snorted at the television—and brief interviews with several people who happened to be in the gallery at the time.

"Lovely show ... no, I have no idea who the model is ... oh a senator's wife? Really? ... Well, beautiful paintings anyway ... I would buy one if I had the money ..."

The report cut away to Richard standing behind a lectern, flashbulbs popping in front of him. *"At a press conference earlier today, Senator Macintyre reported that his wife has been under a great deal of stress lately but was now home resting. 'It has been a difficult year for us but we are trying to put that behind us now. We ask that you respect our privacy while she recuperates.'"*

CNN cut to a commercial and Marie reached for the remote. She clicked off the television.

Luc looked back and forth between Marie and the dark television, confusion clouding his features. He pushed his hand roughly through his hair and closed his eyes for a moment. "I'm missing something here."

"Richard has called off the divorce."

"I see."

"He wants us to reconcile." She used air quotes around that last word. "The divorce is causing problems for his re-election campaign, so he has withdrawn the filing."

The look of panic on Luc's face nearly broke her heart. She tugged his hand from where it was tangled in his hair and held it tight in her own.

"You're going back to him?"

He tried to pull his hand from hers but she held tight. "No. Of course not."

"But he said you are—" A look of confusion crossed his face again. "—that you're at home ..."

"But I'm not, right? I'm here with you." She pulled his hand in against her collarbone and held it tight. "I am not reconciling with him. And it's not something he really wants, either, but his campaign manager has told him he needs to do it. Apparently his opponent is making a big deal out of Maya, out of his having an affair and leaving his wife."

"But if he's telling people you are ..."

She glanced over at the dark television. "I need your show to get a lot of press. I was hoping for it, in fact."

"Wait ... you knew before Wednesday? Why didn't you tell me?"

"I didn't want to upset you. Sam knew, too."

He took a deep breath, struggling to stay calm. "I'll call Sam. Tell her to take down the show."

"No. I need this to happen, Luc." She squeezed his hand tighter for emphasis. "I need this to be all over the news. I can't afford to divorce him myself. He has threatened to bankrupt me if I do. So I need him to change his mind. If I am too much of an embarrassment to him—and to his campaign—he might do that. Not that I'm embarrassed by the paintings, personally," she added hastily.

"But I hate to watch him lie about you. You're not at home with him. And for them to be discussing you like ..."

"Nishi says the news cycle for this sort of thing is short. A few days, tops. His opponent will probably be able to stretch it out a little further, especially if he uses it in TV spots." She pulled his fist up to her lips and kissed his knuckles tenderly, one by one. "It will be ugly for a few days, then Richard will decide I'm more trouble than I'm worth, and he'll refile."

"Well, I guess if everyone thinks you're at home with him, they won't look for us here." Luc reheated their plates in the microwave, then turned on the television again. "We might as well know what they're saying."

Every news channel had a story about it. It had been a slow news day, as Fridays often were. Even Maya had scored an appearance as a "society reporter" on Fox News. "The Senator's wife is turning into more of a liability than an asset for his campaign. She may no longer be ready for prime time."

Luc watched the screen worriedly.

"This is terrible, Marie. They make it sound like you posed for Playboy." He toyed with the calzone on his plate, pushing the tines of his fork into the crust, watching the tomato sauce ooze out.

"That can be my plan B if this doesn't work. And Plan C, making a sex tape. Are you up for that?"

He shot her a pained look. "Please don't joke about this."

She slid down from her stool and stood between Luc's knees. She cupped his face in her hands, tenderly. "Don't worry about it, Luc. This will all be over a week from now. Then they'll be on to Black Friday and holiday shopping. The two of us, we're nowhere near as important as forty percent of the year's retail sales," she joked again, trying to get him to smile. No go.

Her hands slipped from his face as he stood up and clicked off the television. She let him lead her out onto the deck. The November air nipped at her face and insinuated itself beneath her loosely-knit sweater. Beyond the railing of the deck, the dunes and ocean dissolved into black nothingness. A bank of dark clouds hovered overhead, hiding the moon and stars, and the large houses on either side of Sam's stood unlit and empty. In the off season, the beach towns were mostly deserted, entire neighborhoods essentially abandoned for the winter.

Luc stretched out onto an oversized chaise longue and pulled her into it with him. She sat stiffly on his lap.

"Relax, love," he said, tugging her shoulders back to his chest.

"What are we doing?"

"Listening to the ocean."

She was quiet, listening to the rhythmic push and pull of the waves.

"The water sounds like it's right beneath us," she observed.

"It's not."

"Does it ever come all the way up to the house?"

"I don't think so. Maybe in a hurricane it might. None of those forecast for this weekend, though."

She felt his hands begin to massage her shoulders.

"I wish you had told me earlier about your husband."

"I didn't want it to spoil your show. Sam didn't want that, either."

"You could have told me yesterday. Or this morning."

She sighed. "I'm sorry, Luc. But you were so happy, I wanted you to just enjoy that. And it's not like it's actually happening."

"So you don't want to go back to him?" His words were laced with uncertainty.

She turned around on his lap and straddled his thighs. "I can't believe you would even need to ask that." She buried her face in his neck and hair. He smelled like oregano and wine, salty ocean air. She inhaled, filling her lungs with him. "I wouldn't be here if that were the case."

She felt a rush of cool air as her sweater's hem lifted, then the warmth of Luc's hands on her bare skin as he slid them up her back. It was utterly unnecessary in the dark but she closed her eyes anyway, so she could focus on just the feel of his hands against her skin and nothing else. She swayed drunkenly in his arms even though she hadn't had nearly enough wine for that yet.

He added his mouth to the cocktail of sensations she was swimming in, ravishing kisses along her neck and jaw, until he found her lips.

"I can't let you go, Marie. Not anymore." He kissed the words into her breath, then gently eased her back down onto the lounge. He peeled off her sweater, then bowed his head to her breasts.

"We're going to catch pneumonia out here," she pointed out. Her arms prickled with gooseflesh.

Luc swirled his tongue around her nipple. "I would nurse you back to health, Marie."

She pushed her hands between them and unzipped her jeans. Luc made short work of the rest of it. She pulled him back down to her and wrapped her legs around his hips. When he pushed inside her, she let her eyes close again. She wanted to feel him simply with her skin.

"Marie, look at me."

She opened her eyes and shook her head, amused. "You need to make up your mind. See. Not see. How can a girl keep it all straight?" she teased.

He made no reply to her teasing banter. Instead he thrust into her slowly and deliberately, letting her watch the play of emotions across his face. Restraint as he patiently pushed her body along. Isolated moments where he was drawn irresistibly to the edge of desire, before regaining control. The shining desire in his eyes as she fell, spiraling, into her orgasm—and, Marie's favorite, the peaceful smile that curved across his lips as he came down from his own.

21

When Marie returned to the bedroom the next morning, freshly showered and wrapped in nothing but a robe, Luc was awake and looked aggrieved.

"You didn't wake me?"

She leaned over the bed and kissed him. "I let you sleep."

"Sure you don't want another shower?" He threw back the covers and made a show of stretching for her.

She watched him rise from the bed, all feline grace stalking toward her. His tactics were working, she had to give him that. Her secret places were tingling, no longer relaxed from the hot shower. His eyes were saying that she had no secret places, not from him.

"A cold shower, maybe. Otherwise we'll spend all day in bed."

He chuckled as he slid his hands inside her robe and pulled her to him. "And how is that so terrible?" He gave her a long, deep kiss. "Ah well, I will settle for some hot coffee, then. The least you can do if you won't shower with me."

She pulled on jeans and a clean sweater, then headed out to the kitchen. It was easy to find the coffee supplies. Sam's kitchen was large but impeccably organized. No drawers of random utensils and tools in here. Marie plugged in the large combination coffee-espresso maker and ground some beans, Quartermaine with a roast date of only two weeks ago. She made a mental note to buy Sam another bag when she got back home.

While the pot brewed, she turned on the television to see whether she was still in the news cycle. Finding nothing at the moment, she settled on CNN, only half paying attention as she retrieved two coffee mugs from a cupboard. An older couple were holding a framed photo of a young woman. The couple's eyes were red-rimmed, but there was as much anger behind them as sadness. Marie poured milk in one mug for herself; Luc took his coffee black. She stared out the window at the ocean she hadn't been able to see last night. Weak morning sunshine glinted off the dark water.

"George and Marian McKinley say that the artist at the center of a controversial new art show in the nation's capital was responsible for their daughter's death ten years ago."

Marie's attention snapped back to the television. How many controversial art shows could there be in DC at one time?

"Grace McKinley was a graduate student at the University of Virginia when she began an affair with a professor, Dr. Luc Marchand."

Marie froze. *Doctor* Luc Marchand. University of Virginia? He'd been a professor? She ran through her memory, trying to recall if he had ever told her that.

"The relationship ended badly and Grace McKinley committed suicide just before Christmas."

Marie was barely breathing now. So this was what it felt like when time stood still.

"Senator Macintyre needs to keep his wife away from that man. He uses young women and then tosses them away like they're trash

when he's through." Mrs. McKinley wiped her eye with a lone finger.

"Marie."

She looked away from the television to see Luc standing in the doorway of the kitchen. The stricken look on his face mirrored her own.

Suicide. Uses young women. Keep his wife away from that man. Trash.

Marie felt as though she was about to be sick. She made a mad dash for the deck— barefoot, no jacket—and took the steps down to the scrubby dune two at a time, leaping onto the sand at the bottom. She began to run toward the beach, faintly aware of pounding footsteps on the steps behind her, Luc calling her name.

"Marie! Wait! Stop!"

She ran across the cool sand until her lungs burned and she stumbled, doubling over to catch her breath. Luc was still shouting her name. She ran into the surf, the cold water sloshing around her toes and ankles. This wasn't supposed to happen. The press, it was all supposed to be about her. Salacious paintings of a senator's wife. Luc was just supposed to be the artist ... sans secrets of his own.

Why hadn't he told her? Was that who Samantha Smith was referring to the other night? Grace McKinley?

Dr. Luc Marchand. He had never told her that, she was certain of it. Come to think of it, he hadn't told her much about his past. And she hadn't asked. *Idiot.* She had strapped on those sex goggles like she was the Red Baron. Everything looked like love when you were getting great sex all the time.

She needed to clear her head. She waded in further, letting the water numb her knees and then her waist. The cold cut right through her jeans and sweater but she welcomed it, welcomed the pain. She heard Luc swear sharply as he sloshed through the waves behind her. She refused to look at him and headed out further. She was in up to her breasts and neck. The waves slapped against her face, her eyes stinging from the salt.

She saw the wave rising on the horizon, swelling and filling with water. It rolled closer and closer. She just wanted to be alone for a moment. Why couldn't he leave her alone? She needed to think. Why couldn't he just let her think?

"Damn it, Marie, stop!" Luc shouted at her.

"I believed you," she whispered into the salt spray, knowing he couldn't hear her. *Art requires honesty.* Isn't that what he said? *You have to let yourself be seen.* Apparently, that was a one-way mirror in Luc's world. She hadn't been seeing him at all. He hadn't let her, hadn't wanted her to see him. Hadn't trusted her to see him the way he really was.

A hand gripped her arm and yanked hard just as the wave reared up and crashed over them both. She tumbled into the roiling froth of the surf, Luc's hand ripped away from her. The water was loud in her ears. She held her breath and another wave broke overhead, setting off another frenzy of bubbles around her face.

Something grabbed her shoulder, then wrapped itself around her chest. She was being dragged through the water, sand and shells scraping her arms and feet. Suddenly the water fell away from her and cold air hit her face, threaded its fingers through her dripping hair. Luc dropped her onto the wet sand, collapsing next to her. He spit after the surf, then began muttering angrily in French.

He wasn't wearing a shirt, she noticed, and now his skin was red and raw looking. His jeans were as soaked as her own, his hair tangled and plastered to his scalp.

"You could have gotten us killed," he said finally, switching to English.

"I can swim."

"I can too, but the ocean is about fifty degrees this time of year." His voice was as sharp as the waves had been. "What the fuck, Marie. You didn't even wait for me to explain. Just ran out here—"

"You could have told me!"

"You didn't tell me your husband wants to reconcile."

"A girl killed herself, Luc! Hardly the same thing!" Marie knew she was practically shrieking. She stood up and began trudging back toward the house.

"Maybe you should have waited to hear my side of the story," Luc said, right behind her, scrambling to catch up.

She whirled around so quickly, he nearly collided with her. "Well, I'm waiting now."

The next thing she knew Luc had picked her up like she was weightless and tossed her over his shoulder. They were moving toward the house.

"You sleep with all of your students!" she yelled.

"I do not!" Luc yelled back.

"According to CNN you do!" It felt good to yell at him. She was mad and he deserved to be yelled at.

"According to CNN, you're at home with your husband, recuperating from—something! Like I'm some disease!" Luc could give as good as he got, when it came to yelling. He launched into another outburst of French she couldn't understand.

"How many then?" she yelled.

He was quiet, gulping in air as he struggled to move them both across the soft sand.

"How many!" she repeated.

"Two." His voice was quiet. "Just two, okay?"

Marie began to cry as she watched the sand bounce below her.

"Marie."

She pounded her fist on his ass. "I'm not special, am I?" she choked out. "I'm just one more."

He stopped walking and set her down.

"You are not just one more." He brushed his hands against his wet jeans to get the sand off, then cupped her face. "Why are we yelling at each other?"

"Because you lied to me. You never told me any of that stuff."

"It wasn't a good chapter in my life. Not really the sort of thing you tell someone when you're trying to woo them."

"Exactly the thing you tell someone," she countered.

"You could have googled me. I'm sure that's how CNN found out."

"You should have told me."

"You should have told me that you're no longer about to be divorced. *Putain,* now I really am having an affair with the wife of an American politician. I can't delude myself about that anymore."

"Do you have a green card?" It had never occurred to her before to ask and she wondered now why not.

"I'm a U.S. citizen now. They can't deport me over this."

Marie wasn't so sure. Maybe not officially, but lots of things got done unofficially in Washington. Richard could probably make life miserable enough that Luc would self-deport.

"So tell me about her."

Luc cocked his head toward the house. "Let's go back first."

She looked at him warily. "You're trying to avoid answering me."

He sighed and took her hand in his. "I will tell you everything, Marie. But back at the house. You need to get into dry clothes and I need to get you away from the water." He glanced at the ocean. "You are not to do that again."

"I'll do it again if I feel like it."

He pulled her roughly into his arms and squeezed her sandy face between his sandy hands. "If you drown, Marie, then I can't do what *I* feel like."

His kiss was hard and angry. She tried to soften it by kissing him back, but he wouldn't let her. When he finally released her,

her lips were swollen and tender. She was about to protest this treatment when he leaned his forehead against hers.

"I can't lose you, Marie," he whispered. "I just can't."

"You won't lose me." She sought out his lips and gave him the tender kiss she'd tried to just seconds earlier.

"I scare easily when it comes to you. Remember that. Please."

She let him pull her in the direction of Sam's house. She didn't want to argue anymore, certainly not out here on the beach. The sun was beginning to break through the clouds and it was pleasant enough for November, but not in wet clothes.

Luc was quiet on the walk back and she didn't force any conversation. She still needed to know what had happened with Grace McKinley. He wasn't getting off the hook on that, but she didn't want any more yelling. She had started it, and it had felt good—cathartic—for a few minutes. She had never been able to yell at Richard. Now, though, she was ashamed of her behavior. He should have told her about this girl a long time ago—and he would, she would make sure of that—but he didn't deserve to have it splashed all over the television. If it hadn't been for her, if she weren't who she were—Senator Richard Macintyre's wife—it would never have happened.

They trudged up the stairs to the deck, her thighs burning with the effort. At the top, Luc released her hand. She brushed the sand from her jeans.

"Go inside and shower. Change into dry clothes."

She reached for his hand but he pulled it away. "You aren't coming?"

He shook his head. "I'll wait out here."

"Why? Come inside where it's warm."

"Just go, Marie. Don't argue with me anymore."

She backed away from the flash of anger in his eyes, and retreated into the house to do as he asked. She showered quickly, combed out her hair and changed into a dry pair of jeans and a clean blouse.

He was still on the deck. She ventured cautiously outside. He was lying on a chaise longue, still in his wet clothing, one foot planted on the deck floor, the other leg stretched out before him. His eyes were closed but he gestured toward a chair. A sketchpad and pencil lay on the chair.

"Sit," he said.

She lifted the pad and pencil and sat down.

"Draw me," he said.

She quietly took a deep breath, trying to tamp down a flare of anger. "I thought you were going to tell me your side of the story."

"I will tell you as you draw." He sat up, planted his feet on either side of the lounge and leaned forward.

"Why are we doing this?" she asked.

"I want you to see me."

She flipped open the sketchpad, the pencil poised over the page. How could she see him when he was being so distant? So stubborn? She felt miles away from him—was that what she was supposed to draw? Looking at him, let alone *seeing* him, was almost more than she could bear right now. She was used to Richard being angry with her—that was the usual state of affairs with him—but not Luc. She didn't want him angry with her.

"Marie."

She took a deep breath and looked across the miles at him, then began to draw in faint, tentative lines. His eyes were dark on her, his stare unwavering. His hair was wild from the sand and ocean, like some modern-day Poseidon. His legs and the end of the chaise longue formed the tines of a trident. She bit her lip. She could draw him that way, as god of the ocean. She suspected he wouldn't be amused. Not today.

"I used to be a professor at the University of Virginia," he said. "Art history."

He paused, letting this information sink in for her. She took quick glances at him, just long enough to capture enough visual information to draw a few more lines, and tried to imagine him as Dr. Marchand standing in front of a room filled with students.

"I became involved with one of my students. As you know. She was a grad student, not an undergrad. So she was just a few years younger than I was." His voice was measured, deliberate. "The university had a policy against this, as most do, but I loved her. I love unwisely, perhaps. At least, that is Sam's opinion."

It was impossible to capture with mere pencil the absolute flat darkness in his eyes. Impossible for her, anyway. And the way the weak late morning sun made the sand in his hair glow. But she tried. She tried to see him.

"I planned to propose to her at Christmas. I bought a ring. I was ready to spend the rest of my life with her. Then she disappeared one week."

Marie's pencil stilled.

"I called everywhere to find her. No one knew—or would tell me—where she'd gone. When she returned, she refused to tell me. But eventually, she confessed. She'd gone to Richmond to have an abortion. A friend drove her there and back. I couldn't ask her to marry me after that. I just couldn't. And I told her that. I told her that I'd been planning to propose but that now I couldn't. I should have kept my mouth shut, but I was so angry ... I said things I shouldn't have."

Pain was etched all over Luc's face. She couldn't draw this, even if she wanted to. She didn't have the technical skill to corral emotions beneath her pencil. The physical difference between a smile and a grimace could be so slight.

"She hung herself in her apartment." His voice cracked, and he closed his eyes against Marie's gaze. Even he didn't want her to see this. "She killed my child, and I killed her."

"You didn't kill her."

"I did. I drove her to it. I said terrible things to her." He ground the heels of his hands into his eyes, as if he were trying to push the memory back into his brain. "And you and I, we were yelling at each other today—"

"I'm not her, Luc."

"Please let's not yell at each other anymore. Promise me that."

"We have to be able to disagree."

"You were running away from me. You could have drowned. There are riptides all along the shore here."

"I can swim ..." Marie was beginning to remind him when, suddenly, she *saw*.

Luc was afraid. Terrified. That's what he wanted her to draw, his fear of losing her. He had already lost Grace and now Richard was running around telling the whole world that their marriage was back on.

"When you walked into my studio that first day, I didn't think *I want this woman,*" he said. "I thought *I want to belong to her.*"

"But you sent me away ..."

"Because I knew even then that if I ended up losing you I would lose myself too. You would take me with you and leave me with nothing. I am yours, Marie."

22

Thanksgiving had always been Marie's favorite holiday as a child. Christmas was a rushed affair, a slap and dash through presents, then off to the National Cathedral to be seen with her parents at one of the services. Afternoons were spent serving meals at a soup kitchen or delivering gifts to local nursing homes. Not that the childhood Marie hadn't appreciated the value of doing all that, but it was a day of work. Even Richard had been surprised, initially, by how her parents' careers didn't cease even for Christmas.

But on Thanksgiving, the Witherspoon family stayed home and allowed everyone else to come to them. Instead of a traditional sit-down dinner, Eileen Witherspoon hosted a day-long open house with a never-ending parade of important people marching through the house. People stopped by on their way to or from other dinners, dropped in for a drink and dessert, or plopped down on the sofa to watch a quarter or two of the Redskins-Cowboys game. The Witherspoons' turkey could be eaten traditionally, on a plate piled high with sweet potatoes and stuffing, or layered into a sandwich and washed down with cider or beer. Within a certain stratum of Washington society, the

Witherspoon house was the place to see and be seen on Thanksgiving.

For a child like Marie, the combination of grazing for hours on hors d'oeuvres and desserts (because no one was particularly watching what she ate) and being expected to stay under the radar and in the background made for a darn near perfect day. Thanksgiving awarded her, for one blissful day, a cloak of invisibility. She could do as she pleased and no one noticed. Extra slice of pie? Disappear to her bedroom to make whispered phone calls to friends? Sneak a juice glass filled with wine? No problem.

This year, however, Marie was dreading the day. She drove around and around the streets of her parents' Cleveland Park neighborhood, passing up open parking spots. *Maybe I'll find one closer.* Even she knew that was a lie. The longer it took to park the car, the longer she could put off having to make small talk with the dozens of people who were already at her parents' house. She could hear it already.

How lovely that you and your husband are getting back together! I know your mother is dying for grandchildren. She talks about it all the time.

Of course, we didn't go see that awful show. Pornography, I heard it was! Did he drug you, sweetie? Because that's what we heard.

The French. Libertines. What can you expect?

The phone in her purse buzzed. That would be her mother, impatient. She'd been calling every ten minutes for the past hour. Marie sighed and pulled into an illegal spot next to a stop sign. Running up parking tickets all over town was a strategy that might still come in handy. *Senator's wife owes thousands of dollars in unpaid parking fines!*

Her mother had studiously avoided the subject of Luc's show all week and the silence from Richard's camp had been equally deafening. According to Nishi, he'd been busy fending off the press.

Going out of town last weekend had turned out to be a smart move. With her and Luc's whereabouts unknown, Richard and Sam had been the only people the press could talk to. On Nishi's advice, Marie had turned down all interview requests since and stayed home as much as possible. "Just keep forcing them to call Richard," she'd said. "He'll crack eventually."

It had to work. How could it not make him reconsider filing for divorce? Mistresses just weren't that uncommon in Washington. Nude paintings of your wife, on the other hand, were.

On the sidewalk, she took several deep breaths, counted to ten —then twenty—and plucked imaginary lint off her skirt. She'd dressed simply, almost business-like, in a navy skirt and ivory silk blouse, low heels. An outfit that would blend in with the other guests. Her mother would be dressed in a long skirt and autumn-colored sweater. Her father would wear dress slacks, a shirt and tie. The guests would be all over the board, depending on their other social obligations. There would be sequins on some, jeans on teenagers, even the odd turkey-shaped earrings. Money didn't always buy taste.

Marie touched her own bare earlobes, then dug into her purse for a ponytail band. She quickly rolled her hair up into a loose bun. *Should have brought an apron. Then I could pretend to be catering staff.*

Her parents' home was a classic Cleveland Park four-square. Cleveland Park was a quiet city neighborhood whose tree-lined streets and well-tended yards camouflaged its affluence. The homes were not over-the-top huge like in the suburbs, but they were comfortable and gracious, with traditional details and neighborly porches. Small wooden garages were usually tucked in the back, next to flower beds and modest stone patios.

She paused at the front door and took another deep breath before turning the knob and letting herself in. As quietly as she could, she hung her coat in the hall closet. From her father's study at the back of the house came the sound of television. It took her a moment to realize that she shouldn't be able to hear the television today. The house should be filled with the noise of competing conversations, gossip and policy talk, friendly strong-arming and low-pressure pitches.

But it wasn't. The house was eerily quiet, save the sound of a football game on her father's study television. She was reaching back into the closet for her coat, when the quiet was shattered.

"About damn time you got here. My parents are expecting us later, you know." Richard's voice seethed with barely-controlled fury.

She turned to him, a polite smile on her face. "How would I know that your parents are expecting us later? I had no idea *my* parents were expecting *you.*"

Richard grabbed her arm roughly and yanked her toward the dining room. "You haven't exactly deserved the courtesy of information lately. But we'll discuss that later."

"I'm looking forward to discussing the nude paintings of your wife. Sounds like fun."

Richard dug his fingers deeper into her flesh, but she bit her lip to stifle any reaction. She wouldn't give him the satisfaction.

"You. Are. A. Whore," he spit out, his voice low and mean.

"Well, that does seem to be your taste in women," Marie replied brightly. She refused to be intimidated by him.

He pulled her against his chest, his eyes cold slits. "You belong to me. Understand? And you are going to do as I tell you to do from here on out. After the election, I'll be well rid of you. But until then, I own you. And you're not going to forget it."

She rolled her eyes at him. "Or what, exactly?" She laughed and pushed away from his chest, then went in search of her mother.

I don't belong to you.

She found her mother in the kitchen, slicing a rather smallish turkey with an electric knife. A green apron was tied around her mother's wool pants and sweater.

"Mother. What gives?" Marie gestured to the empty kitchen. "Where is everyone?"

Eileen Witherspoon looked up. "Oh, there you are. I've been calling your cell phone. Here." She nodded her head toward a bottle of wine. "Take that into the dining room. Your father is waiting for it."

"Where is everyone?"

"We're having a quiet Thanksgiving this year, dear. Your father and I thought it was a good idea."

The unspoken words, *given the circumstances,* hung in the air between them.

So she was too much of an embarrassment to hold the usual Thanksgiving open house. *Well, good. That's what I wanted.* A cornucopia of embarrassment. She picked up the bottle. A riesling, her parents' usual Thanksgiving wine.

"Did you have to invite *him* though?" she asked.

Her mother shot her a disapproving look. "He is your husband. And after, you two are going to the Macintyres for a late dinner."

"I am doing no such thing. No one even told me."

"Let's not ruin today any more than it already is." Eileen dropped slices of white meat onto a platter.

"I'd have been happy to stay home and let you invite everyone else. That way, I wouldn't have *ruined* the day."

"We're not discussing this any further, Marie. Take the wine in. I will follow with the turkey."

The dining room table was decked out with her mother's formal china and crystal wine goblets. An elaborate floral centerpiece stood on the table, as usual. Marie set the wine in front of her father, who was sitting at the head of the table. Then she surveyed the place settings—two on the other side of the table, one directly in front of her. No way was she sitting next to Richard, who was currently on his phone in her father's study. She pulled out the chair closest to her and sat.

Her mother made bright happy small talk during the meal. Occasionally, her father and Richard lapsed into some discussion of college bowl game predictions or first round draft picks for the Redskins. Marie nodded her head at appropriate times and ate. It was all thoroughly awkward. What were her parents thinking? Neither she nor Richard wanted to be there. Luc had invited her to spend Thanksgiving with him at Sam's house, but Marie had been too chicken. Sam must be furious about the media digging up Grace McKinley after all these years.

She reached for a second helping of sweet potatoes, but her mother's pointed throat clearing stopped her.

"There's something we need to discuss," Eileen said.

Yeah yeah, the nudie paintings my lover made of me.

"After the New Year, you will be going into rehab for awhile," Richard said.

Marie looked around at the three faces staring at her from across the table. She could swear the earth had just stopped revolving on its axis.

"What?" she said.

"People will excuse all this ... unseemly behavior if it's the result of substance abuse," her mother chimed in.

"But I don't have a substance abuse problem."

"You do now," Richard said. "Prescription painkillers. Alcohol."

"You don't like what I'm doing so you're going to put me away?"

"Don't worry. We've found you a nice, upscale facility. Think of it as an extended spa stay, dear."

She couldn't believe her ears. She turned to her mother in disbelief. Her parents had always been on Richard's side but she'd never imagined they would go along with a scheme like this.

She pushed back her chair and stood up. "You all are fucking crazy if you think I'm just going to meekly give in to this crap-shit idea. You can't make me go into rehab." This was nuts. What were they thinking?

"It's the best thing for everyone, dear," her mother said.

"No. It's the best thing for Richard." She glared at him. "It's not MY fault that your constituents are unhappy. YOU made the decision to cheat on your wife. YOU made the decision to file for divorce. That was all YOU. And if it's not working out for you, well I'm sorry but it's not my problem to solve. We are not getting back together and I am NOT going to rehab just because your campaign is circling the drain."

Her father was maintaining his usual poker face. Marie whirled on him next.

"And you're selling me out so your company doesn't lose funding on projects that the Pentagon *doesn't even want.* Yeah, I read the paper too. I guess you'll just have to find another member of Congress to kiss up to."

The expressions on her mother's and Richard's faces were priceless. Clearly, they'd expected her to just acquiesce. *Yes, sure, I'll go into rehab. I have nothing better to do after the holidays. A little spa experience, sounds like fun!*

"And what was Maya doing on Fox News saying I was a liability to the campaign? It didn't look to me like she's just licking her wounds. More like jockeying for position." She shot her mother a meaningful look. "Still."

She grabbed her coat and purse from the hall closet, then charged out of the house, slamming the front door behind her for good measure. She didn't even wait to get out of sight of the house before allowing herself a little skip and fist pump into the air. It was working. The publicity about Luc's show was working, if Richard felt he had to shunt his wife off to rehab to rehabilitate her image. It took all her willpower not to dance down the middle of the street.

23

Luc saw her as soon as he pulled into the driveway. She was leaning against her car, face turned up to the sky. Her hair was pulled up, her neck long and graceful above the collar of her wool coat. The light was perfect, clear and blue, unobstructed by the heavy tree canopy of summer. In the distance, a line of geese dotted the sky.

Everything about her was beautiful, timeless. And he was helpless before her.

Déesse.

He had meant it when he'd said that he belonged to her. An artist always belongs to his art.

He memorized the scene in the moment it took her to turn toward him and smile. Then she was running toward him and all he could do was open his arms and catch her. *Once you see, you can never un-see.*

She snuggled into his chest, warm and solid in his arms. He pressed his lips to her head and took a deep inhale, breathing in the faint flowery scent of her hair. He loved the way she smelled, her shampoo, her perfumes—she had two that she wore, he had determined that—the soap on her skin ... he loved the Marie-ness of her.

"What happened, ma chérie?" He left Sam's house the minute he'd gotten her text. He wasn't fond of Thanksgiving anyway. Too much food for a Frenchman's stomach, not to mention American football.

She shook in his arms, and he was momentarily alarmed until he realized she was laughing. She looked up at him.

"They want to send me to rehab, to fix my image as a senator's wife."

"That's ridiculous. They can't do that."

"And my parents were going along with it. I had to leave or else I was going to bludgeon them all to death with a twenty-pound turkey."

"Now that would be a story for CNN." He kissed her. "You should have come with me."

"I wish I had. But Sam must hate me."

His hands found the bun at the back of her head and tugged it free from the ponytail holder. He ran his hands through her loose hair, releasing a bloom of scent around her. There came a tightening in his groin. That never took long with Marie in his arms. He wanted her lovely naked body in his bed or on his floor or anywhere he could have her. He wasn't particular.

"Are you kidding? She's never had so many reporters in her gallery. She's loving the attention." He caressed her soft cheek, warm against the cold air. "She still thinks I'm an idiot, of course. But that's nothing new."

Inside, they shed coats and shoes, grasping for each other's body beneath layers of fabric. Luc unbuttoned her blouse, unzipped her skirt, unrolled her stockings. Quickly, quickly. Then he stepped back to look at her, clad in nothing but lacy ivory panties that were barely distinguishable from her porcelain skin.

Art or sex? Suddenly he was torn. At their best, they were one and the same.

"You want to draw me," she whispered.

She knew him so well. But of course she did. He belonged to her.

If he did this quickly, he could have both. He lead her to the sofa, posed her just so. Her legs stretched out along the leather upholstery, one arm resting on the back of the sofa, the other dangling toward the floor. He lowered her panties just enough to expose one flawless hip.

L'invitation. That's what he would call it.

Lines flew easily from his pencil. She was here, and he was happy. He could keep her safe here, in his home. No ocean, no husband, could reach her here. He drew her curves against the curves of the sofa, her pale skin fairly glowing against the dark leather.

"What is that little smile for?" she asked.

His smile widened to a grin. "In my next life, I am coming back as a sofa. As your sofa."

"Are you saying you wish you were lying beneath me?"

He closed his eyes with a groan, and allowed himself a moment to enjoy that image. Marie's body stretched out on top of his. He had a raging hard-on now. All he could think of was being inside her, her warm heat around him, holding him tight. When he opened his eyes, she was staring back at him with heavy-lidded eyes of her own. Her breasts rose and fell above her ragged breath.

Fuck the art. He was done drawing.

He went to her. She sat up, making short work of his jeans, popping open the button fly, then cradling him in her hands. She kissed him, exploring his hard length with her lips, softly. When she found the vein and ran her tongue alone it, he closed his eyes again. He wanted simply to feel this, to be blind to everything but her touch.

She slid her lips over him, pulling him in and out of her mouth, slowly, patiently. With his eyes closed, it was all sensation, just the soft velvet of her lips and tongue caressing him, soothing him and urging him on at the same time. When she splayed her fingers across his hip, it was more than he could take.

"Marie. Please. I don't want to come this way."

She let her lips slide slowly off him, then pulled him down onto the sofa next to her. She stripped off her panties and climbed onto his lap.

"You wanted to be beneath me?" She pushed him back into the sofa cushion.

"I want to be anywhere in your general vicinity."

She lifted her hips above his lap and slowly eased him inside her. She moaned as he filled her inch by slow delicious inch. When her hips reached his again, she paused, sighing, savoring the feeling of him inside her. Completely, fully inside her.

"The look on your face right now, Marie. I will draw that someday. Just for me."

She began to rock her hips, letting him slide in and out of her. She gasped for air with each stroke. He rolled her nipples beneath his thumbs, but she seemed not to notice. She was lost in herself, his déesse filling herself with pleasure, with desire, with him. He folded his arms behind his head, a smile on his face, and silently watched her skin and hair and breasts bob and sway before him.

She stilled her hips and her eyes came back into focus, taking in his amused smile, his casual posture. "I'm sorry, Luc," she whispered.

"Sorry for what, love?"

"For—"

She began to lift her hips off him. He pulled her back down.

"It's just that ... posing for you ... I got carried away."

He pulled her head toward his and kissed her deeply. "Shh. I know what modeling does to you. It's okay."

"It's not right to just ..."

"Use me?"

She nodded shyly.

"Who says it's not right? It's just the two of us here. I am yours, Marie." He kissed his way over to her ear, sucked gently on her earlobe for a moment—long enough to feel her squeeze around him—then added quietly, "Do you need to just fuck me tonight?"

He leaned back to watch the rosy blush warm her face.

"You do that on purpose," she protested.

"Guilty as charged. I'm an artist, ma chérie. I like to see color. I also like to see you come."

He pulled her breast to his lips, heard her sharp intake of breath as he closed his mouth around her nipple. Her hips began moving again, slowly at first, then faster. He held her away from him so he could watch. Her breathing fell shallow and ragged again, but her eyes were no longer a million miles away. They were right here, trained on him. Her entire being was here and intent on claiming the pleasure she needed. He had never loved her more than right this very minute, when she was taking exactly what she wanted. And what she wanted was him.

He would paint this, too, someday. Just for himself. He contemplated the logistics of such a painting to hold back his own orgasm until she came. There were so many paintings he wanted to make, it would take a lifetime to complete them all.

"L—Lu—" She was trying to get his name out and failing miserably, charmingly.

He felt her muscles contract around him and he let himself go with a loud moan, accepting the weight of her body as she collapsed onto his shoulder.

"Come with me to New York tomorrow."

"What's in New York?"

"Some collector Sam wants me to meet with. But that won't take all day." He kissed her warm shoulders.

She sighed, and he knew by the tenor of the sound that he was about to get turned down.

"I'd love to. But I have finals next week and I'm behind on studying." She twisted around in his arms to face him. "I'm sorry."

"No apology necessary. Professor Marchand believes in studying."

She smiled ruefully. "I just can't picture you in a classroom. I've been trying but I can't see it."

He ran a finger along her collarbone, imagining another drawing. "There are videos of some of my lectures on YouTube."

"Maybe I'll look those up."

He didn't want to discuss teaching. Unless it was teaching her. And not even that today. Her teacher was the last thing he wanted to be today.

"I never intended for your past to get dragged into this. If I'd known, I would have done things differently."

He pulled her toward him and kissed the words back into her mouth. "It's not your fault, Marie. It doesn't change anything for me. If it gets you free once and for all from your husband, then it will be worth it."

24

Marie set down her bag of groceries and inserted her apartment key into the lock. It was early Friday evening, and she shivered in the cold. The forecast was for an early snow, unusual for Virginia. Well, no matter, she told herself. Studying was the only thing she had planned for the weekend anyway. She'd left Luc's house early that morning, picked up her books from the apartment and headed to the university library downtown. The apartment complex was noisy when the local schools were out. But if she had to study here all weekend, snowbound, she'd manage.

The key turned easily in the lock. Too easily. There was no heavy thunk of the deadbolt dropping. Had she forgotten to lock up when she left? Probably, she figured. It had been early and her brain had been fogged with memories of Luc and lovemaking. *Fuck me, love* and she'd been putty in his hands.

It would be hard to settle for an ordinary Thanksgiving in the future. She turned the doorknob and pushed open the door.

It was the aroma that hit her first, ginger and the yeasty smell of rice. And a faint odor of smoke. The lights were on, that was the second thing she noticed. She had not turned on the lights when she was here that morning. She definitely knew that. She had rushed in, changed into jeans, grabbed her bookbag and left.

Richard stepped around the corner from the small dining nook next to the kitchen. She let out a tiny cry of surprise, then braced herself for the yelling. Instead, his smile was affable and relaxed. He wore casual jeans and a button-down shirt.

"Hungry?" he asked, not a trace of anger or animosity in his voice.

He held out his hand to her, as if he really expected her to take it.

Who are you and what did you do with the real Richard?

"I got Chinese."

Slowly she inched toward the dining nook. Surely there was a catch here. It had been easily over a year since Richard had spoken to her without yelling or accusing her of something or other. The table was set, two candles lit in the middle, a bottle of white wine already opened and poured. He took the bag of groceries from her hand.

"Sit. I'll put these away for you."

Marie was stunned. Something was off here, but what?

"How did you get in here?" she finally managed to say.

"The building manager let me in. He didn't want our dinner to get cold while I waited for you to come home."

She listened to Richard opening and closing cupboards in her tiny kitchen. The building manager let him in. Of course, he would. Her husband was a senator. But still. Not good.

"What do you think of that wine? Your mother recommended it."

The wine glowed in the light of the candle. Marie picked up her glass and took a sip. "It's okay."

"Really? I thought it was quite good. It's from New Zealand."

She glanced at Richard's glass. Half empty. Or half full, she supposed. If that was all he'd had, it wasn't enough to make him drunk. Not that Richard had ever been a big drinker. His military family was wound too tight for that.

He came out and sat down at the table, began dishing out kung pao chicken.

"Why are you here?" she asked.

"We need to talk. Rice?" He handed over the white carton.

"About what, exactly?" Marie could think of a dozen things, *exactly*, that they needed to talk about. But then again, none of those really required any further discussion.

"About us. I had a really good conversation with your parents yesterday."

I bet you did.

He went on. "I'm sorry about everything with Maya. That was stupid of me. Monumentally stupid of me. But that's over now."

She rolled her eyes at him, took another sip of wine. The wine wasn't bad, actually. If her mother had recommended it, it wouldn't be, of course.

"No no. I don't expect you to believe me right away but I'm going to prove it to you, Marie. I want you back."

"Your campaign manager wants me back. You said so yourself when you came to my office."

Richard sipped at his own wine. "Can't we just give this a try? If you think it's not working, then we can quietly separate after the election."

She drank more wine. She needed it. "I'm seeing someone else, Richard."

Now it was his turn to roll his eyes. "That artist is bad news, Marie. Haven't you seen the news reports? One of his students killed herself. He got fired by UVa for ethics violations. He'll never teach again."

"That's in the past."

"Marie, he's using you. Can't you see that? He's a two-bit has-been artist who needs to sell some paintings. What better way than selling nude paintings of a senator's wife?"

"That's not true." This conversation was making her head hurt, and she was tired. Studying all day had wiped her out.

"Your parents really helped me see the light yesterday. We are good together, Marie. We're a good match. We'll be players in Washington for the rest of our lives, like your parents."

She closed her eyes. All she could think of was sleep.

"Don't your parents have a good life? We could have that, too, Marie. Please don't throw this away for us."

PEOPLE WERE SHOUTING NEAR HER. She was being jostled. Now she was floating on air. In the distance, car tires whined on the street. Behind her eyelids, lights were flashing around and around. Her head felt like it had been split open. She reached a hand to her hair.

"She's coming to!" someone shouted above her head.

A hand grabbed her wrist and pressed on her pulse.

She opened her eyes a crack. Faces peered down at her. She *was* in mid-air—and then she wasn't. She was set inside a room with a thud. *Where am I? Damn weirdest dream.*

"How are you feeling?" someone else asked.

She felt a sharp pinch on the inside of her elbow.

Okay, she'd play along with this dream.

"Fine. Where am I?"

"You're in an ambulance. We're taking you to the hospital."

"Why is that?"

"You took a bit of a spill back there on the street. Knocked yourself out cold."

She heard a door open, a blast of air on her ankles, then another voice. "How much have you had to drink tonight?"

She thought for a moment. How much of that wine did she drink with dinner? Well, she couldn't really say *with dinner*. She'd barely eaten any of it. "Half a glass of wine, maybe?"

"Are you sure? That doesn't sound like enough to make someone black out on a street corner."

She laughed weakly. "No. No, it doesn't."

The voice was irritated this time. "Did you take something else then? We need to know what you have in your system, dear."

"Some kung pao chicken. A sandwich from lunch. That's about it, I guess."

"She's still high. Oh well." The voice was no longer talking to her. "They'll figure it out at the hospital. Doesn't look the type, eh?"

They were moving.

"Where are we going?" she asked. She willed herself to wake up.

"To the hospital, remember? Inova Loudoun. In Lansdowne. It's not far. We'll be there in a minute. Can you tell me your name, dear?"

"Marie. Marie Witherspoon. Where is Richard?"

"Who's Richard?"

"My husband. We were having dinner in my apartment."

"Can't tell you anything about that, sweetie. We got a call about a woman lying unconscious at the corner of Ashburn Village Boulevard and Farmwell Road. Showed up and found you."

When the bright lights of the emergency department hit her eyes, Marie realized she wasn't dreaming. But how did she end up on the street? She was having dinner with Richard in the apartment. That was the last thing she remembered.

The EMTs lifted her onto a bed, then swished the green curtain shut around her. She closed her eyes and tried to think it through. It made no sense. Where was Richard? Maybe *that* had been a dream? Maybe Richard had never been at her apartment.

That had certainly been weird anyway. But it still didn't explain why *she* wasn't at home.

There was a commotion out in the hallway.

"I need to see her. I know she's here. Marie Witherspoon. She's a senator's wife. Yes, you have a senator's wife here. How do I know? It's on the freaking wires."

Nishi.

Marie called out for her, weakly.

"I hear her. Marie? Where are you?"

She heard other curtains being swished open followed by Nishi's hurried apologies. Finally, her own curtain was swept aside.

"Marie! What's going on?"

"I'm not sure ... I woke up and some people were putting me into an ambulance?"

Nishi swiped and tapped at her phone, shrugging off a young nurse.

"She can stay," Marie said to the nurse, who stalked off.

"The wires are reporting that you were found unconscious on an Ashburn street. Were you out for a walk? Did you get hit by a car?"

"No. I was having dinner ... Richard sort of broke into my apartment—"

"Wait? He *broke* into your apartment?"

"Well, he got the building manager to let him in."

"What the hell did he want?"

"To talk. Apparently, my parents put the fear of God into him yesterday or something. I don't know. I was so tired, all I wanted to do was go to sleep. He had Chinese and wine. That was weirder than this." She waved her arm at the curtain. "Maybe I dreamed it. I don't know."

An ER doctor came in and Nishi excused herself. Marie heard her talking on the phone while the doctor poked and prodded her, drew some blood and made her pee in a cup. Nishi was waiting with her when he returned.

"Your urine sample tested positive for rohypnol. That explains your blackout. Were you at a party or a bar? This stuff often gets dropped into drinks."

"I was just at home ..."

"Richard brought the wine?" Nishi asked, then fell silent as the rest of it sunk in.

"He poisoned me?" Marie said quietly. "Why would he do that?"

"The bigger question is how you ended up lying on a sidewalk in the middle of Ashburn." She turned to the doctor. "Could she have walked out of her apartment? Like sleep-walked?"

"No. Rohypnol knocks you out cold for hours."

"What time is it now?" Marie asked, looking around frantically for a clock.

The doctor checked his wristwatch. "Nearly eleven."

"I got home around six, six-thirty. How long was I outside?"

"Don't know. Not long probably. You were found at a pretty busy intersection," he said.

"Oh my god. He must have stayed with you in the apartment for a few hours, then took you to ..." Nishi's words trailed off as two other familiar voices leaked in beneath the curtain.

"He was supposed to stop with her, Bill. I won't ask my donors to help him if he continues to cheat on my daughter. It makes me look bad."

Nishi raised an eyebrow at Marie and mouthed, "Your mother is pissed about Maya."

The curtain swished open to usher in her parents. Both were impeccably dressed in slacks and sweaters, when anyone else would have thrown on jeans and a sweatshirt to run to the emergency room to see their only child. Her mother's face was tight and unhappy.

"Marie! What happened?" Eileen turned to glare at Nishi, who was already backing out of the exam room. "What was she doing here?" Eileen asked as soon as Nishi was gone.

"She has a Google alert set up for me. Anytime I turn up on the wires, she knows about it."

"I see."

Yes, Marie was beginning to see too. Nishi wasn't supposed to have been the first person here. Clearly, her parents forgot that Nishi and Imran lived in Ashburn.

"You got here quickly from the city," Marie pointed out.

"We left as soon as Richard called." She looked around. "Where is he?"

"Probably back at my apartment. That's the last place I saw him." She rolled her eyes at her mother's expression. "Oh come on. He breaks into my apartment with dinner and wine, and the next thing I know I'm being transported from some street corner to the hospital in an ambulance. I'm just hoping you two were in on it and I wasn't just dumped on the street and left there alone."

The enormity of what had happened was beginning to hit her. The diciness of the scheme. She'd been in real danger, lying unconscious on the sidewalk. What if some good Samaritan hadn't called 911? She could have been hurt—or worse.

The doctor looked from Marie to her mother and back again, clearly confused by the conversation. "Are you the parents?"

"Yes," her father answered. "Senator Witherspoon. And this is my wife."

Marie rolled her eyes again. Her father still referred to himself as a senator, when he deemed it necessary or it would prove useful. The doctor looked taken aback.

"I see. Well, I can't let her go tonight by herself. But if you're here to take her ..."

"Actually, we're waiting for her husband. He'll take her home," Eileen replied.

"I'm going back to my apartment."

"You heard the doctor, dear. You can't go home alone."

"Then I'll go to Nishi's house."

Her mother gave her a pitying stare. "Richard will be here shortly and will take you home."

Marie looked at the doctor for help, but he was filling out paperwork on his clipboard.

"Great. I'm supposed to trust the man who poisoned me and dumped me on the street to take me home safely."

The doctor was pretending not to hear.

"Marie, I don't know what you're talking about. You're still a little ... under the influence. Richard did no such thing. If anyone, it was that artist friend of yours."

"Don't you mean my artist lover?"

Her father pulled his phone from his pocket and read a text. "Richard's here. He just pulled into the parking lot."

The situation was sinking in. Richard hadn't come to her apartment to make nice. He had come to prove a point. If he could drug her and dump her on a street at night, he could drug her and take her to a rehab facility.

25

Below him, Manhattan looked like a toy city. Luc was speechless, even though there was no one around at the moment to speak to. When Sam had told him that a collector wanted to meet with him, she hadn't mentioned that the collector was a Russian bazillionaire with a penthouse condo. Luc couldn't even begin to imagine what a place like this must cost.

A young woman in a painted-on dress and ridiculously high heels had brought him up, and then disappeared. Wife? Daughter? Girlfriend? Personal assistant? He wanted to laugh at some of his clients in DC. Their wealth was pocket change compared to this.

Well, whatever this guy wanted, Luc could charge him a princely sum for it. Which wasn't a bad thing, considering. When he'd told Marie that the press coverage didn't change anything for him, that wasn't entirely the truth. Some of the sales from Sam's gallery had fallen through because the buyers were upset about what had happened to Grace. So a commission from someone wealthier than God wouldn't be entirely unwelcome right about now.

"Monsieur Marchand."

Luc turned to see a youngish man—no more than thirty, certainly—wearing dark slacks and an elegantly tailored shirt. Bespoke, Luc guessed. An untied tie was draped around his neck as though Luc had interrupted his dressing, though he knew that not to be the case. The man himself had stipulated the date and time of their appointment. Black Friday, eleven am. The man's feet were bare, and bony.

"I am Vitaly. People call me Max."

He strode across the gleaming floor of the vast room, simultaneously shaking Luc's hand and clapping him on the back. "What a view, eh? Was it worth fifty-eight million, do you think?"

Luc wondered what Max's line of business was. He seemed altogether too young to have fifty-eight million dollars, period, let alone to drop on a New York condo.

"Ah well." Max didn't wait for Luc to reply. He waved an arm carelessly at the window. "Even that can't compete with your paintings." He lead Luc over to a cabinet, pulled out a bottle of scotch and two glasses. "I can't tell you how excited I was to see that you had a show of new work. Total random on my part. I just happened to be in Washington that week."

"Why is that?"

Max handed Luc a glass. "Why I happened to be in Washington? Ah, business. You know."

Right. Luc knew better not to ask. In Washington, when someone was evasive about their work, you just let it drop. Better not to know these things, sometimes.

"No. I meant why were you excited that I have a new show? I'm not exactly a household name."

Max knocked his whiskey back. "Ah, but in this household, you are. Come."

He set his glass back on the cabinet and headed down a long hallway. Luc followed, intensely curious. Truly, he wasn't being modest. He was a household name nowhere. At the end of the hall was a cavernous master bedroom with the same floor-to-ceiling windows that the rest of the unit had. Luc followed Max to the middle of the room, mesmerized once again by the view.

Max laughed. "No, no." He gestured toward the back wall of the bedroom. "Only drawback to these buildings. You can't hang art on the windows."

Luc turned around to see what Max was pointing at.

Grace. The two interior walls were hung with his paintings of Grace, all five of them. Sam had sold these for him years ago, not in a show but in a private transaction. Luc had just wanted to be rid of them. Now here they were again, in some stranger's bedroom.

"This is my favorite." Max walked over to a portrait of Grace sleeping, a thin white sheet pulled up to her waist, her lovely budded breasts exposed. Her yellow hair swam around her delicate, serene face, her cheeks flushed like the first moment of sunset. "I have these on my wall for couple of years now. But—well, it's not so much that I am tired of them, because she is lovely, eh? But your Marie Witherspoon, now she is more interesting. Yes? Senator's wife? Ooh la la?" He laughed. "You're in big trouble for that, right? No trouble for me, though. More valuable, too, right?" He waved his hand dismissively at Grace. "Grace McKinley, pretty but no one important. Died before she could do anything in life."

Luc was nearly in shock. The whole point of having Sam sell the paintings of Grace was so he would never have to see them again. And Max had mentioned Marie. He knew where this was going.

"So I'll take these down," Max continued. "Put them in storage, maybe. I don't know. Sell them, perhaps. What do you think? They'd probably sell for more than I paid for them these days, thanks to CNN. And they're nice, sure. Nicer than internet porn when you want to go to sleep."

Luc was in danger of vomiting. And then after that, of punching this obnoxious Russian in the face.

"Then I'll put your Marie paintings up in here. Only thing, I need five. See? To replace these. And I only have four that I've purchased. Wrote Samantha Smith a check on the spot, just so you know. So I need one more and I don't want the ones of her sitting outside drawing or eating. Or those little ones that show just a shoulder or something. Those are cute but not appropriate for—"

Max tilted his head back toward the gigantic bed which was, Luc now noticed, positioned closer to the paintings than normal furniture placement would imply.

"So what are you asking for?" Luc asked, knowing full well that he was going to turn down whatever this piece of shit kid wanted.

"Putain, I need a fifth painting, man. That's what I'm asking for. Another nude. Preferably a part of her body I don't already own. I have her tits, her ass. What would something a little more explicit cost?"

Luc lunged at the man, but Max was both faster and stronger than he'd anticipated. Max pushed him off and laughed.

"Oh come off it," Max spit out. "You paint your women and then put them up for sale. Kill the outrage, dude. I'll give you double what I paid for the other four. Deal?"

Outside, Luc gulped in the cold air then coughed it back out again. New York air. Car exhaust and urine and garbage. He couldn't bear to get back on the subway. He'd walk back to the hotel.

He called Sam's cell.

"Luc! Are you in New York?"

He grunted in assent.

"So how'd it go with Vitaly?"

"Max, to his friends, apparently. I won't sell him those paintings."

"Why? What does he want?"

"He wants a fifth painting of Marie to go with the other four you're selling him. Refund his money. I don't want him to have any of them."

"Oh whoa whoa, Luc. He's already given me a check. And we have people backing out of other sales. You can't really afford to lose these four, too."

"I don't care. Did you know he has the paintings of Grace, too?"

Sam was silent on the other end. Then, "No. I didn't know that. Honest, Luc. He didn't buy those directly from me. The original buyer must have resold them."

The wind between the buildings was slicing painfully against his face. It felt good. Luc considered staying outside all day.

"Luc?" Sam was still on the other end. "Why don't you sleep on this? I'm sure it will look different in the morning. I know it must have been a shock to see those other paintings after all these years."

"That's not it, Sam. He has his bed set up right in front of them. What do you think he's doing with them?"

He heard a long sigh on the other end. "I don't think about what people do with the paintings I sell them. You know, if you don't want to share your women with the rest of the world, then don't paint them. It's like taking photographs. Once you do it, they're out there. Someone will own them eventually, unless you destroy them."

"I don't paint to share with others. I always got marked down for that in nursery school. Does not share well with other children. I paint people in order to see them."

"Well, you're not the only person with eyes, Luc."

Luc lay on the rumpled hotel bed in his underwear, a bottle of whiskey on the nightstand. He was well and truly drunk. He hadn't gotten wasted on hard alcohol like this since the first anniversary of Grace's death. He was more of a wine drinker, normally. Grappa, at the hardest.

It was nearly two in the morning and he was tired but wide awake. He clicked on the television and began flipping through channels, settling on CNN after finding nothing else remotely interesting.

That was a mistake.

The wife of Senator Richard Macintyre was admitted to a hospital after being found unconscious on a street in Ashburn, Virginia. Mrs. Macintyre is suffering from exhaustion and addiction to prescription painkillers, according to the senator's office, and will be entering a rehabilitation center for treatment after the New Year. Mrs. Macintyre has recently been at the center of a minor scandal in the nation's capital, when it was revealed that nude portraits on display at the Samantha Smith Gallery are of her.

Marie was in the hospital. He stumbled across the room, looking for the patch of floor where he'd left his pants. He tripped over them before he saw them, then swore as his big toe made contact with his phone in the pants pocket. He kneeled down and fumbled with the tangle of cloth before finally extricating the phone. He hit dial.

"Hello." Marie's voice was quiet, barely audible in fact.

"Marie!" His voice sounded muffled, like his mouth was full of oatmeal.

"Luc," came the whispered reply, then nothing. The call was dropped.

He hit redial again but got only her voice mail. Before he could think better of it, he hurled the phone across the room.

Luckily, it landed on the hotel's plush luxury bed, where it began ringing.

He lunged for the bed, as best he could in his state. He didn't want to miss her call.

"Marie?" he slurred into the phone.

"No." The voice was not Marie's. He couldn't place it. It was clear and clipped, with a slight accent. "Mr. Marchand? I am Marie's friend, Nishi."

"Nishhhi."

"You sound drunk."

"Mariesssinthehospital?"

"Not anymore. She's fine."

"I need to talk to her, Nishhhi."

"Don't call her anymore tonight. Call me at this number tomorrow morning. When you'll actually remember what we talk about."

"Nishhhi?"

"Yes?"

"I love her."

"Don't call her, Mr. Marchand. Let her sleep."

The next morning, Luc awoke with a splitting headache. He tried to sit up, then collapsed back into the gazillion thread count pillows, moaning in pain. This was why one shouldn't fall in love. There always came that morning when you woke up wrapped around a hangover instead of a lover.

He rubbed his eyes, trying to remember last night. Marie was in the hospital. It had been on the news. And she was addicted to ... something. She was going in for treatment? None of it made any sense. He would have noticed if she had those kinds of problems.

He brushed his teeth and scrubbed at his face. He looked like hell. Dark shadows, bloodshot eyes, pale skin—the works. He looked like a vampire. A hungover vampire. Had he talked to that friend of Marie's? The one who bought the lessons for her—or had that been a drunken dream? He went to look for his phone, shaving foam still on his face.

Yes, there was an unfamiliar number on the call log. He dialed it back.

"Nishi here," a bright, crisp voice answered. Luc held the phone a centimeter further from his throbbing head.

"Nishi. Luc Marchand here."

"Ah, Mr. Marchand. You sound better this morning."

"What happened?"

"Richard drugged her and she ended up in the hospital."

"The news said she was found outside, unconscious."

"I'm still trying to sort that out. It appears that Richard did that, called 911 and then left the scene."

"What kind of asshole does that?" Luc yelled into the phone, then winced. His own voice was too loud for his headache.

"An asshole in danger of losing his Senate seat."

"Marie said he wants her to go into rehab."

"Yes. I think that's what last night was about. He is setting the stage for that."

"I've really fucked up her life, haven't I?"

Nishi was silent for awhile. "No, I think you just walked into it at a bad time. No one could have predicted Richard's behavior of late. Not even me, and I always expect the worst from him."

After a shower hot enough to burn off any lingering alcohol, Luc went to the concierge station to ask where he might find a stationer in New York. When he boarded the train back to Washington, he was in possession of a box of overpriced cotton writing paper—in an elegant silvery gray—and a fine French fountain pen with gold nib. He settled into his seat with a fresh cup of coffee and pulled out a sheet of paper.

He needed to apologize and it seemed best to do it in writing. He'd made a complete and utter mess of everything. He should have told Sam that she needed to delay his show until he had other work to give her. It wasn't wrong to want to paint Marie, but he should have kept those paintings for himself.

He put some words down, then crumpled up the paper and started over on a fresh sheet. If he wrote in French, the words would flow. But, of course, Marie didn't read French. By the time the train rolled into Philadelphia, he'd gone through a third of the box of paper and still had nothing. He was shit writing in English.

It would be easier to draw what he wanted to say but after the meeting with Vitaly-Max, the very idea of drawing made him ill. Not to mention, if he hadn't gone to New York to meet with Max, none of this would have happened to Marie. She would have been with him yesterday, not in a hospital, not being drugged by her asshole husband.

He stared out the window at the train platform, at students with their backpacks returning to school after the holiday, at lovers reuniting after weekends with separate families, at people disembarking by themselves and dragging their suitcases—alone—toward the light of the station. That would be him when the train pulled into Union Station. He would gather up the mess he'd made with the paper and lug his bag off the train and past the shops in the station. He would get in his car and drive to Marie's apartment where he would grovel and beg for her forgiveness. Plead to still be hers.

He scratched his pen across the grey paper, trying to will words from his brain into the nib of the pen. He just wasn't a words person. He didn't interact with the world through his mind. Luc saw. That's where he was most articulate, with his eyes. But this apology had to be in writing. It needed a permanence beyond mere speech, to be something she couldn't just knock away with a smile and a kiss.

He took the outside steps up to Marie's apartment two at a time, the envelope in his hand. It wasn't poetry, but it would have to do. Several times he had to press himself to the wall as movers carried down furniture and boxes. Strange time to move, he thought, on a holiday weekend.

At the top of the stairs, the door to her apartment stood wide open and his heart soared. She was home!

Then a burly man staggered through the doorway, a stack of boxes strapped to his back.

It hit Luc like a piano dropped from a New York penthouse. The movers were in Marie's apartment. He pushed his way inside and frantically began looking for her.

"Marie!" he called.

"Hey buddy," one of the movers said. "No one's here. Just us."

"Where is she moving?"

The mover shook his head like Luc was an idiot. "Can't tell you. What I can tell you is that if you're not out of here when I come back up, I'll have to make some calls."

Luc figured that gave him five minutes, tops, to find a place for the letter. The kitchen was already cleared out. The movers were working on the living room so he slipped down the short hallway to what used to be Marie's bedroom. The bed and mattress were gone, but stacks of boxes still littered the room. He flipped open a few lids. Toiletries, socks, shoes, books. Some of these boxes she might not open right away.

Then he spotted her backpack, leaning against the wall. She had finals next week. She would have to open her bookbag. He pulled back the zipper a few inches, pressed a kiss to the envelope, and slipped his apology inside.

26

Marie dragged her mother into the walk-in closet. "What's wrong with this picture?"

Eileen Witherspoon peered into the closet. Dozens of hangers hung empty. More lay discarded on the carpeted floor.

"I don't know, Marie. You haven't unpacked your clothes yet?"

Marie pointed to the far corner where, on a shelf, a pile of clothing was neatly folded and stacked. Jeans, tee shirts, a sweater. Next to them sat a small leather toiletry case. She unzipped the case and dumped the contents out onto the floor. Lipsticks, compacts, a vial of perfume, tampons.

"Not mine!" She took a wild swipe and knocked more hangers onto the floor. "Maya hasn't *completely* moved out of this house, has she? When I'm in rehab, who do you think will be here?"

"So throw her things out," Eileen replied. "Richard isn't seeing her anymore."

Marie rolled her eyes. "Oh my god. Please. He'll never give her up."

He didn't have to, after all. Marie would spent some undetermined number of months in rehab, then make the campaign rounds with him. After the election, he would dump her again and Maya would be back in her rightful place. She just had to bide her time.

"I informed him that he must. Otherwise, I will not press my donors to support his campaign. It makes me look bad if he's cheating on you."

Marie blew out a big, exaggerated sigh. "It makes you look bad. Heaven forbid. But it's okay that it's been making me look like an idiot for years now. Why the fuck didn't you *inform* him earlier?"

"Marie, I'm leaving. If you can't behave better ..." Eileen turned on her heel and marched down the hall, her heels clicking against the hardwood floors.

Marie followed her downstairs. "Well, I'm addicted to painkillers, right? I'm a little unstable, or so I've been told."

Her mother retrieved her coat from the foyer closet.

"He made me miss my finals, mother. I thought that was part of the deal you negotiated. That I could finish my MBA. Well, I just wasted an entire semester. All that money down the drain."

"You can file for incompletes and make it up."

"Filing for an incomplete gives me an additional six weeks to make up the work. What am I supposed to do? Phone in the exams from rehab? And where is this rehab anyway?"

"I don't know, dear." Eileen opened the heavy front door.

Liar.

The word was on the tip of Marie's tongue, but she let it die there, swallowed the bubble of anger in her throat. Her mother probably didn't know. Oh, if she were to ask Richard he would tell her but she knew better than to ask. Her mother saw the world the way she did—the way she wanted to—and no matter how much Marie tried to clean the lens or angle the light differently, Eileen Witherspoon was never going to see things the way her daughter did.

Marie had asked Nishi once, after one of Nishi's clients had self-destructed in a very public way, how she stayed so calm around people like that. Nishi had replied, "We get angry with people when they aren't the people we want them to be. But our anger doesn't change them. I can't really make my clients behave the way I'd like them to even though it would make their lives easier in some cases. All I can do is change course when they don't—or fire them as clients."

She looked at her mother standing there on the slate walkway to Richard's front door, her black Mercedes parked in the driveway. Her mother was wearing a crisp knee-length coat over one of her St. John's suits—on a Saturday. She'd never seen her mother in sneakers, ever. Not even on vacation. Loafers were as casual as Eileen Witherspoon got.

She looked down at her own feet, bare against Richard's gleaming hardwood floors, and her grey leggings beneath an oversized black sweatshirt. She would never be her mother—and her mother would never be able to see that.

How do I fire my parents?

"Thanks for stopping by, Mom. Will I see you at the reception tonight?"

"No. Your father and I have a dinner to go to. But you'll enjoy it, I'm sure."

Marie stood in the doorway and watched sadly as her mother's silver Mercedes drove away. She almost felt bad for her mother. Richard was thumbing his nose at her little request that he stop seeing Maya. Few people did that to Eileen Witherspoon—or got away with it. Marie knew her mother thought she was helping but Richard had neatly inserted her between a rock and a hard place. Her husband's career or her daughter.

I will always let her down and she will always be disappointed. There was no way to change that.

When the car was out of sight, she waved jauntily to the guy sitting in the rented SUV at the curb. He pretended to ignore her, the ever-present cable of his earpiece snaking along his jaw. She had nicknamed him T. Rex because he looked so stiff all the time, even just sitting in the car. His bearing screamed military. He was practically her new best friend these days, following her every time she left the house, which she did frequently to get meals. The coffee shop for breakfast, a deli for lunch, grocery store for dinner. The last thing she wanted was to eat or drink anything Richard had in the house.

Even when they went out to dinner, Marie abstained from drinking anything. Not a single drop of anything liquid that a pill could be dissolved in. He had more. She just didn't know where he was keeping them. She'd searched the house from top to bottom, but found nothing.

She closed the door and retreated back into Richard's large, gracious home—the home she had lived in during their marriage. It felt completely foreign to her now, even though their wedding photos had been conspicuously planted throughout the rooms. She looked happy and hopeful inside the fancy frames. She wasn't that girl anymore. Maybe she never had been, and just hadn't stopped long enough to notice.

Her bare feet softly padded into Richard's study. She yanked open the paper drawer on the laser printer and pulled out several sheets of paper, then opened one of the desk drawers. No pencils, only pens. That would have to do.

Plopping her butt in the big leather executive chair, she began to marshal her thoughts for the first time in weeks. After Richard brought her "home" from the hospital, she'd spent a week "on bed rest." Or house arrest, as Marie termed it privately. She was put on leave from her job at Witherspoon & Associates, no surprise there. After a week, Richard began taking her out, having them seen in public together. Dinners at nice restaurants in the city, the Nutcracker at the Kennedy Center, the lighting of the White

House Christmas tree. All conspicuously unmentioned by the J Street Chronicle though, Marie was sure, not unnoticed.

At home, Marie was nearly always alone. Congress and the White House were trying to hammer out a last-minute budget deal before the end of the year, keeping Richard on the Hill most days. The rest of the time, she assumed, he was with Maya. That was all well and good—Marie had no desire to spend any more time than she had to with Richard.

But he was also deliberately keeping her isolated, and that was a problem. She had set up three separate lunch dates with Nishi, only to have all of them thwarted at the last minute. A sudden lunch date with Richard's mother, shopping with his sister for a New Year's Eve gown, a policy briefing session with his legislative assistant.

"He's having your phone and e-mail monitored, dear," Nishi had finally pointed out. "He knows when you contact me." Richard had simply shrugged when she confronted him about it.

And Luc. She missed him so much it physically hurt, a gnawing ache in the center of her chest that never subsided. It even woke her in the middle of the night, just to remind her that it was still there. How could *nothing* hurt so much?

She didn't dare try contacting Luc, though. As much as she hated to admit it, putting rohypnol in her wine had done exactly what Richard intended: put the fear of God into her. She had been rather foolish to think there was no way he could force her into rehab. Not if he was prepared to take measures like that.

She sketched in a head on one of the sheets of paper. She'd been drawing constantly since she had been moved in with Richard. There was little else to do, anyway. That and visit Samantha Smith's web site to look at the tiny images of Luc's paintings. According to the site, the show was coming down on Christmas Eve, a month earlier than originally planned.

She shouldn't have let him paint her. She should have known

better. There had been that voice in the back of her head warning that her parents and Richard weren't going to be happy with nude paintings of her. But she had thrown a blanket over the voice and smothered it. She'd been too infatuated with Luc Marchand, too *take that Senator Macintyre!* A man like Luc had been interested in her—no, crazy about her—and she let it go to her head. Well, who wouldn't, right? Still, it was no excuse.

Then again, who could have predicted that Richard would call off the divorce? He had sucker punched her with that. It all seemed so ridiculously hopeful now, the idea that Luc's paintings would make Richard change his mind. Instead, she'd drop-kicked herself right back into her old life and ruined Luc's show in the process.

She sighed as she continued drawing, only half paying attention to the lines materializing on the paper.

Luc had been wrong. Seeing like an artist wasn't enough, not when other people couldn't see you that way. In Luc's world of paint and canvas, paper and pencil, seeing clearly was enough to fix any problem. In Marie's world, not so much. In Washington, she would always be her parents' daughter, always be attached to Richard, even if they did divorce for good someday. People would always see her through their eyes.

It was time to change course.

She needed to leave Washington, go someplace where no one knew her parents or Richard. Someplace where people would look at her through their own eyes and form their own opinion of her, good or bad. But where to go? That was the question. New York wasn't far enough away. Chicago likely wasn't, either. It had to be someplace out of driving range and further away than just a few hours' flight. California seemed like an obvious choice, but Marie had never been there.

She needed expert advice, and there was only one person she knew who had been just about everywhere. Nishi. Nishi could put her in touch with people and help her find a job. But how to reach her without tipping off Richard? Where could they meet that wouldn't make T. Rex suspicious until it was too late?

She stared down at the sketch she had made almost without thinking. It had a head and hair, neck and shoulders. But no face. It reminded her of Elizabeth Calhoun and her faceless portraits. Everyone, it seemed, assumed that she had hidden her face because she had needed to hide her identity. But what if Alistair, despite being her lover, just hadn't been able to *see* her? To see past her public face as a senator's wife? Maybe she had even recognized that and, knowing that, refused to allow him to paint all of her.

Suddenly, Marie wanted to know. *Needed* to know whether Elizabeth Calhoun had been hiding her face from everyone—or just her lover. If she saw the paintings again, would she be able to tell for sure? She pulled up the Phillips Collection web site on her phone. The show was probably already closed, moved on to the next tour stop or packed back into storage. She scrolled down the tiny screen. There it was. *Alistair Smith & Elizabeth Calhoun: A Model Revealed, closing December 20.*

December 20. That was the day after tomorrow.

She palm-smacked her forehead. The museum! That was the perfect place to meet Nishi. The Phillips had a café but she doubted T. Rex knew that. Doubtful even Richard did. He only went to museums to be seen, like he was a work of art.

Well, he was a piece of work. That was for sure. He could keep her from seeing Luc, but he wasn't going to keep her from seeing Nishi.

She would have to contact Nishi without tipping off Richard, however. It would have to look innocent.

A secret message, that's what she needed. Best friends used to have secret codes they used to communicate with each other. She suspected kids no longer bothered with that. In the age of Facebook, nothing was really secret anyway. Marie never used Facebook herself, although Richard had made her set up a page a few years back so she could develop a platform on preschool education. She dropped the platform after the divorce filing.

Alistair Smith & Elizabeth Calhoun: A Model Revealed, closing December 20.

There had to be a way to contact Nishi. She stared at her phone's screen. A box alternating images from the exhibit was surrounded by buttons. *Enlarge. Event admission. Curator's Notes. Share This.*

Share this. She tapped on the plus sign. Facebook was the very first site listed. She tapped that too. She could post this on Nishi's page. Richard might not be checking Facebook since Marie's page had never been a personal one and she hadn't used it in months.

She added a message to the post: Closes Dec. 20. Noon is a good time to see it. Not crowded. She tapped "post" with her thumb, then crossed her fingers that Nishi would understand. She was running out of options.

27

Washington and Paris shared two famous architects, Luc thought as he stared up at the glass and steel geometric ceiling—Pierre L'Enfant, who provided the original vision for Washington, DC, and I.M. Pei, who designed both the pyramid at the Louvre and the east wing of the National Gallery of Art. It was the latter's ceiling Luc was staring at.

He preferred the west wing, personally. It was infinitely more intimate. Quieter, too. The east wing was more like a train station, a cavernous space where everyone was surrounded by hundreds of people and yet they were all completely, utterly alone. Even the giant Alexander Calder mobile suspended from the ceiling left him cold.

But Marie was here and so he would stay. He had guessed right. A senator from Pennsylvania was inclined to attend an opening reception for a retrospective of Philadelphian Stuart Davis. Luc's own connection to Stuart Davis was tighter than Senator Macintyre's. Luc's grandfather had known Davis in Paris.

But that was neither here nor there. Luc had seen plenty of Davis' paintings in museums.

He was here to see Marie.

Getting an invite had been easier than expected. His renewed notoriety had brought all sorts of faces out of the woodwork. Some, like the asshole in New York, Luc wanted to shove back into the woodwork. But others proved to be more beneficial. One of his former students, it turned out, was now a senior curator at the National Gallery. She'd been only too happy to procure an invitation for Luc.

Now he just had to figure out how to pry Marie away from her husband. From the looks of it, that wasn't going to be easy.

Marie looked lovely in a floor-length skirt and some sort of fussy white blouse with layers upon layers of fabric. It didn't escape him that she was covered up from neck to ankles. He wondered whether that had been her choice, or her husband's. Not that Luc minded so much. After all, he'd been the one to expose too much of her to too many people. He regretted that.

Her hair was pulled up into an arrangement on her head that rivaled the elaborateness of her blouse; small diamonds twinkled from her ears. Her cheeks and lips were rosy with makeup. This was a Marie he hadn't seen before, official Marie, senator's wife.

The senator's wife did not look happy.

Luc wasn't surprised by the stabbing pain in his chest. It had been nearly three weeks since he'd seen her, touched her … kissed her. The withdrawal was killing him. Sam was closing down his show early due to the precipitous drop-off in sales that had occurred—people were fine with naked pictures of a senator's wife, but an ex-girlfriend who had killed herself was another matter, apparently. Luc couldn't bring himself to care.

All he cared about was seeing Marie again.

He called her cell phone daily—hourly, some days. But her phone merely rang once, then rolled over to voice mail. She wasn't returning his calls. But surely she had read his letter by now? It wasn't like her to simply not respond. He knew her better than that. *He did.*

Her asshole husband might have taken away her phone. That thought had crossed his mind more than once. When his imagination ran away with him, late at night in bed—alone—he feared that she was being held hostage by him, even. Was he really going to send her away for rehabilitation, as the news kept reporting?

Her husband was keeping an iron grip on her tonight, that was certain. Senator Macintyre steered her this way and that, never allowing more than a few inches of daylight between them. Marie smiled brightly at everyone they spoke to. But Luc could see the flatness in her eyes and it took all his willpower not to run to her and tear her away from that man. He was showing her off like she was a pony at a fair.

I would treat her like a goddess.

He looked around at the crowd, well-dressed, well-heeled. Happy. Had it been just mere weeks since he had felt that way? Marie had illuminated his life—no, his heart—and the future had looked brighter than it had in years. Now his heart was black as midnight again. And he had no patience for Sam's I-told-you-so's.

"Professor Marchand?" It was his former student, the curator. She had done well for herself, and that at least pleased him. A post at the National Gallery of Art? It was what he had wanted for all of his students, a position where they got to continue their study of art, of the greatest art. It was what he had hoped for himself, long ago. A life spent immersed in scholarship and learning.

"I'm about to start a tour of the exhibit. Would you like to join me?" she asked. "Feel free to chime in whenever you like. I remember all the stories you used to tell us about your grandfather and Stuart Davis."

Luc glanced back to look for Marie, but she was gone. Fear sliced through his heart. Had she left? How much of an appearance did a senator need to make at one of these events? She couldn't leave before he had a chance to speak with her and ask why she was ignoring his attempts to contact her. Perhaps she wanted his apology in person. He could understand that. A letter was cowardly. He was a coward, which he freely admitted. A braver man would have rescued her, somehow.

His former student was looking at him hopefully. She had been kind enough to get him an invitation, so he turned and followed her into the gallery. It was the least he could do.

"Ladies and gentlemen," she announced, "We have a special guest with us here tonight, Dr. Luc Marchand. Dr. Marchand's grandfather—the French artist Philippe Marchand—knew Stuart Davis during the year Davis spent in Paris."

The crowd turned to gawk at him, but he felt only her eyes on him. Marie and her husband were ensconced in the center of the group. That's where she had disappeared to. The senator pulled her closer to his side, and irritation flashed briefly in her eyes before her face settled back into a neutral blankness. The senator narrowed his eyes at Luc, in warning. The message was unmistakable. Stay away.

Luc followed the small crowd through the gallery, keeping to the periphery. He didn't want to provoke a confrontation with Marie's husband, and spoil his student's performance. But he kept his eyes on Marie, every fiber of his being aching with need. They had been together for nearly three months and to have her just yanked away from him—it was like those dreams where you found yourself naked and wandering around some city that looked by turns familiar and completely strange.

He loved her. He *belonged* to her, and his heart was utterly indifferent to any evidence to the contrary.

For her part, Marie listened in rapt attention to every word of the tour, despite her husband keeping her too far from the actual paintings to really see them. Luc would never do that, taunt her with pleasure that way. He would take her right up to the art, explain it to her, ask her opinion, share his passion for it with her.

The museum had managed to borrow enough paintings to show the progression of Davis' style, from Ashcan through his explorations of European modernism. The group was paused now before his Parisian paintings. The curator was speaking about the streetscapes and the delicacy of Davis' lines, which lent them an appearance that was as much drawing as painting.

"These always remind me of delicate pastries," the curator said. "Wouldn't you agree, Professor Marchand?"

Luc pretended to consider one of the paintings. "Or a delicate woman, perhaps. Yes?"

His former student was an excellent tour guide, enthusiastic about the art and affable in the face of elementary questions. When she deflected a more complicated question to Luc, he answered it easily. He missed lecturing, missed the give and take with students, missed seeing their eyes light up when they finally understood something, missed—yes—showing off his knowledge. Teaching suburban housewives to draw or helping high school kids polish up their portfolios for college was nice, but not the same as commanding a classroom.

When the tour ended, the group began to disperse. Luc lingered, hoping for an opportunity to speak to Marie. He saw his chance when a man in a tailored suit angled into Senator Macintyre and extended a hand to shake. The senator turned away from Marie.

Luc hurried over to her and before she could stop him, kissed her on each cheek. Not how he wanted to kiss her, of course, but with her husband mere inches away, it seemed the prudent course of action. When he drew back, her eyes were a mirror image of his—filled with longing and sadness. And desire. A frank, desperate desire.

"I have missed you." He wanted those four words to convey

everything he'd been feeling for weeks, even as he knew they were entirely inadequate.

"Night and day," she whispered in reply.

And then their moment was gone, too brief for Luc to say all that he had rehearsed, to ask her why she hadn't returned any of his calls. The reason was obvious now, anyway, especially with her husband reeling back around to face them.

"Good evening, Senator," Luc said politely. He had a pretty good idea of how this scene was going to play out—after all, this was a man who had drugged his wife and dumped her on a street corner—but Luc wouldn't be the one to start it.

Sure enough, Senator Macintyre extended his hand. But not to shake Luc's. When the senator's fist collided with his jaw, Luc staggered, stumbling backward. He heard shocked gasps in the background. He was willing to bet money that no punch had ever been thrown in the National Gallery before. There was a disgustingly self-satisfied look on the senator's face as he grabbed Marie's arm and jerked her toward him. She winced at the sudden pain and Luc lunged forward.

Punch me, you bastard, but don't hurt her.

He tried to put his body between Marie and her husband. If he was going to punch him again, he'd have to punch him in the back, hardly a manly move.

"You don't have to stay here," he said to her. "I'll take you home."

She looked at him sadly but, bafflingly, made no move to leave. "Luc. Just go away. Please."

Senator Macintyre butted Luc's side with his shoulder, attempting to reclaim Marie. Out of the corner of his eye, he saw a black-suited security guard running toward them. Getting arrested wasn't going to improve the situation. He gave Marie one last—confused—look, then let go of her. The crowd was parted behind him, having already sensed that he was going to lose this battle. Just as quickly, they swallowed her back up.

28

The Phillips Collection was unusually noisy. Dozens of teenagers scattered throughout the galleries, defying the attempts of their teachers and chaperones to stay together. Marie's eyes lit up at the sight of all the kids—and not just because she was remembering the joy of a field trip from her own days at school. She wove her way through the crowd of kids, to the staircase. That the museum was filled with rambunctious kids was a stroke of good luck for her. T. Rex had looked none too pleased when she pulled into the Metro station parking lot in Vienna. She was making him get out of his car and follow her on foot.

Well, if you're going to shadow me today, you're going to work for it.

Not to mention, the noise that dozens of teenagers could produce would make it harder for him to eavesdrop on Marie and Nishi. If Nishi showed, that was.

She trudged up the stairs in her jeans and winter coat, her mood torn between hope and despair. What was Luc doing at the National Gallery last night? She sighed. She knew why he'd been there. To see her. But it had been a dumb idea on his part, monumentally stupid. Now Richard was even angrier than he was before. He would have her watched more closely, which would only complicate her plans to get away. And she had to do it. It was her only option.

But god, for a moment there, it was wonderful to see him again. For an instant, she had imagined herself shoving people out of the way and running to him, grabbing his arm and the two of them running out of the museum and into a magically waiting cab. Speeding off into the sunset.

She had wanted to kiss those lips and run her fingers through that thick luscious hair ... unbutton that crisp white shirt and flatten her palms against his chest ... wrap her naked body around his and never let go. No one had ever made her feel the way Luc Marchand had, and she missed it.

Desperately.

But it couldn't be. She had to leave this area if she were ever going to have a life of her own. She'd meet someone else. She exhaled loudly at the top of the stairs to drown out the voices in her head shouting *no no no.*

"Damn. You need to get in shape."

Marie looked up just in time to see a security guard shoot Nishi a sharp look.

"Oh, right. Sorry." She glanced over at a pair of teenagers closely inspecting Elizabeth Calhoun's breasts. They gave no indication that they'd even heard Nishi's four-letter word, not that "damn" would arouse much attention from a high schooler anyway.

Marie nearly fainted with relief at the sight of her friend sitting on a bench in the middle of the room. "I didn't know whether you'd understand."

"Yeah well, I'm smart that way."

Nishi rose from the bench and Marie let herself fall into her friend's hug, her leather jacket and perfume-scented scarf warm and comforting. “I know you are. Is there a guy behind us?” She felt Nishi’s head tip up.

“Leather jacket, cargo pants, obnoxious earpiece? Yup. Richard’s having you followed?”

“That’s T. Rex.”

“He has a code name?”

“From me anyway. God, it’s good to see you again. I’ve been sequestered in that house.” Marie relaxed in Nishi’s embrace. She was going to miss her when she moved.

Nishi shot T. Rex a withering look, then laid an arm casually across Marie’s shoulder and pulled her over to a row of paintings. “Saw a photo of you and Dickhead from the National Gallery last night.” She squeezed Marie’s shoulder. “Killer blouse. But you’re losing too much weight.”

Marie sighed. “I’m afraid to eat anything that’s had any contact with him.”

“Makes sense, but still. You need to eat. How was last night?” Nishi chuckled.

“Please tell me that’s not out there.”

“In certain circles, alas. If you’re plugged into the right information sources. Which I am.”

“He’s an idiot, showing up there like that. Then Richard punched him, making it worse.”

She had wanted to cradle Luc in her arms, kiss the bruise blooming on his skin. But that might have gotten him killed, so she had told him to leave. The hurt look on his face had broken her heart. It had been almost enough to throw caution to the wind and run after him. But she couldn’t let emotion overrule her head, not if she wanted to escape Richard once and for all.

“He’s an idiot but you love him,” Nishi said.

“We’re both idiots. Can you do me a favor?”

“Anything, you know that.”

“Since I don’t have a clean phone, can you call him and tell him not to pull any more stunts like that? It just sends Richard's rage into the stratosphere."

"I've taken care of the first thing. But yes, I'll call him."

"What do you mean?"

"Shh. Later."

Nishi leaned the two of them in closer to the painting, Elizabeth Calhoun seated on a wooden chair, her head lowered, her face obscured by a then-fashionable cloche hat.

"So was this show the inspiration for ...?" Nishi spoke in a low voice, mindful of prying ears.

Marie sighed. "Yes. He needed new work for the show and I wanted him to paint me. It was a stupid idea."

"I don't think it was stupid. The paintings are gorgeous."

They were gorgeous. And modeling for Luc had made her feel gorgeous, too.

"They didn't work, though. Not the way I had hoped."

"Yeah, we were wrong about that making him refile." Nishi glanced over her shoulder to check on the whereabouts of T. Rex.

"I can't believe he'd rather have a wife in rehab than just divorce me."

"I hate to say it, but a wife in rehab gets him sympathy points. People will give him a pass on not accomplishing jack for his constituents because he's been dealing—" Nishi made air quotes with her fingers—"with his wife's health issues. You need to be more embarrassing than a wife in rehab."

"You'd think nude pictures would be pretty embarrassing."

"I would have thought so, too. His re-election prospects must be looking really grim. That's my only guess."

They began to stroll toward a group of smaller canvases, attaching themselves to the small cluster of teenagers gawking at them. As long as they stayed near other people, T. Rex would have a hard time hearing what they said.

The smaller paintings were close-ups of Elizabeth Calhoun's

body. A wrist and hand draped with an elegant diamond bracelet. A calf and the back of a knee. A long spine, punctuated with rose petals.

"These are hot," Nishi said. "I can see why you wanted him to paint you."

Modeling for Luc had been hot, even hotter than the recurring dream that had started the whole thing. It had made her feel mysterious and sophisticated, too. Special. Nothing had made her feel that way, until Luc.

The teenagers moved, en masse, down the wall several more feet. Nishi and Marie followed. They stopped in front of a medium-sized canvas, not as large as the big stately portraits on the wall behind them, but larger than the tiny ones they'd just left. Elizabeth Calhoun was lying in the grass, her face tilted up to the sky. A sheer scarf fell over her nose and closed eyes and gently parted lips. It was the one in which she could most readily be recognized.

Marie wondered why Elizabeth would take that risk, after going to such lengths to hide her identity in the others. Was she feeling more comfortable with Alistair? Had she made plans to leave her husband? Or did she just not give a fuck anymore?

"Why do you think she hid her face in all of these?" she asked Nishi.

"Well, the introduction back there said it was because her husband was a senator." Nishi studied the painting in front of them. "That's what I would have done, I guess."

"Is that what I should have done?"

Nishi responded without taking her eyes off the painting. "Only you know the answer to that question. But whatever it is, I don't think it should depend on Richard's reaction to it."

Then she launched into a dramatic reading of the letter hanging on the wall. Out of the corner of her eye, Marie could see T. Rex just a few feet behind them.

"My most beloved A, you must think clearly about this. I will survive, but they will ruin you," Nishi read.

If I stay, Richard will ruin Luc. There was no question in her mind about that.

She was leaving her heart behind in DC. Who had ever said that before? Washington wasn't the kind of place where you lost your heart. Your soul, maybe. Your moral compass, certainly. But not your heart. It wasn't that kind of city.

Maybe it was best to put some distance between herself and her heart anyway. It might hurt less if it was no longer with her. But damn, it hurt now and seeing him last night had only made it worse.

"I'm going to move away," Marie said.

Nishi looked at her in surprise.

"You think that will make him file again?"

"I don't know. I guess I'm hoping that if I'm not around, just not an option, he'll go ahead and marry Maya. He's still seeing her anyway."

"And you're going to just walk away from Luc?"

Marie shrugged. "I don't know what else to do. If I stay, I'm going to find myself drugged and waking up in rehab. I'll be stuck with Richard at least until the election, after which he won't need me anymore. And Luc will have moved on by then." Her voice cracked as tears threatened to spill. "It's just not meant to be."

"Hey." Nishi turned and gently took Marie's face in her hands. "You get to decide if it's meant to be. After you move, call him. If he loves you, he'll come see you. These are all decisions you get to make, love."

Marie shrugged again. "That still leaves us living in two separate places."

"You need to really force Richard's hand on this. Just running away might not be enough. He can just spin that as his wife went on another bender, blacked out and woke up in Phoenix. You need to *humiliate* him. Do something that is so beyond the pale he won't want you back."

"Jefferson High students, bus leaves in ten minutes." A chaperone appeared in the doorway of the gallery and the teenagers—their cover—began moving toward the exit.

T. Rex stood up from the bench where he was sitting, sensing the opportunity the exodus of students presented. Marie and Nishi were about to be alone in the gallery. But he was outmatched in Nishi. She was a professional, too.

"Are you hungry?" Nishi asked, checking her watch. "The café here isn't bad."

They strode arm in arm past T. Rex and went downstairs to Tryst. Marie bought sandwiches while Nishi scanned the dining area for the best table. When Marie turned away from the register, Nishi had settled in at a small table in the corner, fronted by two occupied tables. T. Rex wouldn't be able to get close enough to listen in. Nishi gave him a little finger wave.

Marie dug into her sandwich. She was hungry all the time these days because she was afraid to eat at home and it was a hassle to run to the store or the deli for every meal.

"I might buy you a second sandwich, the way you're inhaling that one," Nishi observed.

"Sorry," she mumbled through a mouthful of chicken caesar wrap. "I didn't bother with breakfast this morning." She chewed and swallowed, one eye on T. Rex who was impatiently giving the stink eye to everyone sitting at a closer table. "So where do I go? New York is not far enough away, I'm thinking."

Nishi took a long swallow of iced tea, considering the question. "L.A. or San Francisco. Dallas, maybe. A place that has bigger fish to fry than you. It can't be a small town with a two-bit police department that will jump when a pissed off senator calls and says 'jump.' Not Chicago, either. They'll trade you to Richard for something."

"San Francisco. I might like that. Not that I've been, but I've seen pictures." She smiled. "Fly or drive?"

"Fly, definitely. You don't want every cop from here to the west coast looking for your car. Just dump it at the airport and go. I know *a ton* of people in San Francisco. Friends from college, an aunt and uncle, a bunch of cousins. You can stay with somebody until you get on your feet. Plus, we have an office out there. Smaller than DC but I might be able to get you an interview there."

"It's expensive there, isn't it?"

"Yup. But what price for your freedom?"

Just my heart.

Nishi's phone buzzed. She glanced at it quickly. "I've got to get back. But I need to use the ladies room first. Care to join me?" She tapped her phone with her finger, before putting it back in her purse. "I've got an early Christmas present for you."

T. Rex followed them to the ladies room, where Nishi turned and addressed him directly. "Ladies only. Sorry guy. See you in a minute."

Inside, Nishi flipped the lock. "I wouldn't put it past him." She pulled Marie to the back of the room and reached into her purse. She pulled out a cell phone in a black case.

"Here. Your new phone, in Imran's name. We picked one that's identical to your other phone, but don't let Richard get too close to it. Just in case."

Marie threw her arms around her friend. "I owe you, I owe you, I owe you."

"Nonsense." Nishi extricated herself from Marie's death grip. "This is what friends do. Help each other go on the lam."

29

Christmas Eve dawned sunny and bright, with a blinding white winter sun. Melting snow dripped past the windows. If ever there was a candidate for worst Christmas ever, this was going to be it.

When she came downstairs, Marie was surprised to find Richard standing in the kitchen, pouring coffee into a mug. She never saw him at home in the morning. She assumed that was because he was spending his nights at Maya's apartment, which was—granted—more convenient to the Hill than Great Falls. She took in his suit and tie.

"Working on Christmas Eve?"

"Yes, goddammit," he spit out like *thanks for reminding me.* "We need to get an emergency spending bill nailed down before the end of the year. Why we have to debate the debt ceiling every five fucking minutes, I don't know."

Because you're in Congress and that's all Congress does these days? But she held her tongue. It served no purpose to get Richard riled up.

He pulled a second mug from the dishwasher, filled it with coffee and held it out to Marie. She took it, warily and with zero intention of drinking anything that had been touched by Richard. Once burned, twice shy and all that.

"There are bagels on the counter," he added. "I put the cream cheese back in the fridge."

Again, no shot in hell of her eating those. Was he doing this on purpose? Taunting her with food?

Just act normal.

"So my parents are expecting us tomorrow morning. Then we're going to your family in the afternoon?" She already knew this to be the case—her mother had been over it with her multiple times already—but she needed to lull Richard into complacency, if she could. Make him think she was "with the program" now, had come around to his position on things.

"That's the plan. Provided I'm not in session tomorrow, too."

He brushed past her on his way to the garage. He never did take a drink of his coffee, curiously enough. As soon as she heard the garage door open and his car start, she poured both cups down the drain. Then she leaned back against the cold granite countertop and looked around. How had this place ever felt like home? How had she ever imagined raising children here? Or even raising children with *him*? And why couldn't her mother see how arctic cold he was?

She walked through the first floor. When they bought the house, she had been so excited to move in. The house was gorgeous! The kitchen was huge! With pro-style appliances and a walk-in pantry! The great room had a soaring ceiling and a massive, custom stone fireplace. She had imagined years of family celebrations in that room.

How easily she had been taken in by appearances ... by mere *things.* None of that mattered to her now. She hadn't been any happier in the beautiful house than she had been in her tiny apartment. Less happy, actually. The house was a perfect metaphor for her marriage. All shiny on the surface, hollow on the inside.

She peered out one of the front bay windows. T. Rex sat in his SUV, his earpiece cable caressing his cheek, as usual. She almost felt sorry for him, having to sit out in the cold, babysitting her on Christmas Eve. Did he have a wife or a girlfriend? Kids? What a crappy job he'd chosen. Maybe Richard would give him Christmas Day off.

She was hungry and dying for coffee, but it was cold out and she'd rather wait to venture out until closer to lunch time. Traffic would be nuts on Christmas Eve. Best to deal with it just once. And she wasn't up to toying with T. Rex today. She suspected he hadn't reported the little museum trip to Richard because Richard had said nothing to her about it. Richard certainly would have wanted to know what she and Nishi had talked about, and T. Rex didn't know. Maybe he didn't want to admit that to Richard.

She sunk into the oversized sofa. Just six weeks ago, she'd been entertaining the idea of spending Christmas Eve with Luc at his home in Middleburg. They'd cook dinner together or maybe go out to the Red Fox Inn, his favorite restaurant, then spend the evening in front of a roaring fire in the fireplace. And "by spend the evening" she meant ravish each other's body into the wee hours of the morning. She had even pictured snow falling outside. A white Christmas. If you're going to dream, why not go all out?

Now there would be none of that. Luc would probably spend Christmas with Sam, who would chew him out over the show. Marie would spend the day pretending to be happy with Richard, in front of her parents and his. She hadn't even bought anyone presents. The prospect of shopping with T. Rex in tow hadn't exactly put her in the Christmas spirit.

Her sketchpad and pencil were lying on the floor, right where she'd left them last night. She picked them up and gazed around the room, looking for something to draw. After a month, there wasn't much left that had escaped her pencil. Luc would be proud of her. Her heart clenched at the thought. Even though her lessons had ended, she continued to work on it, to try and "see" the way he did. She would be taking that with her into her new life, if nothing else.

When she got settled into San Francisco, she would write him a letter and thank him for all he'd done for her. Even though it had ended horribly, she was grateful for the time he'd spent with her ... and for all he'd taught her. But she wouldn't invite him to visit. A clean break would be easiest, for Marie at least. If he visited, she would just have to say "goodbye" at the end of the visit. She didn't think she could bear that.

She tapped her pencil against the blank page. Something was off about the great room and she suddenly realized what it was. There was no Christmas tree. Richard hadn't gotten one this year. In the past, they had always put it right there, in the corner next to the fireplace. She wouldn't have predicted that this would be the last straw, no Christmas tree. It was though. Hot tears began to spill over her lower lashes, and she let them.

What a crappy, shitty, sucky year it had been. First, the divorce. Then, no divorce. She lost her job—with her own mother for god's sake. Then she got her job back. Then she lost it again. Her husband drugged her, then told the whole world it was her fault and she needed rehab.

And she had fallen in love. Oh yeah, that too. Really, truly fallen in love for the first time.

She needed a good cry—a long, heaving, soul-wracking cry—and she let herself have it. Why hadn't she thought to cry before? It felt good to cry. And terrible. And exhausting all at the same time. But she let herself do it, sobbing until the top pages of her sketchpad were buckling beneath the weight of her tears.

When there were no more tears to heave out and she was cried dry, she took the sketchpad upstairs into the guest bathroom. She sat down on the edge of the cold porcelain bathtub, looked at her pathetic face in the mirror and began to draw on the wet paper.

She drew the puffy eyes. The splotchy cheeks. The mouth that was swollen into a vague parody of lips. The forehead creased with worry and fear and disappointment.

For a few brief weeks, her life had felt great. Really, truly great. Then it all went to hell.

The drawing wasn't bad, if you overlooked the subject, she thought. Maybe it was easy to capture ugliness. Ugly was simple, raw, elemental. It didn't change. It didn't have to. She let the sketchbook slip from her fingers and fall into the tub. Then she crawled back into bed.

When she awoke, it was grey outside, the morning's bright sun gone. She squinted at the alarm clock. Three pm. Her stomach rumbled. She was starving. She had skipped both breakfast and lunch. She stretched her arms and legs, listening to the rest of the house, trying to determine whether Richard was home yet. But all was quiet.

She had to go out for food. If she waited any longer, the Christmas Eve panic shopping traffic would make it impossible to get anywhere. She changed out of her sleep-rumpled clothes into more presentable jeans and a red sweater—her one nod to the holiday—then hit the road. The sight of T. Rex's head snapping up as she drove past him on the street drew a smile from her. He must have been napping if he had missed the sound of the garage door opening. He recovered quickly though—she gave him credit for that— and easily tailed her to the gourmet grocery store.

The store buzzed with a mixture of holiday cheer and holiday stress. She hurried past people picking through the turkeys and hams, squeezing freshly-baked loaves of bread, and trying to make up their minds about cookies and pies. Christmas carols floated through the air, while the red-coated Salvation Army folks rang their cheery bells just inside the door.

Marie headed straight for the salad bar, where she built a huge salad with all the toppings. Chicken, bleu cheese, avocado, walnuts, olives. She piled it all on. At the flower shop, she picked out two large bouquets of flowers—one for her parents, one for Richard's. They would serve as her gifts, even though they all deserved lumps of coal this year. A dump truck's worth of coal, in fact.

At the bakery, she perused the stacks of cakes frosted in red, green and blue; cases of neatly-arranged muffins in every imaginable flavor; and exquisite chocolates, dark and gleaming like that one last chance to be naughty. She selected two tarts laden with berries and carefully set those into her cart with the flowers. Her mother would be mildly offended by the gift. Eileen Witherspoon prided herself on her holiday desserts, but Marie was mindful of the facade she needed to maintain tomorrow. Both families would be watching her like a hawk. *Normal. Everything has to look normal.*

She was at the very edge of the bakery department when she suddenly pulled up short, causing T. Rex to bump into her from behind.

"Sorry," he mumbled.

She ignored him. *Cupcakes.* Cupcakes were like a third party in Washington, practically. Georgetown Cupcakes. Cake Love. Baked and Wired. She and Nishi considered themselves to be connoisseurs of them all.

The store had a decent selection: salted caramel, lemon coconut, strawberry buttercream, red velvet. She stood there for a moment, trying to choose.

What the hell. It's Christmas.

She had the girl behind the counter package up a dozen, six to a box. She would eat one box after her not-so-healthy salad and then ... champagne. She would drink a glass or two of champagne tonight and gaze upon an imaginary Christmas tree. Those were her big Christmas Eve plans.

She glanced back at T. Rex. She would give him the other box of cupcakes, as a Christmas gift. He could take it home to his wife and kids, if he had any. Or just sit in his car and eat them himself.

A tiny bit of Christmas spirit was beginning to seep into her Grinchy heart.

"There's one more thing I need to get," she said to him.

"Take your time, ma'am. I got all night."

She wove her way between the oak wine barrels and stacks of wooden crates. She stopped to eye the specials written in white chalk on the blackboard. A local photographer was selling prints of his trip to Tuscany, creating a small traffic jam of shoppers around his table.

Her eyes scanned the shelves of foil-capped bottles, sparkling beneath festive strands of white lights. The labels were gibberish to her. She knew nothing about champagne.

The ache in her heart, which had been dulled temporarily by her incipient holiday spirit, flared to life again. Luc would know what to buy. He would have strolled right in here, gone straight to the bottle he wanted and plucked it from the shelf like he was a damn sommelier.

The one thing she wanted for Christmas was the one thing she couldn't have: Luc Marchand. Her holiday spirit was deflating so rapidly, there was about to be a sonic boom. The bottles blurred. Apparently she was not as all cried out as she had thought. She took several deep breaths and bit her lip almost to the point of blood. The pain cleared her mind, not entirely, but enough. When she felt composed, she turned to T. Rex.

"Do you know anything about champagne?"

He looked startled at being directly addressed again. "No, ma'am. Not really." His face flushed slightly.

"It must really suck for you to have to work on Christmas Eve."

Surprise flashed in his eyes, but he recovered himself quickly. "A little. But I'm being paid."

"Well, that's more than I can say."

She turned back to the shelf. "Eeeny meeny miney mo." She pointed at a bottle and added it to her cart.

At the express lane, she turned to him again. "If it were up to me," she said, "I'd give you the night off."

"It's not up to you though, is it?" His professional demeanor was returning.

She shrugged. "Richard probably won't be home tonight anyway. I won't tell if you leave."

He gave her a small smile. "Nice try there. But no."

"I could drag you all over the place tonight. Back to the museum, eh? How did you like that?"

"The art was lovely, ma'am. I imagine the museum is closed tonight, though."

"I could make you go to Samantha Smith's gallery. Bet you haven't seen *that* show." She laughed bitterly.

"Actually, I did check that out. Your husband is a lucky man."

Marie felt her face grow hot. "Maybe you could put that in your report when you're through. That he's a lucky man."

"I'll take that into consideration." He nodded toward the register behind her. "Your turn, ma'am."

30

Marie settled in at the kitchen island with her salad and laptop. She typed in "noradsanta.org" to track the big man's progress around the world. Someday, she'd be sitting with her own children, eating cookies and drinking milk, and watching the little animated sleigh and reindeers zip from country to country. Next stop, Rome!

She had to believe that was in the cards for her, with someone. She just had to.

After an hour of shoveling lettuce into her mouth and mindlessly watching Santa, she looked up at the clock. Six o'clock. Congress had to have let out for Christmas by now, not that Marie expected to see Richard until tomorrow morning. She pulled up the J Street Chronicle to see what fab dinner party Maya and Richard were going to that evening. Would it be black tie? At a fancy restaurant—she frowned at the remains of her own salad wilting in its plastic clamshell case—or a multi-million dollar townhouse in Georgetown? She was living vicariously through ... her husband. Good grief.

If he wants to send me to rehab, at least I should get some good parties in exchange. Richard, of course, did not work that way.

There were no photos of fab parties on Maya's blog, however. Not yet anyway. Instead, there was a grainy photograph of Marie standing on a street corner in Foggy Bottom, her bookbag slung over her shoulder, looking tired and haggard. It had been taken one evening after she left class, not that the caption noted that.

No, the caption said something else altogether.

Marie Witherspoon, wife of Sen. Richard Macintyre of Pennsylvania, was admitted to a rehabilitation facility outside Pittsburgh today. A spokesperson for the senator said that Ms. Witherspoon would remain in the facility for an undetermined amount of time. "Doctors are still evaluating treatment options."

Marie pinched her arm. No, still here. Not dreaming. Last she checked, she had not in fact been admitted to rehab *today.* She wondered where Maya had gotten that information. No reason for Richard to lie to her about that, not that Marie could see.

Then she glanced at the header on the post, and her heart stopped. *December 25.* This posting was dated for tomorrow. She gripped the cold granite edge of the countertop to steady her. She was swaying on the stool. Maya had post-dated the article. Probably because she planned on doing normal holiday activities tomorrow and figured no one was reading the J Street Chronicle on Christmas Eve.

Marie stared at the words on the computer screen until they began to waver. She looked at the two bouquets sitting in vases on the island. She wasn't going to her parents' home tomorrow morning. Nor was she going to the Macintyres' home in the afternoon. She was headed to rehab.

Merry-fucking-Christmas.

Well, that explained the lack of a Christmas tree. Hell, Richard probably wasn't even planning to go with her. He'd drug her and hand her over to T. Rex with driving directions. And to think she'd been concerned about him missing Christmas with his wife and kids. When they were in the store, chatting, he'd *known.*

So this was it.

She jumped off the stool and dug through her purse for her new phone. The Batphone, Nishi called it. She hit Nishi's name–the only name—in the contacts list. *Please answer. Please.* Tears were welling. *Please.* Her call rolled over to voice mail. She left a tearful, hiccuping message that was surely unintelligible on the other end and ran to Richard's bedroom. She shouldn't have been, but still she was stunned to see a small suitcase on the luggage stand in his closet—packed with some of her clothes. Jeans, sneakers, tee shirts, underwear. Underwear! Who had packed this and when? Her mother? T. Rex?

She had to leave.

She stood stock still in the closet. *Think, Marie, think. You need to leave. So you need to pack a bag. A different bag. You'll need to get past T. Rex.* She leaned against the doorjamb and took a deep breath. *You need to find the rohypnol pills. They have to be around here somewhere, if he plans to use them on me tomorrow.* She felt up his suit jackets, checking the pockets. Nothing. She ran out to the bed, unmade, and yanked open the nightstand drawers. She pulled out each drawer and upended it, dumping the contents onto the carpet. She tossed aside loose change, parking garage receipts, guitar picks, ATM slips, photos of Maya.

Wait. She turned those back over. *Nude* photos of Maya. She slipped those into the back pocket of her jeans. They might come in handy. But no pill bottle. She didn't even really know what she was looking for. She had no idea what color or size or shape rohypnol pills were.

She rubbed her temples, trying to think like Richard. Where would he be? What would he be doing? *In the kitchen, pouring me something to drink.* The kitchen was too obvious a hiding place, but ...

She ran down the hall and then down the grand curving staircase to the first floor. Richard's study. She yanked open more drawers, in his desk, his filing cabinet, the cupboards beneath the bookcases. Nothing! She wailed in frustration.

She scanned the room. It had to be in the house somewhere. And she was running out of time. Then her eyes stopped on the small wooden box tucked away on a bookshelf, the kind of box you'd dump a handful of change into. The box was exotic and expensive-looking, with an intricately designed inlay on the top. She'd always suspected it to be a gift from Maya.

She lifted the lid gingerly, like it was about to explode. Inside lay a smattering of coins. And a clear plastic sandwich bag of pills. She unzipped the bag and pulled one out. It was white and round, with no identifying marks on it. But this had to be it.

She ran back out to the kitchen and uncorked the bottle of champagne. Shame to waste a perfectly good bottle like this, but hell she didn't even know whether it was any good or not. She poured some into a lovely crystal flute—these were new, she noted—and dropped the pill in. While it dissolved, she pulled one of the cupcake boxes from the grocery bag and wrote "Merry Christmas from the Macintyres!" on the lid. Then she carried the box and the glass out to T. Rex's SUV.

A tiny part of her was horrified at what she was about to do. Then she pictured herself squashing that tiny part like a bug.

T. Rex looked up, warily, as she approached his car. He rolled down the window.

"Merry Christmas," she said as she reached through the window and laid the box of cupcakes on the passenger seat. "If I can't give you the night off, at least I can give you dessert."

"Uh, thanks."

It was an awkward moment in a "friendship" full of awkward moments, she thought.

"And this." She held out the champagne. "Richard will probably want that glass back, though."

He nodded. "Understood."

Marie turned to leave.

"Merry Christmas, Ms. Witherspoon."

She glanced back at him but he was already sipping from the glass.

Merry Christmas to me, too.

Upstairs in the guest room, Marie threw clothes willy-nilly into every bag and suitcase she owned. She would have to leave most of her wardrobe behind, but so be it. She lugged them downstairs to the garage and stashed them in the trunk. Then she returned to the guest room for her bookbag. She had no idea when —or if—she'd ever resume work on her degree. It had been aborted twice already now. Maybe that just wasn't meant to be. She stopped at the island and closed her laptop. She unzipped the bookbag to slide it in.

She was closing the zipper when she noticed something sticking out of the top of one of her textbooks. A grey envelope. She tugged it loose. Nice paper, stationery. She turned it over. Her heart stopped for the second time that evening. Her name was spelled out in Luc's spidery handwriting.

Marie.

She could hear him say it, in that sexy French accent of his.

How did this get in here? There was no way he had been in Richard's house. She tore it open to find a letter, handwritten.

My dearest Marie. Who was the genius who decided that there should be 24 tedious hours in every day? And 365 tedious days in every year? And every tedious year of the rest of my life ... without you. I can't believe that must be so and yet your friend Nishi tells me I must leave you alone. I have caused trouble for you, my love. I apologize. From the sorry depths of my heart, I apologize. I never meant to cause all these difficulties. I should never have painted you. I should have known better. Yet, I don't entirely regret doing so and for that, I am also sorry. Your husband is the vilest sort of man. I apologize for saying that, as well. But I am angry and sad. Hurt. My heart is not merely broken, but crushed. I hope he tires of you so that you may come back to me. I belong to you, Marie. Please never forget that. I love you deeply -- forever your Luc.

He was beautiful even in writing. He had poured his heart out to her. Her eyes misted over. But she still had no idea when he'd written it or how he had gotten it inside her bag. She turned it over, looking for a date, but there was nothing. It was a mystery.

Yet, I don't entirely regret doing so.

I don't regret it either.

Even though it had royally screwed over both their lives, she couldn't say she wished it never happened. Those weekends with him had been the best moments of her life. The absolute best moments and she wouldn't trade them for anything, nor would she ever forget them. And the paintings? They should have been kept private, just for the two of them, but modeling for Luc had changed her. And for the better. It had forced her to open up, to trust someone, to let someone *see* her.

That's what she wanted from here on out. For other people to see her—unafraid, open, loved.

She slipped the letter into the bookbag again and left Richard's house for the last time. She backed her car slowly down the driveway, holding her breath as she turned around and came abreast of the SUV. But T. Rex remained slumped over the steering wheel, out cold. At least he was in his car and not lying on a street corner.

She pulled out of the neighborhood and headed west. It would be west all the way to the Pacific Ocean. She had no airline ticket so she planned to drive for awhile, until Ohio or Indiana maybe. Then she'd catch a flight from there.

But she had one stop to make first. She would drive to Luc's house in Middleburg and leave him an apology of her own. She wasn't sure what to write yet, but she had a few miles to compose her words. Luc wouldn't be there anyway. He would be at Sam's house for Christmas Eve. For Christmas Day, too, in all likelihood. Sam was a good friend to Luc. She took care of him. She'd probably warned him about Marie. Too bad he hadn't listened. It would have saved him a ton of grief.

Traffic got lighter the further west she drove. No shopping malls out this far, few strip malls, even. She still checked the rearview mirror every few minutes, convinced she'd see T. Rex's SUV or the flashing lights of a police car behind her. It wasn't until she was off the highway and on the twisting country road that lead to Luc's house that she began to relax. Just a tiny bit. There were a lot of miles between her and San Francisco and a lot could go wrong, but she was out of Richard's house. Unescorted. That was progress.

She turned into Luc's driveway and parked in front of the house. The windows were dark, as expected. Not even the front light was on. She composed her own apology letter beneath the dull wash of the car's interior lighting. It was nowhere near as nicely written as his had been, but it would have to do. It was dangerous to linger here long—Richard surely knew where Luc lived.

A light snow had begun to fall. The sky was moonless. Luc's property looked different in the dark, and in the winter. The last time she'd been here had been Thanksgiving, and the bright autumn leaves had been hanging tenaciously to branches that were now bare. She stepped out of the car, looked at the dark house, then followed the old red brick path around to the back one last time. She would tuck the letter into the door of the studio.

A light glowed behind the studio's windows. A faint light, but light all the same. She peered through a window, but all she could see were vague shadows of furniture, Luc's easel, boxes stacked about.

On a whim, she tried the door. The knob turned easily in her hand and she hesitated. As someone whose own life had been infringed upon so many times, trespassing wasn't something she took lightly. But he wasn't home, she reasoned, and she would stay just a minute. Just long enough to leave the note and look around one final time.

The memories hit her as soon as she stepped into the dim, quiet studio. They slammed into her like an unexpected wave, the force of them taking her breath away. She stood there, letting them pummel her. She had learned so much in this room. Not just about art, but about men ... about herself. About love. She blinked back hot tears and looked around. The light was coming from a floor lamp, partially hidden behind a stack of boxes. Luc probably forgot to turn it off when he left for Sam's.

Boxes were everywhere, she noticed. He'd been packing. The old battered work table that normally was topped with cans of brushes and half-squeezed tubes of paint, empty coffee mugs and paint rags was completely bare. The studio had never looked so neat ... or so empty.

There was a sharp pain in her chest, like someone had reached in and squeezed her heart. Luc was leaving, too. Suddenly she hated Richard with renewed fervor. Luc had left Charlottesville after Grace. And now he was leaving here ... after her.

She jumped when she heard a low snuffling, like the sound of someone waking up briefly before falling back into sleep. She peered harder into the gloom of the empty studio. There, tucked behind the easel, was Luc sitting at the tiny metal bistro table. His shoulders were hunched over, his head resting on his forearms on the table.

"Luc?" she whispered as she tiptoed closer.

Two bottles of French wine sat on the table, but no glasses. She picked them up. Empty. His breathing was heavy and labored.

"Luc," she said again, this time a little louder. But he slept on. He was sleeping off a drunk, she realized.

She pulled the letter from her purse and dug out a pen, then sat down at the table, across from him. On the back of the letter, she sketched his sleeping form, tentatively at first, then with more confidence. His bedhead of hair, the shadows on his muscled forearms, the tension in his shoulders. She caught it all on paper.

She folded the letter in half again and placed it right in front of him. It would be the first thing he saw when he woke up.

She was halfway to the door when Luc's breathing stuttered again, and he lifted his head. He looked across the studio at Marie, rubbed his eyes, then put his head back down.

"Luc," she said quietly.

He looked up again. "Marie." He rubbed his eyes again and shook his head. "Oh la la. I've never been this drunk before. Not to the point of hallucinations."

He tried to stand, but immediately fell back into the chair. She ran to him.

"Don't stand. You're—"

"Shit-faced. Isn't that what you Americans call it?" He covered his head with his palms. "Why did I do this?"

She wrapped her arms around him from behind, laid her cheek against his warm back. She breathed him in, and her body started humming. This was all it took. Just a second's touch and she was caught up in him. Her head may have been trying to forget everything they had shared in this room, but her body was stubbornly remembering.

He touched the sheet of paper. "What's this?" He spun it around and regarded it for a long moment. "You've been practicing. Bon." He unfolded the paper and read.

Beneath her cheek, the rise and fall of his chest slowed. He was holding his breath.

"How did you get the letter into Richard's house?"

"Hmm?"

"I found your letter today. But how did you get inside the house?"

"I didn't. I went to your apartment when I got back from New York and found movers taking away your things. I put it in your bag."

"Wait. It's been in there since November?"

"Yes. I waited and waited for you to call."

"I haven't opened that bag in weeks." She pressed her forehead into the back of his neck, inhaling, taking the warm masculine scent of his skin deep into her lungs. God, she had missed him. "I missed my finals."

She felt him inhale sharply.

"I'm sorry, Marie. I am so sorry about all of this. I never *never* intended—"

"It was my fault, too. You didn't fully appreciate my situation. But I did. Or I should have. And I dragged you into it anyway."

"I don't recall much dragging, ma chérie. I think I dove in headfirst."

He tried to spin around to face her, but stopped. His face contorted in pain.

"Don't move. Let me."

She carried the other chair over to his side and sat down, her knees cradled inside his. She pulled his hands into hers. His eyes were shadowed and rimmed in red. He was only a day or two away from a full-blown beard.

He was beautiful.

"Are you leaving?" she asked.

He glanced at the boxes behind her. "For awhile."

"Can I ask where?"

"Paris, to stay with my sister."

"I forgot that you had a sister." It was hard to imagine Luc with anything so ordinary as siblings.

"I forgot you had a husband."

His words knocked the wind out of her and she stared at him, speechless. Was he mad at her for that?

"You did know," she said quietly, when words returned to her.

"I thought he was on his way out."

"I'm sorry!" Tears spilled down her cheeks.

"Ma chérie. I'm not angry with you." He tugged her onto his lap. "I'm angry with your husband." He wiped tears away with his fingers. "Don't cry."

But she couldn't stop. Once she started, all the stress and disappointment of the past month poured out of her. He let her cry into his shoulder and held her shaking body in his arms. As she sobbed, all she could think of was that she never wanted to leave his embrace. When finally she stopped, he spoke again.

"What are you doing here?" He looked toward the door. "Nishi told me you are being followed."

"I drugged him."

"Drugged who?"

"The guy Richard hired to babysit me. I found the pills and put one in a glass of champagne and gave it to him."

He looked at her with a combination of disbelief and respect. "Remind me to always open the champagne around you."

"I'm leaving, too, Luc. If I stay, he's going to put me in rehab tomorrow. On Christmas."

"Oh, Marie," he breathed. "Tomorrow? Where are you going?"

"San Francisco. Nishi knows people out there. And it's far away. Away from Richard."

He lifted her hand to his lips and kissed her palm, his breath tickling her skin. How was it that something as simple as her hand being kissed could send her stomach into flip flops? She could sit here for hours and be content with just his lips on her palm.

"Come with me to Paris. It's ... San Francisco on the Seine."

She made a weak attempt at laughter. "They don't call it that."

"No. They don't. But it's farther away than San Francisco."

His tongue lightly caressed the sensitive skin between the base of her fingers. She closed her eyes and gave in to the sensation.

"Have you ever been to Paris?" he asked when he reached her pinkie finger.

Marie couldn't answer. She couldn't take her eyes off his mouth, sucking her finger in and out. What made her finger so lucky? She wanted those lips on hers. It had been too long ...

"Kiss me, Luc."

He looked up from her hand. "If you come to Paris with me."

Paris with Luc. The thought made her breath catch in her throat. He curled her fingers into a gentle fist, then kissed her knuckles slowly, one by one.

"You're blackmailing me for a kiss?"

He kissed the inside of her wrist and every vein in her body lit up. She'd forgotten that he could do this, touch one tiny part of her and make her feel it everywhere. He trailed kisses up her arm.

"Mmm, Paris is hardly blackmail."

"What would I do there?"

"I'm sure we'll think of something," he murmured against the soft interior of her elbow. "It's not hard to find things to do in Paris."

She closed her eyes. It was easy to see the two of them there, together. Ridiculously easy, in fact. Strolling hand in hand down wide boulevards, ducking into cafés, kissing beneath the Eiffel Tower. Luc would show her the Louvre, the Mona Lisa. The Mona Lisa ... that right there nearly sealed the deal. Paris! A giddy excitement bubbled up inside. An hour ago, she thought she'd never see Luc again. And now she was going to Paris with him!

"Say yes, Marie. I want you to see my country, and I want to be the one to show it to you."

She threw her arms around him.

"Yes."

His lips had barely brushed hers with the promised kiss when she heard the faint ringing of her phone.

"I have to get that."

"Mmm. Why?" He nuzzled her nose with his.

"It's Nishi."

"And how can you know that?"

"She's the only one who has the number."

He released her, reluctantly. By the time she dug the phone out of her purse it had stopped ringing. She tapped call back.

"Where are you? I just got your message." Nishi sounded frantic.

"I'm at Luc's."

"Luc's? I thought you were leaving."

"I made a stop on the way."

Luc was walking uncertainly toward her. She frowned and held out her arm to steady him. He snatched the phone away.

"I'm taking her to Paris."

Marie snatched the phone back.

"He's drunk, isn't he?" Nishi said. "Don't let him drive anywhere." Nishi's voice was loud enough for Luc to hear.

"Not drive. Fly," he shouted at the phone, wincing at the volume of his voice.

"You have to get out of the area tonight, Marie. Luc's house will be the first place Richard looks. Does Luc have tickets yet?"

Marie's heart clenched in panic. She looked at Luc. "Do you have tickets to Paris?"

"One. For me. For next week."

She turned back to Nishi. "No, he doesn't."

"Put him on the phone."

Marie handed Luc the phone. A deluge of French poured out of it as soon as he held it to his ear. Luc replied in kind, wincing some more under Nishi's withering tirade. After several minutes, he handed the phone back to Marie, a sheepish look on his face.

"We won't be able to get a flight out tonight," Marie said. "It's Christmas Eve. And getting late. And I don't know if he'd even be allowed on a plane the way he is now."

She watched Luc stumble into the kitchen and begin grinding coffee beans. He grimaced at the noise.

"Sit tight. I need to make a call," Nishi said.

"Wait—" But Nishi was already gone.

She went into the kitchen. "Here let me." She took over the making of the coffee. "Go sit down."

They weren't flying anywhere tonight with him two sheets to the wind, not unless she could get him sobered up. But she had to leave before Richard came looking for her. And this time, he probably wouldn't be content with merely punching Luc in the face. They could drive—or rather, she could drive—and get out of the area, then fly out of another city's airport tomorrow. More people would be looking for her then, though. A senator's wife? Who was she kidding? They would never get through security. Tonight was their only shot at flying, and you couldn't drive to Paris. She was dizzy trying to think through all their options, and the roadblocks to each.

The coffee brewed, hissing and spitting. It matched the sound her heart was making, deflating rapidly. There was no way they were going to Paris together, not if she had to leave tonight. And she did. What she had done this evening, it could only be done once to Richard. She'd had the element of surprise on her side. Richard was not the sort of person to be surprised twice.

She followed Luc to the table and straddled his lap.

"I believe you still owe me a kiss," she said. "Even though I feel like I am taking advantage of someone who's—"

"Incapacitated?" He enunciated each syllable slowly. "I am always incapacitated around you, Marie."

She leaned in, pressing her lips to his. "You hide it well, then."

She wound her fingers into his hair and pulled his mouth hard against hers. His hands slid down her back and cupped her bottom, pulling her in closer. He kissed her back like his very survival depended on it and she let herself sink into the kiss helplessly. She had missed this fiercely. How had she gone an entire month without it? Her skin tingling, her insides going all hot and liquidy in the way only he could make them.

More importantly, how was she going to live without it in the future?

"You have spoiled me for other men," she murmured against his lips.

"That was always the plan."

Her phone rang again.

Luc grumbled but let her go.

"Okay," Nishi launched right in. "You're set. I have a client taking his private jet to Paris tonight. His daughter is in school there and he is spending the holidays with her. He has agreed to let you two stow away. You need to be at the private aviation terminal at ten. He knows Luc is a little ... well, you know."

Marie was speechless, partly because her brain was still addled from the kiss and partly because what Nishi was saying couldn't ... *they were going to Paris.*

"Hello-o-o. Marie? Are you there?"

"You're getting us out?" she whispered.

Luc beckoned to her from the chair. She went to him and sat sideways on his lap, leaned into his arms as they wrapped around her. Even when he was drunk as a skunk, she loved him. She wanted to sober him up, fix pot after pot of coffee, take care of him so she'd never have to see the look that had been on his face at the National Gallery.

Hopelessness.

"I'm going to try and round up a few reporters to see you off, too," Nishi added.

"Reporters? Why?" Reporters were the last thing they needed.

"If you're going to run away from Richard, you have to do it publicly. If you leave secretly, he can bring you back secretly. But if everyone knows you've run off to Paris with your sexy—well, drunk—French lover, that puts him in a bind. Clearly the two of you aren't as reconciled as he has told people."

"It's Christmas Eve, Nish. No one's going to schlep all the way out here tonight."

"I think I can get a few to do it. If they're not covering the Hill, it's been a slow news day. And to get a senator's wife skipping town with her lover? Some reporters will drop anything for that kind of story."

"But what about your client? Surely he doesn't want to be on the news."

"He'll stay in the background, I'm sure. I saved his company a few years ago. It's a long story, but he promised to fly me and Imran to Paris on his jet. I've just made some passenger substitutions."

Marie was silent for a moment, her heart re-inflating. "Nish. I will make this up to you."

"You will make it up to me by getting away from Richard. And by letting me come visit you in Paris."

Marie laughed lightly. "I think you scared him a little." She looked at Luc, who was gazing at her with a dazed, besotted smile. This was the expression she wanted to see. She wanted to see hope in his eyes.

"He'll get over it. He loves you, Marie."

"I love him, too."

"Now go get his bag packed and get to the airport. You can't miss that flight."

31

"What did Nishi say to you on the phone?" Marie poured two mugs of coffee and offered one to Luc.

"Oh, just all the things—painful things—she will do to my balls if I in any way mistreat you or make you unhappy in the slightest ... she's very fluent in French, your friend." He grinned. "She, ah, knows words that aren't generally taught in school."

Marie laughed. "I believe she knows lots of things that aren't generally taught in school. Or anywhere else. You'll want to keep her on your good side."

"Well, for the record, I don't plan on mistreating you or making you unhappy in any way. Or losing my balls."

Marie set down her coffee and slid her arms around Luc.

"Good. I have plans for your balls. And a few other parts of your body."

Luc groaned, a sound that rumbled through her body, shaking loose all manner of desires. How were they going to make it all the way across the ocean without devouring each other?

"You could start those plans now if I weren't so ..." He shook his head. "Next time you decide to drug someone and run away, call me before I get ... shit-faced."

She took a deep breath to clear her head. *Richard.* "We don't have time right now, anyway." She checked her watch. "You need to get showered and packed. And maybe shaved?"

He rubbed his chin with his thumb and forefinger. "Yeah. Sam told me yesterday that I looked like a terrorist."

A silence fell between them. Luc was looking at her softly, but something more intense flickered in his eyes.

"We're going to Paris," she whispered. "I can hardly believe it."

"I can hardly believe you're here. I thought I'd lost you." He kissed her again, his lips soft and gentle on hers, as if he couldn't quite believe he was being allowed to.

"No," she replied. "You belong to me."

THIRTY MINUTES LATER, their bags were packed and stowed in the trunk of Marie's car. Nerves were battling excitement as she drove down the dark country lanes to the highway. She tensed at the sight of every oncoming car, worried that it was Richard or T. Rex or the police on their way to Luc's house. Until they were in the air, she wouldn't be able to completely relax. It was nine o'clock. Surely Congress was out by now. T. Rex was probably awake again. Richard had to know she was missing.

Up ahead blue and red lights flashed, around and around. She felt Luc's hand on her thigh.

"They're not for us. Don't worry," he said.

But they could be for us. That's what Luc hadn't understood before. Richard, her parents—they could have the police looking for her. In fact, they probably were. Traffic was light now, making her car that much easier to spot. Her only hope was that they wouldn't guess she was headed to Dulles.

When the lights of the airport came into view, a nervous excitement began to take hold of her. Paris! It was starting to feel like reality. Tomorrow she would be in Paris with Luc. She took the exit and merged into the heavy traffic on the access road. She squinted at all the signs, trying to find the lane that would take them to the private aviation terminal. If she missed it, she'd have to drive around the airport another time—and every minute was another minute that Richard could be getting closer.

There! She signaled quickly and cut across two lanes, making it just in the nick of time. She parked, Luc grabbed their suitcases and they headed into the terminal, where a small crowd of people stopped milling about and rushed toward them.

"Mrs. Macintyre! You're running away to Paris? Why?"

People shouted questions at them from all sides.

"How will this affect your husband's re-election campaign?"

Luc put his head down and pressed his hand to Marie's back, urging her forward and scanning the room for anyone who might look like their benefactor.

"Wait," she murmured. "We need to play this up."

She couldn't look like she was skulking out of town, under the influence of whatever substances Richard had her addicted to today. She had to look sober, in control and fully aware of what she was doing. She couldn't look like she was running away, terrified and desperate. She was going to Paris with her lover for the holidays, which she had every right to do, and Richard was just a non-factor in all of that.

She beamed her biggest, brightest smile at the reporters. "Merry Christmas! You all are crazy to come out here tonight."

"Aren't you going to rehab?" a woman shouted at her. "What kind of substance abuse problem do you have?"

Marie turned toward her, leaned her body cozily into Luc and made a show of slipping her hand into the back pocket of his jeans. "No. I am not going into rehab. I have never had any substance abuse problem—"

"Although I personally am drunk on love," Luc cut in, his syllables still a little fuzzy.

"So you're not going into the Allegheny Rehabilitation Center tomorrow?" someone else shouted at her.

"No. Could you relay that message to Senator Macintyre, please? He seems confused about whether or not he can force another adult into medical treatment."

"He has said the two of you are reconciling."

"Does it look like we are reconciling?" She turned her most loving, admiring, infatuated expression on Luc. "No, we are not. Drugging someone and essentially kidnapping them does not constitute reconciling. Nor does it make a solid basis for a marriage. Not to mention that the senator is still seeing his mistress, Maya Redfearn." She craned her neck to look over the crowd. "Maya? Are you here tonight?" She let the silence swell and fill the room. "No? Guess we know where she is."

The reporters tittered along with her. Marie was suddenly grateful for the media training she and Richard had taken years ago with Nishi. It was an easy mask to hide behind.

"Mr. Marchand! Do the French like bondage?"

Where the hell did that question come from?

She heard Luc's low chuckle vibrate through her arm. "Oh, oui." He winked theatrically at the cameras. "The things she does to me when she ties me up. American women are—" he shook his head as though he were speechless,"—oh la la." Luc's accent was thick and comically exaggerated, the very parody of a French lover.

Marie felt her face grow hot. Media training had never covered *this* scenario.

"Do you have more nude paintings of the congressman's wife?"

"Not yet," Luc replied. "But check back with me in a few

months." He looked down at Marie, who was still blushing furiously. "Actually, check back with me in a few days."

Several of the reporters were biting down hard on their lips, struggling to keep a straight face.

"What are your plans for Paris, Mrs. Macintyre?"

Luc didn't let her answer that one. He spun her into his arms and kissed her long and deeply as the cameras clicked furiously away around them.

"That's classified," he announced when he broke off the kiss. "I'm sure you can use your imaginations. You look like smart people."

Marie spotted a fortyish man standing by a door across the room, a bemused expression on his face. He was wearing a tailored suit, his tie loosened around his neck. Another man in a pilot's uniform stood next to him.

"I think that might be our ride over there," she said quietly to Luc.

She heard cameras clicking away as they pushed through the crowd.

"You really don't want to cross your friend, hmm?" Luc said. "If she can call out that much of the Washington press corps on a holiday night."

"Best to have Nishi on your side," Marie agreed.

The man in the suit approached them and extended his hand. "Hello, Ms. Witherspoon, Mr. Marchand. I'm George Brown. Bit of theater back there, eh? I've been told to get you on board as soon as you arrive and close the doors. I have my marching orders." He smiled at Marie, acknowledging a shared fear of Nishi Bhat.

George Brown. CEO of a *major* technology firm. Even Marie had heard of him. Nasty divorce a few years back. She vaguely remembered something about their computer systems being hacked into, exposing sensitive client data—including some from a particularly sensitive government agency. Maybe that was what Nishi had been referring to when she said she had saved his company. There must have been a ton of bad press over that. In a crisis, Nishi was your best friend. Marie had learned that over and over.

They followed George Brown and his pilot out onto the tarmac. There were a half dozen smaller planes parked and one large, airliner-style jet. Surely that wasn't ... but George Brown and the pilot were indeed headed toward the jet. She poked Luc in the ribs.

"This is how the other half lives," he said.

"Wow," was all Marie could say. "This is beyond first class. Not that I've ever flown first class." She'd been expecting something like a Cessna or a commuter jet, though now that she thought about it, those probably weren't suitable for flying across the ocean.

Inside, they settled into the buttery leather seats. She fingered the soft cashmere blanket draped over the armrest. No worries about leg room on this flight. She could see Luc's thigh muscles flex beneath his jeans as he stretched out his legs. Maybe in Paris she would attempt drawing him again. All of him. Maybe Paris would magically transform her into a better artist, too! She allowed herself a tiny smile at her silly, insane thought. That was probably asking too much of a city. Then again, Paris wasn't just any city, right?

George Brown emerged from the cockpit, told them to help themselves to anything in the galley once they were airborne, and then disappeared into the back of the plane. A door shut behind him. Apparently, they were to have this part of the cabin to themselves.

"I'm going to Paris." She squeezed Luc's hand.

He slung his arm around her shoulders and pulled her into his chest. "Yes, you are. You're going to love it, too."

"Will you kiss me at the top of the Eiffel Tower?" Marie snuggled closer into his chest, imagining a cinema-worthy shot of herself and Luc silhouetted against the Paris skyline.

"I'll kiss you anywhere you like," Luc replied, in a tone of voice that said he did indeed mean *anywhere.* He nuzzled a kiss into her hair.

Marie was just turning to accept a kiss on the lips when her phone buzzed with a text.

"Let me guess," he said.

Marie pulled the phone from her pocket and swiped the screen. *Only thing more embarrassing than your wife posing nude and going into rehab is your wife running away to Paris with sexy French artist the night before Christmas. Bonne courage!*

Marie handed the phone to Luc, then gave into the giddy laughter bubbling up from her chest.

"Wait ... I'm more embarrassing than rehab? Not sure that's a compliment."

"Oh, it's a compliment. Trust me." She gave him a wicked smile. "He will resume the divorce now." An idea popped into her head, a deliciously wicked idea. "Especially if we send Maya photos."

Marie held up the phone in front of them, stretching her arm as far as it would go. "Say cheese."

"We look terrible," he said afterward, looking at the photo.

Her hair was tousled and unstyled. Dark circles shadowed his eyes. They looked like two people who had stayed up until dawn making love. She hoped they looked this terrible every morning in Paris.

"It'll do," she said, typing in a message for Nishi—*Pls forward to J Street Chronicle*—and hit send.

32

Marie pressed her nose to the window of the taxi. In the early morning light, the city looked like a black and white photo. Or a charcoal drawing. At this hour, no one was out but still it was hard not to expect to turn a corner and see lovers strolling hand-in-hand over a lovely bridge or impeccably-dressed women sitting in a café window, sipping espresso. It was December, too, meaning she and Luc weren't exactly going to be sitting outside at cute side-walk cafés. She tucked that fact back into the recesses of her mind. None of that mattered now.

"I'm in Paris," she whispered to the window. Who cared about the weather?

Luc squeezed her hand. He'd been holding it almost continuously since lift-off at Dulles, even as they dozed during the flight. It was comforting to her, the warmth of his skin, his strong fingers laced between hers. They were en route to a hotel, where Luc had booked a room for a week. Just the two of them.

"I want you to myself for a few days, before we go visit my family. We've been apart for weeks, Marie. I am a starving man here."

A week, just the two of them. That was fine with Marie. She was starved for him, too. She had tried not to think of it too much during those interminable weeks, but now that they were together again she wondered how she had ever believed she could simply leave and live without him. She knew now that she couldn't. Just lying next to him on the plane had filled her with such a sense of contentment, a feeling that she was in the right place, with the right person. At last.

She had no idea how long they would stay in Paris, or how long she *could* stay, even. But it didn't matter for now. She wanted to be with Luc. That's all that mattered.

"Are you hungry, love?" he asked, rubbing his thumb over her wrist, a wrist that was bonier than the last time they'd been together.

Surely, with all the French food she'd be eating, she'd gain that weight back soon enough.

"A little." She wouldn't have to be afraid to eat in Paris. Well, except for snails maybe. Luc would never drug her. How had she ended up married to such a man? Why hadn't she said no earlier and more often? Why did she wait for Richard to file for divorce? She shook her head. That didn't matter either, now.

Luc pulled her hand up to his lips and covered it with kisses. "What is that for? You're not having second thoughts, are you?"

"No. Of course not." She looked at him, her eyes blazing with passion and certitude. "No, I was just thinking of my life ... and how *stupid* I was for so many years. To put up with all that."

He pressed a finger to her lips. "Shh. You're not stupid, Marie. You're just *seeing* your life, finally."

"I owe that to you."

He shook his head. "You don't owe me anything. Well, except for that kiss. I'm not sure that was ever consummated last night." He smiled. "You asked me to help you see as an artist does. Sometimes we don't like what we see. But seeing is always better than not seeing."

That night at the Pancake Palace, the night when she had finally come up with a reason for wanting drawing lessons, seemed light years away now. So much had happened since then.

She reached into her purse to turn off her phone, then climbed onto his lap. She caressed his face. He closed his eyes and let himself enjoy the touch of her hands on his skin.

"What if I had never come up with a reason for taking lessons with you?" she asked.

A wry smile twisted his lips, his eyes still shut. "I would have come to your apartment and begged you to take lessons with me. I can be a complete idiot sometimes. You'll have to remember that, Marie."

She ran her thumb along his lower lip and something beneath her thighs stirred. She brushed her fingers over his eyelids, gently closing them. "Keep them shut," she said.

Her kiss was slow and soft, but definitely not sweet. She teased him, her tongue running along his lips, then slipping inside to find his tongue. His hands pushed up under her coat and sweater, stroking her stomach, cupping her breasts. He was hard beneath her now, but his eyes remained closed as she had asked.

She let her spine unfurl, pressing her breasts more fully into his hands. Her body always responded this way to him, wild and needful. She felt his lips curl into a smile beneath her kiss. Her desire for him was no secret. If it ever had been.

"How far to the hotel?" she groaned, not caring whether the cab driver heard.

"If we stay in here much longer, you're going to fall asleep, I think," Luc observed from his side of the hotel's deep tub.

From her side, the view was spectacular. Luc leaned back against the ceramic, his long arms stretched along the rim. The lavender-scented water lapped at his nipples and the steam was causing the ends of his dark hair to gently curl.

Just then she felt a mischievous foot exploring her calf beneath the water. She couldn't hide the chill that rippled down her spine.

"The coffee will keep me awake," she asserted.

As soon as they arrived at the hotel, Luc had called room service for a pot of coffee and they were now drinking it in the tub, which felt oddly decadent to Marie. Lots of things felt decadent around Luc, of course. Especially taking a bath. The heat and gentle movement of the water relaxed her completely. For the past month, she hadn't felt comfortable letting down her guard even for a minute or two, so now the idea of just sitting here with a man she trusted absolutely was comforting ... and seductive.

"Just a few more minutes," she begged. "This is the first time I've been able to relax in ages."

"I have some ideas for helping you relax." Luc's voice was low and husky as he ran his foot along the outside of her leg.

"What's on the agenda for today?" she asked.

"Whatever you like." His foot was pushing apart her legs. "But I've never made love to you in Paris, so that's at the top of *my* agenda."

He opened the drain and stood up, his body rising from the water like some ocean god. He did it slowly enough, too, for her to watch every inch of skin emerge. Nothing like a glistening wet Luc with rivulets of water running off his chest and stomach and thighs to change her mind. He held out his hand and she let herself be pulled up.

He toweled her off, then dried himself and pulled her into his arms. His body was warm and hard against hers, particularly a certain part of his body.

"Just a quick one," he said, "then we'll take a nap."

Marie wasn't sleepy, though, even considering how few hours she had slept on the plane. Plus ...

"If I fall asleep, this might all be over. When I wake up, I'll be back in Virginia."

He cupped her bottom with his palms and pulled her hips in tighter against his hard length. "Ah ma chérie, you're afraid this is just a dream? What if I promise that you'll be in Paris when you wake? And if you're not, then you have my permission to do whatever you want to me."

Her body needed sleep, no doubt about that. But it needed *him* more. Already her legs were unsteady with desire and he was making it worse, trailing kisses down her neck and nibbling at her shoulder.

"Do I have permission *today?* To do whatever I want?"

He chuckled roughly against her cheek, searching for her lips. "As long as it involves orgasms and me inside of you, then yes. Whatever you want."

He caught her lips in a kiss, and she nearly gave in right there. But no. She didn't want a quickie and a nap. Not their first time making love in Paris. It had to be special ... it had to be *more.*

"You used to tell me," she said between his kisses, which were growing more determined and more heated, "that not all seeing is done with the eyes."

"Mmm ... true."

He slipped his hands between them and rolled her nipples between his fingers. She reached up and stopped him. She didn't want fast, and fast was where he was headed.

"And when we started lessons, you blindfolded me to help me see things better."

"Yes." There was a tightness in his voice now, a forced patience, like he was holding his breath. Which he probably was.

"I want to see you make love to me." She took a deep breath. "See it without my eyes."

He lifted his head and cocked an eyebrow at her. “You want to use a blindfold?”

She nodded, watching his face as he considered the idea.

“Hmm. But I left mine in the studio, packed up.”

Her face fell. He probably hadn’t brought a necktie either. They had packed so quickly last night, throwing things pell mell into suitcases.

“But maybe …” he mused.

He stepped away from her and immediately she regretted her request. The loss of his skin against her was cold and nearly painful. She followed him out to the main room, where he began pulling on clean pants and a shirt.

“I’ll be right back. Wait for me in bed.”

He glanced back at the pristine bed with its fluffy covers and pillows. It wouldn’t be pristine for long. She crawled beneath the covers and waited for his return. Her body was so charged with desire—with lust, let’s call a spade a spade, she thought—she could practically feel the individual threads of the cool sheets against her skin.

Ten minutes later—the ten longest minutes of her life—Luc returned, a gift bag from the hotel shop swinging from his hand. He pulled out the yellow tissue paper and tossed it aside. Then he unfolded a gorgeous scarf. It was silk and intricately patterned in deep reds and golds.

“It reminded me of our first date, at the ballet.”

A rush of heat flooded her body. She wanted him now, and yet she had requested something he would take slow. Excruciatingly slow. God, she was an idiot.

He pulled another scarf out of the bag, this one in muted tones of grey and cream. “For me,” he said. “But another time.” He smiled. “I do want to see you with my eyes today.”

He stripped out of his clothes and then tied the blindfold

around her eyes. "Are you sure you want to do this?" He tugged at the silk.

"Yes. I just want to feel this."

"D'accord. But you have to let me know if it becomes too much."

And then Luc's body was against hers, his hands warm on the bare skin of her back, pressing her into him. When his lips closed over hers, it was no simple kiss. Blindfolded, Marie had only taste and touch to interpret it. It was like tasting a wine for the first time and trying to identify its notes. The first taste was a rush of desire, overwhelming and uncomplicated. Then came the dark smokiness of desperation, teeth against teeth, bruised lips, and a faint hint of earthy sorrow.

When Marie tasted the final note, the distant sweetness of long-aged hope, she gasped at the intensity of it.

"Déesse," he murmured against her lips.

She parted her lips to take in the word. She would accept his compliments from now on, every one of them. His breath was hot with the scent of coffee and she pulled his mouth harder against hers. She wanted to disappear inside him, wanted him to swallow her whole.

Luc kissed her back. He was trying to give her what she was asking for, she could tell, but she needed more. Every inch of skin on her body was clamoring for his touch. *Touch me touch me touch me.* Every nerve ending competed for his attention. *Touch me first.*

"Slowly, love." He pulled his lips away from hers.

"I'm sorry," she panted. "It's so ... was it this way for you, when ..." She struggled to get words out.

"When I was blindfolded with you? Yes. When you take away one sense, the others become more concentrated, pure. We rely too much on sight when we're trying to see."

"It's more intense than I realized."

Luc's lips were at her ear now, the softness of his tongue like the finest velvet on her lobe. "Just relax into it."

"It's the anticipation ... I don't know where—"

"Shhh." He curled his tongue around her ear. "Don't talk. Just feel it."

She felt fingers working their way into her hair, a light tugging against her scalp, then his hands cupped beneath her head. She sensed Luc's lips in the instant before they found hers again. This time, she lay there and let him kiss her, let his mouth explore hers. She felt his nose rub gently against the tiny dip above her lips.

"The philtrum," she said. "I remember."

She felt Luc's groan vibrate against her chest before the sound drifted into her ears, then his hands pulled out of her hair, the way water retreats before a tidal wave. His chest lifted from hers and her nipples hardened at the sudden rush of cooler air. His hips settled lightly over her own, straddling her.

She felt nothing for awhile, for what seemed like an eternity.

"Are you looking at me?" she asked.

"I am, Marie."

"Good." She smiled.

Just like that, his body was on hers again, heavier this time, his erection hard against her. Her lips were crushed beneath his, her mouth filled with his tongue searching for hers. Heat spread like liquid fire through her body and she ground her hips against him. He ground his back.

"Marie," he moaned.

She reached between their bodies and tried to pull him into her, but he lifted his hips away.

"Non. Not yet. You haven't seen everything."

She gasped when his mouth closed over her left breast and he began to suck, gently, patiently, as if he had all the time in the world. Not being able to see what he was going to do next made every touch a surprise—and almost unbearably intense. She was simply waiting for whatever would come next.

"Can I change my mind?" She forced the words out.

"I'd rather you didn't."

Luc moved to her other breast and dropped soft kisses on every swell and curve, pausing only to nip at the hard bud of her nipple. The contrast sent shivers of desire rolling through her spine. When he kissed his way down her stomach, tracing a lazy circle around her navel with his tongue, she was certain her body was about to disintegrate from sensory overload.

"Luc," she groaned.

"If it's too much, take it off," he said as he bared his teeth and scraped them lightly across the point of her hips. Then he pushed her arching hips back onto the blanket and held them there as he kissed lower and lower.

She couldn't wait any longer. She cupped his head in her hands and pushed it down, between her legs. "Touch me. Please," she begged. He didn't need to coax open her thighs this time. She wrapped her quivering legs around his shoulders as he dipped his tongue into the heat between them.

"I never want another man to see this," Luc growled. "Whatever your body needs, I will give it to you. All you have to do is ask. Promise me you'll ask, Marie."

By now, her ears were keenly attuned to the inflections in his voice and she recognized what she was hearing now. Luc Marchand was pleading with her. He wanted her, and only her.

"I promise, Luc. I'm yours for as long as you'll have me."

"I'm going to want you for a long time."

He kissed the ache between her legs and she was lost in a torrent of sensation, beset on all sides by things her senses had been too lazy to notice before. The gentle pressure of the pillow beneath her head. The lingering scent of lavender on their skin. The sound of Luc's breathing, ragged and barely under control.

The way his tongue was both soft and hard against the softest place on her body. The way the air around her was dense with his patience and generosity.

That was love, wasn't it? Surrounding another person with your patience and generosity. Putting their well-being ahead of your own, secure in the knowledge that they were doing the same for you. She had never loved someone before, not like this. She would have to figure this out, how to love Luc Marchand, this man who had been ill-treated by love in the past and yet had dared to open himself back up to her.

She would have to try to *see* him as he saw her. She would start today. Now.

She touched his head, wound a lock of his smooth hair around her finger. "Switch places with me," she said.

He did as she asked, without a word. He took her hand and pulled her up, then slipped beneath her. Marie pressed her body on top of his, then pressed her lips to his mouth.

"You said I should ask if my body needed something."

"Oui."

"What if my heart needs something?"

"I will give that to you, as well. Of course."

"My heart needs this. I want to see you, too." She kissed his lips once more than slid her body over his until his erection caressed her face. She kissed him, exploring his hard length with her lips, softly, blindly. She found the vein and ran her tongue along it.

"Marie," Luc groaned. "My heart may not survive this."

"I know CPR. Don't worry."

"Have you ever actually resuscitated someone?"

"There's a first time for everything."

She kissed the tip, then slid her lips over him.

"Marie—"

She pulled him in and out of her mouth. With Richard, she

had always hurried, wanting to get this over with, her mind elsewhere, ever alert for the signs that he was almost done so she could move away and avoid swallowing. With Luc, she would be patient and generous. She brushed her fingers over his tightly-coiled hair. She took note of every change in his breathing, the speed of his hips rocking beneath her. She pulled on him harder, tightened her lips.

"Marie. Please. I don't want to come this way."

She let her lips slide slowly off him, taking him into her hands to ease the change in temperature. His skin was like the softest silk, softer even than the blindfold she was wearing. She leaned her head to caress him with the scarf, warmed by her skin now.

He groaned again and she knew what his eyes looked like. Even with the blindfold tied around her head, she could see the expression in his eyes. It was the same one she'd seen after he kissed her that first day, kissed her to help her see colors better. Wild. Dark. Desperate.

She positioned her hips above his and eased him inside her. She moaned as he filled her inch by slow delicious inch. When her hips reached his again, she paused to savor the feeling of Luc inside her, completely, fully inside her. She began to rock her hips, letting him slide in and out of her. She gasped for air with each stroke.

"I didn't know it would feel this way."

"How does it feel, love? Tell me."

"Like you're touching me everywhere. Even though you're barely touching me at all."

She leaned over his chest and quickened her pace.

"I can't wait, Luc."

"Don't wait."

He pulled the blindfold off as she got closer and closer to the edge. He was watching her, studying her face, memorizing the details of the moment, looking for the planes and shadows, the light and dark … he was planning to draw her like this. He *saw* her. She'd been planning to run away to another city so people would see her the way she really was, when the one person who had always seen her was right here. Seeing her right now.

When the orgasm hit her, she felt her body split open and flood with a dancing swirl of color, almost too bright to bear, like looking into the sun. Luc had made her see color. Finally.

His hips bucked beneath her, into her, and she collapsed onto his sweating chest, spent physically and emotionally. She struggled to get her breathing under control, leaning her forehead on his shoulder, watching the colors fade and recede over the horizon in her mind.

"Ma chérie. My love."

He caressed her cheek, then tugged gently at her parted lips. *Someday I will paint you like this.* He made that promise the evening he told her he was in love with her.

She looked at him tenderly. His eyes were no longer dark and desperate. Instead, they glowed, eager and hopeful with a question only she knew the answer to.

"Yes," she whispered. "Draw me."

PART TWO: CHIAROSCURO

33

Eleven months later

THE PAIN WAS its own anesthesia. Marie fought to stay alert as the gurney sped down the hallway. A tornado of French swirled around her head, with the occasional lapse into English to calm her. Valerie Marchand clutched her hand as she ran alongside. It wasn't supposed to be Valerie's hand, though Marie was most grateful that Valerie had been home when her water broke. And eternally grateful for all she'd done for Marie in the past nine months. Housed her, fed her, cried with her.

When the gurney hit the doors to the operating suite, Valerie's fingers fell away.

"I'll be waiting outside. You're doing great, Marie. She's almost here."

Marie wasn't doing great. Not generally and certainly not at the present moment. The umbilical cord was wrapped around the baby's neck. This wasn't how her daughter was supposed to be born. Marie had envisioned the birth of her first child as a happy, joyous moment. Physically painful, sure. But she would be surrounded by love as she struggled valiantly through labor, then overcome by a wonderful peace when her red-faced and wrinkled daughter was laid, swaddled in a blanket, into her waiting arms. Followed by a passionate, grateful kiss.

Instead, she was headed into surgery alone—in a foreign country where she still barely spoke the language—to have her daughter cut out of her womb. They might as well cut out her heart while they were at it, as far as Marie was concerned. Her heart was a dead organ, and she had no more use for it.

She felt the wheels of the gurney lock into place, then a needle stab her arm. Her legs and back and stomach were already numb from the epidural. Her eyes struggled to focus on the whirl of activity around her, the doctor and nurses prepping for surgery. She was frantic to wipe her eyelashes but afraid to move her free arm and even more afraid to call attention to her tears. To her terror and cowardice and despair. A big blue screen appeared in front of her face, blocking her view of what was to happen next.

Even then, she had been certain he was going to burst through the doors at any moment, call her name, grab her hand. There would be apologies for being late and she would tearfully forgive him. But when she felt the tugging sensation in her abdomen and heard the startled cries of her daughter, she knew.

Luc Marchand—her lover and friend, her teacher, the only person who had ever really *seen* her, the father of her child—wasn't coming back.

34

On October 31, Luc Marchand stepped off a plane at Charles de Gaulle Airport with little more than the clothes on his back. And while he wasn't home exactly, at least he was no longer away.

What do you do when you run out of places to run to, when your heavy heart has followed you to the far corners of the earth and back like a bad hangover? Luc knew the answer to that question now.

You grow the hell up.

He had no idea what awaited him in Paris, or the States. It wouldn't be pretty, he knew that. It wouldn't be a lovely Claude Monet landscape. Here's your life back, Luc, just painted in a slightly different light, at a slightly different time of day, in the gloaming instead of at high noon.

No, best case scenario he was returning to a Van Gogh. Moody, the colors a little sickly and sour, but still recognizable as his life. Worst case scenario? Hieronymus Bosch was waiting for him.

The cab ride to his sister Valerie's house on the outskirts of Paris passed in a blur. He was tired. So very, very tired. He never wanted to sleep in a hotel bed again. Or on a park bench. In truth, Luc had no idea what he wanted. Everything he had wanted had gotten on a train to London nearly two years ago, but only part of it came back.

He no longer believed that his heart would heal. Twenty months of running had proven that. His heart was irreparably broken—and still so heavy that he could no longer carry it around with him. He needed to set it down somewhere and walk away. Burn it, bury it, smother it with a pillow. Marie had killed something in him that day when she and that horrid woman she called her best friend boarded that train for London. She had taken his heart, his soul, his future, all capacity to love someone with her that day.

And she had taken his art.

Luc hadn't picked up a pencil or brush since she left.

He ran his hand through the tangles of his long hair. *Putain.* He'd barely picked up a hairbrush.

When the cab arrived at his sister's house, he paid the driver and walked to the door. He said a quick prayer that Denis, his sister's husband, wasn't home from work yet and rang the doorbell. When the door opened a minute later, he watched his sister's face roll through a gamut of responses—from blank non-recognition to disbelief to anger.

"Luc?"

"Oui."

"You're back."

"Oui." He couldn't go wrong with yes. To anything she said.

She stepped back and opened the door wider, an invitation for him to enter. As soon as the door closed, she smacked him hard against the face. He rubbed his palm over his stinging cheek.

"I guess I deserved that."

"You guess?"

She stalked deeper into the house, coming to a stop in her

small neat kitchen. Then she pushed past him and stomped up the stairs to the second floor. Luc didn't follow. He knew Valerie's house like the back of his hand, but he didn't want to presume his welcome there. Muttered cursing floated down the stairs, followed by Valerie herself carrying her laptop. He followed her to the kitchen.

"Sit," she ordered. She took a seat herself and flipped open the computer.

Luc pulled out a chair and waited for the motivation behind all this. When the computer stopped its soft startup purring, she clicked open some files. Many files, in fact. Then she spun the screen to face him.

"There. You bastard."

On the screen was a photograph of a little girl. Dark hair, big chocolate eyes, pink rosebud lips, creased forehead that could convey skepticism or irritation or a plea for forgiveness depending on the situation. The same creased forehead that had been staring back at Luc from mirrors around the world.

He sucked in a sharp breath, trying to clear the darkness that was closing in on him from all sides. It couldn't be. He couldn't be seeing things right. Valerie didn't move a muscle to help. No doubt she would be satisfied to watch him lose consciousness, fall from the chair and split his skull wide open on the hard tiles of her kitchen floor. His fingers gripped the edge of the table in an effort to remain upright.

Breathe. Breathe.

When the smoke finally cleared from his brain, he began clicking on the other photographs. The little girl asleep in a crib, clutching a stuffed bear. The little girl in a dress and hair ribbons. The little girl standing up, clutching the edge of a sofa for balance. The little girl, younger now, being baptized in a church. The little girl, even younger, lying in a one-piece sleeper, wide awake in a crib.

The photos went on and on, and each one broke the heart that Luc thought had already been broken as much as it could be. She was beautiful. So beautiful it took his breath away. And she was clearly a Marchand. You'd have to be blind not to see the resemblance. Luc was a bastard, an asshole, an idiot. But he wasn't blind.

By the time he found his voice to speak, tears were rolling down his cheeks and into the scruff he hadn't shaved off in days. Valerie made a choked noise that could have been sympathy or could have been a warning that she was about to clock him again.

"What's her name?" he said quietly, the salt of his tears sharp on his lips.

"A father shouldn't have to ask his daughter's name."

Fair enough. He held up his hands in surrender. "I fucked up, Valerie. I know that." He glanced at the computer screen and had to stuff a fist into his mouth to stop another sob. "Fucked up more than I realized."

"Are you kidding me? She was waiting for you to show up even as they wheeled her into the operating room. She still thought you would come back."

"Operating …"

"Yeah, operating room. Your daughter—whose name is Olivia, by the way—was delivered via c-section. Major surgery, Luc. And you weren't here. You were—" Valerie waved her arm perilously close to his face. "—off drinking, by the looks of it."

Luc clicked through to the last photograph and realized just how not forgiven he was. Valerie had opened a photo of a newborn swaddled tight and lying in the arms of her wan and exhausted-looking mother. Marie's eyes were watery, drowning in depths of sadness that Luc realized were deeper than even his own had been. Fathoms deeper.

He pushed the computer back to Valerie, dropped his head to his arms folded on the table, and cried for hours.

He ran out of tears—and energy—eventually. He heard Valerie

speaking to someone. On the phone, he guessed, since hers was the only voice he heard. When he lifted his face, Valerie was pouring a cup of coffee and sliding it across the table to him.

"Thanks," he mumbled.

She poured another cup for herself. "Denis will be home soon. I assume you need a place to stay."

"Would love to stay here," he replied between gulps of burning coffee. "But I can go, too."

"No. You can stay." She eyed him thoughtfully, more calmly than she had a few hours ago. "Where have you been, Luc?"

"Everywhere. Nowhere. I was traveling. Germany. Russia. Finland. Mexico. I went everywhere."

"You sound like a damned Forrest Gump. Running until you ran out of places to go."

He managed a wry smile against the lip of the mug. "Basically, yeah."

"And why did you feel the need to run in the first place? I thought the two of you were happy about the pregnancy. I mean, unplanned obviously but you seemed okay about it."

He filled his lungs with a long, deep breath, then let it out. "When her friend. Nishi." He struggled to organize the words in his mouth. "When Nishi came to visit, she and I argued. She told me she was taking Marie to get an abortion and then she was taking Marie home."

"And you assumed that Marie went through with it. Like that other girl did."

Luc's hackles rose, suddenly. "Why wouldn't I? Her friend, she's a fixer. That's her job. She takes care of unfortunate situations for people. And she didn't like me. On the night when she arranged for a private jet to fly us here, she told me—in fluent French, mind you—that if I ever hurt Marie, she would cut off my balls and stuff them up my ass."

A snort of laughter burst from his sister. "I'm looking forward to watching that."

"God. You're my sister. Can't you be on my side here?"

"Luc, no one is on your side. You knocked up your girlfriend and took off. For damn near close to two years now. Olivia is ten months old. Ten months. Two weeks, a month—maybe understandable. But you've been gone a long time, Luc."

"How is she? Marie?"

Valerie shrugged. "Fine, I guess. She sends us an email every couple of months with pictures of Olivia, but she doesn't write much otherwise."

"Where is she? In Paris?"

"Are you kidding? No. She went home to the States after the baby was born." Valerie hesitated. "She lives in Pittsburgh now."

"But you have her email."

"And I'm not giving it to you. I will give you her address in Pittsburgh. I don't know what you're planning to do, Luc, but whatever it is can't be done via email."

"She might not want to see me in person again."

"That would not surprise me one bit." Valerie looked past Luc's head. The front door was opening and closing. "Denis is home. I asked him to pick up dinner for us."

Luc stood to greet his brother-in-law only to find himself slammed hard into the kitchen wall. Denis pinned him there with one hand to his chest. Dinner dropped to the floor from the other hand with a thud. Denis was a soft-spoken man and he said nothing now, just nailing Luc to the plaster with an angry glare that said more than words ever could. Luc steeled himself for a punch but after a long moment of silence, his brother-in-law shoved off him.

"You're not worth the sore knuckles." He walked over to Valerie and dropped a kiss onto her forehead. "But I reserve the right to change my mind," he added, not bothering to turn back and face Luc.

Luc picked up the dinner bag from the floor. He set it on the table and began pulling plates and flatware from the cabinets.

"I'll be out of your hair as soon as I can get a flight to the States."

35

Marie had to read the email through three times before she grasped the message. Her mother was inviting her to the family's annual Thanksgiving open house. She didn't go last year; she had remained in France until shortly after Livie was born in early December. And the year before … that was when her estranged husband and her parents informed her she was going to rehab to salvage Richard's re-election campaign.

And bring that boy you're dating.

She took a deep breath. This was progress if her mother was inviting Aidan. Marie hated to admit it but she would feel a lot better going if Aidan were by her side. Richard's parents, the Macintyres, would probably be there. Richard and his former mistress-slash-new wife, Maya, might be there as well. If they could tear themselves away from the pressing duties of the ambassadorship to Estonia. Richard had lost his re-election campaign. Marie had not gone into rehab.

And bring that boy you're dating.

She rolled her eyes. Richard had never been a "boy." Luc had always been "that … that …" furious sputter. But Aidan was a boy.

True, Aidan did have a certain boyish quality to him that neither Richard nor Luc had. Given how those relationships worked out, there was something to be said for boyishness, all things considered.

Marie tapped in a quick reply. *We'll be there. I'll ask Aidan if he can come.* The more she thought about it, the more she wanted him there but there were the logistics to consider. They could do the drive from Pittsburgh to Washington, DC and back in one day. It would be a lot of driving but Livie would sleep most of the way. Making it a day trip would allow her to sidestep the issue of spending the night, getting one hotel room or two. She'd been dating Aidan for nearly two months, since the beginning of the semester, but they had yet to take that next step. Sleeping together.

She tapped out another email to her mother. *Can we stay at the house Thursday night?* Her parents had never let her and Richard sleep in the same room until they were married.

Of course, dear. There's plenty of room. We bought a crib for Olivia, too.

Marie gave a small shake of her head. Her relationship with her parents was not entirely mended but a grandchild could work wonders. Especially the grandchild from an only child. The matter of Livie's paternity had been little discussed so far. Since Luc had washed his hands of her and Livie, it didn't much matter.

Marie leaned back in her cushioned office chair and stretched out her neck and back. Life was good. She had a job she was good at, working in alumni relations at the University of Pittsburgh. Alumni relations being a kinder, gentler way of saying "fundraising." No, she hadn't fallen far from the tree after all. She was back in fundraising, not a career that was her first choice but one she had the requisite experience for and one that paid well enough to support herself and her daughter.

She had more sympathy now for some of her mother's choices and compromises in life. Older and wiser and all that. She had grown up a lot in the past two years. No one needed to tell Marie that. When you had a child, you did what you needed to do. Suck it up, swallow your pride and deal. Practically her motto these days.

Marie worked for an old family friend of Nishi's, Asma Khan. Asma was kind and generous, and had not once asked Marie to trade on her parents' connections. Initially, Marie had been apprehensive about moving to Pittsburgh. Richard had represented this district in Congress. But Nishi had been right, as usual. Hardly anyone knew who represented them in Congress, and Marie had never taken Macintyre as her married name. She could count on one hand the number of people in Pittsburgh who had recognized her, and all of them were major donors to the university whom she'd met at receptions and fundraising events.

Her phone pinged with a text. *Getting sandwiches now. Meet you in five.* Marie shrugged on her jacket and gathered up her sketchpad and pencil. It was their daily date, Marie and Aidan. Eating sandwiches on the lawn of the Cathedral of Learning while Marie drew. Those halcyon days were numbered; it was November already and winter was bearing down on them.

Aidan Janssen was a thirty-three-year-old math professor at Pitt, and as different from Richard and Luc as a man could be. Aidan radiated the light of his southern California upbringing with his tanned skin and sandy, sun-streaked—even in Pittsburgh—hair. He was sweet. Devoted. Patient. And if Marie wasn't feeling the chemistry yet, she was certain it would arrive eventually. And if it didn't? Well, chemistry was overrated in her opinion.

She had to allow the doors of two elevators to open and close before one arrived with enough room for her to get on. Aidan always went to Primanti's to pick up sandwiches and sodas for them. He was … nice. And he wasn't pushing her on the sex front, which only reinforced her belief that he was a truly, genuinely nice guy. The lack of chemistry she was feeling was probably just due to the strains of being a single mother. At the end of the day, she barely had enough energy to brush her teeth, let alone make love to someone.

Was she afraid that Aidan wouldn't be as good a lover as he-whose-name-shall-never-be-uttered-out-loud? She was honest enough with herself to admit to that fear. But some things were more important than sex. Just being around, for starters. Aidan was here. Luc had simply disappeared without any explanation. Without even the courtesy of goodbye.

Well screw that. As Nishi would say.

She wasn't waiting around anymore for him to return. If he were going to come back, he would have done it before his daughter was nearly a year old. Aidan was here, constant and patient and nice. Marie would come to love him eventually. She had no doubt of that. She was just being more careful with her heart this time around.

The elevator shuddered to a stop and Marie exited into the medieval gloom of the Commons Room. In another week or so, they would have to start eating in here beneath the soaring arches and vaulted ceilings. It would be harder to draw in the dim light of the Commons Room, Marie reflected, as she threaded her way through the crowd of students waiting for elevators, waiting for friends, waiting for a professor to show up. It was a strange building, the Cathedral, a forty-two story gothic revival skyscraper plunked down in the middle of Pittsburgh, a city more known for its bridges and hills and sports teams than its architecture. Marie liked it. It revealed its charms when you weren't looking for them.

Kind of like her life these days.

Outside, she spotted Aidan's tall form and blonde hair immediately. She hurried down the stone steps to the lawn.

"Hello sweetheart." He leaned down to drop a kiss on her lips, then folded her hand into his as they looked for an empty patch of grass on which to eat. As the air grew chillier with the passing days, the number of frisbee and football games on the lawn declined and opened up more dining real estate.

"How about here?" he said.

They sat and Aidan unwrapped their sandwiches. He tucked napkins into her lap. He was gentlemanly, and wasn't that a novelty? He wasn't constantly trying to seduce her. He had made it clear that sex was on the table whenever Marie was ready, but otherwise he didn't push the matter.

They ate in companionable silence for awhile, then Marie balled up the remains of her sandwich and picked up her sketch-pad. She was still trying to draw the exterior of the Cathedral. A daunting ambition, to be sure, and one that Aidan thought was nuts. That was how they had met in the first place. Marie was sitting on the lawn drawing over her lunch hour and Aidan had plopped himself down next to her and introduced himself.

"Aidan Janssen."

Marie had looked at him dubiously that day but accepted his handshake. "Marie Witherspoon."

He glanced up at the skyscraper then back down at her sketch-pad. She fought the urge to close it and cover up what was turning into another failed attempt.

"It has over twenty-five-hundred windows, you know."

Marie looked back up at the building. Yeah, that was definitely the challenge. Way too many windows.

"Hmm. Maybe that's my problem. I need a bigger sheet of paper."

Aidan Janssen laughed. "I'm a mathematician. If you let me take you out to lunch tomorrow, I'll help you figure out how big a sheet you'll need. We mathematicians are good for that sort of thing, you know."

Marie smiled even now at the memory. It was the corniest pickup line ever but it had worked. And Aidan Janssen had proven himself good for a lot more than just calculating the ratio of windows to drawing paper.

By now, the Cathedral had turned into a bit of a personal nemesis for her. It was beyond her skills as an amateur artist, and probably beyond her talent as well. But she added some lines and shading to the drawing she started yesterday.

"Are you feeling okay?" she asked after a few minutes. "You're unusually quiet today." Normally, Aidan's mouth ran a mile a minute about his classes, his students, math department politics. He could be charmingly unfiltered. She'd heard none of that today.

He took a deep breath and immediately Marie tensed. *Please let him not break up with me. Not here on campus. Not in the middle of a work day.* She kept her head bent to her sketchpad, afraid to look at him and read the inevitable on his face.

"I know you didn't want me to look up those paintings …" he began.

The tension flooded from her muscles as quickly as it rose. This was it? She *had* asked him not to look her up online, but she wasn't surprised that he had. She was only surprised it had taken him this long to finally do it.

"But you couldn't resist?" She turned and smiled at him. He looked charmingly regretful. "I knew you would do it sooner or later." She reached over and touched his arm.

"I'm sorry. They are good paintings, though."

"Yes. They are."

He leaned over and kissed her, slow and thoughtfully. When he released her lips, he kept his head close to hers. "I know I'm not some oh la la French artist. But I'm not too bad, am I?"

Marie nipped at his lips. "No, you're not bad at all." She could sense where he was going, though. This was his first little nudge. His much-admired patience was wearing thin.

"I can provide excellent references from ex-girlfriends." He grinned.

"Like that wouldn't be awkward."

He ran his thumb over her lower lip, and her heart did race a little—although she couldn't tell if it was from his touch or from her apprehension over having this talk.

"I am but a mere math professor. I can't paint sexy, beautiful paintings of you. I could maybe write theorems on your skin, draw some mathematical symbols if you need that. If that's your particular brand of kink." He pulled back to look her in the eyes. "But really. I'm not too bad in the sack."

The amusement glittering in his eyes a second ago was now a dark question. Part of her, a large part actually, wanted to just give in and sleep with Aidan. She didn't want to lose him, and certainly not over this. It wasn't like she was a virgin or had some deeply held morals on sex. She had a daughter out of wedlock. There were paintings of her nude all over the internet. She had run away on the eve of a major religious holiday with her French lover even though, technically, she was still married at the time. Although since her husband had spent the very same evening with his mistress, the "technically" could be put in quotation marks.

But sex wasn't something she took lightly. She hadn't slept with anyone since Luc, not that she'd had many opportunities until Aidan. Most men weren't as patient and persistent as Aidan was. Or as understanding of her limitations as a single mother. If—no, when—she slept with Aidan, she knew one of two things would happen. She would be in love with him. Or she wouldn't.

And she wasn't sure she was ready for either of those things yet.

36

"Cute little girl."

Luc looked up from the stack of photographs Valerie had printed for him, once she was done slapping and yelling at him. He wasn't forgiven yet, he knew that. Nor did he deserve to be forgiven yet.

He turned to the woman sitting next to him on the plane. He'd been feeling her attention ever since she shoved her carry-on into the overhead compartment and sat down. She was American, not French, with the faint trace of a Boston accent.

"Yes, she is. Thank you," he replied.

He knew where this was going, and it was a place Luc had no intention of ending up. He had never understood the whole "mile high club" thing. There was nothing appealing about having sex with someone in a cramped, odorous airplane bathroom while right outside the door small children whined about having to wait. He was not a club member and wasn't going to become one now.

"Is she yours?"

He bit back an annoyed sigh. This was going to have to play out to its inevitable conclusion, and Luc was really short on patience these days. Well, he'd always been short on patience. Probably the largest source of his problems in life. Going off half-cocked, as they say.

"Yes. My daughter. Ten months."

He felt the woman's stare on his face while he kept his eyes resolutely on the photo of Olivia. He'd had plenty of opportunities with women while on the Drunken World Tour. Turned them all down. Not interested. *Still not interested, sweetheart.* He had meant it when he told Marie that he belonged to her. Luc admitted that half the time he was totally full of shit with his grand pronouncements. It was hard to resist when Americans so easily let him get away with it.

But the other half of the time, he was serious. When Luc loved, he loved completely and without reservation. He loved to the point of pain—his and others. His friend Samantha Smith had said more than once that if only Luc opened his eyes, he would see that point earlier. In time to avoid it. More than once, he had scoffed at Sam. Luc Marchand? He always had his eyes open. He was an artist.

Now he wasn't so sure.

"You must miss her," the American woman said.

"I do. Terribly." He had missed ten months of his daughter's life. Nothing more terrible than that, a fact his sister had made abundantly clear.

He felt a light warmth settle on his knee beneath the tray table. The squeeze of her fingers.

"I can help you forget about that for a little while."

He wanted to ask exactly how having sex in a dirty airplane bathroom was going to make him forget about the daughter whose life had begun without him. Forget about the woman who was raising her alone. Forget about the only woman he would ever want.

The warmth slid higher up his thigh. Maybe this worked on

other men, but it was doing nothing for Luc. He reached beneath the tray table, halted the hand's journey to his crotch and returned it to her.

"Not interested." He almost said "sorry" but stopped himself in time. He had plenty of things to apologize for, but this wasn't one of them.

"Not interested in forgetting or not interested in me?"

He made no effort to hide the sigh of annoyance now. "Both." He tapped the photographs of Olivia into a neat stack and tucked them back into the inside pocket of his jacket. "I'm a family man."

"You're not wearing a wedding band."

"The wedding band is in here." He tapped his chest, the spot right over his heart.

The American woman snorted. "Your loss," she said bitterly.

He pushed up the tray table and retrieved his tablet from the bag at his feet.

"I have lost a lot of things in my life," he said, "but you're not one of them."

He didn't have to look at her to see the effrontery, the indignation, the anger at being rejected on her face. He took his tablet out of airplane mode and resumed reading the parenting book he had downloaded in the airport. Another of Valerie's snarky suggestions.

"I'm a family man," he said again.

THE PLANE TOUCHED down at Dulles only twenty minutes late. The American woman stood up like her seat was suddenly electrified and began waiting impatiently for the crew to unlock the doors. Luc ignored her. He had spent the rest of the flight reading, then sleeping.

He really was a family man. That wasn't one of his full-of-shit grand pronouncements. And it was a fact no one seemed to believe about him. Not even Sam. Just because he was attractive and French and women had been throwing themselves at him since he was fourteen didn't mean he wanted all that. Sure, there were times in the past when he had availed himself of the easy sex. He was human, like anyone. But it had never been what he really *wanted.* He wanted a family of his own. Wanted to be a devoted husband. Wanted a houseful of noisy French-American children. Why was that so damned hard for people to believe?

He thought he had come so close to it with Grace, until she had tossed it all away. She hadn't wanted a family with him. Sam had been right then too. Grace had wanted to be an artist's muse. She had wanted the boost she thought her career would get by sleeping with her professor. But she had never wanted a future with Luc.

How had he been so wrong about Marie?

What hadn't he seen about her?

Those questions had been on his mind constantly since Valerie had shoved her laptop in his face and he had seen the first image of his daughter. His lovely French-American child. The start of a family of his own. Somehow he had gotten so close to exactly what he wanted again and this time, he had been the one to toss it away. He closed his eyes as the line of people crowding the aisle began to shuffle slowly toward the exit.

It couldn't be too late to fix things. It couldn't.

But he knew in his heart that it could be. He no longer had the unblemished optimism of youth. He was nearly forty years old. Still unmarried. Still without a family of his own. Currently unemployed. Currently unloved—okay, utterly despised—by everyone he loved. It was entirely possible—hell, entirely likely—that he would never have the one thing he wanted more than anything else. A family with Marie and Olivia.

"Sir?" He opened his eyes to see a flight attendant standing over him. "This plane is going out of service. We need you to deplane. Is there a connecting gate I can help you with?"

Luc mumbled "no," pulled his bag from beneath the seat in front of him and shuffled his weary heart to the jetway. Whatever it took, he would do it. Beg. Plead. Grovel. Crawl over broken glass. Throw himself at her feet. Anything. Everything. He would do it. Whatever she wanted. He had no pride anymore.

Only a weary heart that wanted to come home.

37

"Your parents have invited me for Thanksgiving?" Aidan chewed his spring roll and nodded his head thoughtfully.

"If you don't have plans," Marie added.

Aidan shook his head. "I don't. I don't usually go to San Diego to see my folks over Thanksgiving. Flying cross country is a nightmare that week. Last year, I volunteered at a soup kitchen but going to your parents sounds like more fun." He smiled and took a swig from his beer.

"Well, I don't know that I would characterize it as fun. My parents don't really do a traditional sit-down meal on Thanksgiving. More of an open house with an endless stream of people parading through. But they've invited us for afterward, just them and us. Trust me, it'll be more fun spending the day at Nishi and Imran's."

Now that she had issued the invitation out loud, it sounded more serious than she had realized it would. She was taking Aidan to meet her best friend and then her parents. In her parents' mind, the day was more about seeing their granddaughter than meeting the new boyfriend, but it ratcheted up the seriousness quotient for

Marie and Aidan. She still wasn't sure she was ready to be more serious with Aidan. In her heart, she knew she wasn't ready, but she also wasn't ready to lose him yet.

She dug into her lemon chicken and brown rice. She tried to imagine herself living here, in Aidan's neat Squirrel Hill rowhouse. It wouldn't be quite so neat with all the accoutrements that came with Livie. Crib, high chair, play mat, toys, children's books, binkies. Aidan's home was tidy and sparely furnished in that way men seemed to like. Marie took another bite of chicken and looked at his large screen television, the audio equipment, the tower of CDs and DVDs, the cables and cords.

Definitely not child-proof, she thought ruefully as she glanced over at Livie, sound asleep on the cushions Aidan had removed from the sofa and spread on the floor. The three of them had spent the afternoon at an apple orchard, picking apples and just generally enjoying a crisp fall day. Aidan was good with Livie, patient and silly, but still a little awkward around her. He was reluctant to bond too closely with her, lest his relationship with Marie not last. Marie appreciated that. It had terrified her, too, to bring a man into her daughter's life.

At the same time, Marie felt pretty comfortable in Aidan's house. At ease, even though she had never spent the night here. They were sitting on the floor, eating takeout from the coffee table. Aidan was drinking a beer. Marie was sipping green tea.

"Penny for your thoughts?"

Marie laughed quietly. "They're a nickel these days, you know. Inflation and all that."

Aidan smiled that sexy smile of his, the one that should make her weak in the knees and set her spine afire … but didn't.

"I'll give you a dime then. How's that?"

"I was going to ask you what you wanted to do while we're in Washington."

He shrugged. "Museums. Monuments. I'll let you be my tour guide."

"That could be dangerous, you know, turning your tourism fate over to a native Washingtonian."

"I trust you."

Marie ate her last forkful of rice. *I trust you.* She heard the other words in there, too. *Why don't you trust me?* Aidan knew the outlines of what had happened with Richard and Luc. It was on the internet for anyone to find. Only her side of events was missing. But Marie was reluctant to talk about any of that, any more than she had to. Eventually, she would have to open up about those chapters of her life if she wanted this thing with Aidan to go anywhere.

But how do you talk about the fact that your husband cheated on you openly? Called off the divorce he had initiated not because he had a change of heart, but because his re-election campaign was in trouble. Richard had drugged her and dumped her on a suburban street corner to be found by good samaritans who called for an ambulance. How do you explain that you have trouble trusting men because a man painted you as a drug addict and was going to very publicly force you into rehab? Marie was ashamed that she hadn't been a stronger person back then, that she hadn't pushed back or run away sooner.

And what was there to say about Luc? She was a single mom. The father of her child had dumped her. Hadn't even stuck around for the birth. What did that say about her? Nothing much good.

"The new Air and Space museum is nice," she said, gathering up her plate and tea mug.

Aidan followed her into the kitchen and for a few minutes, they rinsed plates and loaded the dishwasher in silence. They both knew what was coming next, Marie's departure for the evening, but neither wanted to give voice to it. Marie dried her hands on a dish towel. Aidan closed up the dishwasher.

"I know you have to leave." He stepped toward her, his arms reaching out to her, pulling her in close. "You can bring a portable crib here anytime you like. Or just leave one here. I won't take it as a sign that you're moving in."

Marie let him pull her hips into his. "It's not that. I'm just not comfortable with her waking up in an unfamiliar place."

"Won't she be doing that on Thanksgiving? You don't visit your parents much."

"That's different. It's her grandparents."

When he stroked his thumbs over her cheekbones, she closed her eyes and tried to give into the sensation. When Luc had done this, her heart had raced, her legs trembled—all from just a simple, gentle touch to her face. But still there was none of that from Aidan's touch. It was nice. Pleasant. Nothing wrong with his technique, not too rough, not too soft. But the pleasure of it didn't reach past her cheeks.

She wished she knew why. Aidan was a very handsome man, smart, witty, kind, thoughtful, fun to be with. There was no earthly reason why she shouldn't feel explosive chemistry with him. He ticked all the boxes on her list of The Ideal Man.

Except for sexy foreign accent.

Aidan tipped her head up to his and kissed her. She kissed him back and willed her body to respond. But it didn't. There was none of that swirling, liquidy thing going on in her body that happened when Luc kissed her. After a minute of Aidan's nipping and sucking he pulled back, breathless and hard.

"I'm falling so hard in love with you, Marie."

She couldn't say it back so she pulled his head back down to hers and kissed him again.

38

Luc took a cab to his home in Middleburg and found that his car started after sitting idle for two years. Thank god. He took a much-needed shower. Flying always made him feel unclean afterward, even when there weren't creepy women hitting on him. By noon, he was on route 50 driving toward the city, and Sam's Dupont Circle gallery. He needed to get this over with. Sam was another person on the long list of people who were probably not ready to forgive him yet, but the longer he was in the States without contacting her the less likely he was to renew that friendship. He and Sam had been through a lot together over the years, but she was not a woman to be trifled with.

The gallery was empty when he pushed open the glass door. He let his eyes adjust to the lower light inside then scanned the pale grey walls. Large paintings. He didn't recognize the artist. An abstract sculpture sat in the center of the floor. A thin young man, impeccably dressed in a black shirt and black slacks came out from the back.

"Can I help you?"

"Is Samantha in?" Luc asked.

"Oh holy hell no." The sharp words came from the back of the gallery only seconds before Sam herself appeared. Sam was also impeccably turned out, as usual, in a severe black skirt and jacket, her mass of amber ringlets somewhat restrained by a ponytail.

Her gallery assistant had the good sense to step out of the way as Sam strode toward Luc like a woman on a mission. When Sam slapped Luc hard across the face, the young man quietly turned and disappeared.

"Oh my god, that felt so good," Sam said. "I might want to do it again."

Luc took a quick step back. He was getting used to being slapped, but still. He didn't want to show up in Pittsburgh black and blue.

"Luc Marchand. Everyone thought you were dead."

He sighed. "Not dead. Just off being an asshole."

One of Sam's perfectly penciled eyebrows shot up nearly to her hairline. "You can say that again." She shoved at Luc's chest. "Why the hell didn't you ever answer your phone? I left you dozens of messages. I was worried about you! Hell, everyone was." Her eyes went shiny for a moment, then she blinked and the shine was replaced by fierce, dry anger. "We've been friends for a long time, Luc. It doesn't surprise me, really, that a man would walk out on his pregnant girlfriend. But I'm pissed as hell that you couldn't bother to stay in touch with me."

"I didn't stay in touch with anyone."

Sam held up her hands. "And that's supposed to make me feel better? You blew off everybody and I was just one of the many? How did you ignore your phone all this time?"

"The phone's at the bottom of the Thames."

She rolled her eyes, looking at him with disbelief carved all over her face. She seemed on the verge of saying something, then turned away. "I don't even know what to say to you."

She headed toward the back hallway that led to her office. Luc remained where he was.

Two steps into the hall, she turned. "Are you coming?"

"I have a new phone," Luc said as he followed her into her office. She closed the door behind him. "I'll call you so you have the number."

She sat down heavily in her office chair and waved a hand at the visitor's chair, indicating Luc should sit.

"So what are you going to do now?"

"Go to Pittsburgh. I just got into Dulles this morning. I'll get a few things from the house, then drive to see her. She had the baby."

"Yeah. You're the only person for whom this is news."

Luc winced.

"Well, good luck with that," she continued. "What if she doesn't want you?"

"That may be the case."

"If I were her, that would be the case."

"Good thing you're not her."

"I might call ahead and advise her not to want you."

"You wouldn't do that."

Sam sighed. "No, I wouldn't." She shook her head. "I really don't get you, Luc. You ran out on your pregnant girlfriend. Disappeared for nearly two years. What the hell? In what alternate universe is any of that forgivable?"

"No alternate universe. But she's my daughter, too."

Sam's breath came out in a chuff of disbelief. "So you're just swanning back in here and suing for custody?"

"I hope it wouldn't come to that." Luc leaned forward in the chair. "I do want her back, Sam. I love her. I love Marie."

"Again, good luck with that. Paint me some pretty pictures and I'll see what I can do about your career."

"I don't give a shit about my career."

"You say that now. But when she tosses you out on your ass like she should, what will you have then?"

Luc had no answer for that. Or no answer he wanted to vocalize. He would have nothing.

"Whatever you do, don't go back to painting rich people's cars and horses, Luc. Go back to teaching instead."

The snort escaped before he could stop it. "Like anyone would hire me."

"It's been fourteen years, Luc. Work your network. You were a gifted teacher. You *are* a gifted teacher. Stop letting your mistakes define who you are."

STOP LETTING your mistakes define who you are. Easy for Sam to say, as he wandered the sunny streets of Dupont Circle. His stomach was tight with hunger, but he had no appetite.

Other people defined him by his mistakes.

He walked up and down the neighborhood streets with no purpose or destination in mind. After thirty minutes, he found himself standing in front of the venerable Phillips Collection. His favorite museum in Washington and the place where he had agreed to paint Marie. He went in, paid the entrance fee and perused the brochure. The Alistair Smith and Elizabeth Calhoun show was long gone, naturally, on the road taunting some other city's cultural mavens. He wondered what really happened to their relationship in later years. He should never have painted Marie. He had enjoyed it immensely and loved the resulting canvases, but he should have had better judgment. Been a stronger man and resisted the easy temptation of it.

He skimmed the description for the current traveling exhibition on the third floor. It wasn't one he was interested in, so he wandered the permanent galleries instead. It was a day for wandering. His last day for wandering before starting a new life.

He ended up in the Rothko room. Luc had never been a big fan of Mark Rothko's paintings, but the quiet of the small room drew him in. He had noticed in years past that other people didn't generally enter this room if there was already someone in there. It was a room people wanted to experience alone and other people respected that.

He sat on the slatted bench in the middle of the pale blonde wood floor. On each ivory wall hung a single large canvas. Luc freely admitted that he was a representational painter. Most abstract art left him cold. He couldn't stare at washes of ochre and maroon and tangerine and imbue them with any kind of emotion. What did he feel when he looked at a green slab of paint over a smaller maroon one? Nothing. The colors were pleasing to him, but it was just something to look at.

He sat in the Rothko room for a full hour, just staring at each painting in turn. Then starting over again. Luc had always looked to art for answers but whatever answer people found in this room was eluding him. He hadn't drawn so much as a single straight line in nearly two years. He wasn't sure he still could draw, for that matter. He'd been so certain he saw Marie clearly. But clearly he had not. There was some truth about her he had missed.

39

Maybe it was better if she didn't feel any chemistry for Aidan. Marie turned that thought over and over in her mind as she walked from campus to Livie's daycare. Without blazing intense chemistry, it wouldn't hurt so much if she and Aidan broke up at some point. And Marie really didn't want to go through that again, the deep aching emptiness she had felt when Luc left. Month after month he didn't return, and there were days upon days when the pain and the betrayal had been more than she could bear.

She couldn't withstand that kind of pain again. Not for herself, but for Livie. She had a young child now. She couldn't lie in bed and cry all the time, not worrying whether she ate or slept. She was a mother and her daughter came before all else now. Before men, before heartbreak, before her own desire to be loved. Before chemistry.

She couldn't afford to be devastated by a man leaving the way Luc had devastated her. And maybe it wasn't a matter of chemistry at all. Maybe the issue was that Livie—with her dark curls and darker eyes, her perfect rosebud lips—had laid claim to all of

Marie's heart. There was no room in her heart for anyone else. No vacancy at the inn.

When Luc never came back, Marie's heart had shattered into a million pieces. The pain had been excruciating, all those tiny shards of glass swirling like a tornado in her chest. Livie had put it back together again, made it whole, gave Marie's life a focus and center that had never been there before.

She pushed open the door to the daycare, greeted the woman at the desk, then headed down the hall toward one of the toddler rooms. Livie's face broke into a wide grin when she saw Marie step through the door. Really, could a person smile any harder than Livie did when Marie walked into a room? Marie hadn't planned to be a mother this soon but now that she was, it was hard to imagine anything else. The overwhelming happiness she felt when she looked at Livie … one could get drunk on it.

She scooped up Livie, gave her a kiss, asked how her day was. She imagined Livie thinking, *Fine, maman, I played with Chelsea and Chloe. Russell is cute, don't you think? We had applesauce for snack. Again. Yes, I napped, dearest maman.* Marie smiled into the sweet soft crook of Livie's neck and nestled another kiss there, then retrieved her tiny coat from the cubby.

The days were getting shorter. Already it was dark by the time they got home and soon it would be too cold to walk. They would have to begin taking the bus. But for now, they both enjoyed the crisp evening air on their cheeks, the pink of the sky as the sun dipped below trees and houses, the lights popping on in houses and shops as the sun faded.

Marie did the complicated dance of getting the stroller through the daycare's front door, pushing open the door with her hip, pulling the stroller through, pivoting back around on the sidewalk outside, turning right toward home. She was so content, so utterly happy to be reunited with her daughter after the work day, that it took her mind several steps to process what her eyes had just barely seen. She stopped the stroller, turned around. Her heart froze.

Luc.

He dropped to his knees on the sidewalk.

"*Déesse*," he said.

"No." She had given up on this ever happening. Made peace with it not happening.

"Please, Marie."

The way her name sounded on his lips, she didn't want to like it.

"No." She tightened her fingers around the plastic of the stroller, to steady herself. She would not soften her heart for him. Not after all this time.

"I'm sorry."

The apology hit her like a punch to the chest.

"It's too late to be sorry."

"I didn't know—"

"Didn't know what?" Marie took a deep breath, modulated her voice. She felt like yelling, screaming, tearing her hair out. But not in front of Livie. "That I was pregnant? Having your baby? You knew that."

Tears began to run down his face.

She shook her head. "You can't do this to me, Luc. You cannot."

"Just let me see her, Marie. I beg you."

She used to imagine this moment, the moment he returned to her. Over and over, examined its every line and plane, rehearsed her words, rehearsed her feelings. And now that it was here? All of her scripts were swept away, their lines, their carefully-planned control, whooshed into the evening air around her. Faced with Luc—faced with his irresistible Luc-ness—she no longer remembered what she was supposed to do. Her mind was screaming for her to turn on her heel and walk away. *He left you! Alone! In a foreign country!* Her heart wanted to kiss him as though the past eighteen months had never happened. *It was a horrible, horrible dream. And now they had awakened. Everything was fine.*

But her body. Oh la la. The things it wanted could probably only be described in French. The chemistry she so desperately wanted to feel with Aidan was here, right here and right now, with the man who had betrayed her beyond all forgiveness.

She peeked back at Livie, who had fallen sound asleep beneath her blanket, her stuffed bear clutched tight against her cheek, totally oblivious to the standoff happening between her parents. She took a deep breath and gently wheeled the stroller around and pushed it toward Luc, who was still kneeling like a penitent on the sidewalk. There was no amount of penance he could do to make up for what he had done.

Luc wiped the back of his hand across his eyes, then touched the blanket where it covered Livie's tiny foot. He stared in awe at her for a long moment.

"Valerie said her name was Olivia."

"Yes. Your sister helped me choose the name. She was there when she was born."

Luc flinched. "I'm happy to hear that, that she was there. She is beautiful."

He unfolded himself from the sidewalk and Marie got her first good look at him. Her first look in nearly two years. He was thinner, it seemed. His jacket was too light for this time of year in Pittsburgh. His dark hair was a little shaggy, his cheeks covered in a light beard. The shadows beneath his dark eyes were a little deeper. Still, she would have recognized him anywhere, just from the thrumming that had started up in her chest.

In her traitorous heart.

"Where are you staying?" she asked.

"A hotel downtown."

"How long are you staying?"

"I don't know. That depends on you."

"Nothing depends on me, Luc." She forced herself to turn the stroller around and take the first few steps toward home.

"Let me walk you home."

"You can do whatever the hell you want." Yes, she was angry. Angry at him for daring to come back after all this time. Angry at herself for still wanting him to come back.

She saw his hand reach out to touch her arm, and her heart skipped a beat. But then he pulled it back and shoved it into the pocket of his jeans. *Damn it all.* She had wanted him to touch her. She was feeling it again, the attraction to him, the way his voice plucked at every nerve in her body, setting them all vibrating and humming. Her mind remembered all those nights alone, each one another step toward the certainty of never seeing him again. Her heart remembered pain, the sheer blinding agony of his absence. But her body, it remembered other things.

She didn't want to be attracted to him now. It was the last thing she needed. He couldn't be trusted. He had abandoned her. Abandoned their daughter. *Whywhywhy?* A litany of questions skittered across her tongue, pushed at her pursed lips, but Marie bit them back. She didn't want to know. There were no answers that would be good enough.

They walked in silence to the apartment. She didn't invite him up. He didn't ask.

"Goodnight, Luc."

40

Luc went back the next day and waited for Marie and Olivia outside the daycare. He went back every day. She never asked him up and he never invited himself. He knew better than to push too much. He had screwed up, and he had no right to ask for a second chance.

Then came the evening when Marie and Olivia weren't alone. When they emerged from the daycare, Olivia bundled into her stroller in her coat and blanket, a tall man with blonde hair and the open, unguarded face of an American was with them. When the man adjusted the collar of Marie's wool coat and draped his arm casually—familiarly—across her shoulders, Luc's stomach clenched so violently he nearly doubled over from the pain.

This was a scenario he hadn't considered. He had been faithful to Marie, but there was no reason for her to have done the same. She was a beautiful woman, loving and passionate. Of course, other men would be attracted to her—and giving her what Luc had taken away.

He crossed the street toward them. Marie might not want him back. By all indications so far, she did not. She had spoken fewer than twenty words to him all week. But that was his daughter in the stroller. No man was going to move in on Olivia. He was her father and nothing could change that.

The blonde man spotted him before Marie did, and pulled her in closer. His open, unguarded expression shuttered. Luc ignored the two of them for the moment, instead kneeling down to the stroller and tweaking Livie's nose.

"Bonjour, ma chérie. How's my little girl today?" he cooed. The other man might be staking his claim to Marie right now, but Luc was staking his claim to his daughter—and through her, his claim to her mother.

"What are you doing here, Luc?" Marie asked.

"I walk you home every evening. Isn't that right, Olivia?"

A smile lit his daughter's face. Marie might not be happy to see him night after night, but Olivia had taken to him more quickly than he had expected—or hoped for. Luc stood and extended his hand to the blonde man.

"Luc Marchand. Olivia's father."

The man, who was clearly younger now that Luc could see him up close, accepted the greeting. Marie's jaw was tight, her blue eyes lit with anger.

"Aidan Janssen. Marie's boyfriend."

The gauntlet has been thrown. Luc smiled inwardly. He hadn't expected this turn of events but he was up to the challenge. He had to be. His daughter, his firstborn, his flesh and blood, was regarding him thoughtfully from the stroller. *Don't worry, Olivia. I'm not going anywhere.* Walking away from her was not an option.

"Well then, Aidan, we should probably get to know each other."

On Saturday morning, Luc waited for them by the fountain

in front of the Carnegie Museum of Art. He'd been a little surprised that Aidan—and Marie, grudgingly—had accepted his invitation. But he was here to stay, and he intended to spend time with his daughter. Plus, he did need to get to know Aidan if he was going to supplant him in Marie's life. On the walk home to Marie's apartment, he had sensed that their relationship was still fairly new. There was a familiarity, a friendship between Marie and Aidan, but there was distance, too. And he suspected that distance was being enforced by Marie. That bode well for him.

He had gotten a haircut yesterday and was shaving regularly again. His outfit today was chosen carefully to contrast as much as possible with Aidan. Luc was wearing his black leather jacket and a black shirt, a dark grey tie knotted loosely at his collar. He shoved his hands into the pockets of his jeans as he watched the three of them approach. Marie was pushing the stroller. Whatever she might feel for the other man, she didn't feel close enough to him to let him handle the stroller.

When they reached the fountain, Luc shook Aidan's hand and dropped a light, French kiss on Marie's cheek. Her demeanor was as chilly as her skin. He scooped Olivia out of the stroller and hugged her tight to his chest.

"So you can check the stroller," he said to Marie. As they marched toward the entrance, he asked Aidan, "Have you been to this museum before?"

"A few times. And you?"

"First time. But my grand-père had work in the Carnegie International here. Many years ago, of course."

"We're not going to see any of your paintings here, are we?" the other man responded.

"Certainly not. I am not the painter my grandfather was, sadly."

Luc stepped up to the desk and paid their admission. When

Marie began to protest, he waved her off. "My invitation, my treat."

"I admire the paintings you did of Marie," Aidan remarked as Marie checked the stroller and their coats. "I've only seen them online, of course. Would love to see them in person someday."

Luc caught the other man's wink to Marie and the resulting flush to her lovely skin. Luc took a deep breath and swallowed his jealousy. There was a time when Marie blushed for him and if he wanted that time back, he would need to be patient.

"I could make a few more."

"Stop it!" Marie nearly shouted. "We are not talking about these paintings."

If Luc hadn't been holding Livie in his arms, Marie probably would have slugged him. The urge to was painted all over her face. She unfolded the museum map and directed her energy toward studying it.

"What should we go see first?" Luc murmured to Olivia. "Should we find some French paintings?"

Marie let out a loud, dramatic exhale. "I can't believe you did this, Luc."

He looked up from Olivia's twinkling eyes to face her mother's angry ones.

"Did what, chérie?"

"Stop with the terms of endearment."

Aidan took a step closer to her. Marie snapped the glossy museum map in the air, then lifted Olivia from his arms.

Luc scanned the map. *Merde.*

"I didn't know it was here, Marie. Truly."

She rolled her eyes, while Aidan took the map from Luc's hand.

Alistair Smith & Elizabeth Calhoun: A Model Revealed.

"We don't have to see it again."

"And we're not." She shifted Olivia's weight in her arms.

"Come on." She marched off, leaving Luc and Aidan to hurry behind in her wake. She lead them to the museum's Water Lilies painting. Monet. It was the first thing that came to mind. French.

"Ah oui," Luc exclaimed when he and Aidan caught up to her. He lifted Livie from Marie's arms. "Let me carry her. Give your arms a rest."

Luc's hand brushed hers—an accidental touch, barely anything—and yet Marie felt it burn down her spine like a shot of whiskey. Her reaction surprised and dismayed her. The last thing she needed in her life right now was to be this affected by Luc.

Aidan's warm hand wrapped around hers and the firm but gentle pressure held her back, while allowing Luc and Livie to move closer to the painting.

"Nice of him to finally come back."

Marie made no reply. She understood Aidan's bitterness over Luc's sudden reappearance. She shared some of that bitterness herself. It was nice for Luc that he could decide to be a father on his own timetable, show up when he felt ready for the job. Marie hadn't enjoyed that same luxury, and she'd had to shoulder all the responsibility of motherhood by herself. On the flip side, she had enjoyed all the joys of motherhood by herself, too—and now here was Luc asking to share those joys.

But watching Luc hold Livie while cooing softly to her in French, pointing out elements of Monet's brushwork that Livie of course couldn't understand, Marie realized it *was* nice of him to finally come back. "Better late than never," her mother used to say about donors. Sometimes she had to spend years cultivating a person before they finally gave money.

The sentiment applied here, too. It was better for Livie to have a father—her father—a year late rather than never at all. And never at all was the outcome Marie had finally made peace with. Livie was never going to remember that Luc was AWOL her first year. That wasn't a grudge she was ever going to bear against him.

Marie, of course, was a different matter.

"It's nice for Livie," she replied at last.

"But is it nice for you?"

Marie heard what he was really saying. Their relationship was on solid footing, as far as dating relationships go, but her refusal to sleep with him thus far left a certain gap in intimacy between them.

"It has nothing to do with us. He's her father. I can't keep him away entirely."

From the look on Aidan's face, that wasn't the answer he wanted to hear.

41

When Aidan excused himself to use the men's room, Luc saw his chance. Marie had retrieved the stroller and was shaking and pressing it open. It was a complicated contraption. His daughter was asleep in his arms, her head resting heavily on his shoulder, her back rising and falling beneath his hand with her every breath. He buried his nose in her and took a long inhale of her baby scent, warm skin and milk and the sweet perspiration curling her dark hair.

Marie gave him a tiny smile, her first of the day. Her first since he'd come back. "She smells good, doesn't she?"

Tears pricked at Luc's eyes as he nodded. He had to be quick. Aidan's absence gave him no more than five minutes, tops.

"I'm sorry, Marie. If it takes me a lifetime to show you how very sorry I am, I will do it."

Marie gently peeled Olivia from his shoulder and chest, laid her softly into the stroller, tucked a blanket around her, then her warm coat.

"What do you want, Luc? Why are you here?"

"I want you—us—back." She began to shake her head, but he

pressed on. “I want to be Livie’s father.” He used the shortened name that he’d heard Marie use all week. He hadn’t wanted to be presumptuous by using it earlier, but now it felt right on his tongue.

She shook her head like she just couldn’t believe the words she was hearing. “You don’t get to come back after two years and just expect that everything will go back to the way it was. Everything is changed now, Luc. I have my own life here. And you’d have to stay. You can’t just drop into Livie’s life when you feel like it.”

“I’ve been looking at apartments here.”

“I’d want to see a lease.”

“Please give me a chance, Marie. If not with you, then with our daughter. I want to be a good father to her.”

“You broke my heart.”

“I know that. I will be forever sorry.”

“You can’t break hers.”

42

Thanksgiving at Nishi's house was everything that Thanksgiving at the Witherspoons was not. Nishi's home was filled with the warm conviviality of close friends and family members, and the barely controlled chaos of nieces and nephews everywhere underfoot. It was the kind of Thanksgiving Marie had longed for as a child—that Norman Rockwell-esque timelessness of family and food and tradition. The table and sideboard in Nishi's dining room was laden with turkey and curry, stuffing and saffron rice, mashed potatoes and samosas, dinner rolls and naan, pumpkin pie and kheer.

After dinner, Marie put Livie down for a nap in a guest room while Aidan huddled around the videogame consoles with Imran's nephews.

"He's nice. I like him," Nishi said as she and Marie carried dirty plates and flatware from the dining table to the kitchen. "He seems very steady."

"He is. Steady, nice, attractive." Marie pulled open the dishwasher.

"So why am I hearing a problem in there?"

"Luc has come back."

The plate in Nishi's hands bobbled before Marie reached out and steadied it.

"Son of a bitch. When?"

"Couple weeks ago. He wants to be Livie's father now." Marie sighed. "And I don't know what to do about him."

"What has to be done? I suppose you can't keep him from his daughter, but other than that …"

"I don't feel around Aidan the way I feel around Luc." There, she had admitted it.

"That's probably a good thing. A very good thing."

"I know. And I keep telling myself that, but …"

"But he left you. Has he explained the why of that?"

Marie shook her head. "I haven't asked, either. I really don't even want to know. I mean, there's no good reason why he did that."

Marie opened the cabinet beneath the sink and retrieved a dishwasher pod.

"Other than that he didn't want to have a baby with me. Although he's good with Livie," she added.

With the dishwasher loaded and running, Marie went back to the guest room to check on her daughter. Livie was sound asleep, splayed out on her back, open and unguarded like children were in sleep. Unlike their parents who tossed and turned, clutched at pillows and blankets, and woke bleary-eyed before the alarm.

Marie's heart swelled the way it always did when she looked at her daughter. How could Luc not have wanted her? He'd never said that he didn't. The pregnancy was a surprise, sure, but he had seemed okay with it. Obviously, he wasn't though. He'd taken advantage of her absence to leave. Nishi had come to Paris to visit her and the two of them went to London for a weekend. A girls' weekend together. When they got back, Luc was gone. He took the cowardly way out, without even saying goodbye or explaining himself. He just vanished, as if into thin air.

And Marie didn't care why anymore. Nor did she particularly care why he'd come back. He could have time with Livie. She wouldn't deny him that. But he wasn't going to be part of Marie's life beyond that.

Livie sighed in her sleep, a long sound of sheer contentment. Marie had never not wanted her. Motherhood had always been an abstract, someday-in-the-future hope. But from the minute she suspected she was pregnant, she had wanted Livie with a surprising fierceness.

And it wasn't as though she didn't have other options. Nishi had offered to pay for an abortion since Marie couldn't work in Paris and her bank account in the states had been frozen after she left. Marie never even considered it. Not for a second. She had talked so much about "Luc Luc Luc" and starting a family with him on the train to London, even Nishi—who possessed a bottomless well of patience with Marie—had gotten tired of hearing it.

Marie had needed even more of that patience when they got back to Paris Sunday evening and discovered him gone. They'd called Valerie, his parents, everyone. No one knew where he was. No one could get through to him on his phone. She had cried on Nishi's shoulder until there were no more tears left to cry.

She tucked in Livie's blanket and returned to the kitchen, where Nishi was waiting with desserts.

"Pie or kheer?"

"Oh kheer, totally. I can get pumpkin pie at my parents'."

"Aidan is getting his butt kicked on Xbox with the kids." Nishi handed her a bowl of kheer and a spoon.

"How's he taking that?"

"Better than Imran does." Nishi pushed her fork into a slice of pie. "I like him, Marie. I really do. I'm glad things are working out for you."

Marie felt her friend studying her.

"What?" Nishi said. "Things aren't working out?"

Marie shrugged. "He ticks all the boxes on the list of what I should be looking for, but ..."

But I don't think about him when he's not around. I don't ache for his kiss. At night, I don't wish he were sleeping next to me.

"You're just not feeling him," her friend finished the sentence.

Marie shook her head. "And I really want to feel more for him."

What was it she had said to Luc once, back when things were still good? *You're spoiling me for other men.* And his reply? *That was always the plan.*

"Give it time. Luc is messing with your pheromones. He probably won't stick around again anyway, when he realizes you don't want him back."

Except she hadn't been feeling much for Aidan before Luc came back either. She kept waiting for the chemistry to kick in, and it just wasn't. When he kissed her or held her hand, she didn't feel anything special. With Luc, all he had to do was look at her—even now, after all he'd done—and her whole body practically went up in flames. But her body clearly wasn't to be trusted in all this. Her body had been wrong about Luc Marchand's heart.

"Yeah. I need to be smart about this. For Livie's sake."

BY THE TIME they arrived at Marie's parents' house in Cleveland Park, Marie had re-convinced herself of Aidan's desirability. She'd run down the list of all the boxes he ticked off. Nice. Attractive. Smart. Funny. Her best friend liked him. Good job. He was steady, stable.

Boring.

Boring was good, she countered. Luc had been exciting, sure. While he was around.

There were still open house guests around when Aidan held open the front door of the Witherspoon home for Marie and Livie. The appearance of the lone Witherspoon grandchild created all the commotion Marie had expected.

"Eileen! Your granddaughter is here!" "Adorable!" "Precious!" Fingers were tweaked, cheeks lightly pinched. Livie recoiled from the sudden onslaught of attention and buried her face in the crook of Marie's neck.

"Oh sweetheart." Eileen Witherspoon threaded her way through the group of guests surrounding Marie and Livie. "Come to grandma."

Livie's face remained buried in Marie's neck.

"She was asleep in the car. She just woke up," Marie said.

Eileen rubbed Livie's back softly. "Well, there'll be plenty of time for just the two of us later," she cooed.

The fearsome Witherspoons, one of the most powerful power couples in Washington, had been reduced to mush by one tiny eleven-month-old girl. Marie's smile was genuine for a moment—until she saw her ex-husband and his former mistress-now-wife stride hand in hand from the back of the house, just steps behind her father.

"You must be Aidan. Welcome and happy Thanksgiving," her father said when he reached Marie and Aidan. Aidan gave him a strong, firm handshake. Her father leaned in to kiss Livie on the top of her dark hair, then kissed Marie's cheek.

Marie tried to will Richard and Maya to disappear into thin air and, if not that, to return to the back of the house. But no such luck.

Maya walked around Marie to get a better look at Livie, then turned and squinted at Aidan. "She doesn't look a thing like you."

Aidan stood there, unsure what to do while Marie fumed inwardly. She didn't want to disrupt her parents' party. On the other hand, she was disappointed they had invited Richard and Maya at all. Maya knew damn well that Aidan wasn't Livie's father.

"She looks everything like me though," came a French-accented voice.

That moment when things get weirder.

Marie looked past Richard and Maya to see Luc headed straight for her. The question of what Luc was doing at her parents' house was immediately answered by the sight of Samantha Smith standing in the doorway to the kitchen.

"Hello sweetheart."

Livie perked up at the sound of her father's voice and gave a little kick of excitement. Stunned, Marie simply let Luc lift her away and cuddle her against his chest. He walked back toward Sam. Without the ballast of Livie, Marie felt faint. Aidan reached out to steady her arm as she watched Luc introduce their daughter to his friend.

"I didn't know he was going to be here," she whispered to him, as they turned away from the curious crowd.

"Why *is* he here? I assumed your parents had no relationship with him." Aidan steered her toward a settee in the front parlor and helped her sit down.

"They don't. But my mother knows his friend, Samantha. Socially. They don't know each other well but tons of people get invites to Thanksgiving here."

"Do you want me to go get Livie?"

Marie shook her head. "She's okay with Luc."

"Are you sure?"

She nodded. She was sure. Livie had been almost immediately comfortable with Luc, a fact that both heartened and disheartened her.

"I wish I had known he was going to be here."

Marie bit back a sigh. "I wish I'd known, too. I also wish I'd known my ex-husband and his wife were going to be here. She was the one who said Livie doesn't look like you. She knows who Livie's father is."

The day was going from bad to worse, and Marie wasn't feeling thankful for any of it.

43

Luc's nerves were getting the best of him. If he weren't holding Livie in his arms, he'd be shaking like a leaf. He hadn't expected Marie to take so long to show up at her parents' house. Several times, he had almost told Sam they could go. Especially given the presence of Marie's ex-husband, who had been glaring malevolently at him all day.

The feeling's mutual, pal.

The man had cheated on his wife in a very public fashion, drugged her and left her on a street corner for good samaritans to find, lied about her having a prescription drug addiction, and was planning to drug her again and hold her hostage in a rehab facility just so he could get re-elected. Yeah, Luc's feelings toward the man were pretty damn malevolent, too.

Luc was spending the Thanksgiving weekend with Sam and her family, as he'd done for so many years in the past. Sam's husband, Peter, had been only too glad to let Luc be Sam's guest at the Witherspoons' party.

"I'm going to sit right here on the couch, eat leftovers and watch football," Peter had said. "Then take a nap."

So Luc had accompanied Sam as her plus-one in the hopes of getting to see Marie and Livie again. He should have warned Marie ahead of time that he would be here, but he knew she would have stayed away.

"Can I have Livie back?"

He turned to face Marie. She was wearing a grey wool dress and black suede knee boots like they were a suit of armor.

"You can't hide her away in the kitchen," she added. "People want to see her. My mother wants to see her."

Livie squeaked in protest as he handed her over.

"Where's Aidan?" he asked.

"I dropped him off with my father. They're discussing cars or something."

"I'm guessing you wanted to speak to me alone."

"I want to know what you're doing here."

"Sam invited me. And I wanted to see you."

"You see me nearly every night after work."

"But you barely talk to me then."

"I don't know what to say to you, Luc. I'm not sure there even is much to say."

Luc knew she couldn't possibly feel that way. They had so much to talk about, to hash out, to come to terms with.

"We should be talking about Livie," he said.

"I want you to see her, Luc. I do. I want her to know her father. I just don't know how to incorporate you into our life. And I'm dating a wonderful man who understandably feels threatened by you showing up out of the blue."

"I signed a lease this week on a studio and an apartment in East Liberty." He watched her expression change slightly, then change back, as she absorbed this information. East Liberty wasn't far from her apartment in Shadyside. Far enough that he wasn't living down the street, but close enough to see Livie every day.

"What are you going to do there?"

"Paint. Take on some students. Sam knows some people at one of the other colleges in town. I might try to get a teaching job or at least some adjunct classes."

Marie adjusted Livie's weight in her arms. He gave her a moment to let his news sink in. He wasn't going anywhere this time. If Marie and his daughter lived in Pittsburgh, then he would live there. If they moved somewhere else in the future, he would follow. He had to. He belonged to them both now.

"I'd like to host a birthday party for Livie next weekend. Unless you had other plans."

"No. I hadn't made any formal plans."

"I spoke to your parents about it. They said they'd be happy to come."

"My parents? Wait—you spoke to my parents?"

"I'm a guest in their house. Of course, I spoke to them. Hard to avoid it in any case. I'm the father of their only grandchild."

"Who else were you planning to invite?"

Luc shrugged. "I don't know that many people in Pittsburgh. So you can invite whomever you want. Aidan. Coworkers. Nishi." He winced.

"Why did you leave, Luc?"

The question he had been waiting for. Dreading.

"I was scared." That was only part of the truth. He couldn't very well tell her he thought she was going to London to terminate the pregnancy. She would think he was making that up. She would never believe that her friend had told him exactly that.

"I'm sorry," he said. "Is there any chance we can put that behind us? That's all I ask, Marie. A chance to make things right between us again. What we had was good, wasn't it?"

"It was wonderful," she whispered. "But I don't know if I can see my way back to that place again."

Her honesty made his heart soar. It wasn't exactly what he

wanted to hear, but at least she was thinking about them and the way they used to be. It was a start.

"I'll help you see the way. We'll find the way together."

LIVIE WAS sound asleep by the time Marie finished changing her diaper. It was blissfully quiet in her childhood bedroom, and Marie wanted to just stay there for awhile, escape from the noise and drama downstairs. She lay back on the bed, next to Livie, and stared sightlessly at the ceiling. After a minute, she closed her eyes and allowed herself to hover on that soft field between sleep and wakefulness. She could take a nap. Just five minutes, enough to recharge and refresh. No one would begrudge her a quick turkey coma, would they?

She wasn't sure how long she'd been asleep when the sound of angry voices awakened her. The voices were muffled, as though they were coming from outside. She stood and drew back the window drapes. The bedroom overlooked her parents' long, narrow backyard. It was a typical city yard, fenced and bordering an alley. Richard and Luc were in the yard yelling at each other, Luc gesticulating wildly with his arms.

This wasn't going to end well. The only question Marie could see was who would throw the first punch.

Richard.

Luc made no effort to duck her ex-husband's fist. Blood spurted from his nose.

The bedroom door opened behind her and her mother slipped in. Eileen Witherspoon wrapped her arms around her daughter's shoulders in an uncharacteristic show of motherly affection.

"What's going on?" Marie asked.

"I think a score is being settled."

"Why isn't anyone stopping it?"

"There aren't many people left downstairs, sweetie. You and Livie have been asleep for awhile. And Richard has been taunting your baby daddy, as he has called him a few times, all day. I think Monsieur Marchand is defending your honor at the moment."

Marie sighed. "Unsuccessfully, it looks like."

"I told him to let Richard hit first. Legally, that's a better idea."

"Wait—you sanctioned this? Where's dad?"

She felt her mother's shrug against her back.

"Some things you just have to let work themselves out."

Like your lover working through his ambivalence over you and the child you were carrying? Even if it took nearly two years? Was that it? Was she supposed to simply be patient and wait for Luc to come around?

Marie stared down into the yard as Richard bobbed and weaved in some grotesque parody of a boxer. Luc wiped his bloody nose on the back of his sweater sleeve.

"Why did you invite them today? Richard and Maya."

"We can't cut out the Macintyre family, dear." Her mother squeezed her shoulders. "But we're not responsible for their son's behavior either."

Marie understood what her mother was saying, even as she didn't like it. Richard was always going to be on the periphery of her life. Like Luc, now that he was back. How did she keep ending up with men who weren't fully in her life, but couldn't be completely cut out of it either?

In the yard, Richard's dance moves stopped. Luc stepped in and hit him with a hard uppercut to the kidney. Richard doubled over in pain, his curses loud enough to be heard upstairs in her bedroom. She watched as Luc strolled calmly to the end of the yard, unlocked the wooden gate and left.

"I'm sorry about this, mother," Marie apologized.

Eileen unwrapped her arms from around her daughter. "No

apology needed, sweetheart. Your father and I were glad to meet Livie's father."

Marie pinned her mother with a look of pure skepticism.

Eileen patted Marie on the back, then gazed at Livie on the bed, still asleep and oblivious to what had just transpired in the yard. "You've got a choice to make, don't you?"

44

Luc ripped the sheet of paper from the sketchpad, crumpled it up in his fist and threw it across the room, where it scattered among its already discarded comrades. He was sitting in his new studio, surrounded by stacks of boxes he hadn't bothered to unpack yet. They all needed to be unpacked if he was going to host a party for Livie's first birthday that weekend. But it had seemed more important to sit down and draw.

Only he couldn't draw anymore. Whatever talent he had once been in possession of was gone. It had been drunk away while he was wandering the globe. Karma had finally caught up to him. Or whatever.

It had been easy to blame Marie back when he was convinced that she had ended their pregnancy. Even then, though, he had chalked it up to a simple lack of interest in drawing. He hadn't been interested in too much more than alcohol in those days. But now he was intensely interested in making art again—and it was still gone.

He wanted to draw his daughter. He had missed nearly a year of her life, a year he hadn't seen, had no memories of, no drawings or paintings. It was unfathomable—unforgivable—that he had missed even a single day of Livie's life. He was not going to miss any more. But the lines weren't coming.

He'd tried drawing her from memory. Tried drawing her from the photographs on his phone. But nothing was working. He could see her face perfectly in his mind but that image wasn't making it to his fingers, to the pencil, to the page.

He hurled his pencil across the room, where it hit the wall and snapped neatly in two.

How could he not draw the one thing that was more dear to him than anything else?

And what was he going to do if he couldn't draw or paint? Couldn't credibly teach drawing lessons? Go back to teaching art history, as Sam had suggested? He had promised Marie he would stay in Pittsburgh, but what if he couldn't? What if there was nothing for him to do here? Then what?

He leaned back on his stool and kicked the easel over, too.

45

The bus stop was directly in front of Luc's studio-slash-apartment. That was convenient for Marie, given that she hadn't bought a car yet. Pittsburgh was easy enough to get around without one, at least the parts of it she needed to frequent. The bus stop would be convenient for Luc's students, too. She pushed down at the little twinge of jealousy she felt at the thought of him taking on students. After all, look what happened the last time he took on a new student.

She reminded herself that Livie gave her a claim on Luc that his new students wouldn't have. Unless he knocked one of them up, which wasn't entirely out of the realm of possibility. He'd done it twice already.

She hitched the diaper bag onto her shoulder and adjusted Livie's weight in her arms. She scanned the building in which Luc was living. From the outside, everything he'd told her about it was true. It was a former auto body shop, its grey cinder block exterior and large grey garage doors still there. It lacked the charm of his studio in Middleburg, no question about that. It was hard to imagine that he didn't miss his old place.

According to Luc, the interior had been divided up into three live-work units. The other two units were occupied by a photographer and a fabric artist. Luc's unit was number three, and the door sported a sign with his meticulous penmanship. *Bonjour. Please come in.* Birthday balloons had been artfully drawn around the words. She should snag the sign when she left. She would keep it for Livie, an original Luc Marchand drawing from her first birthday.

She tested the door handle and it opened easily. They were an hour early, having turned down Aidan's offer to pick them up and drive them here. Her polite declining of his offer had sparked their first fight. She wasn't entirely sure he would turn up at Livie's party later. The fact that she had turned down rides from Nishi and her parents, too, hadn't assuaged Aidan. It wasn't her mode of transportation that bothered him, but her coming here alone.

Aidan had still not acclimated himself to Luc's presence in her life. Marie wasn't acclimated either. Spending time with Luc was difficult. She was still angry with him for abandoning her. Yet, she still wanted him even after all that. There was no denying the way he made her body feel when he was around. If he hadn't left immediately after the fight with Richard, she would have been first in line to clean up his face and take care of him.

That would have made for a tense ride back to Pittsburgh in Aidan's car.

She was early today because she wanted to give Luc some time with Livie alone on her birthday. She owed him that. And she owed it to Livie. She and Luc might not be a couple, but they were Livie's parents. They were a family.

Inside, Luc's new studio was decorated in red, white and blue —the colors of both sides of Livie's heritage. Balloons and streamers were everywhere. Luc had rented tables and chairs. These were also festooned in red, white and blue tablecloths. She recognized the old wooden work table from his Virginia studio.

It was topped with a multi-layer birthday cake and several brightly wrapped presents. It was hard not to smile at the effort he had made. That he had moved furniture from Virginia to Pittsburgh said something about his intent to stay here, she supposed.

She glanced toward the other end of the long room where easels and stools had been pushed together to make space for the party. Fresh canvases were stacked against the wall. She wondered what Luc had been painting in the past two years. Or whom. She pushed that thought away.

A door at the top of a flight of metal stairs opened and Luc stepped through, balancing two baskets of potato chips and a sizable bowl of dip. His eyes widened when he saw them, then a smile split his face.

"Marie! Livie! You're here already."

She watched as his eyes darted around the studio. He was looking for Aidan.

"We came by ourselves. I wanted to be early."

Luc set the chips and dip down on the nearest table and crossed the room quickly. He lifted Livie from her arms.

"Hey baby doll," he crooned to her, kissing her gently—almost reverently—on the cheek.

Livie, as usual, lit up like a neon sign at the sight of her father. Livie had bonded effortlessly with Luc. Marie couldn't have asked for an easier time of it in that regard. Of course, even a one-year-old could probably recognize when someone was a besotted fool over them, and Luc was mostly certainly that where Livie was concerned. Which made the prospect of him running away again all the more worrisome.

"So what do you think?" he asked. "About my new studio?"

"It's big. Nice." She looked around at the stools and easels again. Jealousy reared its ugly head in her, even as she knew she had no right to be jealous. She was dating someone, after all, so

Luc was free to date, too. She knew he hadn't been celibate while he was away. That just wasn't in his nature.

"It'll do."

He stepped in close to her and cupped the side of her head with his free hand. Livie watched them wonderingly.

"I'm thinking about doing after school classes for kids. There's an elementary school a few blocks away."

Her breathing fell shallow and she tried not to let herself hope that he was saying what she thought he was saying. What she wanted him to be saying.

"No mommy and me classes?" She made a feeble attempt at a joke.

Luc slid his hand lower on her head and stroked her jaw with his thumb. She fought the urge to close her eyes and lean into his touch.

"Only if you and Livie want one. I could schedule a private class."

Then his lips pressed gently onto hers and all the chemistry she'd been repressing since his return came rushing back. She wobbled on unsteady legs for a moment.

"Actually I believe you do have a few more classes on that gift certificate." He pressed another gentle kiss onto her lips before pulling back. "Do you want to see the upstairs before our guests arrive?"

Our guests. So many things would be *ours—theirs*—from now on. Anything to do with Livie would be a joint decision. Birthdays. Holidays. Summer vacations from school. If he stuck around.

Marie followed him in a daze as he showed her the rooms in the upstairs apartment. She recognized some of the furniture from Luc's Middleburg home. Other pieces looked like inexpensive things from the mall. All in all, it looked more permanent than she expected.

"You've really moved in."

"I'm living here."

There was a nursery for Livie, outfitted with a crib that would turn into a bed as she got older, a dresser, a toy box overflowing with stuffed animals.

The pride in Luc's voice was evident as he pointed to the back wall and said, "I'm going to paint a mural on that."

The short hallway leading to the kitchen was lined with framed charcoal sketches, the studies he had done for her paintings and the show at Sam's gallery. She was touched that he had moved those, too. At the same time, she hoped Aidan didn't see them later.

"Are you selling the house in Middleburg?" The thought of not seeing that house again—or the studio where so much had happened between them, happened to her life—filled her with a sadness that surprised her.

"No. I'm going to keep it, unless I need to sell it. Financially, at the moment, I can afford to keep it." At the doorway to the kitchen, he stopped and turned toward her. "You can hit me, if you want. I deserve it."

"What? I'm not going to hit you." Memories of Luc's nose spurting blood rushed through her mind. Before she knew what she was doing, she reached out and touched his nose gently. The faint yellowing of a bruise was still on his skin, a shadow from the weekend before. "Why would I do that?"

His eyes darkened. She was playing with fire here, she knew that.

"Everyone else is hitting me. My sister. Sam. You're the person who most deserves that honor."

"I have no desire to hit you, Luc." She let her hand fall from his nose. "Thank you for what you did last weekend. Settling things with Richard."

"I wasn't planning on doing that. Sam got an invitation and

she invited me. She thought I might want to see Livie that day. See you."

"No one's ever really stood up for me like that with Richard. Not even my parents."

Luc touched the fading bruise around his nose. "I was horrified by the things he did to you, before. But … I don't know. Maybe it was seeing you with Livie that made me realize just how beyond the pale he was. The danger he put you in. You're the mother of my child, Marie. No one will ever endanger you like that again."

He shifted Livie onto his hip and she watched the way the muscles in his arms rippled beneath her weight. It was tugging at her again. The chemistry, the draw he had on her. Why was it that he looked even sexier with a child on his hip?

Because it's your child.

"If I ever find out that Aidan—or any man—is mistreating you, there's nothing I won't do to stop that. Nothing." He fixed her with a dark look. "I will protect the two of you always."

46

Luc shook more crackers from the box and arranged them neatly around the cheese slices on the platter. The party was going well. He'd had cordial conversations with Marie's parents, her boss, several coworkers and a woman who lived down the hall in Marie's apartment building. He didn't expect the people in her life to warm up to him immediately, but he did hope that her parents at least saw that she was in no physical danger from him. Honestly, her ex-husband's behavior had been downright criminal.

Sam, Peter and Ellie had driven out for the weekend, too. If he and Marie still lived in the Washington area, they'd have an eager babysitter in Ellie. Not to mention Marie's parents, who were only reluctantly sharing Livie with anyone else.

Luc hadn't gotten much time with Marie either. Aidan and her best friend, Nishi, were stuck to her like glue. Or bodyguards. There was also the possibility that she was actively avoiding him after the kiss. He could tell that she and Aidan still weren't intimate from the way Marie held her body around him. There was a stiffness, an awkwardness to her posture that Luc knew wouldn't be there if she and Aidan had slept together.

Not that he had any right to expect Marie to have been as celibate as he'd been, but it relieved him just the same. He wanted her back. Had never stopped wanting her, even when he was wandering the world like a drunken fool. He belonged to her. Nothing could change that. Not even a new boyfriend.

And her reaction when he kissed her before the party began? She wasn't immune to him either. Not at all. She was still angry with him but part of her wanted him too.

"Bonjour."

The greeting came from the doorway of the kitchen. It wasn't a friendly "bonjour," and Luc didn't have to even look up to know from whose lips the word had come.

"Bon-" he started to reply. The word was cut short by a sudden, sharp pain in his groin. He doubled over in agony. Nishi Bhat had just kneed him in the balls.

A slap across the face. A punch to the gut. He wouldn't have been surprised by those. But this? He sucked in deep breaths, willing the shock to subside.

"You deserve so much more than that," she spit out above him.

Slowly he straightened.

"Pardon?"

She launched into a torrent of French so fast and furious even Luc had some difficulty catching it all. He let her say her piece, which was—predictably enough—about Luc abandoning Marie, being a world class jackass, not deserving her or his daughter and that when—not if—he skipped town again Nishi would hunt him down even to the far corners of the earth.

When at last she paused for air, Luc put in a few words of his own.

"You lied to me."

He could see Nishi Bhat's shoulders rise up an inch. He doubted many people called her a liar and lived to tell the tale. He didn't care.

"You told me you were taking her to London to get an abortion," he said in even, measured French.

"No, I didn't lie," she responded in fluent French. "I did offer to pay for one when we were in London. I was completely serious about that."

"And yet I have a daughter." He waved his arm toward the door of the kitchen behind her.

"She wanted to keep the baby. She refused my offer."

"And you didn't think to call and tell me that?"

"I didn't realize you were going to disappear by the time we got back. We were only gone for a weekend."

Luc's hands clenched into fists. He had tried to talk to Marie about Nishi's plans before they left, beg her not to end the pregnancy—*their* pregnancy—but in the end he'd been unable to do it. Every time he tried, the words had sounded like accusations in his ears. He'd been so careful all along not to get between Marie and her best friend, not make her choose between him and Nishi.

"People were trying to call you, asshole," Nishi added. "If you had answered your damned phone, you would have known."

"And if you had trusted Marie to make her own choices, none of this would have happened."

Nishi opened her mouth to refute that but Luc cut her off.

"Her parents, her ex-husband … no one has ever allowed her to decide the direction of her own life. Then she did that with me. She chose *me*. And you didn't trust her choice either. I am grateful that you helped Marie leave the country with me, and I have tried not to come between the two of you. But it's no longer just the two of you. There's a child involved and with that child, *me*. So don't expect me to step back any more. If I need to do something or say something that doesn't respect your friendship, I will do it."

For what he assumed was perhaps the first time in Nishi Bhat's life, she was stunned into silence.

"Does she know that you told me about your plans?" he asked.

Footsteps sounded in the hallway, coming toward them. He needed to end this conversation.

Nishi shook her head. Her "no" was chastened, and spoken in English.

"I am going to tell her. Not today, because I don't want to ruin my daughter's first birthday. But as soon as the right moment presents itself, she is going to know. I accept my blame in what has happened up to this point. I acted wrongly. But from here on out, things are going to be different."

Nishi opened her mouth again to speak, only to be silenced by Aidan's sudden arrival. He looked back and forth between Nishi and Luc, and Luc didn't like the little smirk on his face. He didn't like much about Aidan Janssen, but he had been respecting Marie's choice there too.

"Marie wants to do the birthday cake," the other man said.

47

Luc looked around his studio in its post-party disarray. The bowls and platters on the tables were empty. The birthday cake had just a few slices left. The tub of ice cream had melted into liquid. Some of the streamers and balloons, now deflated, hung limply toward the floor.

It had been a good party. Only one person hit Luc and so far Luc had resisted the impulse to punch Aidan. Livie was exhausted, of course; Marie had taken her upstairs to nurse. Luc wanted to ask her to stay awhile, but knew that was probably pushing things. Baby steps, he reminded himself. Keep the focus on Livie. Things with Marie would follow.

He hoped.

He felt a soft hand on the small of his back. Sam. She and Peter were clutching their coats, ready to leave.

"Thanks for coming."

"Livie is precious," Sam said and leaned in to kiss Luc lightly on the jaw. "Good luck," she whispered.

"I need it."

He shook Peter's hand and gave Ellie the French cheek kisses she loved. Sam rolled her eyes behind her daughter's back and said, sotto voce, "Her friends all do that now."

"Glad to have been an influence," Luc snarked back.

When the door closed behind his friends, Luc gave the room another once-over. Sam's family weren't the last guests to leave. No, there was one person still there and Luc took the stairs two at a time to find him. When he entered his living room, what he saw did not please him. Marie was sitting on the sofa, her blouse unbuttoned, Livie at her breast. Aidan sat next to her, watching.

"Sorry pal. You gotta go," Luc said, stepping to the side and pointedly leaving the door down to the studio open.

"I'm waiting to take Marie home."

Aidan's voice was low and steady, but Luc heard the challenge in it. *Fine buddy.* Luc had fought Richard Macintyre the week before. *Happy to do it again.* His bruises hadn't entirely faded yet, but for Marie? He'd gladly take on a few more.

"I'll give them a ride home," Luc said. "I want to spend some time with my daughter on her birthday, alone."

Luc didn't expect a father's prerogative to mean a thing to Aidan. He was exercising it anyway. Luc was giving space to Marie's relationship with him—hell, he'd even offered to babysit Livie some evening so the two of them could go out. That was far more generous than he wanted to be, but he was doing it for Marie. He didn't want to pressure her, but Livie was another matter. Aidan had no standing with Livie, as far as Luc was concerned, and if Luc wanted time alone with his daughter he was damn well entitled to it. Other men did not have to understand that.

Aidan made no move to leave. Marie's posture had stiffened.

"She's feeding my daughter," Luc said. "I get to say who watches."

Then Aidan launched into French. Fluent French. *What the hell?* Did everyone in Marie's life speak fluent French?

"You want a say in things a year after your daughter was born," Aidan was saying.

His accent wasn't perfect, Luc noted.

"A daughter you thought Marie was going to abort."

A wary look filled Marie's eyes at the sound of her name. Her French still wasn't that good, and Luc knew she couldn't follow Aidan's rapid-fire speech. And how did Aidan know about … then Luc remembered Aidan's arrival interrupting his fight with Nishi in the kitchen. It hadn't occurred to him at the time that Aidan could understand French.

"You're a dick, you know that?" Aidan continued. "You don't deserve Marie. You abandoned her in a foreign country when she was pregnant. That might be your daughter, but you're not getting her mother back."

Luc took a step toward Aidan but then Aidan whirled around on Marie.

"Did you know the reason he left you was because he thought you were getting an abortion?" Aidan spoke in English now. "He thought so little of you that he—"

Luc grabbed the other man by the shoulder and pulled him up off the sofa. Before he could resist, Luc had Aidan pinned against the wall.

"Leave."

"Not without Marie." Aidan was defiant.

"This is my home and you will leave."

"Not without—"

Luc loosened his grip on Aidan, then pushed him back into the wall. "This is my family. I will see that they get home. Without you." Livie let out a wail.

"Guys, please …" Marie said.

"He thought you were going to *abort* her, Marie." Aidan

shoved back at Luc.

Enough. He and Marie needed to have this conversation, but not with someone else around. And definitely not with Marie's boyfriend around.

"You know, I'm getting good at beating the shit out of the men in Marie's life. Happy to do it again today, pal." Luc swung Aidan around and gave him a hard shove toward the stairs.

"Aidan, please. Just go. I'll call you when I get home," Marie's voice was barely audible over Livie's crying.

Luc gave Aidan another shove. "We're taking this downstairs."

LUC AND AIDAN's angry French seeped up the stairs, even though Luc had slammed the door shut behind him. Aidan spoke French? Why hadn't he mentioned that? Not that they had ever discussed how many languages they each spoke, but given that Luc was French she would have expected the subject to come up.

And Luc knew that Nishi had offered to pay for an abortion? How? And how was it that Aidan knew that too? So many questions. It was making her head hurt. Up until a few minutes ago, Livie's birthday party had gone perfectly. Or as well as could be expected anyway, under the circumstances.

Livie's wailing had subsided to sleepy hiccups, but Marie couldn't just sit there, waiting for the shouting below to be interrupted by the sound of punches. She carried Livie back to her nursery and laid her in the crib. By the time she had changed her diaper, Livie was sound asleep.

Let sleeping babies lie.

Luc's living room was quiet again. The shouting was gone and no sooner had Marie collapsed back into the sofa then the studio door opened and shut hard. Luc stomped up the stairs.

"Shhh. I just put her down."

Luc immediately softened his footsteps. As far as she could tell, there was no blood on him, no fresh bruises, no broken nose.

"We need to talk," she said.

Luc cocked his head toward the hallway. "Let's talk in the kitchen. I'll make coffee."

48

“I didn’t know Aidan spoke French.” Marie wrapped her hands around the warm coffee mug. She sat at the kitchen table while Luc fussed around the room, cleaning and straightening, releasing nervous energy.

“I didn’t either.”

She got up, poured another mug of coffee and made a show of setting it next to her own.

“So what was he talking about?” She patted the table. “Please sit, Luc. You’re making me anxious.”

He pulled out a chair and dropped himself into it. Shadows darkened his eyes and stubble had sprouted along his jawline. He was still the sexiest man she’d ever seen, and the impulse to pull him up and lead him down the hall to his bedroom was strong.

“He overheard a conversation Nishi and I were having earlier.” He took a big gulp of coffee.

She doubted they’d merely been having a “conversation,” but she didn’t press the matter. That wasn’t important. Nor did she want to repeat what Aidan had said, in English, before he left. She wanted to hear Luc's side of things. She wanted to hear what he would say when he had to tell her himself.

"When Nishi came to visit you in Paris, she was very angry with me for getting you pregnant. She said I had rescued you from one bad situation only to put you into another." He sighed and dug his hand roughly into his hair. "I'm sorry I didn't tell you this at the time. I have always tried not to come between you and your best friend."

His hand dropped from his head and moved toward her, as if he was going to take her hand. But then he pulled it back.

"But you're *my* best friend, chérie. And I am sorry I didn't trust you more. I've never been sorrier about anything."

"Nishi told you she offered to pay for an abortion, didn't she?"

Luc's head snapped up and he looked at her. His face was drawn in pain and regret.

"She told me she was taking you to London to get one, and then taking you home."

Marie drew in a long, deep breath. "And you assumed that I did."

"Yes. I did. And I shouldn't have. I should have spoken to you before you left."

"I never even considered it, Luc. Not even for an instant. Yes, Nishi was willing to pay for it since I didn't have much money of my own then. But I wanted our baby."

"I'm sorry."

"Why didn't you say something before we left? If you were that worried?"

"I didn't want to get between you and Nishi."

"Why didn't you wait until we got back then?"

"I wasn't sure you were coming back. She said she was taking you back to the states."

"So you thought I was leaving you for good, and you didn't say anything? Not one word? Not even 'please don't leave me?'" She looked down into the now-cold coffee that she had no stomach for. "You're the only man I've ever been in love with, Luc. And you didn't fight for me. You thought I was leaving you and you let me go without a word."

The pain of that idea had her struggling for a next breath.

"I was afraid, chérie. Afraid of what I would do when you came back. I loved you too much—I *love* you too much—and I didn't trust myself."

Marie was quiet. What was there to say? He didn't trust himself? Well, he hadn't trusted her either. She was upset with Nishi, too, for getting between herself and Luc. Nishi was used to fixing things. She got paid well by very large companies and important people to take care of things. But her relationship with Luc wasn't a problem to Marie, nor had her pregnancy been. Unplanned, yes, but not unwelcome.

"I fucked this up," Luc said. "We had a wonderful thing and I ruined it. We could have been a perfect family—" His voice broke on the word. "We could have gotten married."

She looked up from her cold coffee to see his stricken expression. Tears welled in his eyes. He held her gaze for a moment, letting her see him, before burying his face in his hands and giving in to his sorrow.

He had left her because of his own fears. Not because he didn't want her, or didn't love her. She supposed that was some small relief. But could she live with him, always wondering whether his fears would get the best of him? They had a child—there were even more things to be afraid of now, most of which Marie was sure she couldn't even imagine at the moment. Livie getting behind the wheel of a car for the first time … falling in love … falling ill … but being a parent meant taking a deep breath and facing those fears head on. She had spent the entire past year learning to be strong enough for Livie, to put someone else's needs ahead of her own. Was Luc even capable of that? Richard certainly hadn't been.

The men in her life had been such polar opposites. Richard had no emotions, and Luc was all emotion, raw on-the-surface emotion. He was all in or all out on everything, from teaching to painting to sex. His intensity, she had loved that about him, but it magnified everything else in his life. In their life.

She went to him and straddled his lap. She pulled his head and hands to her chest and let him cry. His heart was big, but his fears were bigger.

"What time did he take you home last night?" Aidan set two lattes onto the table and sat down. It was Sunday morning, and he had called at eight o'clock on the dot to invite her out for coffee.

"How about an apology for picking a fight with him?"

"I didn't—"

"Yes, you did. And just for the record? I don't appreciate it when people speak in another language just so I can't understand what they're saying."

"He did it, too."

"Oh my god, Aidan. Can you hear yourself? You sound like a five year old. I don't like it when he does it, either. It's wrong for both of you."

Marie pried the plastic lid off her drink and took a sip of the milky coffee. Then she glanced down at Livie, happily playing with her new stuffed dog, one of the presents Luc had given her for her birthday yesterday.

"Is this decaf?" she asked.

"What? No." Aidan took a sip of his own. "Oh shoot. I forgot." He started to unfold his long body from the chair.

"Sit. I'll go get it."

Marie got back in line to order a decaf, this time simply a drip coffee because it was faster. She didn't want to leave Livie for too long. Livie was comfortable around Aidan, but Aidan still wasn't at ease around her. She added a splash of cream to the cup, then returned to the table. Livie was still preoccupied with her stuffed animal. Aidan was watching her like she might explode at any moment.

Marie couldn't blame him. Lots of people weren't comfortable around children until they had one of their own. Still, it was hard not to compare him to Luc, who had instantly bonded with Livie.

"What time did he take you home last night?" Aidan repeated as she pulled out the wooden chair and sat back down.

Marie fought the urge to roll her eyes. It was nine-thirty on a Sunday morning, too early for this. Yesterday she'd been dealing with Luc's fears. Today it was Aidan's.

"We stayed another hour and a half." She sipped cautiously at the hot coffee, then added, "Livie napped a little and Luc and I talked."

"Talked about the fact that he left you because he thought you were going to—"

Marie cut him off. "Let's not use that word in front of my daughter. Please."

Aidan glanced down at Livie. "She won't understand."

"I know that, Aidan. Alright? I still don't want to use that word."

It's none of your concern. She knew he wouldn't see it that way, though.

"How can you take him back after that?"

"I'm not taking him back. He's Livie's father. I want him in her life."

"What are the odds he'll stick around?"

She shrugged. "I don't know. I don't have much choice but to assume he will."

The look of disgust that flashed across his face annoyed Marie.

She understood that he didn't like having Luc around but it also wasn't entirely his business.

"What kind of man does that?"

A man who is not as secure as he pretends to be.

"To not even talk to—"

A man who can't separate what he feels from what he thinks he sees.

"I mean, he thought so little of you that—"

A man who wants everything to be as lovely and controlled as art, when life is messy and unpredictable.

"Aidan! I don't want to discuss this with you. He's here. He's Livie's father. End of story."

She drained her coffee down to the halfway mark. She didn't have the patience for Aidan's insecurities today. She should have declined his invitation to come out this morning, said Livie was fussy or whatever. But Aidan wouldn't have taken "no" for an answer. He would have pressed her until he got the reason he really wanted to hear, that she had stayed late at Luc's place last night. That wasn't true, but Aidan always believed the worst when it came to her and Luc.

She was getting tired of people believing the worst of her.

49

"Say bye bye to maman."

Luc held out Livie for Marie to kiss one last time. If she and Aidan didn't leave soon, he was going to have to kick them out. Or withdraw his offer to babysit for the evening, an offer he was beginning to think he was crazy to have made in the first place.

What had he been thinking? Make it easier for Marie and Aidan to go out by watching Livie for a few hours? He must have been crazy.

Marie was lingering with Livie. She was clearly unused to leaving her alone when she wasn't at work.

"Love, the longer you draw it out … she'll be fine," he murmured.

Aidan opened the door, a hint if Luc had ever seen one.

"Go," he whispered. *Before I change my mind.*

Aidan snaked his hand around Marie's waist and pulled her toward him and the door … and away from Luc. Luc held his breath. *What are you doing?* He was letting her leave with another man. *You're an idiot.*

But he wanted Marie to choose him. If she wanted him. He

wouldn't pressure her or try to persuade her. Nor would he try to seduce her, though he was sure he could. Their bodies still craved each other. Neither of them could deny that.

When the door closed behind them, he jostled Livie gently in his arms.

"Alright, mademoiselle. It's you and me tonight." He gave her a loud kiss on each cheek, which never failed to make her laugh.

He set her down on the padded mat that was covered with her toys, and she set happily to playing. She was a happy kid. He shook his head, amused. In that respect, she did not take after the Marchands. Luc had been fussy and temperamental, according to his mother. He was still fussy and temperamental. Or temperamental at least, he acknowledged, as he retrieved two sketchpads, a pencil and a box of chubby crayons from his backpack.

He laid the smaller pad and the crayons next to Livie's mat. They were for her. Marie had said Livie was fascinated by pens and pencils already. In that respect, she was a Marchand. Luc rolled his eyes at the pride he felt swelling in his chest.

My daughter.

How much love could one person feel for another? His heart had expanded at least tenfold since the evening he'd first laid eyes on his daughter. Of course Marie should kick him to the curb for missing out on the first year of their daughter's life. If he were given one wish to make, it would be to go back in time and undo all the mistakes he made in Paris. He would have told Nishi Bhat that Marie's pregnancy—*their* pregnancy—was none of her business. He would have proposed marriage to Marie the minute she told him she was pregnant. He had been talking to jewelers in the city anyway. He'd wanted to design a one-of-a-kind ring for her.

How pointless that all seemed now.

He couldn't go back in time. He was stuck with the consequences of his own stupidity.

He flipped open the brand new sketchpad. His art was still

missing. Maybe it was gone for good. That was beginning to feel like a real possibility. He had drunk his talent away. *Serves you right.* Nonetheless, he wanted it back. The after school classes had begun this week at his studio. He still drew well enough for kids—and most of their parents. But Sam would be appalled at the junk he'd been turning out. In fact, she'd been appalled at Livie's party that he had no new work to show her.

The teacher needs a teacher. It had been a long time since he was a student. His grand-père had been his favorite teacher. Then Philippe Marchand died and Luc had thought, with the arrogance of the young, that he would step into his grandfather's shoes. His first small gallery show in Paris had been a disaster. Roundly panned, only one sale. His parents had made it clear to him that he was not to drag down his grandfather's legacy with his own immature ambitions. That was when he left France. Ran away.

Running away had always been his modus operandi. But he couldn't run anymore, no matter how bad things got. The reason was sitting on the floor with him, happily cooing at her stuffed dog and slamming plastic blocks onto the mat, then laughing at the sound.

He had to stay now. Even if he was never able to draw well again. Even if Marie stayed with Aidan. Or left Aidan and fell in love with someone else. Livie was his anchor, his reason to muscle through pain he would have avoided before.

He began sketching her, quickly laying down the lines and planes before they moved. Children were hard to draw. They were constantly in motion. He made a dozen tiny drawings of her on the first sheet of paper. None of them were good.

How could he not draw his own daughter? He was looking right at her. He had her face memorized. Seared into his heart. He could close his eyes and see her perfectly. But what he saw wasn't making its way down his arm and into his pencil.

He laid down on his stomach, stretched his legs out behind

him. He picked up Livie's sketchpad and opened it to the first page. Her hand, holding a plastic block, paused in midair. She watched her papa as he opened the new box of chubby crayons and laid them all out on the mat. Luc picked up the blue one and began scribbling on the paper. Livie watched for a moment before wrapping her hand around the yellow crayon. She stretched out on her stomach too, and began making awkward marks on the page.

Luc made a mark, then Livie tried to imitate him. He drew lines and squiggles and circles. None of which Livie could really approximate but she drew her hand across the paper and then looked over at Luc for approval. He reached over and tweaked her tiny button nose.

"You are a Marchand through and through," he said. "Pleasing your papa with art."

Livie lost interest as the paper filled up with blue and yellow marks. When she dropped the crayon entirely, Luc pushed back up onto his knees and surveyed their masterpiece. It looked like that damn exercise he'd made Marie do in their first lesson. Draw blue. What the hell. He had pulled that one straight out of his ass. He'd been so flustered by her presence, he'd known he wouldn't really be able to teach. Part of him had been trying to chase her away. That might have worked out better for both of them, had he possessed more willpower.

Livie laid her head down on the mat, her stuffed dog clutched tight in her arms.

"Oh sleepyhead." Luc picked her up. "We need to get a bath before you fall asleep for good."

She laid her head on his shoulder as he carried her to Marie's bathroom. His heart was about to burst from his chest.

"I love you, sweetheart," he whispered into her dark hair. "More than anything."

As he bathed Livie, trying to soap her up without getting a faceful of water splashed on him, he thought back to that silly exercise again. Draw blue. You could no more draw blue than you could draw love or passion or heartbreak. Who could even say what blue looked like? One person's blue could be another person's red. One person's passion could be someone else's heartbreak.

Marie had tried to draw blue though. She had trusted him as a teacher, and he hadn't failed her there. But as an artist, a lover, a friend? He was a failure on all three counts.

He rinsed baby shampoo from Livie's hair, careful not to get any water or suds in her eyes. The bath seemed to wash away her earlier sleepiness and getting her into her zippered pajamas became a game. Or a battle of wills. One that Luc eventually won after some fancy sleight of hand. He combed her dark hair, then warmed milk for a bottle. Livie grabbed the bottle from his hands before his ass had completely sunk into Marie's sofa.

He was happy, right here, in this moment. Happier than he could ever remember being, actually. With the weight of his daughter nestled against his body, he felt safe. Secure. Fathers were supposed to keep their children safe, but Livie made him feel safe too. Grounded. The storms in his soul stilled when Livie was in his arms.

Marie was trying to wean Livie off breastfeeding. As he watched Livie suck down the cow's milk, her chubby fingers splayed around the bottle, he suspected that it was Marie who was being weaned. She always looked most at peace when she was nursing Livie. That was the face he wanted to capture beneath his charcoal or brush. His déesse at peace.

He watched as Livie's eyelids began to droop, her hands relaxing on the bottle, her lips growing slacker and slacker. The bottle was still half full when she finally slipped under into sleep. Luc gently removed the bottle from her grasp, then slowly stood up, careful not to jostle her awake. In Marie's bedroom, he laid her in the crib and tucked a blanket around her.

So beautiful. Love her so much.

Maybe it wasn't possible to capture on paper something you loved as much as your own child. Maybe he would never see Livie clearly enough to draw her, never be able to see through his love for her to see the real person.

He stripped off his still damp tee shirt and draped it over a towel rack in the bathroom. He cleaned up Livie's bath toys, put away the baby shampoo, stared at the mirrored medicine chest over the bathroom sink. He should go back out to the living room, pick up his sketchbook and try to draw again. Maybe brew a pot of coffee. He should not open the medicine chest. He should not snoop through Marie's apartment. But he was a man, and a weak one at that.

He tugged gently on the edge of the mirror, heard the little click as the latch gave way. Inside, the metal shelves were neatly lined with Marie's toiletries—her toothbrush, a tube of whitening toothpaste, eye drops, bottles of cleansers and lotions. He stared hard at the items, making sure he wasn't overlooking anything. Overlooking what he feared he would find.

But there was no second toothbrush, no man's razor, no man's deodorant. Relief flooded his body. He wasn't sure how much time Aidan spent at Marie's apartment but he wasn't spending nights here regularly if he didn't have so much as a toothbrush and razor here.

AIDAN PUT the Jeep into park in front of Marie's apartment building. It was after midnight, and Marie felt a twinge of guilt about not seeing Livie before bedtime. She and Aidan had gone out to dinner, then to a late movie. Luc's unexpected offer of babysitting had enabled her first real date with Aidan. She still wasn't quite sure what to make of Luc's offer. It was nice, but out of character.

Aidan opened his door, came around to her side and helped her out.

"You don't have to come up," she said. "Livie will be sleeping."

"You sure?"

"He's not going to hurt me."

The look on Aidan's face said he wasn't sure about that. But Marie knew Luc would never physically hurt her. He wasn't that kind of man. He was the opposite, in fact. When he felt he couldn't trust his behavior, he ran away.

"Alright." Aidan gave in. "Call if you need me."

"I will."

She let Aidan cup her jaw softly with his hands and kiss her. She hoped Luc wasn't watching through a window. The kiss was nice, as all of Aidan's kisses were. There was nothing wrong with it, nothing she could put her finger on. They should be quite nice, really. She liked Aidan. She did. Nishi liked Aidan. Her parents had seemed to like him. She should like his kisses more by now.

But she just didn't.

Upstairs, the apartment was quiet. The living room was empty. She peeked into the kitchen, where the aroma of coffee was faint but still lingering. There were only two rooms left to check, the bathroom and her bedroom. She and Livie shared the bedroom, a situation that had so far allowed Marie to fend off Aidan's desires to spend the night. She wasn't letting a man sleep over with her daughter in her crib a few feet away.

As she tiptoed down the short hall, she could see the bathroom door open and the light off. So Luc had to be in her bedroom. Maybe Livie hadn't gone to sleep for him. Livie was used to Luc but not used to someone other than her mother putting her to bed.

The bedroom was dark but the street lamp outside provided enough light for Marie to see the tableau on her bed. Luc, shirtless but in his jeans, was lying on his back with Livie in her pajamas splayed across his chest. Luc's hand rested on the small of her back, as if holding her in place. Both were sound asleep.

Marie grabbed her sleep shirt from the closet and returned to the bathroom, where she brushed her teeth and washed her face in the dark. She considered her options. She could sleep on the sofa in the living room. That was probably the safest option. She could try and lift Livie off Luc, put her back in the crib, then wake Luc and send him home. The odds of doing that without waking Livie were slim and none.

Then there was the third option.

Ever so slowly she stretched her body out on the bed and watched Luc and Livie sleep. Here in her bed was the man whose child she had chosen to bear. Her daughter's papa. *Their* daughter. This was what she had wanted when she made that choice, the three of them falling asleep together under the same roof.

50

In the morning, Marie awoke in an empty bed and for an instant her heart dropped at the thought of last night being just a dream. Then the sounds of French drifted down the hall, followed by the smell of coffee and eggs. Luc was cooking breakfast. Another thing she had envisioned them doing together as a family. Meals, weekend outings, quiet evenings in.

Not that her family had done those kinds of things. Her parents had worked all the time. But Marie had wanted a different kind of family for her children.

And you got that alright.

Punctuating Luc's stream of French was the occasional outburst of babble from Livie. She wondered whether Livie was babbling in English or French. She hoped Livie would learn French from Luc. That was another thing she had pictured in their life together. Their adorable bilingual children, equally at home in France and the United States.

Everything she had wanted was right here in her apartment, this very morning. And yet she didn't have any of it. Not for real.

She threw on jeans and a sweater and went to join Luc and

Livie. Luc had dragged Livie's high chair to the doorway of the kitchen, where she seemed mesmerized by the sight of Luc scrambling eggs and popping toast from the toaster.

Marie had to admit, it was certainly a mesmerizing sight. Luc had regained some of the weight he had lost, filling his clothes better now. And he still had that way of moving that was careless and graceful at the same time.

"Livie, sweetheart, is your maman checking out my derrière?"

"Luc!"

"What?" Luc glanced back over his shoulder.

"Your language."

"She doesn't know that word yet." Luc popped two more slices of toast from the toaster and plated them. He added a scoop of eggs to each plate. "Besides, it's French."

"Are you going to teach her French?"

"You know I am. But we haven't gotten to body parts yet. Have we, sweetheart?"

Luc's grin was mischievous as he picked up Livie and her high chair and moved them back to the small dining table. "And then she can teach her maman," he added.

Marie carried the two plates to the table, then pulled a small bowl for Livie from the cupboard and spooned eggs into it.

"Has she had a bottle this morning?"

"Yes. Sorry. I didn't want to wake you. I wasn't sure how late you got in last night."

"A little after midnight."

"Ah Livie, we need to set a curfew for maman." Luc poured two mugs of coffee. "And I apologize for appropriating your bed. She woke up and couldn't get back to sleep."

She shrugged. "It was nice seeing the two of you together like that."

They ate breakfast like a family, a perfectly normal family, except Luc was asking Marie about her date. A subject she didn't really want to discuss with him.

"We had dinner then we saw that new spy thriller."

It made her uncomfortable to tell Luc about her date with another man. She had been more intimate with Luc than with any other man. Not just physically, but emotionally. She had shown him sides of herself she had shown no one else. Sides she hadn't shown anyone since. And after all that, she was sitting across from him at breakfast talking about another man's efforts to woo her.

"So what did you two do last night?" She rerouted the conversation back to Luc and Livie.

"We created a masterpiece in crayon, didn't we?"

Her heart nearly stopped at the sight of Luc affectionately ruffling Livie's hair.

"We'll show it to you after breakfast," Luc added. "Then there was bathtime in which papa got almost as wet as if he'd been in the tub himself." He winked at Livie, earning him a big smile.

It would be so easy to just sink into this, she knew. To let herself be pulled under by this easy feeling of family and what-could-have-been. Was there any good reason not to? It was hard to remember, when her heart skittered all over the place every time he looked at Livie with those dark, adoring eyes.

"Then when Livie couldn't get back to sleep, we discussed our upcoming trip to Paris."

"Oh?" Luc was planning to take Livie to Paris? By himself?

"My parents have invited us—" He gestured around the table. "For Christmas."

"Me too?"

Luc's forehead creased in a frown. "Of course, you too." He drained the last of his coffee. "I'm sure the invitation is mostly for you and Livie. I'm probably more of an afterthought."

"Luc, that's so not true. Your parents were out of their minds when you disappeared. Everyone was." His expression remained doubting. "They told me about your gallery show, the one after your grandfather died."

"Right. Did they tell you that I was dragging my grandfather's artistic legacy through the mud?"

"No, they didn't. They said you overreacted."

Luc rolled his eyes.

"They said you needed to develop more as an artist before showing your work. That, as a Marchand, you would be subject to higher standards."

He waved his hands in the direction of her kitchen. "Yeah well, your trash can is filled with my failed attempts last night at higher standards."

That was the reason right there that she couldn't allow herself to sink into this easy family scene. She stood to wipe Livie's face and begin clearing the table. He had seemed so confident—arrogant, even—when they'd first met. Under the bluster, though, was a man who didn't believe he could meet higher standards. For art or for love.

MONDAY AT NOON, Marie took the elevator down from her office and snagged their usual table in the Cathedral's Commons Room to wait for Aidan. Since the weather had gotten cold, she and Aidan often ate packed lunches together there.

At twelve-fifteen, she checked her phone for messages. Aidan wasn't usually late, but he also hadn't confirmed their lunch date either. Nor had he answered any of her calls the day before. She debated starting to eat without him. Her lunch break was only forty-five minutes today due to a meeting. At twelve-twenty-five, she unwrapped her sandwich and uncapped her bottle of iced tea. Maybe Aidan was stuck in a meeting himself, or had been shanghaied by a student after class. She pulled up a book on her phone.

At twelve-thirty-five, a shadow fell over the table. She looked up to see Aidan pulling out the chair on the other side and sitting down. His expression was grim. He had no lunch in his hand, nor did he pull one from the backpack he carried everywhere with him on campus.

"He spent the night." Aidan's voice was flat and Marie could hear the control he was exerting over it.

She debated what to say.

"Don't try to think up a story, Marie. I sat outside your apartment for three hours. I didn't see him leave."

"You waited outside my apartment?" It took a moment for her to process that information. Aidan had spied on her? Didn't trust her? She felt the burn of anger in the back of her throat. She'd been through this before with Richard—people following her, watching her, trying to make sure she was doing what they wanted her to do. "Yes. He stayed. He and Livie were sound asleep when I got into the apartment. He was holding her." She left out the fact that they had been sleeping on her bed. "I didn't want to wake her."

Aidan's eyes narrowed ever so slightly. He was doubting her?

"Nothing happened." She reached her hand across the table to cover his. He allowed this but didn't flip his hand around to hold hers. After a moment, she pulled her hand back and wrapped it around her bottle of tea. *Fine.* She fiddled with the bottle, but her appetite was gone. "You don't trust me?"

"Hard to do that when your French lover is spending the night."

"He's not my lover. He's the father of my daughter." She calmly rewrapped her sandwich, trying to keep her emotions in check. They were in a public space, and at work for both of them. This was neither the time nor the place for a fight. "I know he wasn't around when we met and I didn't expect that to ever change. But it did."

"You're glad he's back."

Marie let out the breath she'd been holding, and with it her anger. *I am so over this crap.* She was tired of people putting words in her mouth, telling her what she felt and thought. Her parents had done it. Richard had done it. Even Nishi, her best friend, was guilty of it. But no more.

Contrary to popular opinion, I do know what I feel. And I can think for myself.

"I'm glad he is in Livie's life. I don't want her growing up without her father, or having him show up suddenly when she's a teenager."

"And now you have this nice cozy little family."

"Luc and I aren't a family. We are Livie's family, individually. That's it." She shoved her sandwich back into her lunch bag. "But you know what? I don't really have the bandwidth right now to navigate this testosterone minefield between you and him."

"So you want to split up?"

"Yes. I do. I just don't think I have room for this in my life right now."

"Because he's back."

"Because I have a young child and a full-time job, and that's enough."

"Fine," Aidan said flatly and stood up.

She waited until he was on an elevator back up to the math department before leaving the table. She thought about what she'd said to Aidan. *Luc and I aren't a family.* But they had felt like a family on Sunday morning, Luc making breakfast, the three of them sitting at the table together. It felt like family.

51

"We're in Paris, sweetie," Marie leaned over to whisper in Livie's ear as the plane bumped down onto the runway. Livie's eyes widened as the pilot hit the brakes. "It's okay, sweetheart."

Marie took her daughter's tiny hand in hers. Livie was sitting in the seat between her parents. Luc covered her other hand with his until the plane slowed and turned toward the terminal. Marie blinked as she looked out the window into the early morning light. The flight was a red-eye, and Luc and Livie had slept most of the way across the Atlantic.

Marie, on the other hand, had slept only fitfully. Her emotions were in a jumble over the trip. There was her excitement over being in Paris again. There was regret, knowing what she knew now about why Luc had disappeared. Everything that had happened over the past year and a half? None of that had to happen. If it hadn't, they'd be deplaning in Paris a happy family. She glanced over at Luc. Not that they weren't a happy family … she blinked her exhausted eyes again. It was confusing and she was too tired to make sense of it all.

They *were* a happy family together. They just weren't the kind of family she had envisioned. The kind of family she had wanted them to be.

The kind of family she still wanted them to be.

The plane had stopped at the gate and en masse everyone began standing in the aisles, pulling their luggage down from the overhead bins. Livie was entranced by all the activity, the people, the sense of anticipation flooding the stale cabin air.

"You didn't sleep?" Luc asked over Livie's head.

She shook her head. "I kept waiting for her to wake up and start crying."

Luc's eyes were soft as he smiled at her. "You're a good mother, chérie. I don't think I tell you that often enough."

"So many things to worry about when you're a mother."

"Most of which never come to pass, right?" He tenderly smoothed Livie's sleep-ruffled hair. "She was the perfect traveler. Better behaved than some adults."

Livie looked at Luc and then Marie, sensing that she was the topic of conversation.

Marie smoothed her hair, too. "You were an angel, darling. Your papa has more faith than I do."

Luc's smile was crooked, and rueful. They both knew that wasn't entirely true. True where Livie was concerned. Of course, he could rely on Marie to worry about the things that needed to be worried about. But he lacked faith in almost everything—and everyone—else. Including Marie.

She wanted them to be a happy family. She wanted the picture people were seeing of them on the plane—an adorable child and two adoring parents—to be the reality. She could even talk herself into having faith in Luc again. That wouldn't work, though, if Luc didn't have faith in himself.

That he might never have enough faith in himself terrified her. It would be hard on Livie if Luc were to up and run away, and harder still if the three of them were living together all the time and he disappeared again. Marie wasn't sure she would survive losing him another time.

She wasn't sure she would survive not having him again either.

"Are you okay?" Luc asked.

"Just tired." That was the truth, just not all of it.

"You can nap at my parents' house."

"I think I will, if no one minds."

Luc's arm reached over Livie's head to touch Marie's cheek. "We're going to have a good holiday, I promise. We'll relax and have fun with Livie. Valerie has offered to babysit Livie, if we want . . ."

If we want to go out by ourselves. She finished the sentence in her mind. It was probably a bad idea, the two of them going out on what could easily be construed as a date. She wanted to, though. She wanted to spend time with him, just the two of them, like old times. She wanted to discuss art with him. She missed their lessons. She missed cooking in his house with him. Now most of their conversation centered on Livie, not that that was a bad thing necessarily, but sometimes she wanted to be just a *woman* with him.

"Livie won't remember Valerie."

Luc's thumb touched her lower lip lightly, briefly, and every nerve ending in her body began to glow.

"My family is going to pay so much attention to her—and spoil her so much—she won't even notice we're gone." He pulled his hand back. "We need some time, just the two of us, Marie. You know we do."

INSIDE THE TERMINAL, his brother-in-law, Denis, looked like he wanted to hit him. Valerie just burst into tears.

"She's all grown up!" his sister said.

"Hardly," Luc murmured as he pivoted to turn Livie toward Valerie. At least with Livie in his arms, Denis would restrain himself. If he could get through the holidays without a broken nose or a black eye …

While his sister cooed over a bewildered Livie, Denis kissed Marie on her cheeks then opened his arms to hug her tightly. His family's affection for Marie stung him, even as he was glad of it. They had been with her when he should have been, and was not.

"Let me have her, Luc." Valerie lifted Livie from his arms and he let her.

They headed for baggage claim, Marie and Valerie talking excitedly to each other. Seeing his sister and brother-in-law seemed to have given Marie a burst of energy. He and Denis followed behind the women in an uneasy silence. Luc tried to make conversation about the weather, football, new restaurants he and Marie should try. All without much luck. By the time they were all in Denis and Valerie's car, luggage stowed in the trunk and the girls chatting in the back seat, Luc had given up. He and Denis rode in silence to his parents' home.

At least his mother was happy to see him. The front door of his parents' modest home was thrown open before he had Livie out of the car.

"Bonjour!" Kisses everywhere. "Bonjour! Bonjour!" More kisses. "Ma petite-fille!"

Livie was more prepared this time for the sudden onslaught of affection, and she allowed her grandmother to kiss her and ruffle her dark hair.

"There's fresh coffee inside," Juliette Marchand said. "I can make some breakfast, if you're hungry."

Luc glanced over at Marie, who was looking unsteady again on her feet as she hoisted Livie's carry-on bag over her shoulder. He rushed over to her.

"You're exhausted." He took the bag and slipped it over his own shoulder, only to have his mother take it off again.

"Marie, darling. You look like you're about to fall asleep on your feet. Luc's room is cleaned and ready upstairs. Why don't you nap for a bit? We can take care of Olivia for awhile."

Luc's childhood room was just as she remembered it. The bed with a mountain of down pillows in place of a headboard. The French new wave posters on the wall. A dresser that was now filled with some of Juliette's out-of-season clothing and seasonal table linens. A few snapshot photos and tiny sketches tucked into the frame of a mirror. A cardboard box of art books nestled into the corner, behind Livie's crib.

While she was pregnant, Marie had stayed with Valerie and Denis. But when Livie was born, Juliette had claimed a grandmother's prerogative and insisted that they stay at the Marchand family home. Not that it didn't make sense. Juliette was retired so she had more time to help with the baby. Marie and Livie had spent a month in Luc's old room before going back home to the States.

She walked over to the crib. It was made up in brand new sheets and a blanket. A new stuffed puppy sat smack in the middle, as if Livie would ever miss it. Luc's students were endlessly entertained by Livie toddling around the studio, her arms filled to the brim with as many stuffed animals as she could hold.

She smiled—then other, older memories rushed at her. Livie sleeping in the crib as a newborn. Herself sleeping, sore and tired, in Luc's bed. Alone. Sitting cross-legged on the mattress, nursing Livie in the wee hours of the morning, too tired to contemplate any longer where he had gone or why.

"There are diapers and extra sheets in here." Luc was peering into his closet. "And a hamper."

Marie turned. "I know where everything is," she said quietly, sadly.

"Right."

They stared at each other, Luc's bed between them.

"I can sleep in another room," he said.

She shook her head. "Let's not make the holiday awkward for your parents."

"Valerie knows we're not together."

"Still. Better not to thrust it into everyone's face." She sat down on the edge of the bed. "Besides, we're adults. We can sleep in a bed together."

Luc gave a little smile. "I don't mind, if you don't."

DOWNSTAIRS, Livie was all set up in his old high chair, happily munching on slices of cheese.

"Did you keep *everything*?" he asked his mother.

"I've been waiting years to bring these things out of storage." Juliette looked pointedly at Valerie. His sister and her husband had long ago decided not to have children. Juliette's grandmotherly ambitions rested entirely on Luc's shoulders. "Don't give me grief now."

"Where is Denis, by the way?" he asked, looking around. Not that he wanted to see his brother-in-law but it was best to keep tabs on him. Luc didn't want to be caught off guard when Denis finally gave in to the desire to clock him.

"He had some shopping to finish," Valerie answered. "He'll be back for dinner."

Great. Denis had gone to the airport just to glare menacingly at him? Maybe Marie and Livie should have come by themselves. They were the ones his family really wanted to see.

Juliette handed him a mug of coffee.

"Marie all settled in?"

He nodded and took a sip, savoring the burn all the way down his throat.

"You're sleeping on the floor?" his sister asked.

"No."

"Why would you sleep on the floor?" Juliette asked, looking from her son to her daughter, then back again.

"Thank you," Luc said to his sister. "I brought Marie and Livie over. Can you at least be nice to me?"

"Children. No sniping at each other over the holidays. And absolutely not at the reception."

"What reception?"

"The Louvre has mounted a retrospective of your grandfather's work. The opening reception is tomorrow evening."

"You couldn't have mentioned this before?" The expression on his sister's face answered that question. They weren't sure he would have come if he knew about the show. "We didn't bring formal clothes with us."

"I can take Marie shopping this afternoon, after she wakes," Valerie offered.

"And what about me? I don't particularly want to buy a new suit."

"I've already called Alain. You can go to his shop today and borrow a suit. He'll make alterations today for you," Juliette said.

"Would have been easier just to tell me and I could have brought a suit."

"Well, easy isn't the Marchand way, is it?"

52

The dress shop was very French and very crowded with shoppers. Marie lifted her chin as she and Valerie walked in, and remembered Nishi's advice from years ago. *If you look like you belong somewhere, you will.* Besides, she had tried her best to dress like a Parisian. No going shopping in jeans the way she did in the states. Today, she wore slim black pants and heeled boots, a scarf wrapped around her neck the way Valerie had taught her.

Inside, Luc's sister strode straight to the back of the shop like a woman on a mission. Which they were—a mission to find a dress for Marie to wear to the Louvre while Luc searched elsewhere for a suit. Valerie took on one rack and Marie another.

After several minutes of fruitless searching, Valerie asked, "What about this one?"

Marie turned away from the rack of dresses she was perusing to see what Valerie was holding up. The dress was a dusky pale blue with a deep pink abstract floral pattern.

"It's very arty," she said. "Appropriate."

She considered the dress further. The bodice was fitted with a skirt that flared out in gentle gathers. She patted her stomach. "Would hide the problem areas."

Valerie rolled her eyes. "You look great. Is that a 'yes' to this one then?"

"That's a yes. If we can find some dressy shoes to go with it." The impossibly chic saleswoman was watching them; Marie sucked in her stomach a little bit harder. She'd lost the baby weight, but her body still seemed, well, curvier.

"And what about you? Are you splurging on a new dress?"

"I wasn't going to, but I'm on the verge of changing my mind. Too many pretty dresses in this shop."

Marie took the blue and pink dress from Valerie's hands. "Let's find you something, then we'll get a dressing room."

It was good to spend time with Luc's sister again. She missed having a close female friend. She'd had that kind of friendship with Nishi for years, and now she didn't because they lived in different cities. And with the revelation that Nishi had misled Luc—or made an incorrect assumption about Marie's wishes—she wasn't sure where that friendship stood now. Nishi had been traveling a lot for business since Livie's birthday party, a circumstance that had made it convenient for Marie to avoid the conversation she needed to have with her friend. It was not a discussion for the phone or email.

She looked through a rack of dresses, searching for something that would look good on Valerie. Valerie had that perfectly casual chic look that Marie simultaneously hated about French women and wanted to emulate. A black dress with ivory trim caught her eye. Very Chanel. She pulled it out, but kept looking.

Life was simpler before Luc came back. For a long time, she'd been desperate for him to return. She realized now that what she'd been desperate for was for things to magically go back to the way they were. For Luc not to have left in the first place. His return certainly hadn't solved every problem.

Valerie seemed to read her mind. "I wouldn't have taken him back." She fingered the black and ivory dress Marie had set aside.

"I haven't. Exactly."

"Oh?" Valerie lifted the black and ivory dress from the rack. "Luc said you're not seeing that other guy anymore."

"No. We split up. But that wasn't so Luc and I could be together. It just wasn't working with him."

The impossibly chic saleswoman found them a dressing room while Marie checked her phone for messages from Luc and Valerie's mother.

"She'll be fine. They became fast friends yesterday while you were napping."

"She and Luc became fast friends too. A little faster than I was ready for."

Valerie laughed. "Yeah, she was working on 'papa' yesterday. She has the 'puh' down."

"Really slays me, too. She's going to say papa before maman or mommy." Marie sighed as she closed the dressing room door behind them. At least the impossibly chic saleswoman gave them a larger room. "Your brother has a way with women, that's for sure."

"He seems to have jumped right into fatherhood."

"He has. I can't fault him for that."

"I do. Luc's never had to earn anything. Either something comes easily to him or he gives up. That's how he ended up in the U.S. in the first place. He had a gallery show in Paris, no one liked it, so he picked up and left the country. Instead of staying and listening to the criticism, then maybe applying some of it."

Marie undressed and neatly laid her clothes on the dressing room's upholstered bench. She slipped the blue dress from its hanger, unzipped it and wriggled into it.

"It must have been hard, growing up with such a famous grandfather," she said.

"Zip me up?" Valerie turned her unzipped back to Marie. "It

was hard for Luc because he decided he wanted to follow in grand-père's footsteps. Our father went into banking and I can't draw a straight line to save my life."

Marie zipped up the black and ivory dress, then turned around for Valerie to do the same for her.

"Do you think he could have?" She turned to look at the blue dress in the mirror. "Followed in your grandfather's footsteps?"

"Our grandfather thought so, or he wouldn't have encouraged him to the extent that he did. But Luc wasn't willing to work hard enough for it. Raw talent isn't enough. And the art world is different today than it was when our grandfather was younger. It's more commercial now. Corporate. Luc has to decide if he wants to be part of that."

"He'll have to work hard for Livie."

"I wish you had made him work harder when he came back, Marie." Valerie indicated for her to turn around. "That dress is perfect on you."

Marie swiveled her hips back and forth, admiring the way the full skirt on the dress swished back and forth. The dress was definitely a keeper.

"I can't keep him from Livie, for her sake as much as his. I'm hoping she'll change him. Or anchor him, at least." She crossed her fingers and waved them in the air.

Valerie waved her own crossed fingers. "Let's hope."

53

Marie lay in bed listening to Livie's soft, rhythmic breathing. What would she do when she and Livie were no longer sleeping in the same room? It had to happen someday. They couldn't live in a one-bedroom apartment forever. She would miss falling asleep to the gentle flow of her daughter's breath.

Next to her, Luc's breathing had a forced cadence to it. He was feigning sleep, just as Marie was. The conversation she and Valerie had while they were waiting for Luc outside the men's shop kept running through her mind.

"Do you still love my brother?"

Marie was surprised to discover that the answer came to her immediately.

"Yes. I do."

Which only made the whole situation harder. She was determined to do what was best for Livie. Emotions only complicated that. Emotions she hadn't been able to make herself feel for Aidan.

"You're a brave woman. Or insane. One of the two." Valerie's voice held amusement, and admiration.

"Insane, is what I'm thinking right now. Because I don't know if I can trust him. I can't go through him leaving me again."

"He seems very attached to Livie. Even mother commented on that."

"He is a devoted dad. But I worry about adding a relationship between us in there. He won't leave because of Livie. But if something goes wrong between us, he might."

She loved him. Still. But it was more important to keep him around as Livie's father than to have him as a lover, a partner, a spouse. She sighed and felt Luc's warm hand close around hers beneath the covers.

"Did my sister spend all day telling you how horrible I am and that you should stay a thousand miles away from me?"

"More or less."

"Are you going to take her advice?"

She squeezed his hand. "I'm not exactly a thousand miles away from you right now."

On the contrary, she was perfectly aware that the distance between them could be measured in inches. Plus a few millimeters of fabric when you took into account the sleep shirt she was wearing and the pajama bottoms Luc had politely donned. They were close enough for her to feel the body heat radiating from his bare chest.

She wanted to reach over and touch that bare chest.

Luc made no move beyond holding her hand. Even that was chaste. There was no thumb tracing practiced circles on her wrist, or his long fingers feeling every scar and scratch on the back of her hand.

"What are you thinking?" he asked quietly.

How much I want you to kiss me, run your hands down my ribs, make me feel the way we used to feel.

"Nothing."

How naive they'd been. Both of them. She'd thought things

were complicated back then, back when he'd been just her prickly, sexy drawing teacher. *It's like seeing with your skin.* He'd said that the first time they made love, on the floor of his studio. Skin was pretty blind, actually. It was more like seeing with your libido.

"Liar." The word slipped quietly from Luc's lips.

She smiled in the dark.

"It's okay, chérie. I know what you're thinking." He released her hand. "It's what I'm thinking too."

The watery winter sunlight gradually seeped into Luc's consciousness. Then his consciousness became aware of the gentle warmth lying next to him. Marie. He stretched his legs a little, trying not to move the mattress and wake her. His muscles were tight and aching from the effort of lying perfectly still all night, resisting the urge to roll onto his side and pull her into his arms. Three hours, that was about how much time Luc estimated he'd slept.

A *sproing* came from the other side of the room and he opened his eyes fully. Livie was standing up in the crib, her hands wrapped around the top rail for balance. She gave another little bounce. Next to him, Marie stirred and he laid a hand lightly on her shoulder.

"I'll get her. You sleep."

Marie's gratitude was expressed in a sleepy mumble.

He grabbed a diaper and wipes, then laid Livie back down in the crib to change her.

"Hungry, sweetheart?" he whispered. "We're going to let maman sleep in. She gets up early with you all the time."

He tossed her pajamas into the hamper and dressed her in a pair of stretchy black pants and a red top. He kissed the top of her head as he lifted her from the crib into his arms.

"Ready for Santa to come tonight? Hmm? I know you've been a good girl."

He nuzzled another kiss into the sweet, warm crook of her neck. He wanted ten Livies. Okay, maybe not ten. Marie would never go for that. But more, he wanted more Livies, more sweet-smelling children he could carry downstairs in the morning. That's what he wanted Santa to bring. A fresh start, another chance at a family with the woman he loved.

Too bad he hadn't been that good lately.

Downstairs, his mother was already up and busy in the kitchen. When she held out her arms for Livie, Luc was surprised by how eagerly Livie reached for her grandmother. His recollection of Sam's daughter, Ellie, was that she had been awkward around people she didn't know, reluctant to go to them. Or reluctant to go to him, anyway.

Livie seemed much more trusting of people.

"Let go of her, Luc," his mother said. "I'm your grand-maman," she said to Livie. "We got to know each other very well yesterday, didn't we?"

Luc let his mother lift his daughter from his arms. "Sorry. I don't want her to be uncomfortable."

Juliette rolled her eyes theatrically. "Please. She has Marchand blood in her veins. Don't you, sweet child? You know we're family, even if your papa doesn't bring you to visit often enough."

She cuddled Livie closer. His daughter was basking in her grandmother's affection and attention.

"Things are still … new. With Marie and me. I can't just whisk Livie off to Paris without her."

"I know, Luc. I'm just expressing a grandmother's wishes."

He opened the refrigerator and pulled out the milk. He poured some into a measuring cup and opened the microwave.

"She drank it cold last night," Juliette said.

He lifted an eyebrow. "She always drinks it warm."

“Or you always give it to her warm.”

He shrugged and closed the microwave, then poured the milk into one of Livie’s sippy cups. He handed it to Livie, still in his mother’s arms. Livie promptly began sucking down the cold milk.

“See?” Juliette settled Livie into the high chair his parents had dug out of storage for her. “But you and I, we’ll drink it warm.” She smiled mischievously and set about pouring two bowls of café au lait. “I apologize for putting you all in the same room. I assumed you and Marie … but Valerie set me straight on that.”

“It’s okay. It was fine.”

“Marie has a beau?”

He grimaced as he accepted the warm bowl from his mother.

“She did. Not any longer.”

“So …”

“She doesn’t trust me.”

Juliette started to speak but Luc raised his palm to stop her.

“I know. I don’t deserve her trust. If you were her, you wouldn’t trust me either. I’ve heard it from everyone.”

“May I offer slightly different advice? As your mother who might know something about matters of the heart?”

He shrugged. She was going to anyway. His mother, his sister. Everyone had advice for him on matters of the heart.

“You live large, Luc. That always worried your grandfather. Your grandmother, too, for that matter.”

“So did he. All artists live large.”

She sipped her own café au lait, then tapped the spot above her heart. “In here, Luc. Artists live large but you also have to be willing to sit in front of an easel for hours every day and just do the work. Attend to the brushstrokes, the light, the perspective—even when your fingers are cramping and the sun is shining brilliantly outside your window and you’ve just realized that the horizon is in the wrong place on the canvas. That’s what worried your grandfather, that you weren't willing to stay inside on a beautiful day and work."

Livie set her cup down loudly on the highchair tray. Her upper lip was coated in white milk. More milk dribbled down her chin. Luc moved to go to her, but his mother got there first, wiping Livie's face.

"I'm not painting anymore," he said as Juliette lifted Livie from the chair. "I've lost it. I can't do it anymore, it seems. Can't even draw."

"Nonsense. Your grandfather would say that too, if he were here."

He reached out his arms for Livie but Juliette shook her head. Instead, she set his daughter down on the floor, on her feet. She toddled toward him and wrapped her arms around his leg.

"I can't even draw my own daughter."

Just as he was about to reach down and scoop up Livie, she let go of his leg and toddled away.

"Let her explore."

"You have all your Christmas things out. She might break something in the process of exploring."

Juliette gave a Marchand shrug. "And what if she does? It's not like you and Valerie never broke anything. Life went on."

"I was planning to take Marie and Livie to his studio this afternoon. Is that okay? We'll be back before Christmas Eve dinner."

"That's fine. But you won't find your art there either, Luc."

54

His grandfather's studio looked just as it had when Luc was a child. The whitewashed walls, the faint tang of paint, his grand-père's denim shirt draped over a chair—it never failed to squeeze his heart and make him long for all the afternoons he'd spent there.

The house and the small cottage that had served as Philippe Marchand's studio belonged to Luc's parents now. He knew they had permission from his grandfather to simply use the property as a weekend retreat outside the city, and to convert the studio into a guest house. But they hadn't. The Marchand family was a sentimental bunch, and no one had the heart yet to change a thing. Maybe they never would. Part of Luc hoped that would be the case.

He shifted Livie's weight on his hip and dropped the key onto the small wooden table just inside the door. On the wall above the table were three iron hooks. His grandfather's hat still hung on one of the hooks. Luc lifted it off and placed it on Livie's head.

"Meet your granddaughter," he whispered quietly as Livie looked around the studio from beneath his grand-père's hat.

Luc followed her gaze, trying to imagine what she saw and remembering the way the studio had always looked to him as a young boy. His grandfather's presence was still strong here. It was easy to imagine him walking out from the tiny back room with a cup of coffee in one hand and a mug of water for Luc in the other. Even the easels were set up in the same manner—his grandfather's by the window, Luc's a few feet away.

"Are you okay?" Marie touched his arm.

He nodded and carried Livie over to the easels. Marie had been in this studio numerous times when they were in France before. Before the pregnancy. Livie was too young, obviously, to remember this visit or for it to mean anything to her. But Luc wanted to bring his daughter, wanted his grandfather to see her and see that Luc was grown up now. He was an adult, a family man—all the things his family had doubted he would ever mature into.

His mother was right. As a young boy, he *had* lost interest in drawing with his grand-père when the work got difficult. His grand-père had always let him go outside and play. Philippe Marchand had never made his grandson stay inside on a sunny day and do the hard work of being an artist. At the time, naturally, the young Luc was happy to be released from the drudgery. Now he wondered why his grandfather hadn't been stricter, and regretted the too easy freedom he'd been given. Maybe his life would be different now.

Marie lifted Livie from his arms and sat down on his grandfather's stool. Luc stretched the strain from his arm muscles.

"You're getting bigger, sweetheart." He lifted the brim of his grandfather's hat to smile into Livie's twinkling eyes. A realization hit him suddenly. It wasn't just a cliché, that kids grow up quickly. He could see that with Livie already. It wasn't hard to foresee the day when she would be too big—or too unwilling—to carry in his arms. And that day would be here sooner than he would be ready for.

"Draw us," Marie said.

SHE HAD SEEN it in his eyes, the way he was looking at her and Livie sitting on the wooden stool. He was gauging the lines and planes, planning a sketch. She knew he'd been trying to draw Livie, but a one-year-old was a hard subject to capture. Not only couldn't Livie sit still but she wanted to be with her papa, sitting on his lap, twirling his hair around her fingers, rubbing her palm against the rough stubble of his jaw.

But if Marie held Livie? Perhaps then he could manage it.

Nor had he attempted to draw Marie, a fact that left her unaccountably disappointed. He had always wanted to draw her before. He drew her even when she hadn't wanted it, had wanted to eat her dinner or watch the sunset without it being recorded for all time in charcoal. Now she missed those times, those moments of having Luc's focus on her and her alone.

It would never be just her and Luc alone again. Now there was another person, their daughter, holding them together—and keeping them apart.

She saw the doubt on his face.

"Try it, Luc. Or just draw Livie. She's pretty calm right now."

His drawing wasn't going well, she knew that. He was teaching after school art classes to schoolchildren, but his own work was stalled.

Livie blinked her eyes sleepily and Marie gently pressed her head to her shoulder.

"She's about to fall asleep," she mouthed to Luc, who finally retrieved a sketchpad and pencil from a bookshelf filled with art books and leather-bound journals full of studies for Philippe Marchand's paintings.

Livie's small chest rose and fell against her shoulder as she listened to the light scratch of Luc's pencil against the rough sketch paper. A memory came back to her, the first time she posed for him. Nude, on a stool, the weekend after they had gone to the Phillips Collection in Washington together. They had looked at the portraits of the Senator's wife, painted by her lover.

"What are you thinking about?" Luc's voice was quiet, barely above a whisper. They spoke that way a lot these days, quietly so as not to wake Livie.

"The first time you drew me, sitting on a stool like this, and now here I am holding your child. I never would have imagined this back then." Livie's breath was sweet and soft against her cheek. "How did we get here?"

"We fell in love," Luc replied, without looking up from the sketchpad.

"You didn't like that first drawing I did. You said it was depressing."

"You said I looked sad."

"And here we are again."

Marie blinked back the hot sting of threatening tears, glad that Livie's dark head gave her some cover. Here they were back in France, where they had left off—and with Livie now too—and yet it was all wrong. A gaping chasm lay between them, filled with Luc's guilt and doubt—and her fear and worry over trusting her heart to him again. It required a big enough leap of faith to trust him with Livie's heart.

That was the relationship she needed to protect most of all. Father and daughter. Luc and Livie. Marie could live without Luc's love in her life, but she couldn't deny their daughter that love. That was her fear—that if a relationship between her and Luc fell apart again, Livie would lose her father. She couldn't—wouldn't—risk that.

When you became a parent, you put your child's well-being ahead of your own. Her parents hadn't always done that, and Marie was adamant that she would not make the same mistake with her own daughter.

"How do we get back to where we were?" Luc asked.

He tore off the sketch he was working on, folded it in half and let it drop to the floor. He began a new one. He hadn't said anything to her about his difficulty drawing, but Sam had divulged that information to her at Livie's birthday party. That was another thing that gave her pause. Why couldn't he tell her that? Would he someday not share with Marie something that she needed to know concerning Livie?

"There is no way back," she said.

The scratch of his pencil stopped.

"Then how do we find our way to someplace new?"

She lifted one hand from Livie's back and motioned Luc over.

"Take her," she mouthed.

Livie's eyelids fluttered when Luc cradled her against his chest, then closed again. Was there any sweeter sight than Livie in his arms? Marie couldn't imagine one. She stood and indicated for Luc to take her spot on the stool, then walked over and picked up his sketchpad. A quick glance at the drawing he'd been working on confirmed his difficulties. The drawing would have been great for most people, but it wasn't anywhere near as good as his old work.

She flipped the page over and looked at Luc and Livie on the stool. He was watching her warily over their sleeping daughter's dark head. She began drawing.

"Livie is the most important thing in my life," she said quietly. "As I know she is in yours. I don't doubt your love for her. That's the new place we are in. The thing that is most important to both of us is the same person. And you are important to her. My fear is that if you and I try again and it doesn't work, Livie will lose you too. Or grow up with parents who are bitter toward each other."

He closed his eyes, silent for a long moment before speaking. "I won't leave again. I promise that, Marie."

"I know you believe that. I want to believe it, too. More than anything, I want to believe that. I just don't know that I can risk believing it, for Livie's sake."

55

"Luc, dear, can I see you for a minute?" His mother beckoned him through the kitchen and into the small nook tucked away at the back of his parents' house, a cozy space where his mother drank her morning café au lait when there weren't guests around.

It was late Christmas morning. His parents had invited a wide array of extended family over for a midday Christmas meal. He glanced back at Livie sitting on the floor, surrounded by a small mob of older cousins. Marie was standing a few feet away, sipping at coffee and talking to Valerie. If he had known how much his sister was going to bad mouth him while he was here, he might have thought twice about bringing Marie and Livie.

"She's fine, Luc." Juliette tugged at his shoulder. "She's eating up all this attention."

That was true. Livie was pleased as punch to be the center of attention. Everyone under the age of eighteen had already opened their gifts. The older kids were picking up Livie's new toys and dolls, each vying to be the one whose toy she chose next.

He followed his mother through to the nook. He hoped she wasn't planning some power negotiation of her own. The women in his family were not to be underestimated. Luc had learned that many a time. If only the lesson would stick one of these days.

His mother picked up a small box from the table in the nook. "This is a special gift from your father and me."

The box was neatly wrapped in silver paper, a white ribbon wound around it. He slipped his finger beneath the ribbon and tugged it off. He had no idea what his parents could be giving him that required a private opening. He carefully removed the paper to reveal a smooth wooden box with a small gold clasp. He flicked the clasp open and lifted the lid. Inside lay a necklace. Luc frowned. Surely this wasn't for him?

He looked up at his mother.

"Your grandmother wanted you to have this."

"Me? Why not Valerie?" He smiled. "She'd be more likely to wear it."

"You were your grand-père's favorite. You know that."

Everyone knew that. The Marchand family might have secrets, but that wasn't one of them. Philippe Marchand had doted on Luc and, in return, Luc had worshiped him.

His mother went on. "This necklace belonged to your grandmother. She wanted you to have it, to give it to your wife or child."

Luc lifted the jewelry from its padded resting place. It was a distinctive piece, but not something he could recall ever seeing on his grandmother. Not that he had seen her dressed to the nines much when he was a child. His grandparents had led a quiet life, despite Philippe's acclaim as an artist.

The necklace was a gold choker inlaid with emeralds and diamonds. A large teardrop emerald surrounded by tiny glittering diamonds hung at the front. It was a beautiful piece of jewelry and he couldn't help picturing it around Marie's lovely, graceful neck. It was a picture that seemed unlikely to ever exist in reality. He gingerly laid the necklace back in the wooden box and closed the lid and clasp. He was the last person in the family who deserved to inherit this.

"Valerie must want this, surely," he said.

"Your grandmother wanted you to have it."

"I'll keep it for Livie. Maybe when she turns eighteen."

"You won't give it to Marie before then?"

"It doesn't look like she's going to be my wife."

"I would say it's too soon to tell."

"She doesn't trust that I'll stick around if she and I break up. She said she'd rather have me in Livie's life than her own."

"I think she'd rather have both but becoming a parent changes you."

"I know that," he said, not bothering to mask the exasperation in his voice.

"Do you? I spent a lot of time with Marie when she was pregnant. I had never heard of her parents. Or her ex-husband, either. But clearly they were in charge of her life."

"To say the least. And despite my many failings, I am a better man than her ex. For the record."

"I would say that too, sweetheart. But Marie is a woman who is ready to run her own life now. Make her own decisions."

"She seems to have decided against me."

"I don't believe she has. I believe she wants to decide in your favor but she's not comfortable making that decision just yet."

"Hey." His sister's voice came from the doorway. "The grownups want to open gifts."

"*D'accord*. We'll be there in a minute." His mother put her hand on Luc's back and gently pushed him toward the door, in a way only a mother can get away with. "Luc. You made the decision to return home and take up your role as Olivia's father. And you took quite a bit of time to come to that decision. Marie needs some time, too. Allow her to have it."

MARIE LOOKED WARILY at the two small, square boxes on the floor in front of her. They looked suspiciously like jewelry boxes, and both were just the size to be a ring box. *Please no. Please let this not be an engagement ring.*

The grown ups had gathered in the living room to exchange Christmas gifts, now that the kids had opened theirs and were busy playing with new toys—and Livie. Marie had poked her head into the hallway where Livie's cousins were racing cars down the slick hardwood floor, and been roundly ignored. That was fine with Marie. She was happy Livie was enjoying herself with Luc's extended family. It was something she didn't have back in the states with the small Witherspoon tribe.

Marie was sitting cross-legged on the floor, next to Luc. His parents, Valerie, and Denis were sunk back into the upholstered sofa. Aunts and uncles and assorted cousins, most of whom Marie couldn't remember names for, were either perched on chairs or also sitting on the floor.

She tugged off the box's red satin ribbon and undid the green wrapping paper, more carefully than was warranted. *Please not an engagement ring.* Next to her, Luc was stock still. Maybe not even breathing.

She dropped the paper onto the floor, then lifted the lid of the white box. She fought the urge to let out a long exhale of relief. No engagement ring. Instead, the box held a pair of stud earrings in a gorgeous shade of blue

So why was there a sting of disappointment in her throat? *You don't want to marry him. Well, yes you do. But it's not a good idea. No more throwing caution to the wind for love.*

"It's Livie's birthstone," Luc said. "December. Open the other box."

Marie opened the second jewelry box more quickly, less

worried about the contents. The second box held another pair of blue studs, these smaller.

"For Livie when she's older," Luc explained.

She turned to him and smiled. "Thank you. They're beautiful." She touched her earlobes and found them bare. "I'll put them in right now."

"Here. let me do it."

Luc removed the first earring from the box and pulled off the back. His fingers tugged lightly at her earlobe to find the hole. Marie was aware of her breath catching in her throat, of her lungs suddenly refusing to work. He'd always had this ability, to touch her, slur her thoughts, make her body drunk on its desire for him.

She felt Valerie's eyes on her from across the room, as Luc put one earring on her, then the other. She knew her face was flushed red; she could feel the heat radiating off herself.

"They're beautiful. Thank you," she said, her voice barely above a whisper. She wished they were alone so his family couldn't witness her discomfort. At the same time, she was glad they weren't alone. She didn't trust her self control.

"Their beauty is eclipsed by the woman wearing them." Luc's voice barely met the definition of "whisper," clearly not meant for anyone else in the room to hear. He was on the other side of the rubicon, beckoning her to follow him across.

"Please." Her one word held so many meanings, even she wasn't sure which one she truly meant. *Please don't do this to me. Please I'm not ready. Please drag me-carry me-tempt me over to the other side.* Maybe she meant them all.

Luc leaned back and picked up another wrapped box. "Open this one next."

She was glad the moment of intensity was over. She needed to hush the voice in her head, the one that was unhelpfully pointing out that she would never be able to have Luc in her life as Livie's father and not want him there as more. That when the day arrived that Luc was seeing another woman—maybe even married to another woman—Marie's heart would collapse like a dying star, violently.

Inside the next box was the grey and cream silk scarf Luc had purchased from the hotel gift shop their first day in Paris, when she'd been running from Richard. She shook it out to look at it again.

"I still have the other one," she said quietly.

"That's gorgeous!" Valerie exclaimed. "Hermès. Where did you get that? I haven't seen that design."

Luc's family was, naturally, assuming that the scarf was new. Only she and Luc knew otherwise, and the sly smile on his face told her he liked that little bit of intimate, shared knowledge—and that he was remembering what had come next that first day in Paris.

Her body was remembering too, as she expertly wrapped the scarf around her neck and adjusted it against her red sweater.

"Thank you."

Luc leaned into her ear, pressing a kiss just above the earring he had put on her. "This belongs to you. No other woman will ever wear it. Or use it."

He caught her eyes with his own when he leaned back. She knew exactly what he meant by "use it."

"I might give it to Livie when she's older. Minus its complete history, of course."

"Enough with the chit chat over there," Valerie's husband, Denis, called out. "The rest of us want to open gifts, too."

"So don't let us stop you," Luc said. "We don't have to do this one by one."

Marie breathed a sigh of relief when the other adults began exchanging and opening gifts. She had never been one for the spotlight, to begin with, and was only too happy to relinquish it now.

She reached for her gifts to Luc.

"I have one more," he said.

The gift he handed her was wide and flat, and Marie knew as soon as she held it that it was a softbound book. It was the right size to be an art book. The museum catalog to his grandfather's show at the Louvre. It had to be. She eagerly tore off the paper.

Alistair Smith & Elizabeth Calhoun: A Model Revealed.

It was a catalog to a museum show, just not the one she was expecting. It was the catalog to that fateful show at the Phillips Collection in Washington, DC. The one where she had agreed to model for Luc, the one that had inspired her to hatch an ill-advised plan to escape Richard and his political machinations.

The show was still at the Carnegie Museum of Art in Pittsburgh, though she had so far lacked the nerve to go see it again. Too many memories. She rubbed the edge of the book with her thumb. She wasn't sure she even wanted to read the catalog.

"I wanted to give you a portrait of Livie," Luc said, "but I can't draw even her. Sorry."

"You'll get it back. Do a portrait of her then. I can wait."

She set the catalog down and handed Luc his first gift.

"I feel bad giving this to you now."

Puzzlement creased his forehead. "Why?"

"You'll see when you open it."

She held her breath as Luc carefully undid the red wrapping paper and slid out the gift. His eyes teared up as he looked at it. She had taken Livie to a photographer to have a portrait done. It wasn't a drawing or painting, but Marie's skills weren't up to that. She had figured a photograph was the next best thing.

She watched as Luc struggled to keep his emotions in check. Fortunately, no one else in the room was paying attention to them.

"How did you get her to sit still long enough to do this?"

"Well, it involved the photographer's teenaged son, who was there practicing magic tricks after school. And two sittings."

Luc's eyebrow shot up to his hairline. "Teenaged son, did you say?"

"Relax, papa. You have a few more years before you have to worry about boys."

Luc grinned wryly. "I'm a boy. I know how early I need to start worrying."

She wished she could freeze this moment, Luc smiling and relaxed. This was the way it was supposed to be last Christmas. Instead, Marie had been in this very room, with Luc's family, exhausted and with a newborn. In January, she had returned to the states. She shook all that from her mind. Here. Now. This was what mattered. *Live in the present.*

"This is for you, too." She handed Luc a larger box, also wrapped in red paper, then held her breath. She wasn't sure he would like the gift. He might even be offended or hurt. But she knew he would be grateful for it at some point, even if that point was many years down the road.

He pulled off the paper and looked at the packaging, his face neutral. She had bought him a very nice digital camera. The photographer who had taken Livie's portrait had recommended a model to her.

"Livie does things too quickly for pencil and paper. I think you'll be glad later if you take photographs." She bit her lip, still awaiting his reaction.

He leaned toward her. "I'm glad I have it now." With his finger he gently pulled her lip from her teeth. "I wouldn't have bought one for myself. But then again, you probably know what's best for me better than I do."

I can't even begin to know—

He covered her mouth with his and the room fell silent. She knew all eyes were on them. The kiss was more than friendly but it stopped well short of passionate. Disappointment and relief warred in her breast. His lips were soft but firm, not pushing for more but letting her know that more was there.

More. She wanted more with Luc. She also didn't want *more* to blow up in her face, tear her apart so badly that it rendered her an unfit mother for Livie.

Later that night, as she lay in bed waiting for sleep to overtake her, she replayed the kiss in her mind. Right up to the moment where her heart threatened to burst open.

56

The pyramid of the Louvre glowed like a beacon against the night sky. He and Marie had been here before, numerous times, but always in street clothes. Tonight, Marie looked beautiful in her new dress. It skimmed over her curves, then flared out at the waist in tiers of silky fabric, naturally drawing the eye down to her legs. He imagined undoing the tiny buckles on those strappy silver sandals later, and tugging them off her feet.

He imagined that he would be doing no such thing.

She wants me. She wants me not. She wants me. She wants me not.

Her hair was twisted up into some elaborate style and Valerie had loaned her a pair of dangly earrings. It took Luc back to the reception at the National Gallery in Washington, where he'd nearly been arrested for clocking a sitting United States Senator. Marie had that poised, contained "official" presence she could slip on like a sweater. She had been wearing it that night in Washington and she was wearing it now, as she stood in the light looking at him.

"Just take the damn picture," his sister barked. "It's cold out here."

He snapped two shots then caught up to Marie, leaving his complaining sister behind. His whole family was on edge, worried about what he would do tonight. Yes, he had been Philippe Marchand's favorite grandchild. Yes, he had hoped to follow in his grandfather's (rather large) artistic footsteps. Luc no longer knew what he hoped for, other than the beautiful, shivering woman whose hand he clasped in his.

"Are you okay?" Marie asked as they followed the crowd into the museum.

Marie and Valerie had spent most of the afternoon together, primping and getting ready for this event. He loved his sister—most of the time anyway—but she was a busybody. Even as a child, she'd had her nose in everyone else's business. He wasn't sure how Denis put up with it.

He squeezed Marie's hand. "I'm fine, chérie." She squeezed back and he felt the gentle pressure in the very center of his heart. "Tonight I am going to enjoy great art in the company of the best subject I have ever painted."

In the company of the woman I love.

She smiled and rolled her eyes at him and he fought the urge to pull her into his arms and kiss the hell out of her. He could kiss away her resistance. He was sure of that. But he didn't want to wear her down or toy with her body to get what he wanted. He wanted her to let go of the resistance herself.

Problem was, Marie wasn't the passive woman some people saw her as. It had taken him awhile to see it, too. Beneath that perfectly poised "official" Marie was an inner skin made of steel that kept out anything she didn't want to let in. Most people never saw that steely reserve because they weren't trying to get past it. They were content with official Marie.

He wasn't. He knew the woman who lay beneath that shell, and she was strong and loving and giving. And he would wait until she gave herself again.

"DID you know your grandfather did so many portraits of her?" Marie started counting the small charcoal drawings grouped on the wall. There were at least a hundred. Probably more that weren't being shown.

"No. I didn't." Luc stared at the tiny artworks. "I knew he drew and painted her but I didn't realize it was quite this extensive. Or obsessive, maybe."

Marie touched his arm lightly, then strolled away to read the curator's wall label for this section of the exhibition. After a moment, Luc followed. He draped his arm around her shoulders, and she allowed it. Partly because it felt good to have his arm around her and partly because being here reminded her so much of the time they spent in the Phillips Collection. Of course, there were far more people here than on that afternoon she had snuck away from the office to meet him in the third floor gallery.

Philippe and Emeline Marchand were married for sixty-one years, until his death in 1996. Emeline was not an artist but she was, nonetheless, Philippe's artistic partner and "his inspiration for life." Over the course of their long marriage, he captured her likeness in hundreds of casual drawings and nearly a dozen formal painted portraits. These private drawings of Emeline have never been exhibited publicly before; in her will, Emeline requested that the drawings be added officially to Philippe's body of work and gave her permission for them to be shown.

Marie drifted out from beneath Luc's arm to look at more of the drawings. Some were posed; most were casual, like snapshots of Emeline Marchand going about her day. Dressing, drinking coffee, arranging flowers in a vase. Some were lovingly detailed, while others were quick lines and shading to capture a moment.

Marie couldn't help herself. For a moment, she imagined a lifetime of tiny portraits of her … drawn by Luc. Then she pushed the thought from her mind and headed further down the wall. What she found there, nearly tucked into the corner of the room, surprised and delighted her. She glanced back at Luc, who was still studying the drawings of his grandmother. Then she turned back to the wall, on which were hung a dozen small sketches of a young boy. Several depicted the boy sitting at an easel, a frown of concentration on his face.

Marie knew that frown all too well. She saw it on Livie every day. And it was on the man standing fifteen feet away from her. This room didn't only contain Emeline Marchand. It held her grandson, as well.

An older gentleman sidled up next to Marie. The curator. Marie was briefly introduced to him when she and Luc arrived.

"It's not often that I have both the subject and the image together in one gallery," he said in heavily accented English.

"He spent a lot of time drawing the people he loved."

"He did. I knew him only in his later years but he was a man with a big heart."

"His work changed a lot over his lifetime."

"It did," the curator agreed. "He was not a thinking artist. He was a feeling artist. He painted what spoke to his heart, and when it stopped speaking he moved on to something else that did."

Luc was a thinking artist, she thought. Maybe that was the source of his current troubles. He didn't have anything that spoke to him artistically anymore.

"But he never tired of drawing his wife and grandson," the curator continued. "As you can see."

The curator excused himself and left. Marie looked at Luc, who was looking back at her. She cocked her head toward the wall in front of her. Luc joined her and chuckled softly when he saw the drawings of himself.

"I'm surprised these still exist. My grandparents kept everything."

"Do you remember him drawing you?"

Luc nodded. "Yes. But there were also times when he would draw you without you ever noticing. He could get an image down on paper so quickly." He shook his head. "He tried to teach me how, but I still can't do it."

That wasn't Marie's impression of Luc. He had always seemed able to draw anything with a few strokes of his wrist.

"Come. There's more to see." He wrapped his hand around hers.

She took one last look at the drawings of Luc as a young boy. She couldn't really imagine him as a boy, being taught to draw and paint by his grandfather. Most of the time, Luc struck her as a person who was completely unteachable. She wondered if Philippe Marchand had ever felt that way about his grandson.

THE PAINTINGS of Emeline Marchand were large and richly detailed, even more so than Luc remembered. The way the folds of her dress captured the light … the whispery lines along her upper lip … the subtle changes in her hair and skin as the years passed … all of it his grandfather's trademark realism. And yet his grandmother was utterly beautiful in the portraits, despite the unflinching fidelity to painting exactly what was there.

Luc had always struggled with that balance. Even in his portraits of Marie, which he considered to be his best work, sometimes the painting didn't reflect the beauty he saw in her. There was something that got lost between his eyes and the canvas. And now things were even worse. He could barely capture any image, beautiful or not. How could he not be able to draw even his own daughter, the most beautiful thing he'd ever known?

Marie was spending more time with each painting than he needed to. They were new to her. He moved on to the next one. And the next one. And then there it was. The emerald and diamond necklace. The one his mother had given to him on Christmas day.

In the painting, his grandmother was seated in the green upholstered chair he remembered from their living room. She wore a simple black dress, black pumps and the choker. Her dark hair was loosely curled, her lips rouged with red lipstick and smiling softly at the painter, her husband, his grandfather. He had rarely seen his grandmother like this, and in that moment he felt an intense envy of his grandparents' marriage. They'd had a good life together, a long loving partnership. Luc wanted that, had always wanted that.

In retrospect, it was easy to see that he wouldn't have had that with Grace. Sam had told him that at the time and she'd been right, as she almost always was. Sam was his Nishi, the person who looked out for his best interests when he was blind to what those interests were. He knew he shouldn't blame Nishi for what she'd done. She was the only person who looked out for Marie's best interests. Her parents hadn't. Her ex-husband certainly hadn't. Marie thought her parents had come around, but that was a trust he didn't share. They had invited Richard Macintyre and his new wife to their home for Thanksgiving. Even Sam had been taken aback by that, and Sam was hard to shock when it came to people behaving badly in DC.

He felt a hand settle on the small of his back, and he was struck by the knowledge that he would always recognize Marie's touch. Even if she never took him back, he knew in his gut—in his heart—that he would always know her touch. He turned to his left to smile at her. Somehow she had gotten ahead of him in the exhibit, while he'd been ruminating on his grandparents' marriage.

"Come look at this one," she said.

He followed her to the last painting in the room. It was markedly different from all of the earlier portraits of Emeline Marchand. Philippe Marchand had spent his life painting his wife —painting everything, for that matter—in exacting detail. The way he had taught Luc to draw and paint—to see things just as they are, not as the mind wants to see them. Then, in his later years, his work began to grow increasingly abstract.

Luc had noticed that as a teenager. Vaguely. But his grandfather had continued to teach Luc to paint in a realistic manner, and Luc had been too much of a know-it-all adolescent to question his grandfather's changing style. He had scorned abstract art. Truth be told, he had been more than a little contemptuous toward his grandfather's abandonment of representational art.

"His work changed," Marie said. "I mean, I know that's stating the obvious."

She gestured at the painting on the wall. The woman in the painting wasn't recognizable as his grandmother. It could have been anyone, really. That's what Luc disliked about abstract art. It could be anything. Anyone. Not that some of it wasn't beautiful. Luc admitted that. There was a strange sort of loveliness to this portrait of his grandmother. The colors were rich, if muted, and the lines strong even if they didn't coalesce into an image that looked like Emeline Marchand.

But it was a non-specific beauty. In Luc's mind, beauty was better when it was specific. What was the point of painting someone if the end result looked nothing like them?

"It did." He draped his arm across Marie's shoulder and pulled her into his chest. He didn't want to paint Marie and Livie if he couldn't completely capture how beautiful they were to him.

"The curator said to me that your grandfather was a feeling artist, not a thinking one."

"I wouldn't agree with that," Luc said. "I'd say he was a *seeing* artist. That's how he taught me to be. That's what I was trying to teach you. How to just see what's in front of you." He lifted his free hand toward the painting. "I don't know what he was seeing here."

57

"Ah pumpkin, what do you think your great-grandfather was up to?"

Luc kissed Livie's soap-sweetened cheek as he stood before one of Philippe Marchand's later paintings, his daughter in his arms. It was their last day in Paris and Luc had arranged to come see his grandfather's show one last time. It was eight in the morning; the curator was allowing him in an hour before the doors opened.

Livie clutched at the collar of his shirt. She wanted down. Over the course of their short trip, she had gone from standing to toddling. Her older cousins had been happy to hold her hand, help her walk across rooms, hold out their arms in encouragement. The sight of Livie with the kids had stung his heart. He desperately did not want her to be an only child.

He also desperately wanted to know why his grandfather's painting style had changed late in life. After decades of ignoring all the twentieth century art movements, he suddenly transformed the way he painted. If he hadn't been so self-absorbed when he was younger, Luc might have paid more attention. But he was a teenager back then, busy with school and friends and girls. He had been convinced that he had learned everything he needed to from his grandfather.

How wrong he had been. After years spent under the tutelage of one of France's most loved painters, Luc had failed to see what was happening in his own grandfather's studio. Philippe Marchand had spent years teaching Luc to see like an artist, then abandoned all that.

Luc felt a little betrayed.

"Monsieur Marchand." The curator appeared as if out of nowhere and extended his hand in greeting. Luc shook it, then readjusted Livie in his arms.

"You didn't bring your wife?" the man asked.

"No. We let her sleep in. Last day of vacation." Luc smiled. They were headed back to Pittsburgh the next day.

"Well then. What did you want to know about the show? It looks like it's going to be very well attended."

Luc turned to look at the painting he'd been studying. It was a Paris streetscape, according to the wall label, but one would be hard pressed to connect it to any city specifically. Why had he gone back to streetscapes? He painted those before the war, in the late twenties when he was friends with Stuart Davis. After the war though, he retreated into nature. He painted the French countryside, acres of vineyards, the coast, fields of lavender. He painted the French Alps, with almost photorealistic precision, like a French Albert Bierstadt. All holy light and reverence. His devotion to France in that way was what had made him such a beloved national figure.

"Were people upset when he changed his style?" he asked. "For decades, he painted one way and then he abruptly took up another."

The curator slowly looked around the room, scanning Philippe Marchand's late-career work.

"It wasn't that abrupt," he said. "His eyesight was failing for many years. He tried to hide that for as long as he could, but eventually people realized it."

If Luc hadn't been holding Livie in his arms, he would have dropped to his knees. *I never realized it.*

"By the time he painted this one," the curator gestured to the streetscape, "he was nearly blind." The curator paused. "You did not know this?"

Luc shook his head slowly, stunned. He hadn't known it. And why hadn't anyone ever mentioned it to him?

"By the end, your grandmother was doing nearly everything for him but the painting. I met with her several times after his passing, when we were finalizing details of her will and what she wanted to do with his work. And, I must say, her love and dedication was awe inspiring." The curator laughed. "I certainly wouldn't expect that from my wife."

Luc squinted at the streetscape canvas, then closed his eyes for a moment, trying to imagine his grandfather painting without sight. He opened his eyes again.

"How could he paint blind?"

"He was painting from memory, I imagine. Although your grandmother said he was trying to paint the way things felt to him."

"And things felt abstract to him?"

"Well, I suspect the abstraction was due to his failing eyesight and less any intentional change in style. The way your grandmother made it sound, he could barely see the brush in his hand, let alone the canvas or whatever he was painting."

Luc tightened his hold on Livie as he struggled to breathe. How could his grand-père paint without being able to see? The man who had revered *seeing* above all else?

"For the last two years or so of his life, he was only painting your grandmother," the curator added.

As the curator's heels clicked crisply in retreat across the gallery's floor, Luc took one last look at the streetscape painting. Then he carried Livie to the Mona Lisa. They had a few minutes yet before the crowds arrived. As he stood before what was probably the most famous painting in the world, he wondered how much any artist really sees.

Livie turned out not to be much interested in the Mona Lisa and her enigmatic smile. Not that it mattered, he thought. She was too young to remember any of this trip to Paris. She could see the Mona Lisa. But she would never recall it.

Outside, the morning winter sun was weak and pale. He called his sister on the phone.

"Why didn't anyone tell me grandpapa was blind?" he asked when Valerie picked up.

"Everyone knew," she replied. "It didn't need to be said. It was as plain as day."

"YOU AND LUC are not lovers again?"

Marie looked across the small bistro table at Juliette Marchand. She wasn't surprised that Luc's mother had raised this topic of conversation. The two of them had spent countless hours during Marie's pregnancy, dissecting men and love. And Juliette's son. In this very bistro. Marie missed those conversations. She and her own mother never spoke this way. Candidly. From the heart.

"No. We're not."

Marie felt almost as if she should apologize to Juliette for not taking back her son.

"Can I ask why not?"

Marie's gaze shifted to the cozy interior of the restaurant as she considered her words. Butter yellow walls. Dark, gleaming wood. Waiters and waitresses in dashing black and white aprons. And all around them, the intoxicating aroma of warm food and coffee. She imagined this bistro looking exactly like this for the past century. And for another hundred years to come.

She'd be a liar if she were to deny that she'd been thinking about Luc *that way* since they arrived in France. As a lover. A husband. She liked his family. They were so rooted here, so *permanent* in a way her family wasn't. Her parents had invented themselves, invented their lives. And in so doing, invented Marie's life.

But she couldn't get back together with Luc simply because she wanted his family.

"The most important thing is for Livie to have him in her life. If we were to split up again … losing him would be harder for her than for me."

"I am sorry, Marie. Luc is not that emotionally resilient. I failed him as a mother on that count. I let my father-in-law coddle him too much. He wanted his grandson to follow in his footsteps as much as Luc did." Juliette sipped at her coffee. "And some of it was guilt, too."

"How so?"

"When my husband was a child, Philippe spent so much of his time painting. Being an 'artist.'" She made air quotes around her last word. "They weren't close, as father and son, and they never became close. Philippe was trying to make up for that with Luc."

"I haven't been a mother for very long, but I've learned already that you do the best you can," Marie said. "And hope you don't screw them up permanently."

"Marie, dear, you are doing a lovely job with Olivia. Not that any of us ever doubted that. Luc has made plenty of mistakes in his life, but he made the perfect choice for the mother of his children."

Children, plural. That wasn't lost on Marie, nor did she think it was an unintentional word choice on Juliette's part. Luc's mother was nothing if not precise. It was surprising that she had raised a child like Luc who was anything but emotionally precise and contained.

Juliette smiled warmly across the table. “What are you thinking?”

Marie shook her head ruefully. “I’m wondering if Livie will turn out completely opposite of how I’m trying to raise her.”

“Almost certainly. In some ways, at least.”

“I see a lot of Luc in her sometimes, and it scares me.”

Juliette laughed softly. “Well, that should be good for Luc. A taste of his own medicine.”

“He’s not painting right now.”

Juliette’s soft laugh sobered to a frown. “I know. He mentioned it.”

“I think he compares himself to his grandfather.”

“It’s a different time for art. Harder to get attention perhaps, pure talent less of an advantage.” Juliette neatly folded her napkin and placed it on the table. “Luc only knew his grandfather after he was successful. He didn’t see the hard work Philippe put in when he was younger. And the work Emeline did, picking up the slack in their lives. Luc hasn’t worked hard enough. He learned a lot from Philippe, but some things you just have to learn on your own.”

58

The crowd in the lobby of the Carnegie Museum was thinning. The bartenders looked bored. The caterer was circulating fewer trays of stuffed mushrooms and mini tomato tarts. Marie discreetly took a peek at her phone, both for the time and for any texts from Luc. He was watching Livie while Marie worked this evening. The alumni association was holding an Art & Cocktails reception at the museum for alumni under the age of thirty.

Which makes me one of the oldest people here.

She'd always assumed she would be married and raising a family by now. If she had followed the path her parents had chosen for her, she would be.

I'd be miserable, too.

She was happy enough as a single mother, a working mom. But she'd be lying if she said she didn't still want the rest of the package. A husband, more kids, a house.

There were no messages from Luc, and it was twelve minutes past seven o'clock. The reception was scheduled to wind down at seven-thirty. Everything had gone off without a hitch, which was Marie's purpose there. Make sure the caterer didn't run out of food or wine. Introduce herself to the handful of already wealthy twentysomething alums, mostly founders of small technology firms, and gauge their interest in becoming benefactors to the university.

At seven-thirty on the dot, her phone's clock alarm vibrated in the pocket of her blazer and she slipped away from the museum lobby. She had been reading the museum catalog Luc had given her for Christmas, the one for *Alistair Smith & Elizabeth Calhoun: A Model Revealed.* The show was still at the Carnegie and she had wanted to see it again, but Livie had been on and off sick ever since they'd returned from Paris two weeks ago. She had been reluctant to leave her with Luc tonight, but he had practically pushed her out the door.

"I can take care of her," he'd said.

"Call me if she starts to run a fever again."

Luc had rolled his eyes. "Call me if you want a ride home."

"I'll just grab the bus. It's not a late event."

The gallery wasn't empty. Nor was it crowded. The museum was closed to the general public for the evening, but the reception guests were free to wander through any of the galleries. She strolled up to the curator's explanation. She could practically recite it word for word by now.

Alistair Smith was a relatively unknown American artist living in New York in the 1940s when he met Elizabeth Calhoun, the wife of U.S. Senator Teddy Calhoun. For decades, the identity of the woman in Smith's paintings was a mystery and the artist himself refused to say who she was, taking the secret to his grave. Finally, when Elizabeth Calhoun passed away in 2001 and her children discovered boxes of correspondence between Elizabeth and Alistair Smith, the mystery woman was unmasked. For nearly fifteen years, Elizabeth had been Alistair's lover, muse and mystery model. Three years ago, the estates of Calhoun and Smith generously gave their correspondence and his paintings to the Phillips Collection in Washington, DC. The Carnegie Museum is the final stop on the exhibit's nationwide tour.

As much as she liked the paintings, the entire show troubled her. This affair—this very private thing between two people—was now immortalized in a museum exhibit, in a published book and in the minds of the thousands of people who had viewed Alistair's portraits of Elizabeth.

Two years ago, she had taken inspiration and courage from these paintings—and allowed Luc and Sam to show her own portraits. Marie had thought she was being brave by allowing Luc to paint her with her face exposed, unlike Elizabeth. She shook her head as she strolled through the gallery. Amazing how quickly courage could turn to foolhardiness.

And immortality.

Alistair and Elizabeth's heirs had exposed their love affair to the world. Would a grownup Livie do such a thing in the same situation? Livie wouldn't need to, of course. Alistair Smith had been a relatively obscure artist. But Luc wasn't, not in France anyway. Their trip to Paris had driven home that point. Luc was related to a beloved national figure there. It was overly optimistic to think that the paintings Luc had made of her could simply fade away and be forgotten, buried eventually in the basement of the internet. Luc would always be at least a footnote in his grandfather's legacy.

And there was Livie. Alistair Smith and Elizabeth Calhoun never had a child together. But she and Luc did. What would Livie think some day? That her mother was best known for being at the center of a scandal and then running away to Paris on Christmas Eve with her lover?

Nishi was fond of saying, "you have to control the narrative." Marie had thought she *was* controlling the narrative when she had encouraged Luc to show the paintings, when in fact she had simply started another, different narrative. One in which she was the estranged wife of a sitting United States Senator and smack dab in the center of a juicy scandal. At least Elizabeth Calhoun had been smart enough to avoid that narrative while she and Alistair were alive.

On the other hand, their love hadn't survived. The museum catalog contained a few details that the actual exhibit left out. Eventually, Elizabeth's husband retired from the Senate and they moved back home to Texas. She never saw Alistair again.

Marie skipped over the tiny charcoal drawings—those had never been her favorites—and stopped in front of a large painting of Elizabeth lying on a bed, white sheets twisted and tangled around her body. Her face was turned away from the viewer, as it was in so many of the paintings and drawings. Her arm hung limply over the edge of the bed, a necklace dangling from her graceful fingers.

Marie leaned in to look more closely at the necklace. She had looked at this painting countless times in the museum catalog, but in it the necklace was too small to really notice. It was just a line of green. But here, in person, it was almost lovingly depicted in all its sparkling beauty. Emeralds, Diamonds. Gold. It was a beautiful piece of jewelry.

And she could swear it looked just like the necklace Luc's grandmother was wearing in some of her portraits at the Louvre. She pulled her phone from her pocket and snapped a close-up shot of just the necklace. She would show it to Luc when she got home. It was uncanny how similar the two pieces of jewelry were, although it was possible Marie wasn't remembering Emeline Marchand's necklace accurately. There had been so much to take in at the Louvre retrospective.

A pair of hands settled on her shoulders, and Marie stiffened.

"Hey there."

She spun around. It was Aidan.

"What are you doing here?"

"One of the grad students in the math department was invited. He's a young alum. He asked me to come along."

Marie glanced behind Aidan toward the entrance to the gallery.

"Where is he?"

"He headed over to the library. He's supposed to meet one of his students there. He's a TA this semester."

"Oh." Marie stepped back from Aidan. She hadn't spoken to him since the day they broke up. Occasionally, she saw his blonde head towering above the crowd in the Commons Room but she was always careful to hang back and not run into him.

"Do you want to go get some coffee?" he added.

"I have to get home." She pulled out her phone again and glanced at the time. It was after eight, she was surprised to see. "I didn't realize it was this late."

Aidan smiled warmly. "I'll walk you out then."

Marie kind of wished he wouldn't but there was no good reason to be impolite to him. He wasn't angry the way he'd been the last time she saw him. He retrieved their coats from the coat check and tipped the attendant. She allowed him to hold out her coat while she slipped her arms into it. She buttoned it up, tugged her leather gloves from the pockets.

His long legs covered the distance to the door a few steps ahead of her. He held it open for her. She stopped just outside to say goodbye, but Aidan suddenly stumbled as he came through the door. Her arm shot out to steady him. The pavement was covered with a thin film of snow and more was falling. Righted, Aidan brushed his finger over her nose.

"You had a snowflake there," he grinned.

"It was nice seeing you again." She turned to head toward the bus stop.

"How are you getting home? Cabbing it?"

His long legs caught up to her.

She inclined her head toward the bus shelter where a small

group of people were huddled inside against the cold and the snow.

"I'm taking the bus."

"Don't be ridiculous. I'll give you a ride. My car's just around the corner."

She hesitated.

"When does the bus come?" he asked.

"Eight-forty."

"That's twenty minutes from now. I can have you home in that amount of time."

That was true. The bus would take another thirty minutes after that, by the time it wound its way through Squirrel Hill and Shadyside. She did have to work in the morning, as did Luc. The sooner she got home, the sooner he could go home.

"Alright. Thanks."

She followed Aidan to his car, where he dropped his keys into the slush while opening the passenger side door for Marie. She buckled her seat belt and waited for Aidan to round the car and join her.

With each passing block, the snow seemed to get heavier—and Aidan got more talkative.

"How was Paris?"

"Good. It was good."

"You didn't get married or anything while you were over there, did you?"

"No." She waved her left hand, still unadorned.

"Is he babysitting Livie tonight?"

"He's with her, yes. But he's her father so I don't think you can call it 'babysitting.'"

"You know what I mean. Are you—"

"Aidan!" Marie screamed as the rear bumper of the car in front of them got closer and closer. Aidan slammed on the brakes just in time to avoid hitting the other car.

"We're fine. It's nothing."

She looked over at him in disbelief—then in dismay as she saw what she had missed earlier, in her effort to keep some distance between them. Aidan's eyes had the slightly unfocused look of someone who'd had too much to drink.

"Aidan, you shouldn't be driving."

"I'm fine."

"How much did you have to drink tonight?"

The light turned green and the car began moving forward again.

"It was your event. You were serving alcohol."

"Aidan. Pull over. I'll call us a cab."

"I'm fine, baby. You've never almost rear-ended someone?"

No.

"Seriously, Aidan. Pull over."

"No."

The light ahead was red. She would get out of the car the minute Aidan stopped at the intersection. She leaned over to dig in her purse for her phone, then remembered it was still in the pocket of her blazer. She stripped off her gloves, then clumsily unbuttoned her winter coat beneath the straps of the seat belt. She woke up her phone and was about to call Luc when she felt Aidan slam on the brakes of the car. She looked up just in time to see the headlights of a bus bearing down on her. Shouldn't there be noise? Her mouth was open in a scream and the car was skidding sideways. She should be hearing tires squealing, horns blaring, but everything was eerily silent. She felt the side of the car push in against her and then nothing.

59

Luc poured another cup of coffee and tried to rub the tired ache from his eyes. Marie should be home by now. It was a cocktail reception. Those things don't last all night. He stared at his phone on the table. He'd been calling and texting for hours. It wasn't like Marie to not answer. He'd even called the museum, but all he got was a recorded message stating that the museum was closed for the day.

As he watched his phone, the clock on the screen rolled over to midnight. He took a deep breath. There had to be a reason why she was late.

Had to be. Had to be. Had to be.

He took a deep breath and picked up the phone again. He would call the police. Then the hospitals. *Please, god, no.*

His phone buzzed in his hand, startling him. Marie! She was calling him back, finally. But the name on the screen was Eileen Witherspoon. He touched the screen and answered.

"Luc? It's Eileen."

"Eileen." This wasn't good. No earthly reason for Marie's

mother to call him at midnight. They weren't going to just chat about Livie at this hour. But wait! Maybe …

"Is Marie with you?"

The silence on the other end was a beat too long.

"Marie's been in an accident. We're at the hospital."

An accident?

"Montefiore," Eileen clarified.

"What kind of accident?" He looked around Marie's living room, frantically searching for Livie's diaper bag. What would she need? Bottle. Diapers. Wipes. Cereal. What else what else?

"An automobile accident. They were hit by a bus in an intersection."

Who's they? Who had Marie been with?

"What was she doing in a car? She was going to take the bus home. And I told her to call me if she wanted a ride."

"Aidan was driving. That's all I know at the moment. We came as soon as the hospital called us. We took a helicopter out here."

"Is she—"

"She's still in surgery. Apparently, she took the worst of it. The doctors haven't said much otherwise. Is Livie with you?"

"Yes. Of course. She's sleeping."

"Well, don't wake her. Come when you can."

Luc hurriedly packed the diaper bag. Waking Livie was the lesser of two evils, he decided. She'd fall back asleep in the car. She barely protested when he wrangled her into her warm fleece pants and top, then zipped up her coat and tucked the hood around her face.

"Sorry, sweetheart." He kissed her sleep-warmed cheek.

LUC PACED the waxed floor of the hospital's waiting room. Marie was still in surgery. No one had come out to give them an update.

Livie was sound asleep in Eileen's arms, while William Witherspoon was on the phone booking them a hotel room.

He physically hurt. This not knowing how Marie was, being in the dark about her injuries, felt like a knife slashing him open over and over. He tried to ignore the secondary pain, the one engulfing his heart. What had Marie been doing in Aidan's car? Had she not been at a work event after all? Did she meet up with him later? Were they seeing each other again?

It had felt like they'd made some progress in Paris. Now he doubted that. Obviously he'd been mistaken. He needed a drink. He needed to punch something. He needed … he didn't know what he needed. So many thoughts stomping through his brain. He wanted to go to sleep and then wake up to find that none of this ever happened.

He walked toward Eileen, but stayed a few feet away so he didn't wake Livie.

"I'm going to get some coffee," he said quietly. "Do you want some?"

She nodded and mouthed, "thank you." Then she nodded toward her husband. Luc nodded back. Coffee all around.

In the bleary-eyed hours of early morning, the hospital's cafeteria was nearly empty. A handful of employees milled around, chatting quietly. A lone couple sat at a table, staring into their respective cups, silently, their faces speaking everything that needed to be said. Grief, hopelessness, despair. Luc had never been much of a praying man but he sent one their way—and hoped someone else would do the same for Marie.

Helplessness. It was the feeling that pervaded the hospital. It was the feeling Luc tolerated least well. He hated being helpless and unable to fix things. In his studio, he could blend an errant brushstroke or scrape off paint. Or toss a canvas that was beyond salvaging into the dumpster out back.

Here, in the hospital, there was nothing he had the power to do. Beyond wait. Like everyone else in the building, waiting for a loved one to come out of surgery or wake up or heal. Waiting for a doctor or nurse to share some hopeful scrap of information.

He poured three tall cups of coffee from the self-serve station, capped them and nestled them into a cardboard carrier. The cashier silently took his money.

Luc had thought he knew helpless before. But he hadn't. Loving Marie and Livie had shown him entirely new levels of helplessness. It was so easy to imagine Livie getting her heart broken someday or suffering some disappointment in life—and Luc being completely impotent to change it. Or worse, to have to stand by and watch her make her own mistakes. He could be there for her, stay by her side, but he couldn't live her life for her. It was a prospect he wasn't looking forward to.

And now? His entire body ached with the desire to help Marie. To find her, wherever she was in the hospital's maze of hallways, and take her pain into his own body so he could carry it for her. The way he should have done in Paris. Would he have stopped loving her if she had gone through with Nishi's plan and ended the pregnancy? He'd spent hours contemplating that question. So many hours that they probably added up to weeks by now. And the answer he kept coming up with was "no."

He had run because he feared she no longer loved him, and that was a fear he couldn't bear—because he would always love her. He had run, not because he hadn't trusted her, but because he hadn't been able to face losing her. His reasons had revolved around himself.

"Art isn't about the artist," his grandfather had said to him once. "Some day, you'll understand that."

He understood it now. It had taken him to the age of forty, but he finally got what his grand-père had been saying.

It was another hour before the surgeon appeared in the waiting room. Livie, exhausted, was sleeping with her head in Luc's lap.

Eileen had gone back to the cafeteria to get another round of caffeine for everyone. And from the tenor of William Witherspoon's phone conversations, Aidan was headed for something akin to the witness protection program, never to be heard from again.

Luc was doing his best not to think about Aidan Janssen, and why Marie had been in his car.

The surgeon pulled up a chair to sit in front of them. "She's in the recovery room," he began, "but she has not regained consciousness. We repaired the ruptured spleen and reset her arm. It was broken in two places. She also has several cracked ribs."

"When can we see her?" Luc asked. Livie stirred on his lap.

"A nurse will come tell you when she's been moved from the recovery room. May be a few more hours."

The surgeon disappeared back into the depths of the hospital and Eileen turned to Luc. "Why don't you take Livie home and get some rest? We'll call the minute she's out of recovery."

Luc shook his head, even as he knew Livie couldn't stay here for hour upon hour. She could sleep anywhere, but she would need a real meal eventually and a place to run around. He couldn't expect a one-year-old to sit still and be quiet for hours.

"I can't leave," he said. "I have to be here when she wakes up."

"Then let us take Livie back to the hotel."

"We have two queen beds," William interjected.

"See? Just call us if anything changes?"

Luc agreed and nodded at Livie's diaper bag sitting on the floor. Then he eased Livie up from his lap and kissed her. Her eyelids fluttered open, then fell closed again.

"Sweetheart," he whispered, "you're going to hang out with grandmaman and grandpapa for a little while." He kissed her again. "Love you, sweetpea."

When they were gone, he walked up to the desk. "Is Aidan

Janssen well enough to see visitors?" He smiled warmly at the woman on the other side when she gave him the room number.

Luc pushed open the door to Aidan's room and slipped inside. Aidan was awake, a fact that made Luc all the angrier since Marie wasn't.

"Get out," Aidan rasped, his eyes dark with a focused, concentrated anger.

You're angry? That was rich, Luc thought.

"She's still unconscious." He ignored the other man's command.

"I said get out of here."

Luc scanned the man lying in the bed. He looked beat up—his cheeks a sickly green with bruises, blood still matted in his blonde hair, the outline of a leg cast visible beneath the sheet. Still, Luc couldn't find it in his heart to feel sorry for the man.

"We are having this conversation," Luc replied. "And now is as good a time as any."

"She doesn't love you."

"That's not material to this conversation, my man." He leaned back against the heavy hospital door, doing his best impression of arrogant French insouciance. He was dying to ask what Marie had been doing in Aidan's car, but the last thing he wanted was to come across as jealous and insecure. Because he wasn't. This wasn't about him. It was about Marie and Livie.

"She's never going to love you again."

"Also not material. What *is* material is that she is my daughter's mother. That gives me a standing in her life that you don't have."

"She'll be the mother of my daughter too, one day."

Luc fought the urge to roll his eyes. "Doubtful. No, really damn impossible actually. Because you're not going to see Marie again."

Aidan opened his mouth but Luc spoke right over the other man's words.

"As a father, I am responsible for my daughter's well being. Her well being includes having a mother who is alive and healthy. You could have killed her mother tonight. You don't get a second chance on that, pal." *I was an idiot for stepping back and letting you have a first chance.*

"That's not up to you. Marie gets to make that decision."

"When she wakes up."

A flinch seized the other man's face. Also not something Luc felt bad about. Where Aidan Janssen was concerned, Luc's sympathy was locked away in a bombproof vault. And guarded by Cerberus, the three-headed dog of Hades.

"I think you're being overly optimistic about what her decision will be," Luc went on. "Livie's well being is the most important thing to Marie, as well." With his shoulder blades, Luc casually pushed himself away from the door. "I would say that my daughter is never getting in a car with you ever again, but that goes without saying. Her mother is never getting in a car with you again either. You are out of the picture."

60

Luc held his breath as he pushed open the door to Marie's hospital room. He'd been back in the waiting room only ten minutes when a nurse found him and gave him the good news. Marie was out of recovery and he could see her for a few minutes.

She still wasn't awake, though.

He slipped into the room, eager to see her yet fearing the worst. His heart raced as he stood at the foot of the bed, taking her in. Her face was ashen, where it wasn't purple and green with bruises. Her mouth was swollen. The curve of her cheekbone was outlined in black stitches. Tubing from an I.V. snaked into her arm. The arm that wasn't in a cast. Broken in two places, the surgeon had said.

He had to will his feet to remain planted on the waxy hospital floor, because every muscle in his body was screaming to sprint down the hall to Aidan's room and tear him limb from limb. It could be worse, of course. At least she was alive.

But not awake. The doctor and the nurse hadn't seemed overly concerned by that. But Luc was not going to breathe easy until she opened her eyes, smiled, spoke again. Until he was certain his Marie was okay.

She looked so tiny and frail, lying there beneath a thin hospital sheet. He had to look away to regain his composure. He focused on the room. It was standard hospital fare. Dingy, scuffed walls. Uncomfortable vinyl-covered chair. Unattractive drapes covering what was probably a view of the drab city building next door.

And the noise. Even with the heavy door closed, the din of the hospital seeped in. The squeaking of shoes on the floor as they walked past the room. The squealing of cart wheels, the low buzz of serious conversations, the squawking of the intercom looking for Dr. This or That.

He picked up the hard vinyl chair and carried it around to the side of her bed. He leaned over and kissed her forehead, smoothed the hair away from her face. Then he collapsed into the chair, exhausted physically and emotionally. This was all his fault. If he hadn't been such an asshole, Marie would never have met Aidan Janssen. She never would have gotten in his—or any man's—car. They wouldn't be living in separate apartments. They'd probably be living in Middleburg, raising their daughter together and not in shifts as co-parents. He hated that word.

Maybe they'd even have a second child on the way by now.

He covered her small hand with his and watched her chest rise and fall beneath the sheet.

"Marie, please wake up. I love you. You know I do. I love Olivia. I want more just like her. I want us to have the life we were planning to have before I fucked everything up."

She remained asleep, and Luc hung his head and cried out the ugly stew of emotions simmering in his chest. He was too tired and too regretful to even sort out which emotions they were. *Did it matter?*

He had no idea what Marie had been doing in Aidan's car last night. But that didn't matter. He loved her. And he would stand his ground this time—against Aidan, against any other man, against his own fears. Nishi had nothing to worry about. He wasn't going anywhere, ever again, if this woman right here wasn't going with him. He would be the husband and father Marie and Livie deserved. He wanted nothing less, and nothing was going to scare him away this time.

Not Nishi Bhat.

Not even himself.

In his pocket, his phone buzzed with a text. Reluctantly, he pulled his hand away from Marie's and looked at his phone. It was from Marie's mother.

Livie not happy at hotel. We're bringing her back. Sorry.

Luc quickly typed a reply. *No problem. Marie just got out of recovery. Still asleep.*

He leaned over Marie and kissed her on the forehead again. "I'll bring Livie tomorrow. Please wake up, love."

In the hallway, Nishi was leaning against the opposite wall, her eyes rimmed in red. Luc wasn't surprised to see her, though he had to fight the urge to drop his hand to cover his crotch.

"They told me you were in there," she said. "How is she?"

"Not awake yet." He waved the phone, still clutched in his hand. "Marie's parents took Livie to their hotel. But Livie's not having any of it. So they're bringing her back." He sighed. "I don't want to leave, but I can't keep Livie here all the time."

Nishi crossed the distance between them and laid her hand firmly on Luc's forearm. "One of us will always be here."

Luc took a deep breath and tried to take some comfort in that. "Call me if anything changes?"

"We'll call you periodically, even if nothing changes." She fixed him with a serious look and removed her hand from his arm.

He shoved the phone back into his pocket. "I don't want to leave. I want to be here when she wakes up."

"You *will* be here when she wakes up. Maybe not the exact

moment she wakes up. But shortly thereafter. Or I will spend the rest of my days hunting you down."

There wasn't even a hint of humor in her words, not that Luc expected humor—or even forbearance—from Nishi where he was concerned. She had just issued a threat.

"I plan on being here every morning when she wakes up. For the rest of her life."

"Plans aren't worth the napkins they're written on, Monsieur Marchand. You'll need to do better than that."

"I'm not leaving her. Or my daughter." Luc turned to leave, but two steps later he turned back. He nodded toward the far end of the hall. "Room six-twelve."

Nishi caught his meaning immediately, and smiled. "Thanks."

Luc walked back to the waiting room, fighting the sense of evil satisfaction dancing in his chest. Aidan Janssen might not be afraid of a candy-ass French art teacher. But when Nishi Bhat was through installing the fear of God in him, he was going to run straight for the gates of hell.

61

Luc stared at his empty studio. Normally at this time of the afternoon, kids would be coming through the door, laughing and talking, finding their easels and sharpening their pencils. Luc would be asking for a volunteer to model if the day's class was going to include figure drawing.

But today, the studio was quiet and still. When he came home with Livie that morning, he sent an email to his students' parents letting them know that he'd had an emergency in the family and was cancelling classes until further notice. He didn't know when that "further notice" would be.

That done, he had crashed on the bed with Livie and napped for hours. He woke to the sound of Livie's soft "papa papa" and the sensation of her hand patting him on the cheek. They ate lunch, then played on the floor for awhile. Eileen called twice with updates. No news, really, though the doctor had said that Marie's brain wasn't swelling and her vitals were fine. No news was good news. That's what Luc kept telling himself, anyway.

Now Livie was napping again and Luc, restless, had come downstairs to the studio. He walked past the class easels and stools, arranged in a neat circle around the model's podium, and headed for the far end of the room. This was his private painting space. A canvas was propped on his easel, its blankness taunting him for months now. He hadn't even attempted painting. He couldn't draw. Why waste canvas and paint? But he missed it. Art had always been his way of getting out of his head, of not having to think—only see.

Suddenly he hated this taunting canvas, hated it with a passion he hadn't felt in ages. He ripped the packing tape off a cardboard box like he was ripping off a bandage. Inside were his paints, his brushes, his palettes. He squeezed great gobs of paint onto a palette and pulled out a brush at random. It didn't matter which brush. He wasn't going to paint.

He needed to destroy something. Vent. Rage. His first choice was to punch a few walls but he knew what stood behind the sheetrock in his studio. Cement blocks. Luc was, as Sam used to joke, "dumb but not stupid." He couldn't afford to break his hand, not if he were going to take care of Marie and Livie in the coming weeks. Or longer. The thought of that stoked his rapidly rising anger. Not the prospect of taking care of his girls—no, he was going to take care of them for the rest of his life. What infuriated him was that someone had injured Marie. Someone who didn't value her enough to keep her safe. He still wasn't sure what Marie had been doing in Aidan's car but he knew why the accident had happened. It hit him like an uppercut to the jaw when he was driving home from the hospital.

Aidan had been drinking. Luc was as certain of that as he was of anything. He'd observed Aidan at the Witherspoons' house on Thanksgiving. The guy was a drinker. Maybe not an out-and-out alcoholic, but he was definitely one of those people who always have one drink more than they should.

He squeezed out more gobs of thick, shiny paint. He wasn't even careful to keep them separate on the palette. He tossed each tube onto the floor behind him, not caring whether the caps were back on tight or whether paint leaked out onto the floor.

He needed to destroy something. He was going to destroy this damn, taunting canvas.

He dragged the brush through cadmium orange, purple madder and lamp black, then drew back his arm and flung the paint onto the canvas. It made a satisfying splat when it hit so he quickly loaded up the brush with more. Titanium white, cerulean blue, bismuth yellow, chrome green. Over and over, he threw paint at the canvas until it was covered.

He was picking up the tubes to squeeze more paint out onto the palette when he heard the sharp bleat of his phone. He dropped the palette and brush onto the cement floor, not minding that his jeans were now splattered with paint too, and lunged for the phone on the table. It was Nishi's voice he heard when he swiped the screen.

"She's awake."

62

Something was dripping. Water? Rain? No, the noise was more like a tapping, a clicking. What would be making that noise? Luc in the kitchen? Her brain was fuzzy. She was having trouble thinking, waking up. Obviously she hadn't slept well, though she couldn't remember waking in the middle of the night. Or remember Livie waking either.

Tap tap tap tap tap.

Her arm hurt, too. Did she sleep on it the wrong way? She tried to shift it, but it was heavy and leaden. Still asleep. She waited for the sensation of pins and needles to begin. And her ribs ... it stung to breathe.

Taptaptaptaptap.

Was the apartment above leaking? She opened her eyes just as she realized she wasn't hearing Livie's soft breathing across the room. She turned her head toward the window. Why was it almost dark out? Or was it still the middle of the night? It took her a moment to realize that the window she was looking at wasn't the window in her bedroom at home. Was she in Luc's bedroom?

"Luc?" she croaked.

A sudden flash of movement across the room startled her and she let out a raspy yelp. She was so thirsty. Her mouth was like sand.

"Marie!"

It was Nishi. What was Nishi doing here? She closed her eyes. *I'm dreaming.*

"No! Don't close your eyes! Stay with me, Marie!"

Nishi wasn't making any sense, but she opened her eyes again. Gingerly, she turned her head to look around the room. Her neck ached. Her entire body ached, in fact. She hadn't felt this bad since giving birth to Livie. Her eyes dropped to herself. She was covered in a thin white sheet. There was an I.V. in her arm … she was in a hospital.

"Why am I in a hospital? Nish? Are you really here?"

Nishi's face appeared immediately bedside. Dark circles shadowed her friend's eyes and her lips looked dry and chapped.

"What am I doing here?" The words were a struggle to get out. She felt like she was drugged. Drugged! Richard.

"Did Richard …"

"No." Nishi's warm hand settled on her shoulder. "You were in an accident. Night before last. A car accident."

"I was?" She tried moving her legs. Ouch.

"Don't move. Let me get a nurse."

"No. Wait. Just a moment. I don't have a car."

"You were in Aidan's car." Long silence. "Do you remember where you were?"

She thought hard. "I had a work thing. At the museum. A reception." She thought some more. "Aidan was there. But I didn't see him until the end. He offered me a ride. I was going to take the bus but it was snowing."

Just getting that out was exhausting. She closed her eyes.

"No, no! Don't go back to sleep!"

"I'm not," she mumbled. "Just tired."

"I'm getting a nurse. Wait."

A moment later the door flew open and she was being poked and prodded.

"Thanks, Nish," she muttered.

"How do you feel?" the nurse asked.

"Fine. Lousy." She felt the blunt point of a thermometer in her ear. She had one like that at home for Livie. *Livie.* "Where's my daughter?"

"Your husband took her home. She needed some rest. He did too."

Luc had been here. She exhaled the breath she hadn't realized she was holding. He had Livie. Livie was safe.

She tried to sit up but the nurse gently pressed her back into the bed. "You need to rest, dear. I'll let your parents know you're awake."

Nishi had already taken care of that, she was certain.

"How long have I been here?"

"A little over twenty-four hours."

"I was asleep that long?"

"Not unusual after an accident."

The nurse was bustling around the bed, busy but Marie couldn't tell with what. She was still groggy. All she wanted was to go back to sleep. And see Livie.

"I need my daughter."

"You can see her when they come back. I'm sure they're not gone for good."

Gone for good. No. He wouldn't.

"Does my—" She almost uttered the words, "my husband." "Does Luc know about the accident?"

"Yes. He was here all night. He just took your little girl home."

"I need Livie!" The panic was rising in her throat before she could even identify why. Then the why came to her. She'd been in the car with Aidan. He was giving her a ride home but then the bus … there'd been a bus. She couldn't remember anything after that. But Luc would know she'd been in Aidan's car.

"My daughter! My daughter!" Livie was with Luc. And she didn't know where Luc was. But he knew she'd been with Aidan. Except she hadn't been *with* Aidan. She'd just run into him at the museum …

"Please. My daughter."

The door opened and Nishi was in the room again.

"Nish. Where's Livie?"

"Luc took her home."

"Are you sure? Can someone go get her? Make sure?"

"They're on their way here right now. I just spoke to Luc on the phone. He just has to get Livie up and get her dressed. Then they'll be here."

"Nish, it wasn't like … I was in Aidan's car but it wasn't—"

"You need to leave," the nurse said to Nishi, her tone sharp. "She's awake but she still needs to rest. You're getting her worked up."

Marie could see the dress-down forming in Nishi's eyes, but then her friend took a deep breath. "I'll be in the waiting room. The next person you see in here will be Luc. I promise."

"The doctor will be the next person she sees." The nurse took a step toward Nishi.

"The doctor, yep. But after that, Luc. Okay?" Nishi gave a thumbs-up sign before retreating from the room.

The panic wasn't subsiding. Marie tried to talk herself down even as the promised doctor appeared and asked her question after question. She could barely think straight enough to answer him. His questions weren't important. Yes, she was fine. Yes, she was in pain. Yes, she would like some water or ice chips or whatever. A popsicle, fine.

Luc wouldn't take Livie away from her, would he? No, Nishi said he was on the way here. But Nishi and Luc speaking to each other … not a good combination. Look what happened before. She needed to know what Nishi had said to him just now.

A plastic cup of water appeared on the tray next to her bed. The doctor was gone. She looked around. So was the nurse. *Thanks for the water.* It was on the left side of the bed. Next to her left arm, which was encased in a cast. Her right arm was still attached to the I.V. line. She tried to move that arm across her body but the pain in her ribs and side stopped her. She let her head sink back into the thin hospital pillow, and closed her eyes.

Luc's heart stopped. Marie was lying in the hospital bed, her eyes closed. She wasn't awake. He hadn't gotten here quickly enough, despite coming as fast as he could.

"*Put—*" He caught himself just in time. Livie was in his arms, squirming at the sight of her mother. He wanted her to learn French, but not that kind of French. She'd learn to swear on her own, the way most kids do.

He tightened his hold on her, but she stretched her body out toward the bed so quickly he feared she was going to jump right out of his arms and land on Marie.

"Mama mama mama." The urgency in Livie's voice increased with each syllable.

"Shh, Livie. Mama's resting."

"Mama-a-a." Livie stretched out the word as she stretched her arms out toward her mother as far as they could reach.

Marie's eyes opened wide and what Luc saw in them slayed him, ripped him right open. He clutched Livie tighter to his chest, a countermeasure to the sudden weakness in his arms. The relief in her eyes was stark and unmistakable.

She thought I wasn't coming.

He opened his mouth to speak, but no words came out.

She thought I ran away again.

She was still that afraid that he wouldn't stick around?

She thought I took Livie.

"I wasn't … we weren't …" Tears and worry replaced the relief.

He came around to the side of the bed.

"I swear, Luc …" Her voice was raspy and tired.

Livie reached out to Marie, kicking Luc hard in the ribs in the process.

"Sweetheart, maman has to rest."

Marie lifted her right hand a few inches above the bed. The weakness in her movement tore at his heart. He had half a mind to leave Livie with her grandparents in the waiting room and storm Aidan Janssen's room, tear him limb from limb for doing this to Marie.

"Let me touch her. Please."

Luc carefully held Livie next to the bed. He guided her hand toward Marie's.

"Gentle touch with maman," he said in a soothing voice. He stroked the back of Marie's hand with Livie's. "See? Gentle." Marie closed her hand around Livie's.

"We got here as quickly as I could," he said. "I had to take Livie home for a bit."

"It was snowing, Luc. I didn't want to drag you and Livie out of the house." Marie's fingers fell open around Livie's fist. Her arm hovered in midair for a moment before sinking to the bed again. "He offered me a ride home. That's all it was."

"Shh, love. It doesn't matter."

"It does matter." Her words were getting slower and more

labored. “He was at the reception, that’s all. I don’t know why, really.”

Luc could guess why. Aidan had been there to see her.

“He’s okay,” he said. “Better shape than you are. Well, he was when I went in to see him anyway. I can’t speak to what Nishi did to him.”

She grimaced. “You went into his room?”

“Oui. I told him he was never going to see you or my daughter—our daughter—again. It’s a father’s job to keep his daughter safe. If he doesn’t do that, what else matters?”

Luc sat down in the chair next to the bed and settled Livie on his lap. He bounced her gently to distract her.

“And keeping this one safe includes keeping her mother safe, too,” he added.

“I’m sorry, Luc. Please believe me. I didn’t know he was going to—”

“I believe you, chérie.” He did, he realized. Marie had always been entirely upfront about Aidan. If she said they weren’t at the reception *together*, then he accepted that. Marie had never done anything to betray his trust. That had been all him.

“I didn’t realize how much he’d had to drink.”

“Shh. How do you feel?” He didn’t want to talk about Aidan Janssen. As far as Luc was concerned, the guy didn’t exist. Not in Marie’s life. Not in his either.

“I’ve felt better.”

Her voice was hoarse. Luc’s gaze settled on the cup of water on the other side of the bed, then on Marie’s arms. He stood, Livie on his hip, and retrieved the cup. He pulled the chair closer to the bed and resettled Livie on his knee. Then he carefully held the cup to Marie’s lips and tilted it so she could drink.

“Thanks.” Her voice was no more than a whisper.

It hit him. She couldn’t just go home by herself. She wouldn’t be able to care for Livie. She wouldn't even be able to lift Livie for awhile.

"Do you know when they're going to discharge me?"

"I don't think anyone has thought that far ahead yet, love. You just woke up."

She looked at her left arm and its cast.

"My arm is broken."

"And several of your ribs." He held the cup to her lips again. "And you had a ruptured spleen. You were in surgery."

Marie closed her eyes for a moment, then reopened them. She looked over at Livie, and he could tell she was reaching the same conclusion he just had.

"You and Livie will stay with me. I'll take care of you." He didn't say "until you're better" because that was a promise he couldn't make. He couldn't force her to stay, of course, but he had no intention of ever asking her to leave.

"I THINK THAT'S A GOOD IDEA."

Marie had run through all the reasons why it wasn't a good idea.

We'll get in the way of your classes.

One of us will have to sleep on the couch.

Livie will miss her crib.

We'll distract you from painting.

I'll want you to make love to me, and you won't say no when I ask.

And dismissed them all. Even the last. If she were honest with herself, she had to admit that she was more than a little disappointed when Luc hadn't even tried to seduce her in Paris. They'd been sleeping in the same bed!

Maybe she was kidding herself about how much Luc wanted her.

He wanted Livie. He wanted his daughter. Look at how easily he dismissed her attempts to explain why she'd been in Aidan's car. *It doesn't matter.* It didn't matter because he was over it. He'd moved on.

But she had few good alternatives to moving in with Luc for the time being. She would need help with Livie until her arm and ribs healed. She looked at Livie, who had snuggled up against Luc's chest and fallen asleep. Father and daughter.

There was only one serious reason not to move in with Luc. Livie wouldn't want to move back out.

MARIE HAD BEEN MUMBLING in her sleep for the past twenty minutes, and Luc wondered what she was dreaming about. Livie had gone back to the hotel with her grandparents, amicably this time. Luc had spoken to his mother on the phone about the accident. She had promised to fly over immediately if they needed help when Marie was discharged. And Nishi had spoken to her friend, Marie's boss at the university, and extracted an agreement to let Marie work from home for awhile.

Work from Luc's home.

He wished they were living in Middleburg. The house there was so much more comfortable than his apartment here. Not for the first time he pictured Livie playing outside in the yard. Perhaps having her own small easel in his studio. He missed that house. It had been his home for so many years, a fact he hadn't appreciated enough at the time. It was his home, and when he thought of it now he thought of it with Marie and Livie there.

"... necklace ... same one ..."

Marie had been rambling about a necklace off and on. It made no sense to him.

"... phone ... Emeline has it ..."

Emeline? His grandmother? Was she dreaming about that necklace? She couldn't be. He hadn't shown it to her yet.

"... on my phone ... the painting ..."

She was dreaming of his grandfather's show in Paris. Luc smiled. Maybe she would dream of sharing a bed with him in Paris, too. He hoped her dreams were showing her all the things he had wanted so badly to do with her in that bed.

63

Thunderstorm After Midnight.

Crashing Rainbows.

Luc tilted his head and squinted his eyes to look at the painting he'd done last night, after Livie went down for the night. He imagined telling Sam what was in the painting, hence his joking attempts at naming it.

It was just junk, as were all the canvases he'd wasted—or ruined, if one was in a less generous mood—since Marie's accident. They weren't serious paintings and Luc hadn't been serious when he painted them. He was just killing time in the middle of the night when he was too keyed up to sleep. Too worried about Marie. Still too furious about Aidan Janssen. He'd run a red light and been hit by a bus. A bus! Marie had been very lucky, according to the doctor.

Painting No. 145688902

Actually, he hadn't done that many paintings. Yet. He was only on number seven. But about to start number eight. Livie was taking a post-lunch nap after a morning at the hospital. They'd return later in the afternoon. Marie was doing well and the doctor was saying she could be released in another day or two.

Dead Paint, or the Only Thing Keeping Me from Killing Someone.

It was therapy, that's what it was. Even Luc was self-aware enough to see that. He was taking out his anger, his hurt, his every jumbled emotion on these poor, innocent canvases that had done nothing to deserve his mistreatment of them. He had to do something at night, though, to occupy his mind and his body. He was finding it hard to sleep and he wasn't the sort to sit and stare at the wall or count sheep against a black ceiling. During the Drunken World Tour, he would have drunk himself to sleep. That wasn't an option anymore, and not only because he was responsible for Livie.

Drinking was running, and that was off the table. Completely off the table. Instead he was running into his art. Colliding with it might be a more apt description, he thought, as he lifted last night's still damp canvas off the easel and leaned it against a wall. The paintings were awful, garbage really, each and every one of them. But when he was painting, he wasn't thinking—and thinking was what he needed to avoid, because he had no answers for the questions in his life right now.

His mother had shared Marie's fear about him: that if the two of them tried a relationship again and it failed, Livie might lose her father. He didn't know how to allay that fear for her. Words were just words. He thought he'd been doing well on the action front, but he wasn't making any headway there either. He had stepped back and allowed Marie to date another man. Hell, he'd even facilitated it by taking Livie on those nights. He hadn't tried to seduce her, even though every nerve ending in his body banged like pots and pans when he was in her presence. He wanted her to control the pace and decide when she was ready. But so far, there had been no pace at all.

Maybe that's my answer.

He set a clean canvas on the easel and looked over the rainbow of paint tubes on his old work table. When his arm got tired last night, he finally unpacked his boxes of paint tubes instead of simply reaching into the cardboard and grabbing the first color his hand made contact with. They were now arranged by color, all the reds together, all the yellows, etcetera. He ran his fingers over the tubes like they were piano keys until he got to the blues.

Draw blue.

Really, he was extraordinarily lucky she had ever given him the time of day. If someone had said that to him, he would have told them just how many ways they were wasting his time. But Marie had given it an honest try. She had trusted him, trusted teaching methods that he was making up on the fly.

Trust was a fragile thing, and easily broken. He had broken hers and now he had no idea how to repair it.

One by one, he uncapped each tube of blue paint and squeezed some out onto his palette. Prussian blue, French ultramarine, cerulean, cobalt, Delft blue. Nothing but blue.

More than once as a child, he had grumbled about some assignment his grandfather had given him. His grand-père's response had always been, "I never ask you to do anything I haven't already done myself." As a teacher, Luc had never particularly adhered to that philosophy, but he had asked Marie to do something. *Draw blue.* He should at least try it himself.

An hour later, he had a canvas full of blue paint but no greater insight into blue. He went upstairs to check on Livie, who was still sleeping soundly. He was in the kitchen when he heard the studio's exterior door open and close. He frowned. He wasn't expecting anyone. His classes were still cancelled.

"Luc?"

He recognized the voice immediately. It belonged to Jon Randall, the father of two of his students. The youngest was an elementary school student who came for drawing lessons after school. Jon's oldest, Ashley, was in high school and preparing her portfolio for college applications. Luc had been working with her on it one or two evenings a week.

He hurried down the stairs to the studio.

"Hey, Jon."

Jon was alone, which engendered a sense of relief in Luc. At least Jon wasn't there because he had forgotten about the cancellations.

"What can I do for you?" Luc added.

"Nothing. Just stopped by to see how you were doing."

"Oh. Well, fine. All things considered, you know. Marie should be home in a day or two."

He and Jon had become friendly. Not close, but friendlier than Luc was with the other parents. Jon had been a graphic designer before he quit to be a stay-at-home dad to his daughters. Jon's wife was president of a local private school. Jon also painted— "not seriously," he had said.

"Actually, I came to offer my help. If you need someone to help teach the after school classes, I could do that. I'm here most afternoons anyway. I'm not qualified to work with your private students, but the little kids I can handle."

Luc was floored and speechless.

"You're going to have your hands full for awhile," Jon added. "You can't keep your studio closed for long. The parents will take their kids elsewhere."

That was certainly true, and had certainly crossed Luc's mind. Another question in his life for which he had no answer. How to keep his business running and take care of Marie and Livie at the same time.

"Thanks, Jon. I appreciate that. When can you start?"

Jon grinned. "As soon as you can send out another email to parents."

Upstairs, Livie began to wail.

"Can you hold on one minute?"

Jon waved him away. "I'll wait. No worries."

When Luc came back downstairs with Livie, freshly diapered and sucking down a sippy cup of milk, Jon had wandered to the back of the studio and was perusing Luc's midnight canvases.

"What kind of hourly rate do you need?" Luc asked.

Jon turned and waved him off. "You don't need to pay me. You're not charging me enough for all the help you're giving Ashley. I just can't help her anymore. I can't be critical enough with my own child's work."

He pointed to a painting. "Is this new work? These are fantastic."

Luc laughed. "These? That's my insomnia series."

Jon looked at him quizzically.

"That's just me taking out my frustrations in the middle of the night when I can't sleep," Luc clarified.

Jon shook his head. "Well, they're good, man."

64

“I can walk,” Marie protested as Luc lifted her from the car and carried her into his studio. Her father held the door open for them. Her mother had already carried Livie inside.

It felt good to be home. Well, she wasn’t home exactly. It was Luc’s home. Even there, she didn’t really see his Pittsburgh apartment and studio as “home.” Home was his house in Middleburg. She felt a twinge of guilt in her chest. If she weren’t living in Pittsburgh, he’d probably be living in Middleburg.

It felt good to be out of the hospital, anyway.

Inside, Luc’s studio smelled like paint and the pencil shavings that littered the floor beneath his students’ stools. This was a better space for his business. The studio in Middleburg could never have accommodated twenty kids at one time. But Marie still liked it better. It was cozier. It was … *theirs*. It was the place where they had fallen in love, made love, escaped the craziness that had been her life in Washington.

She missed that life. It seemed simpler, even though she knew it had been ridiculously complicated. Maybe it was just that their feelings for each other had been simpler. Straightforward. Detached from reality.

Or maybe she was just seeing the memories through rose-colored glasses.

"I know you can walk." His breath was warm and soft on her ear, words meant just for her. "But if I make you walk, Nishi will probably break my legs. Then *I* won't be able to walk."

"Oh, so this is really all about you," she joked back, quietly, just for him to hear.

He stopped at the foot of the stairs leading from the studio to his apartment above. Everyone else was already up there.

"I'm keeping you safe from here on out. I admit to a certain selfish interest in that. And if I have to be the most selfish man who ever lived to make sure you and Livie are safe, then that's who I'm going to be."

There was no joking in his eyes now, only seriousness and determination and … Marie had to look away. The desire to kiss him, to just fall into everything she saw in his eyes, was overwhelming. And maybe that's where they were headed. Where they had always been headed, ever since he arrived in Pittsburgh. And now, to be living with him again? Where Luc was concerned, she was weak. And he needed someone to be strong.

His nostrils flared as she looked at his face, just inches from hers. He was trying to control his breathing, making himself hold back. He might be selfish but he wasn't going to kiss her. She knew that. She'd spent plenty of time in the hospital wondering why he hadn't tried to make love to her in Paris. The wondering had distracted her from the throbbing pain in her arm.

She knew why he hadn't. He had always waited for permission to make love to her. Once she signaled the green light, he was all systems go but he never tried to move faster than she was ready for. He wanted to kiss her now—just as much as she wanted him to—but he wouldn't until she granted him permission.

But now was not the time.

He carried her up the stairs and into his living room, where he made a big show out of carefully setting her on her feet. It was over the top but even Marie couldn't entirely discount the threat of Nishi breaking his legs. Her stomach rumbled loudly.

"I smell food," she said and her stomach clenched harder. "If I never see Jello or mushed green beans again, it will be too soon."

Nishi and Eileen appeared carrying trays laden with fragrant Indian food.

"Please tell me you didn't spend all morning here cooking."

Nishi grinned. "As tempting as it is to claim all that credit … no. It's all from a restaurant. And, I have to say, it's as good as my own."

"Impossible," Marie countered.

"Well, nearly as good."

The food was delicious. Nishi was right about that. Marie sat on the sofa and stuffed herself with samosas, tandoori chicken and saffron rice. Luc sat on the floor with Livie between his legs, feeding her small bites from his plate. The two of them couldn't be more comfortable around each other, and Eileen caught Marie's eye. Her expression said everything Marie was thinking. *You need to make up your mind about this man.* Marie was worried about Luc taking Livie away from her? After a few weeks of living here, Marie knew she wouldn't have the heart to move Livie back out.

Nishi began collecting everyone's empty plates. Marie stood up too.

"No no no. You're not helping," Nishi said. "Sit your butt back down."

Marie handed over her plate. "Alright, I won't help." She followed Nishi toward the kitchen anyway. "I'll just peek at dessert."

She turned to give a theatric wink to her parents and Luc but at the sight of Livie playfully trying to climb up Luc's back, her wink simply pushed back tears.

"Am I being an idiot?" she asked Nishi in the kitchen.

"From the look on your face out there? I'd say yes."

"So you're thinking better of him these days."

Nishi gave a characteristic shrug. "I'm edging toward forgiveness, as Imran would say. He was there every day at the hospital."

"So were you. So were my parents."

"I'm not even going to explain the difference." Nishi rinsed plates and loaded Luc's dishwasher. "You already know it."

"How did you know that you and Imran were going to work out?"

Nishi laughed and closed the dishwasher. "You know me. I believe I can make anything work." She laughed again. "But Imran wasn't sure. Sometimes I think he's still not sure."

"How can he not be sure? You guys have been together for years now."

"My childhood has left me with a certain wanderlust. He wasn't sure I'd be able to settle down."

"But you get to travel for your job. It's sanctioned wanderlust."

Nishi shook her head. "I'm going to have to cut back on my travel soon." She patted her stomach.

Marie's eyes widened. "You're pregnant?"

Nishi nodded, her eyes glistening. Marie went to her friend and gave her the best hug she could manage with only one arm.

"You can owe me the other half of that hug when the cast comes off. But don't tell anyone yet. Only you and Imran know so far." Nishi turned to pull a cake from Luc's refrigerator. "I'm settling down because I can't imagine being with any other man."

Marie watched her friend plate slices of chocolate cake and garnish each with a scoop of vanilla ice cream.

"I *am* being an idiot."

There was no other man for her. That die was cast the day she had unwrapped Nishi's gift to her, drawing lessons with some French artist she had never heard of.

"Give maman a kiss goodnight."

Marie wrapped her good arm around Livie and hugged her. That was what most angered her about the accident—not that she was hurt but that now she couldn't pick up Livie, give her a bath, hug her properly. Livie was fascinated by the cast on Marie's arm, and Marie had no idea how to explain it to her.

She watched as Luc carried Livie down the hall and into her nursery. Livie was as tired as Marie felt. It had been a long day. A good day, but a tiring one nonetheless.

"You should go to bed." Luc's hands settled firmly on her shoulders and began to massage her muscles.

"That was quick." She fought the urge to turn into his arms, bury her face in his chest.

"She was asleep before her head hit the pillow. I barely managed to get her pajamas on her before she was out."

"Thank you." She stopped fighting and spun around to face him. "For letting us stay here and helping … for everything. Thank you."

His hands slid down her shoulders to lightly grasp her upper arms. "I hope you know by now that it never occurred to me to do any less."

"I do know that," she answered quietly. "You and Livie today, seeing you together …" Her eyes welled with tears. "You're a good papa."

Luc pulled her into his chest and held her tight. She wanted to stay there forever, but her sore ribs had other ideas.

"Luc. My ribs."

He released her immediately. “Sorry, I forgot.” He raked his hand through his hair. “How could I forget? I’m sorry.”

“It’s okay. What are the sleeping arrangements?”

He glanced at the couch behind him. “I’ll sleep out here. You need the bed.”

“What if we both take the bed?”

He looked at her for a long time, as if trying to figure out what she was playing at.

“I mean, I’m out of commission that way,” she forced a soft laugh and used her cast to wave off the awkwardness of her suggestion. “But we can be like Paris.”

“You mean me lying in bed, counting backwards from a hundred as a distraction from the beautiful woman sleeping next to me?”

65

The bed was empty next to her. She knew it the instant she awoke. She swung her legs out of bed and looked around for something to put on over her nightgown. She needed to go to her apartment tomorrow and pack some things, if she and Livie were going to be living here for awhile. Her mother had gone and retrieved a few things but not nearly enough for an extended stay.

She pulled a sweater from Luc's closet and dropped it over her head before tiptoeing down the hall to Livie's room. She was assuming Livie had awakened and Luc was with her. But when she stuck her head into the room, Livie was still sound asleep and Luc wasn't there.

She passed the kitchen, also empty. There was only one other place he could be. She stood at the top of the stairs leading down to his studio. Sure enough, a sliver of light shone beneath the door.

He looked over at her the minute she stepped into the studio. He was wearing the sweatpants he'd worn to bed, no shirt, his feet bare. It was the sexiest thing she'd seen since … the last time she'd seen Luc shirtless. Maybe she should just give in and let him make love to her. It would be fantastic, she knew that. That was why she hadn't slept with Aidan through all their months of dating. He might have turned out to be a lesser lover than Luc, and then where would that have left her? Sex wasn't everything in a relationship. But it wasn't nothing, either.

His eyes reflected what he thought of her outfit too—his sweater grazing her thighs, her legs and feet bare.

"Did Livie wake up?" she asked.

"No. I couldn't sleep."

"You didn't try counting back from a hundred?"

His smile was but a flash. "Three times. Didn't work though."

"You're painting again."

He shrugged. "I don't know that you could call it painting."

She walked around the easel to take a look.

"That's not …" She didn't know what to say about the canvas Luc was working on.

"My usual thing? Yeah. I'm not painting. I'm just screwing around when I can't sleep."

"There's something kind of appealing about it, though … the colors, the strength of the brushstrokes …"

Luc laughed. "You don't have to be polite about it, chérie."

He stood and retrieved a stool for her to sit on.

"Sit with me while I paint away my insomnia." He squeezed more paint onto his palette. "I miss your company, Marie."

"You might be sick of my company by the time my arm heals."

He shook his head as his brush touched the canvas. For someone who was just "screwing around," he looked remarkably focused. "I sincerely doubt that."

She looked around at this end of Luc's studio. He had set it up as his space for painting, separate from but open to the classroom space. He must miss the Middleburg studio. How could he not? It was cozier, with more charm. It suited Luc more than this converted auto shop. This was the kind of place one would expect to find someone making big abstract or conceptual works.

Which wasn't Luc Marchand at all.

And yet against the wall leaned half a dozen other canvases, all covered in bold gestures of paint and brush. He hadn't been sleeping much, by the looks of it.

"In the hospital, you had dreams where you were talking about a necklace. Do you remember that?" Luc asked the question without looking away from his canvas.

"I don't remember the dreams, but I know what necklace I must have been talking about. When I was at the reception, I went into the Alistair Smith and Elizabeth Calhoun show. It's still there. In one of the paintings, she's holding a necklace just like the one your grandmother wears in some of her portraits. I mean, it was absolutely identical."

"Well, probably more than one was made. My grandparents were well off, but not wealthy enough to have one-of-a-kind jewelry."

"I'll show you tomorrow. I can go to the apartment and get the catalog."

"I'll go get it. And anything else you need. So you went back to the show?"

"Well, it was still there. Their story intrigues me, I guess. And I wonder how her family felt when they learned about the affair, all those years later."

His brush stopped. "You worry about what Livie will think someday when she sees my portraits of you."

"And when she reads the articles online. Or some mean kid at school taunts her with it."

"Water under the bridge now, dear. Even if I could get the paintings back and burn them, there are still all the photographs online."

"I wouldn't want you to do that."

“Do you wish I hadn’t painted you?”

It was a question she had posed to herself countless times, and the answer was always the same.

“No, I’m glad we did it. But I wish there hadn’t been a show. I wish we’d kept them private.”

“It was partly your idea.”

“I know it was. And I miscalculated Richard’s reaction. I also wasn’t thinking ahead to a time when I would have a child who would have to deal with that mistake.”

“You might not be giving the future Livie enough credit.”

“I hope that’s the case. I really do.”

66

Marie stepped through the door, leaving the winter gloom and slush of the street outside. Inside, Luc's studio was warm and brightly lit, abuzz with the energy and chatter of his young students. Just the sight of it all made her heart stop. Luc was leaning over a student's easel, holding their small hand in his to show them how to shade. Then he stood back and watched as the boy did it for himself.

"Bon!" Luc's voice was excited.

A tiny, high-pitched echo sounded from Livie, who sat on the floor with a sketchpad and crayons. Occasionally she would make a wild scribble across her page, but mostly she watched the "big kids" and basked in their attention. She was in her element during Luc's after school art classes.

Luc was in his element too. That was abundantly clear to Marie. He was an excellent teacher with kids, patient and enthusiastic. Everything he wasn't about his own art at the moment. Marie wished she could help him. He feared that his time spent wandering the world and drinking had stolen his talent. She didn't believe that, but she did wonder if his talent had changed. Luc had certainly changed. He was quieter, less certain of himself.

But far more patient. A smile curved her lips as she quietly closed the studio door behind her. Having a child will do that, build patience. She had more patience herself. Maybe she and Luc had too much patience though, at least with each other. At what point did patience settle into simply waiting? She knew Luc was waiting for her to give him the green light. She was waiting to feel one hundred percent sure that she was ready for the light to change.

She should just close her eyes and floor it. But she wanted the old Luc back, not the one who got up in the middle of every night to take out his troubles in the studio. She glanced toward the back of the giant room, where Luc's own easels sat. He had three canvases in progress now. She could always tell which emotion he'd been working out by which canvas had the wet paint in the morning. Some mornings, all three were wet.

Luc noticed her standing just inside the door, unbuttoning her winter coat. He came over and kissed her, just the briefest, lightest touch of his lips on hers. But even that faint touch was charged with attraction and enough to set butterflies aswirl in her stomach.

"How's the arm?" he asked.

She waved her arm, newly freed from its cast, and twisted her wrist back and forth.

"Good as new, the doctor said."

Luc's eyes darkened. Any reference to the accident still made him angry.

"Is Jon here?" She changed the subject. "I promised him I would proofread your new web site."

She walked toward the back of the studio where Luc's small office was. Luc had hired Jon Randall, the father of two of his students, to help out with the business side of things. She was impressed that Luc had such a thriving enterprise, but he was a better teacher than businessman. As if on cue, a round of laughter erupted from the kids at their easels. Luc was a natural teacher and a natural with children. Maybe teaching was his real calling, not a career as a painter. She doubted he would ever accept that idea.

"I don't quite have it done yet," Jon answered when she asked about the web site. "I need to use my computer at home to work on it." He glanced at Luc's old laptop sitting on the desk. "I'll send you a link tomorrow."

"Okay. Whenever you have it ready."

Marie and Jon had ganged up on Luc to convince him of the need for a more professional web site for the business. With the new site, parents would be able to register and pay for classes online instead of phoning Luc.

She wandered back out to the studio and watched Luc with the kids, then Livie. Livie hadn't even noticed that her mother had returned. Marie shook her head, then strolled over to look at the paintings Luc was working on in the wee hours of the morning. They were far more abstract than even his grandfather's late work. Miles more abstract. Luc brushed them off as just playing around but there was something compelling about them. They were hard to look away from.

"I like them." Jon came to stand next to her.

She tilted her head to look at them from a different angle. "I do too. He thinks they're not serious."

Jon snorted. "If I come in here some day and they're all gone, I'm diving headfirst into the dumpster out back to rescue them."

She laughed softly. "Be careful what you promise. He's liable to do that."

"I hope not. His talent is bigger than his grandfather's, but he doesn't seem to see that."

Luc's talent was certainly different than his grandfather's. The show in Paris had revealed that to her. Philippe Marchand had been a master portrait painter. Luc was good—very good—at portraits but it was easy to see the difference between Philippe's work and the paintings Luc had made of her. It was easy, too, for the Marchand family to dismiss Luc's insecurities about his painting as a fit of youthful pique, but Marie could see why he felt the way he did. It wasn't that Luc was a lesser painter than his grandfather. He was just a different one.

"I DIDN'T MEAN to wake you," Luc said without looking away from the easel.

"You didn't." Marie picked up one of the kids' stools and carried it over to where Luc sat, painting. It was two in the morning and Marie had awakened to find herself alone in bed. Again. Luc's nighttime painting was happening nearly every night, and the lack of sleep showed in his face during the day. Instead of rolling over and going back to sleep, as she did most nights, she got out of bed this time and came down to the studio.

"Is Livie okay?" he asked.

"Still sleeping."

"When did she start sleeping through the night? How old was she?"

The question surprised her. Luc hadn't asked much about Livie's first year of life, and Marie had been hesitant to volunteer the information. She didn't want him to read criticism into any attempt to fill him in on what he had missed. Even though they'd been living together for weeks now, she still felt like she was walking on eggshells around him, afraid she might say or do something to send him running again.

"At about six months. It wasn't too bad."

Luc made no reply to that, and she offered no elaboration. She didn't want to make him feel bad about that year. She wanted them to be past that even though, being realistic, she knew they might never be entirely past it.

"She's an easy child," she added.

"She must get that from your family."

"I guess." The Witherspoons were hardly an easy family. Nor were the Marchands, though they weren't as difficult as Luc made them out to be. He really didn't see people as accurately as he thought he did. Nor was she sure the Marchands saw him with perfect accuracy. The older she got, the more she doubted anyone ever truly knew another person.

She looked at the painting he was working on. It wasn't as wild as some of the others he had done lately. It was more restrained, like he was trying to find his way back to a more representational style. The lines were still imprecise and the brushstrokes still rough, but she could make out a few recognizable forms. Two easels, one large and one small. Two stools, also one large and one small. A large window through which sunlight streamed. A small boy standing by the window, looking out, his face bathed in a wash of yellow paint.

"Your grandfather's studio," she said.

"Oui."

She left the other observation unsaid. The small boy was Luc. She watched as he daubed paint on the canvas, working it into the scene. His movements were slow and patient. This definitely wasn't the wild painting of earlier nights, but it was still unlike his previous work.

She liked it. But did he? She was afraid to ask.

"How's work been?" he asked.

With the cast off her arm, Marie had gone back to the office.

"Good. I miss you guys during the day, though." She missed Luc in the evenings, too. By then, he was beat from teaching and watching Livie. And from lack of sleep. They were living together and yet they seemed further apart than ever. Luc had retreated into his art, and she wasn't sure whether that was healthy for him or not.

One thing that became clear to her in Paris was that Luc was the outlier in his family. He was right about that, no matter how much his mother and sister protested to the contrary. The Marchands were cool, calm and collected. Rational. Restrained.

Luc was the emotional one, the one ruled by his heart and not his head.

She wondered what he was seeing in his mind as he painted this scene from his childhood. As a teacher, he was all about the seeing. That was important to learning how to draw, freeing your mind of what you wanted to see, expected to see, thought you knew to be there—and just letting your eyes absorb what was actually in front of you. But now Luc was painting something he was seeing only in the past, just as his grandfather did at the end of his career when his eyesight was disappearing. At the Louvre, Luc had insisted that Philippe Marchand had been a *seeing* artist. But what kind of artist had he been in those later years when he couldn't see?

"How do you think he painted when he was blind?"

"My grandfather? From memory, I guess."

"Like you're doing?"

Luc leaned back and laid down his brush. "I'm just fooling around." He waved at the canvas. "This is as fuzzy as my memory."

There was something very arresting about it, though, she thought. All of the little details that Luc prized were missing, obscured by time and paint. What was left was a boy and two empty easels, two empty stools and a window full of light. Everything else was gone.

Luc's memory wasn't fuzzy. It had simply picked out the important elements and, in doing so, had created a very emotional painting. Even though it wasn't finished yet, Marie could sense the loneliness and longing in that little boy by the window. Luc wasn't painting what he saw. He was painting what he felt. That realization made all of his middle-of-the-night paintings make sense.

Luc had admitted that he was painting out his anger when he couldn't sleep, using his brush as an outlet for his emotions. Now that he was no longer painting wildly—Marie was healing, he was happier with her and Livie living here—he was channeling other emotions onto this canvas.

"I wish I could draw you." Luc reached over and touched her knee, bare beneath the hem of her nightgown. "I miss that. Not the making love—well, I miss that too."

He grinned, a welcome sign of the old Luc here in the middle of the night.

"But I miss just us—" He gestured in the space between them. "The time we spent in my old studio. Just the two of us, together."

"Come." She stood up and reached for his hand.

"Where are you taking me?" But he did what she asked and stood.

"To bed."

67

Luc sat on the edge of the bed, waiting. When Marie turned back from rummaging in his bedroom dresser, she was holding the grey silk scarf he had given her on Christmas morning. In the dark, it was more of a pale wash of color than a physical object. He liked where she was going with this. When she approached the bed, he held out his hand.

"I'll tie it on you," he offered.

She shook her head and climbed behind him onto the mattress.

"This is for you."

He felt the soft fabric cover his eyes and cheekbones, then tighten as she tied it securely behind his head. Ah, they were going to recreate their first time together when Luc was blindfolded and Marie explored his body with her hands. He felt the initial stirrings of desire, remembering where that exploration had taken them. He heard the soft swish of her nightgown against her skin as she pulled it over her head and dropped it onto the floor. He allowed himself a tiny smile in the dark. He didn't want to get his hopes up, but if she was undressing first … that could only be a good sign.

He stood and began pushing his pajama pants down over his hips.

"You can leave those on, if you want," she said.

"How are you going to touch me then?"

"I'm not. You're going to touch me."

Luc paused. "With the blindfold on?"

"Yes."

"I'd rather see you while I'm touching you."

"You've already seen me. I want you to *feel* me."

"I don't think this is going to help me draw you."

"We're not doing it for that."

He took a deep breath. "Where are you right now?" In the daylight, the silk would let in some light. But it was night, and he had no vision beneath the fabric.

"I'm on the bed."

He took another deep breath. "I don't know if …" He was aroused already, at just the thought of touching her. "I don't know if I can touch you and then stop when …"

They used to be so open, so frank with each other and now he was stammering like a virgin teenager. It had been two years since he'd been with Marie, and there had been no other women since. He hadn't even been tempted by another woman when he was gone, though a few had tried.

An exasperated sigh floated up from the darkness. "I'm lying in your bed stark naked, Luc, and you're debating the matter?" The exasperated sigh turned into an exasperated laugh. "I've thought this through. I wouldn't be suggesting it if I wasn't comfortable with the potential outcome."

"So you've been planning this awhile?" He grinned in the dark. "Plotting out a way to seduce me?"

"Maybe if you stayed in bed all night, I would have seduced you already."

"Maybe if you had seduced me, I would have stayed in bed. I would have been relaxed enough to sleep. I've heard that orgasms are good for—"

There was a sudden jerk on his pajama pants and he tumbled forward onto the bed.

"Take advantage of this before I have second thoughts," Marie whispered.

He shifted his legs until he was straddling her waist. "What about feeling you with my lips?"

"No. Just your hands and fingers."

He ran his hands up her side, careful not to touch any points of interest. Not yet. He wanted to start at the top and work his way down. He touched her hair, messy from her earlier sleep. He liked watching her sleep. When he woke in the middle of the night, he never jumped straight out of bed and rushed to the studio. He always sat there for a few minutes, watching Marie's peaceful face and her lovely auburn hair splayed across the white pillowcase. *His* pillows.

He pushed his fingers in deeper, until they grazed her warm scalp. Was that a little moan he heard? He cupped her head in his hands and imagined her face, just on the other side of the silk scarf. It was so damn hard to lie in bed with her night after night and not touch her, not pull her into his arms and never let her go. That was what kept him up at night, the physical frustration of having her so close and yet being unable to touch her. That, and just the need to make sure that she and Livie were still there, that he wasn't waking to find them left behind in a dream.

"You have no idea how badly I want to kiss you right now," he said. It was a good thing she made no reply. Knowing that her soft lips were open would have made it impossible for him to hold back.

He gently withdrew his hands from her hair and slid his palms down her face, over her cheekbones. She had gorgeous skin. Even his mother, who practiced the meticulous skin care of a Frenchwoman, had complimented it. Effusively, in fact, and his mother was not given to fawning insincerely over someone.

His thumb settled into the indentation above her lip.

"The philtrum," she whispered. "Latin for love potion."

"At least you learned *something* from me."

"Mmm, one word of Latin."

He felt her smile beneath his fingers, and he let them linger there until the smile faded. He wanted to feel all of her smiles, for the rest of her life. He wanted to be the one to put smiles on her face. Livie was formidable competition in that regard. To watch Marie with their daughter filled him with such peace. All was right with the world when he was with them. Maybe that was his problem with painting. Art used to be the most important thing in his life. Now it wasn't. Not even close.

He traced a fingertip along her jaw, then under to her neck. He knew just how far his finger could go before it reached the slope of her shoulder. Her body was still completely familiar to him. His hands knew exactly where to go, how wide her shoulders were, how much skin before her forearm dipped into her elbow. He interlaced his fingers with hers, both hands, and resisted the urge to bring them up to his lips and kiss each finger in turn. He unlaced his fingers and lightly touched her ribs, one by one.

"Does this hurt?" he asked.

"No."

No one was ever going to hurt her again, not on his watch. If he hadn't disappeared, Aidan Janssen would never have come into her life. He bore responsibility for that.

He ran his finger straight up the middle of her torso, between her breasts, and felt her shiver beneath him. Even he could feel how cocky his grin was.

"Just because you can't see me doesn't mean I can't see you," she reminded him.

"I don't need to see you. I'm feeling you."

I don't need to see you.

But he did need to see her. How could he draw her otherwise? And he couldn't spend his entire life unable to draw the people he loved. His grandfather had an excuse, his failing eyesight. Luc couldn't claim that. There was nothing wrong with his eyes. He just couldn't see with them any longer.

His hand moved to her breast, cupping it for a moment before twirling her nipple beneath his thumb. Her chest began to rise and fall more rapidly. Even after two years, they still had the same effect on each other. He moved from his thumb to his index finger, patiently rolling her nipple beneath each finger. Her hips were rocking, feeling this one isolated touch everywhere on her body.

He slid lower, running his palms over her stomach. She was softer here now, a not unpleasant change. He imagined laying his head on her stomach and resting there. His fingers stopped on a bump in her skin. No, it was a ridge, he realized as he traced the line across her lower abdomen. It was a scar. Livie had been born via c-section. He knew that, but the reality of it struck home now. Marie had gone into surgery by herself. Come out of it by herself.

"Were you frightened?" he asked quietly.

"Yes."

She knew what he was referring to. He missed that, too, the comfort of being understood by her.

He bent his head to her stomach and began kissing the scar from end to end, kisses like stitches in a wound he would never be able to close. He expected her to protest the use of his lips instead of his hands, but she lay silent above him.

When he reached the end of the scar, he crawled back up her body and pressed his lips to hers. If she didn't kiss him back, it would be no more than he deserved. But her lips parted beneath his and he deepened the kiss. He felt her ankles hook around his calves, her hands grappling with his pajamas.

"Take me into you," he murmured against her warm lips. "Don't let me go."

IN THE MORNING, they were back to the usual routine. Luc jumped out of bed at the first squeak from Livie. While he changed and dressed her, Marie hopped in the shower to get ready for work. As the warm water hit her skin, skin Luc had patiently touched every inch of the night before, she could tell that her body felt different this morning. There was no denying that. She'd been made love to for the first time in almost two years. It was worth the wait, and there was no turning back now. Sleeping chastely next to Luc … that wasn't going to happen anymore.

It was more than the physical pleasure of being with him, though that was considerable. Luc had made her feel *loved* last night. That was more compelling and more addicting than any physical pleasures could ever be.

Loved.

Showered and dressed, she popped into the kitchen to kiss Livie goodbye.

"Be good for papa." She pressed her lips to Livie's damp, combed hair.

"Oui."

Was it any surprise that some of Livie's first words were in French? She and Luc spoke French during the day. Luc's students spoke English to her, and Luc switched back to English when Marie got home from work. Livie didn't miss a beat, gliding from one language to another.

She turned to go and ran into a wall of chest. Luc steadied her with his hands on her shoulders. He bent his head and kissed her tenderly, his lips tasting hers for just a moment before he released her.

"See you later," he whispered. In those three words was nestled the promise that they'd be doing much more than seeing.

Marie put on her coat and found her bag in a daze, not trusting herself to look back at Luc before she descended the stairs to the studio. She knew what she would see in his eyes. Love. And her own love for him was right that minute pounding on her chest, demanding to be let out. They had crossed a line the night before, a line that couldn't be uncrossed now. A line she knew now with perfect clarity that she didn't want to uncross.

Downstairs, Luc's studio was quiet. The students' easels sat empty. Here and there a forgotten pencil or piece of charcoal lay on the floor. Maybe this would be enough to anchor Luc, the knowledge that he would be leaving behind lots of people—not just a lover. She walked to the far end of the studio, to Luc's own easel, to look at the painting he had in progress. The more she looked at it, the more she liked it. Yes, it lacked the precision and realism that Luc prized in himself and others, but it had more of one very important element.

Luc himself.

She reached into her purse for her phone, and snapped a quick photo of the painting. Then she hurried out the door to make it to work on time.

68

Luc tucked Livie in for a late morning nap, then retrieved the box containing his grandmother's necklace from its hiding place in his closet. He still hadn't shown it to Marie, or even told her that he had it. He wanted to surprise her with it. He sat down on the living room sofa and opened the box. The diamonds and emeralds sparkled even in the artificial light of the windowless room. He lifted it from its padded bed and held it up, trying to imagine it draped around Marie's graceful neck.

Last night she had opened the door on his hope. Maybe she could forgive him, after all.

He turned the necklace around in his fingers, inspecting it, touching each gem in turn. It seemed incredible that his grandparents had such a piece of jewelry. Even if it had been his grandmother's style to wear a necklace like this, his grandparents surely couldn't have afforded it.

He remembered what Marie had said about the necklace looking like one worn by Elizabeth Calhoun in one of her portraits. He carefully laid the necklace back in the box and went to look for Marie's copy of the museum catalog. It was one of the things she had asked him to retrieve from her apartment, in addition to clothing for her and Livie.

That was another thing that gave him hope—she hadn't asked him to take anything back to her apartment, despite the fact that her arm was healed enough for her to live without his help anymore. She hadn't mentioned the idea, so Luc hadn't raised it either. He hated the idea of being alone here again. Marie and Livie had made this otherwise charmless place a home. To not see the two of them all day, every day … he shook his head to clear his mind of the thought. He didn't want to even contemplate it.

Back on the sofa, he opened the catalog and thumbed through the pages. It didn't take long to find the painting Marie had mentioned. It was one of the later paintings, and one Luc remembered only vaguely. It was also a large painting; Luc had thought it overlarge. In it, Elizabeth Calhoun lay in waves of white sheets on a bed, her face turned into the painting. Her right arm dangled over the edge of the mattress, a necklace laced through her fingers.

He squinted in an effort to bring the necklace into sharper focus. In real life, the painting was large but the photograph in the book was small. He glanced over at his grandmother's necklace in its box. Certainly, the two pieces of jewelry looked similar but it was a stretch to him to imagine they might be the same piece. His grandmother's necklace was not costume jewelry, to be sure, but the odds of her owning a one-of-a-kind necklace were slim.

He blinked and stared at the photo of the painting. The image, her pose in the bed, struck him as sad. None of the other paintings or the small charcoal drawings Alistair Smith had made of his lover had conveyed such an air of hopelessness as this one did. Elizabeth was lying nude in a mussed bed. It was clearly the aftermath of lovemaking but she was alone, her lover already gone. And the necklace was in her hand, not around her throat—like she had just taken it off or it had never been on, a spurned gift in the waning light of a love affair.

That was probably why Luc hadn't paid much attention to this particular painting before. He'd been in the throes of falling head over heels in love with Marie. Such a poignant reminder of where love often ends up—of where it can't go, the hurdles it can't overcome—wasn't something he had wanted to contemplate.

He rather liked the painting now, its directness, the honesty of feeling in it. Whatever could be said of their affair, of the choices the couple had made—and hadn't made—it couldn't be said that Alistair had glossed over the reality of the relationship. Or the emotional turmoil of a love that couldn't be. Alistair Smith had taken both his lover's identity and his love for her to his grave. That's what this painting with the necklace was about, he suspected—the end of a relationship.

In the kitchen, his phone buzzed. By the time he got there, he had missed the call. But it was Sam. He tapped the screen to call her back.

"You called?" he said when Sam answered immediately.

"I love it."

"Love what?"

"The new work."

"What new work?"

He was beginning to feel like he was stuck in some old comedy routine.

"The painting. The one with the little boy in the studio."

"Where are you? Are you downstairs?" That didn't make sense, even as the words left his mouth. Marie wouldn't have manually unlocked the door to the street when she left. It should have locked automatically behind her.

Sam's laugh trilled on the other end. "No. Marie texted me a picture of it. I love it. What else do you have?"

Marie sent a picture to Sam? His heart sunk. Why would she do that? She knew he was just fooling around with these paintings.

"She wasn't supposed to do that."

"Ah. You wanted to wait and show me everything at once?"

"No. There is no 'everything.' That painting is just me goofing off. I can't sleep at night so I come into the studio and throw paint at canvases."

Sam was quiet for a long beat. Luc rubbed at his temple and the headache brewing behind it. Why would Marie do a thing like that? Betray his trust that way?

"You should goof off more then," Sam said. "That painting is really good."

"It's not even finished." What was he saying? It didn't need to be finished. It was junk.

"When it is, send me another photo. And whatever else you have. You've been holding out on me."

"It's not going to be finished, Sam. It's not serious. I'm still having trouble painting. Or drawing, even. I've lost it."

"What do you mean, it's not serious? Granted, I just have a tiny image of it but I think it's the best thing you've done besides the portraits of Marie. Maybe even better than those. I'll reserve final judgment until I've seen the actual painting, but this is good."

Luc's headache was scrabbling at the inside of his skull now. "It's junk, Sam. Junk. It's nothing like my other work. Face it, I drank away my talent. And I deserve to have lost it, too."

There was a long exhale on the other end. "Luc, you spent years painting rich people's cars and horses. Frankly, that was a waste of your talent."

"It was a way to make a living after I was kicked out of academia."

"I don't dispute that. That doesn't change the fact that it was beneath you, artistically. Maybe instead of drinking away your talent, you drank that style of painting out of your system. If it's gone for good, I'm not sure that's a bad thing. Can I offer you my professional advice?"

"You're going to anyway."

"Damn straight I am, because we've been friends for a long time. Trust me and go with this for awhile. Send me pictures of whatever else you've been working on. I don't care whether you think it's any good or not. Just send it to me."

"Don't ask Marie to take pictures of my work. Just don't, okay?"

"I won't. But she was right to send me this."

"It wasn't her place to do that."

"No, and it shouldn't be my place to beg you for new work, either. You need to step up to your own place in your life, Luc."

THE STUDIO WAS dark when Marie got home. Yes, home. She'd begun to think of Luc's place as "home," even if a converted auto body shop lacked a certain traditional hominess. She crossed the studio floor in the dark and ascended the stairs to their living quarters. The apartment was dark too, and eerily quiet. Obviously, Luc and Livie weren't home. It wasn't like Luc to not be home at this time of day.

She switched on the lights and hung up her coat before calling his cell. They might have run out to the supermarket. When the call rolled over to his voice mail, she strode down the hall to the kitchen, to look for a note. But the countertops were empty. She called his cell again. Luc and Livie had never not been here when she got home from work, but it was hard to imagine Luc not leaving a note as to their whereabouts. He would know she would worry about Livie.

Still no answer. She tried a text. No reply to that, either. She double-checked her own voice mail. Nothing new.

She felt her pulse skitter as her mind resisted other possibilities. If Livie were sick … or had an accident … if they were at the emergency room … Luc would have called or left her a message. She slumped into a chair at the kitchen table to think.

And to try and not think.

Had last night scared him? Had she pushed him too far? He didn't exactly put up any resistance. He was fine when she left this morning, or so it had seemed. But Luc's moods were changeable. She jumped when her phone buzzed with a text. Samantha Smith.

Thanks for the photo. He'll come around.

He'll come around? What did that mean? Marie replied to Sam's text. *Do you know where he is? He's not here.*

Five minutes passed with no response, and she found it harder to ignore the obvious. Luc had left again. And this time, he took Livie. She folded her arms on the table and laid her head on them. She took deep breath after deep breath, trying to convince herself that she was jumping to conclusions for which she had no evidence.

Other than his absence. And her daughter's.

He wouldn't do that. He wouldn't take Livie away from her. *He wouldn't. He wouldn't. He wouldn't.*

But the panic began to swell in her chest, crowding out her attempts to be rational, logical, calm. *Hospital. They're at a hospital. Start calling the hospitals.* She picked up her phone, only to have it buzz with a new text from Sam.

He's at the Carnegie Museum.

Does he have Livie? Marie replied.

Yes. Just spoke to him.

So he answered Sam's call but not any of hers? That said everything right there, didn't it? But at least he was still in the area. That soothed Marie's nerves. A little.

Thanks.

She tapped on Luc's name to call him again, then thought

better of it. What would she say even if he answered? Nothing that should be said over the phone. On the other hand, she had precisely zero intention of sitting in his apartment and waiting for him to return.

Been there, done that.

She called a cab instead.

69

Marie hurried through the lobby and into the heart of the museum. She ignored the couples obviously on first dates, the clusters of students taking notes on this painting or that, the lone visitors seeking after work solitude or solace in a cathedral of art. Marie had pondered what she was going to say during the cab ride over. She still wasn't sure, even as she entered the exhibit.

Luc and Livie were easy to spot, their twin dark heads huddled together before a large portrait of Elizabeth Calhoun. As she got closer, she saw it was the portrait with the necklace. She could tell from Luc's lips that he was speaking French to their daughter. It hit her that eventually Luc and Livie would be able to speak to each other without Marie understanding.

Livie saw her first. "Mama!"

It was all she could do not to break into a flat-out run to get to her daughter. Livie stretched her arms out and Marie pulled her into her chest. She buried her face—and the threatening tears—in her daughter's shoulder. When she had regained enough composure, she lifted her head.

"Why didn't you answer my calls?"

Luc gave no answer.

"Never mind," she went on. "I know why. You wanted me to worry."

His silence confirmed her accusation.

"I'm angry," he said, "that you sent that picture to Sam."

She shifted Livie's weight in her arms. Livie was too big anymore for her to hold like this for very long, but she had no intention of letting Luc see that and take Livie back.

"That's what this is about?" She shook her head, disbelieving. "You've got to be kidding me."

"You knew that painting wasn't anything serious for me."

"It might not be serious, but it's good, Luc." Her arm muscles were burning beneath Livie's weight.

"That's not for you to decide."

She coolly aimed a perfectly arched eyebrow at him. "I wasn't deciding anything. I shared it with your *best friend*."

"You're my best friend."

"If that were true, you would know that the worst thing you could do to me is disappear with Livie. And if you did know that and you did it anyway …" She looked away from him. "You obviously don't care about me enough to call me a friend. Let alone anything else."

"I didn't disappear. We came to the museum."

"Without leaving me a note, a text, a phone call. Nothing."

From the corner of her eye, she could see other museum-goers moving around them, moving from one painting to the next. But it all looked like slow motion to her, the way she felt her life slowly tilting, tilting, tilting, on the verge of toppling over and crashing hard to the ground.

"Do I need to tell you my whereabouts every minute of the day? You have to trust me more than that, Marie."

She fixed him with a hard glare. "I need to know Livie's whereabouts. I don't need to know where *you* are. I didn't know where you were for almost two years. And you know what? My life was fine before you came back. I had a job, a boyfriend, a life. So no, you don't need to share with me *your* whereabouts. But Livie's? Yes, you do."

"He wasn't much of a boyfriend." Luc snorted.

"He was better before you showed up."

"I would bet my last dollar he had a drinking problem long before he ever laid eyes on me. You just didn't know it yet."

"He has nothing to do with this, Luc." Her arms were shaking from the fatigue of holding Livie—and from anger. She knew he was probably right about Aidan's drinking. She had been looking so hard for reasons to say "yes" to Aidan that she had missed the reasons to say "no."

"Let me take her."

Luc reached over, but she took a step back.

"I'm not going to run off with her."

They stared each other down over the dark head of their daughter. How did it fall apart so quickly again? Maybe the two of them weren't meant to be. After a minute, Luc turned back to face the painting on the wall in front of them."

I want to show you something. It's why I came here. To think, calm down and look at this painting."

"You want to talk about a painting? Now?"

"Yes, I do."

His hand disappeared inside his coat pocket, then reappeared with a long, shallow wooden box. He lifted up the lid and tilted it toward her so she could see the contents. It was a necklace. She glanced at the painting as he gingerly freed the jewelry from the box.

"That looks like …"

"It's my grandmother's necklace, the one she wore in my grandfather's painting. My parents gave it to me when we were in Paris."

"You? Why not Valerie?" Valerie seemed the more obvious choice to her.

"My grandmother wanted me to have it."

"Why didn't you say anything earlier? When I told you I thought . . ." She lifted one aching arm from Livie's back to gesture at the painting on the wall.

"She wanted me to give it to my wife. That's why I didn't say anything."

They both let his words fade into the chilled museum air between them. His wife, meaning not her.

"Or I will give it to Livie some day."

He took a step toward the painting and held the necklace up to it, for comparison.

"They certainly look identical, though it's hard for me to fathom my grandparents having a one-of-a-kind piece of jewelry."

"It's too distinctive to have been mass produced, though. And it's clearly not just costume jewelry."

Luc ran a thumb over one of the emeralds. "No, I think not. But I can't see any way for these to be the same necklace. This painting here predates the one my grandfather did by years. My grandparents weren't acquainted with Elizabeth Calhoun or Alistair Smith. They never even visited the United States."

He returned the necklace to its box and slipped it back into his coat pocket. He held out his arms for Livie. She started to shake her head, but he cut her off.

"You're about to drop her, Marie. Your arms are shaking."

She let him lift Livie from her arms and tuck her into the stroller he'd brought with them. He began pushing it toward the exit. She skipped to catch up with his long strides.

"Last night meant nothing, did it?" she said.

"It meant a lot to me."

"Not enough for you to leave me a note or simply call and tell me you were angry that I sent Sam a picture of your painting."

"I was upset. I'm sorry."

"And what was I supposed to do? Sit home and wait for you to come back?"

"You found me easily enough."

She felt like tearing her hair out. "Was I supposed to go find you when I was pregnant? Go from country to country looking for you? I still don't know where you were, exactly."

"A little bit of everywhere."

"Oh, well that would have made it easy to track you down."

"I didn't mean that you should have come looking for me back then." He ran a hand through his hair, grabbing a fistful tightly before letting his hand fall back to the handle of the stroller.

"I needed to think today. I was looking at the necklace and the museum catalog when Sam called this morning. That's why I went to the museum. Just to get out and think."

"You could have left a note. You *should* have left me a note. Or a text or something."

"You're right. I should have. I'm sorry." He let her take the stroller while he opened the door to the street outside. "But I didn't run away. I never even left the city."

"What would you have done if I hadn't gone looking for you?"

"I would have come home when the museum closed."

70

He missed Livie. Marie had moved back into her own apartment. He missed her, too. But he had gotten so used to being with his daughter all day long, seeing her first thing in the morning and last thing at night. Marie had agreed to let Livie stay with him during the day instead of going back to daycare while she worked, but it wasn't the same. Better than nothing, of course, but less than he wanted. Much less.

He chewed on the end of his paintbrush, mindless of the paint that had dripped onto his jeans. It was six in the morning, and he'd been awake since three. Marie would be here at eight to drop off Livie. Exhaustion stung his eyes. He would nap with Livie later in the morning, before lunch, but lunch was eons away. He had no idea how to fill the next two hours, even.

The painting of him in his grand-père's studio was finished. He hoped. Maybe it wasn't so bad. Or maybe it was worse. He couldn't trust his judgment anymore. Why hadn't he left Marie a note? He was an ass. He'd let his emotions get the best of him again, when he should have taken a deep breath and been patient enough to let them subside.

The problem, of course, was that he had no patience where Marie was concerned. He wanted her the very day he met her, and that feeling hadn't subsided one bit. Nor did he have any semblance of control over his emotions around her. He wanted her so badly his chest ached.

But I didn't run away. I didn't leave the city. I would have gone home in another hour anyway.

Yes, he should have left Marie a note or texted her. He admitted that. But he didn't leave. Wasn't that progress? He would never take Livie away from her mother.

He carefully lifted the wet painting off the easel and leaned it against the wall, out of the way. He got a fresh canvas and began to paint again. He didn't have a plan—barely an idea—when he painted now. That's what Marie didn't understand. He was just going through the motions here, but it soothed his soul. He couldn't screw up a painting like this. It wasn't serious to begin with. And he desperately needed something he couldn't screw up.

MARIE'S PHONE RANG. She knew without even glancing at it that the caller was Luc. It was seven-thirty. He called every evening at this time to wish Livie a goodnight.

"Papa. Papa." Livie reached out her hand for Marie's phone. "Papa."

Livie knew who it was, too.

This was what Marie had feared, had always feared about staying with Luc after the accident. Living with him, the three of them living as a family, had become the new normal for Livie. Now that they were back in their old apartment, Livie asked for her papa all the time.

And there was no way to explain the whole messy situation to a one-year-old.

Marie answered the call.

"Hi," he said quickly. "Don't let her hang up after I say goodnight, okay? I have something I want to tell you."

She agreed and handed the phone over to her daughter, who immediately pressed it to her ear. Marie sat on the sofa and watched Livie smile and babble to her father. Occasionally, a recognizable word in French or English broke through. Marie fought the smile that was tugging at her lips, and lost the battle. Livie was always so happy when Luc was around. Marie felt guilty denying her daughter that.

Had she been too hasty in moving out? It wasn't like in Paris, when she and Nishi returned from London to find him gone. Then, he hadn't answered his phone—not even for Sam. At least this time, someone had been able to get through to him, even if it hadn't been herself.

And she missed Luc, too. It wasn't only Livie who had gotten used to living with him. Marie had fallen right back into the ease and pleasure of it, of being around him, falling asleep next to him, hearing him sing in French to Livie in the morning as he got her dressed and fed.

Livie was trying to repeat some word Luc had said to her on the phone, her lips and tongue struggling to wrap themselves around the letters. It was hard to believe that he would just up and leave Livie. That wasn't Marie's fear anymore. To believe that he would take Livie away from her required her to believe that he was a terrible person. And she knew him not to be that. Emotional. Rash. Insecure sometimes. But he wasn't blackhearted.

So what *was* she afraid of?

"I'm not a perfect man," he said to her when she was packing up her things at his apartment.

Was she expecting too much? Could she live with an imperfect Luc, for the sake of their daughter? She didn't even have to ask the other question: could she love an imperfect Luc? She did love him. Would probably always love him.

And she loved the way his emotions swept him away, loved him when he acted first and thought later. Like when he fought Richard at her parents' house on Thanksgiving. Aidan would never have done that. Or when he had chased her into the ocean the weekend they'd spent at Sam's beach house. When she had been running away from the reality of Luc's past.

Luc hadn't let her run away that day. He came after her without so much as taking the time to put on a shirt. Shirtless, he had plunged into the November-cold Atlantic to carry her out of the water. After, he sat for her on Sam's deck and let her see him totally exposed and vulnerable, raw with fear over the prospect of losing her. Meanwhile, Richard had been running around telling everyone that he and Marie were back together.

Then in Paris, Nishi had told him she was taking Marie back home.

Marie took a deep breath as she tried to imagine what Luc had been feeling when she and Nishi were in London that weekend. Richard hadn't really been smart enough to take her away from Luc. But Nishi was, and Luc would have known that.

"Mama. Mama." Livie was looking at her. "Mama."

Marie could tell Luc was telling Livie to return the phone to her mother, but Livie clearly had no intention of complying. The phone stayed resolutely pressed to her ear. Marie held out her hand.

"Say *'bonne nuit'* to papa. You'll see him tomorrow."

Livie's lower lip pushed out, quivering. Marie felt hot tears well up in her own eyes. After another minute of whispering from Luc on the other end, Livie held out the phone.

"Hey." Marie blinked hard to dry the tears. "What did you want to tell me?"

"I'm sending the paintings to Sam."

"You are?"

"I am. I still don't think she'll like them when she sees them in person, but at least she'll stop nagging me about it."

"I don't know about that. Sam seems to know what she's doing. In art and with you."

Luc's chuckle was soft on the other end, and just like that the tears were back. She felt Livie's eyes on her, intently watching her maman and coveting the phone.

"She wants me to come to Washington this weekend to meet with her."

"Okay."

"Come with me. You and Livie? Please. I want to take Livie to Middleburg."

Marie closed her eyes and leaped.

"Okay."

If Luc had been smart—had followed his head and not his heart—he would have run away from a woman who was the estranged wife of one senator and the daughter of another. But if he had, they would never have fallen in love. Their beautiful daughter wouldn't exist. Luc was a man governed by his emotions, for better or for worse. She wanted the better. Could she handle the worse?

71

The front room of Sam's gallery was in disarray, as her staff took down one show in preparation for hanging another. Luc shifted Livie's weight in his arms. She was getting bigger by the week, a fact that saddened him more than a little. Every day was a day closer to the time when she wouldn't need her papa, when she wouldn't look at Luc like the sun rose and set on him.

For him, everything rose and set on Livie.

"Text me when your meeting is over." He leaned in toward Marie. "Give maman a kiss," he said to Livie. He could feel Sam's eyes on him, observing, judging. Things had thawed a little between him and Marie, but she was still holding back. He didn't know what to do.

"I will," Marie said and then disappeared back into the bright sunshine and the lunchtime crowds in Dupont Circle.

"You're an idiot."

Luc turned to face Sam. "Yes, that is a well-established fact. Just don't hit me in front of my daughter." Livie squirmed in his arms. "I know you want down, sweetie, but …"

He looked around Sam's gallery. Paintings leaned against the walls, waiting to be packed up. A freestanding sculpture stood in the middle of the room. One toddler could wreak thousands of dollars worth of havoc here.

Sam turned back toward her office. "Ellie? Can you help me out for a few minutes?"

Sam's fourteen-year-old daughter poked her head out. When she saw Livie and Luc, she rushed over and immediately began prying Livie from his arms. Livie's body stiffened.

"It's okay, sweetie. This is Ellie." He leaned over to kiss Ellie on the cheek and show Livie that she was a friend. "You remember Ellie?"

"We'll play," Ellie added.

Livie eyed the girl's riotous blonde curls and then let herself be transferred from his arms.

"Just keep her away from anything valuable," Sam warned.

"So *my* paintings, she can go near those."

Sam punched Luc lightly in the arm.

"I like these new paintings. I'm glad you shipped them to me after all."

"They're just me messing around."

Sam sighed audibly, but didn't argue the point. He and Sam had known each other for so many years now, they could argue with each other without saying a single word.

"So let's talk about how to show this mess." Sam strolled to the back room of the gallery, where Luc's paintings—unwrapped and uncrated—leaned against the walls. "At least I don't have to hang these so they can't be seen through the front window."

She realigned a few of the canvases. "You don't have titles for any of these?"

"Painting number one, painting number two … no, they're not paintings of anything." He pointed at one. "I was angry with Aidan Asshole Janssen the night I painted that one. I wanted to kill him." He walked over and tweaked the corner of another. "I was mad at myself here." He tapped the one next to it. "Mad at the world here."

"I think this is the first time you've let yourself be angry," Sam said quietly. "I think that's why these work. They're powerful, Luc. They're all raw energy and aggression."

He snorted. "I've been angry a lot. It's the chief cause of most of my problems, letting myself lose my temper."

"Losing your temper, sure. And then you remove yourself from whatever situation has pissed you off."

"Yeah, so I don't hurt anyone any further."

"But you couldn't remove yourself this time."

"No. I'm not leaving Marie and Livie. Under any circumstances."

"So you had to stay and stew in your anger." Sam pulled a painting away from the wall.

Now it was Luc's turn to sigh. "What are you trying to say, Sam? I stayed and found an outlet for my anger, yes."

"What I'm trying to say is that you survived staying and nothing terrible happened." Sam faked a frown. "You didn't kill that guy, right? And you got some great work out of it."

Luc squinted at the canvases leaned against the wall, trying to reassess them. There was nothing great in them, as far as he could see.

"Do you enjoy painting like this?"

"I didn't at first." He shrugged. "Now … I guess so. It's easy to enjoy, though. It's not serious." He glanced back to check on Livie, but she was happily playing with Ellie. "What if they don't sell?"

"What if they don't?" Sam countered. "Art buyers are a fickle bunch." Sam rearranged several of the paintings against the wall, trying out different groupings. "You know I will always show your work."

Luc's expression was skeptical.

"Well, unless it gets really awful," Sam allowed. "But as long as it's *good,* you have a place in my gallery."

"Thanks."

"So don't worry about the art, is what I'm trying to say. You don't need to follow in your grandfather's footsteps."

"That's good since that's obviously not happening."

Sam fixed him with a stern glare, then cocked her head toward the front of the gallery where her daughter was making Livie laugh. "Life isn't going to stand still while you look for the right angle, the right light, the right relationship to the horizon line. Livie's going to grow up. Marie will get tired of waiting."

"I'm the one who's waiting for her. I don't know what I have to do to make her comfortable with me."

"It's not what you have to *do,* Luc. It's what you have to *be.* Stop waiting to get your art back, stop waiting for Marie to be comfortable with you again. You already have all that. And if you spent less time looking for it, you'd see it as clearly as everyone else does."

THE CURATOR'S office at the Phillips Collection was surprisingly spare, the white walls bare of any art or photographs, the woman's desk topped with just the necessaries of office life. Computer, phone, a notepad covered with what looked like hastily scribbled phone messages. Or reminders to self.

Marie waited patiently while the curator finished typing an email. The woman looked to be fortyish, roughly Luc's age. Younger than she had sounded on the phone when Marie had called to ask if they might meet. After a pause, the woman gave her keyboard a sharp click. Send. Then she turned to Marie.

"I apologize. I had to get that out."

"No problem. I'm grateful you were able to make time for me while I'm in town."

"I've met your mother a few times." *Of course you have.* Was there anyone in Washington who hadn't met her mother? If so, Marie was still looking for them. "Lovely woman."

The curator had known immediately who Marie was when she called. Of course she would. Marie had only been the subject of the biggest art scandal in DC since … well since forever. DC wasn't the kind of town to harbor art scandals. Political scandals, yes. But to merge the two? She and Luc had pulled off a rare feat there.

"So you're interested in the Elizabeth Calhoun-Alistair Smith show?" the curator asked.

"Yes. I've seen it several times, here and in Pittsburgh. I was wondering whether there was more correspondence between the two that wasn't included in the show."

The curator nodded thoughtfully. "I believe there is, yes. But we don't have it. We have just the letters that were written during the years in which Alistair was painting Elizabeth. Can I ask what your interest is in any additional documents?"

"In one of the paintings, Elizabeth is holding an emerald and diamond necklace. There is an identical necklace in a painting by Philippe Marchand. I know his grand-"

The curator nodded. "I know of your relationship."

"And Luc has inherited that necklace. I am trying to figure out whether it is the same one and, if so, how it came to be in the Marchand family."

Marie fished her phone from her purse and tapped open some photos. Luc was certain the two necklaces were different and that mere coincidence explained their presence in both paintings. But Marie wasn't so sure. She had a feeling that there might be more to it than that.

She slid the phone across the desk to the curator.

"This is the actual necklace," she said.

The curator studied the photographs for a moment.

"Well, I do know which painting you're referring to. The one where she's lying on a bed, her arm hanging over the edge. I don't know anything about the necklace. I did meet extensively with members of both families to discuss the paintings. The necklace did not come up."

Marie's heart sunk. They were at a dead end.

"But I could give James Calhoun a call," the curator continued. "He happens to live in the city, not far from here actually. I can tell him what you're looking for and he can call you directly if he has anything that will help."

Marie's heart soared. Elizabeth Calhoun's son lived here in DC?

"You would do that? I would so appreciate it. Please tell him we won't take much of his time. We're only here for a few days anyway."

Marie left the Phillips Collection nearly skipping with delight and relief. There was no guarantee that James Calhoun would agree to meet with her and Luc, but at least there was a chance.

72

At two o'clock the next afternoon, she and Luc stood on the doorstep of James Calhoun's elegant Kalorama townhouse. Marie took a deep breath. Luc rubbed the small of her back.

"Relax, chérie." He rang the doorbell.

Livie was with Marie's mother for the day. After this meeting, however it went, they would pick up Livie and drive out to Virginia to meet Sam and her husband for dinner.

A minute later, the heavy wooden door opened inward. A plainly dressed man in pressed khaki pants and white button-down shirt smiled warmly at them, then stood aside and gestured for them to enter.

"Ms. Witherspoon. Monsieur Marchand." His eyes twinkled. "Come in. Come in."

They followed him down a short hallway to a parlor, furnished exactly the way Marie would expect a Kalorama home to be furnished. Formal, traditional. A settee upholstered in deep blue velvet. A red and gold Persian rug. Antique tables. And on the walls, exquisite paintings of New York and Paris and London. Luc walked over to one to inspect it further.

"Yes, those are Alistair's paintings. The ones he wanted to be famous for. Ah well. One doesn't always have control of one's destiny, now do we?"

He extended his hand to Marie in greeting. She shook it, then Luc did as well.

"Have a seat, please. I'll bring in coffee, if you'll give me a moment."

He disappeared back into the hall, followed by the sounds of cupboards opening and closing, the light clink of silverware and china. Then he returned, carrying a tray with cups and a silver pitcher of coffee, a small pitcher of cream and a sugar bowl.

James Calhoun was in his sixties but he carried himself like a much younger man. His white hair was neatly trimmed and she took note of his nails—short and buffed—as he poured three cups of coffee. He took a seat beneath a large painting of Central Park. Odd, she thought, that he not only owned paintings by his mother's lover, but displayed them so prominently. Surely his father, the senator, wouldn't have approved. Of course, Teddy Calhoun was long gone now, and perhaps James Calhoun simply liked Alistair Smith's work.

"So you two caused quite a stir a few years back." He laughed at the slightly alarmed expressions on their faces. "Oh come now. You didn't expect me to have no idea who you were, did you? Even if I hadn't gone to the show in person, I do know how to use the internet." He stirred a spoonful of sugar into his coffee, then took a thoughtful sip. "An artist and his model. I'm glad to meet you both, actually. I recently purchased four of your portraits."

"My portraits? Ours?" Luc nearly choked on his coffee.

"Yes, yours. I employ an art consultant part time to help me curate and manage my own collection. She happened across a Russian chap in New York who was looking to sell them."

Marie felt Luc stiffen next to her on the settee. Then it hit her: James Calhoun had seen her portraits. Nude portraits. She regretted them all over again. What had she been thinking? What was Livie going to think someday when she was old enough to be aware of them? Would classmates at school make fun of them? Of Livie? Kids could be cruel. What idiots she and Luc had been. They should have kept the paintings for themselves. Kept them private.

"He said you had refused to sell him a fifth painting, and he absolutely required a fifth." James Calhoun chuckled. "I, on the other hand, have no such requirements. Though it took about three months of negotiations to get him to agree to a fair price. My consultant knew what he had paid for them. He wanted another fifty percent on top of that." He chuckled again.

"Well, he had them up on Ebay for awhile," Luc said. "So you probably still overpaid."

Marie gasped. Ebay? Just when she thought it couldn't get any worse … it did. She felt Luc's hand settle over hers.

"Sorry, love."

She shook her head, incredulously. "You were right, Mr. Calhoun. About having no control over one's destiny."

"James, please. And destiny is overrated, in my opinion. Now what can I do for you two? The curator who called was quite vague."

Marie pulled from her bag her copy of the museum catalog for Alistair and Elizabeth's show, a photo of the necklace, and a photo of the painting of Emeline Marchand that Luc had persuaded his sister to take and email to them. They had printed out the photos at Sam's office that morning. Luc took the catalog from her hand and flipped it open to the painting in question. He turned it around for James Calhoun to see.

"In this painting, your mother is holding a diamond and emerald necklace," he said.

"Hmm. Beautiful, wasn't it?" James studied it for a moment.

Marie held out the photo of Emeline's portrait.

"And in this painting, my grandmother is wearing an identical necklace," Luc continued. Marie held out the final photograph. "My grandmother left the necklace to me. This is a photo of it that I took last week."

James Calhoun looked at the photographs and the catalog for several minutes. Marie began to get nervous. The older man took several deep breaths, trying to hold onto the composure he was struggling to maintain. He shook his head, then wiped a tear from the corner of his eye.

"Of course, there is always the possibility that there are simply two necklaces that happen to be identical," Marie ventured. It wasn't the outcome she had her heart set on, but Luc was right. The odds seemed against the two pieces of jewelry being the same.

James swallowed hard before speaking, his eyes still watery.

"It's not. They are the same necklace." His voice broke on the last syllable. "I always wondered whether they ever met again." Finally, he gave in and pulled a white handkerchief from the pocket of his pants and dabbed at his eyes. He handed back the catalog and photographs, then stood up. "If you'll excuse me for one moment, I can get you some things to look at."

Marie could barely contain her excitement. There *was* a connection between the two couples, after all. It *was* the same necklace.

James returned with a file folder tucked beneath his arm. He sat down across from them.

"Before I go further, I need you to understand that this is to be held in the strictest confidence. Not everyone in the Calhoun and Smith families know that they were in touch again after the affair was over, even just in correspondence. I think it best to keep it that way, out of respect for them, and because I have no need to alter the storyline at this point."

Marie glanced at Luc, before nodding agreement.

"There is another secret my mother took to her grave. Senator

Calhoun was not my father. Alistair Cook was. But this is also not information that needs to be known. Both of them are gone. What's done is done. I was raised by Teddy Calhoun and I bear his name. I'm personally not embarrassed by that, though certainly I wish I had been able to know my real father while he was alive. My mother did what she thought was best."

James opened the folder and slid out the top sheet of paper. "I have no interest in changing the past at this point."

Luc took the sheet of paper James offered and held it so both he and Marie could read it.

My dearest E, I will be spending the winter in Paris with an old friend from the war. I hear through the grapevine that you might also be in Paris soon. I will leave it up to you. Forever your A.

It was the briefest of letters, yet it said so much. Marie could hardly breathe.

"That was written in the sixties. My parents had ended their affair by that time and I was being raised as Senator Calhoun's son," James added.

Luc was one step ahead already. "The old friend was my grandfather."

James handed over three more letters from Alistair.

"As you can see, my father was desperate to see her again. My mother was the more practical one."

"The one with more to lose," Luc said.

James shrugged. "Perhaps. Or perhaps more to gain. Two sides of the same coin, I'd say." James thumbed carefully through the next several letters. "My mother never replied to these initial letters, and I was never sure whether she did meet up with him somewhere in Paris. But this painting of your grandmother and the fact that you have that necklace confirms that they did." He handed over more letters. "These letters were written several months later. I never knew to whom she gave the necklace."

Dear E, I am ashamed to say that I am hurt that you gave away the necklace. What do you have to remember me by now?—A

A—I was sad to give it away, too. But I cannot wear it—you know that—and it is too lovely a piece of jewelry to sit, unworn, in a hidden box. I am sorry you are hurt, A. It was not my intention to hurt you. I remember you by all the time we spent together. Please understand.—Your loving E

Then another quick, follow-up letter from Elizabeth.

What we had was precious, A. I will always remember it. I will always remember you. I love you. You know that. We are the right people at the wrong time. Perhaps in another life we will be together. But I fear him, A. He can ruin you, and he would.—With tears and kisses, E

Tears were pricking at Marie's eyes now. *I will always remember you.* Marie had thought those very same words countless times, in imaginary letters she wrote to Luc while she was pregnant. Luc had changed her life. Made her a better person. Given her a daughter. Even if she wanted to forget him, it wasn't an option.

I am ruined already without you.—A

"Did you ever meet him?" she asked James. "Your father?"

He shook his head, sadly. "He had already passed away by the time she finally told me. She waited until both he and Teddy were gone. As far as I know, Alistair never knew that I was his son."

"I should give the necklace back to you," Luc said.

James touched the base of his throat and smiled ruefully. He shook his head. "It's not really my style. And I have no one to leave it to. I never married or had children." He looked pointedly at Marie. "My mother gave it to Emeline Marchand so someone would have a chance to wear it. I think she had the right idea."

73

Marie checked her phone for the fourth time since entering the restaurant. She looked up to see Sam surreptitiously doing the same thing.

"They'll be fine," Luc said, rolling his eyes.

Ellie was babysitting Livie at Luc's Middleburg house while they went out to dinner with Sam and Sam's husband, Peter. Luc had even magnanimously suggested inviting Nishi and Imran. So the six of them were seated in an Italian restaurant in Leesburg, Virginia. The place was new, opened since Marie and Luc had moved away from the area, and located in the charming historic district of the town.

The waiter arrived with the bottle of wine Luc had ordered and poured glasses for everyone but Nishi, whose belly bump was slight but noticeable to anyone who knew to look. Marie sipped cautiously at her own glass. Livie was totally weaned from breast-feeding, due more to Livie than Marie, so Marie was cleared for wine. Nonetheless, she was mindful of the fact that she hadn't been drinking wine for awhile.

Sam lifted her glass and Marie caught the flash of alarm that passed over Luc's face before quickly disappearing. Her own pulse sped up at the prospect of what Sam might say. Luc seemed to have forgiven her for telling Sam about his new work, but she'd rather not have Sam remind him of it. A tentative truce had been declared—if unspoken—between them. Still, she knew how fragile Luc's emotions could be. How fragile her own definitely were.

"A toast," Sam said. "To friends."

Marie saw Luc let out his breath. *To friends.* That was innocuous enough.

Then Nishi held up her water glass. "I owe an apology. To Luc and Marie." Her voice wavered, then she took a deep breath. "I shouldn't have meddled in your relationship. If I hadn't, none of this—" An anguished hiccup swallowed the rest of her words.

"Nonsense," Sam said. "You were looking out for Marie's welfare. There's no way of telling how other people will react. We all make the best decisions we can at the time."

"Amen to that." Marie draped her arm around Nishi's shoulder and squeezed. She had forgiven her friend for meddling. Nishi shouldn't have done it, but Luc should have confirmed things with Marie before going off the deep end.

"Speaking of making the best decisions." Luc looked pointedly at Sam. "Guess who bought the paintings from that Russian asshole?"

"I'm all ears," Sam answered.

"James Calhoun, the son of Elizabeth Calhoun and—"

Marie shot him a warning look. They had promised James not to spill his—or his parents'— secret.

"Elizabeth and Teddy Calhoun." Luc covered well.

"Apparently, the Russian guy was trying to unload them on eBay," Marie added.

"Ouch," Sam added. "So you're okay with James Calhoun owning them, I take?"

"I didn't get the impression he had acquired them as an expensive spank bank." Luc took another sip of wine.

"Wait—you spoke to Elizabeth Calhoun's son? The Elizabeth Calhoun from the paintings?" Nishi asked.

Marie nodded.

"Why?"

"We just happened to find out that he lived in Washington," Luc said quickly.

Marie felt bad withholding the information about the connection between Luc's grandparents and the other couple from their closest friends. They had promised James, though, and they intended to honor that promise.

At least Livie won't have to keep any secrets about her parents. For better or for worse, Luc and Marie had gone public with their relationship. She raised her glass of wine to her lips, but a new thought stopped her from drinking. What would she have told Livie if Luc had never come back? Would she have told Livie who her father was, that he was the son of a famous French painter? Would she have confessed the circumstances surrounding Livie's birth? Would she have had the courage to admit that Luc had abandoned her? These were all questions she wouldn't have to answer now, because she and Luc had not hidden their love.

"What do you think would have happened if Teddy Calhoun had found out?" she asked Nishi.

Nishi shrugged and took another sip of water. "Who's to say he didn't know? Affairs are usually the worst kept secrets in Washington. And sometimes an imperfect marriage is still more politically advantageous than a divorce."

Silence settled over the table as everyone filled in the blanks. Marie's marriage to Richard had been one of political advantage, and everyone in DC knew it. Maya had never been any kind of secret. Marie had been expected to suck it up and pretend she was the one person who didn't know.

"Maya got away with it," she said at long last.

"I don't know about that," Peter said. "She's not well-liked at the State Department or the embassy in Luxembourg. And his career is falling apart."

"That's true." Nishi clapped Marie on the back. "Maya was the best thing that ever happened to you."

"Any problems with our little terror?" Luc glanced around the living room of his home, as if checking for signs of destruction.

Ellie shook her head confidently. "Nope. She was a total princess all night."

"Ah," he smiled at her. "You wouldn't tattle on her anyway."

Ellie's smile said he was exactly right. He looked around for Marie, only to see her legs and feet disappearing up the staircase to the second floor. She was going to check on Livie. Marie had surprised him by agreeing to come with him to Washington. He hadn't needed her and Livie in order to meet with Sam and discuss his new work, work he still wasn't entirely certain of. He was trusting Sam's and Marie's opinions though. Heaven knew, his own judgment had proved faulty in the past plenty of times. Better to trust other people for awhile. Sam and Marie had his best interests at heart. He couldn't deny that.

He was grateful, too, that Nishi had apologized publicly at dinner. Though what had happened certainly wasn't entirely her fault. She had been looking out for Marie, and a good thing she had since Luc had abdicated that responsibility. But not any more. Marie's interests were front and center in his life now, as were Livie's. He would never walk away from them again. Never.

Sam, Peter and Ellie were ready to go.

"Thanks for babysitting," he said to Sam's daughter. He had

been consumed for too many years by the knowledge that his and Grace's daughter would have been Ellie's age. He had been living in the past.

"You're welcome." Ellie had impeccable manners. He only hoped he could raise his daughter half as well as Sam and Peter were raising theirs. "Livie's adorable. Wish I could babysit her all the time."

He could tell Sam was resisting the urge to roll her eyes. He leaned in to kiss Sam on the cheek, then stepped back and shook Peter's hand. When they were gone, their car crunching up the gravel driveway to the road, Luc took the steps upstairs two at a time.

He found Marie in the guest room, right where he knew she would be. Marie had slept in here with Livie last night, the two of them sharing the queen-sized bed. This was the room Marie had stayed in the very first time she had spent the night here. The drive from Pittsburgh had been tense still, but things had thawed a bit since their visit with James Calhoun. It was hard not to be affected by the story of Elizabeth Calhoun and Alistair Smith, and by their sad love story. Two people who weren't able to be with the person they loved. A father who had never known his son. A son who never knew his father.

Luc leaned against the doorjamb. Marie knew he was there, but she kept her eyes on Livie's sleeping body on the bed. Sam was right. He already had everything he wanted, and it was right here in this room. He had no intention of letting it slip through his fingers again.

He walked over to Marie and nestled his chin on her shoulder. For a minute, they watched their daughter sleep. Then he took her hand in his and led her back out to the hall. Downstairs, Marie grabbed the baby monitor from the coffee table.

"Let's go out back," she said. She held up the baby monitor for him to see. "This will work from the back lawn."

"It's kind of chilly out, isn't it?" Spring was still a week away.

"It's only uncomfortable because we've been conditioned to think it is."

The very words he had said to her on the morning of her first drawing lesson with him. *Their* first drawing lesson.

"I wish I could go back in time and erase that day," he said as he followed her through the front door. "I was such an ass."

She sat down on the stone wall in his backyard. He sat next to her.

"What were you even thinking, coming back?"

The night air was more than chilly. It was downright cold, in fact, and he rubbed at the gooseflesh on his arms.

"I wanted another kiss," she answered. "The way you kissed me that first day … no one had ever done that to me before."

He looked at her incredulously. "That was it? All you wanted was a kiss?"

"I wouldn't go back and erase any of that day, Luc.'

"You seemed pretty pissed when you left."

"I was very pissed. You're lucky I didn't take out your mailbox when I drove away."

"Would have given me an excuse to go find you."

"We found each other again anyway."

"Fate found us."

They sat in silence for a minute, until Luc found the courage to say what he needed to say.

"I love you, Marie. You know that. And I know you're not sure that my love for you—and for Livie—will be enough."

"I know that you love us. I don't doubt that."

"I'm not a perfect man."

Her next words surprised him even more than her agreeing to come with him on this trip.

"You never promised that you were."

He felt her hand inch over onto his.

"A life with you and Livie is the thing I want more than anything," he said. "I admit that I am totally full of shit about art sometimes. Maybe most of the time. But not about you, Marie."

"You've changed as an artist."

"I've changed as a man, too. Changed because of you. Changed for you. For Livie, too." He flipped his hand over and clasped hers tight in his fingers. "And I desperately want to prove that to you. But I don't know how." He was glad that there was no moonlight to illuminate the sheen of tears in his eyes. "All I know is that I want a second chance. Maybe I'm on a third chance here. I don't know. But I want another shot at making things work with us."

His words were tumbling one after the other from his lips. He released her hand and leaned forward. The hand he'd had over hers was warm on his cheek as he leaned his elbows on his knees. He suspected the words he was mumbling into the night were French, and he didn't know why. For the first time in his life, he couldn't recognize his native language.

"Marry me."

The words were there, suddenly, in the crisp night air. Had he said them? Had she? Was he just imagining them, the words he had wanted to speak to her for months now?

"Marry me."

He heard them a second time and knew he was either experiencing auditory hallucinations or rambling like an idiot in the dark. *Wouldn't be the first time.*

74

"Marry me."

The words were out of her mouth before her brain had a chance to even form the thought. But now that they were, they felt right. She looked at Luc, his head in his hands, muttering to himself. Had he even heard her?

"Marry me," she repeated.

She tugged on his upper arm until he turned to face her, then pulled his body into her. She wrapped her legs around his hips and cupped his face in her hands.

"I love you," she said softly. With those words out in the air, she felt like a heavy weight was lifted from her chest. She hadn't realized until that moment how exhausting it had been, keeping those three little words bottled up inside, carrying them everywhere but never sharing them.

His eyes scanned her face and she bit back a smile. He couldn't help himself, memorizing the lines and planes of everything that fell under his gaze. He would always look at things that way.

"Did you just ask me to marry you?" he said. "Or was it me who said that?"

"It was me."

He smiled. "Then the answer is oui. I want nothing more than to marry you."

"Nothing?" she teased.

"Well okay. I want some siblings for Livie. And I want us to live under one roof again." His hands slid into her hair. "No, not just under one roof. I want you in my bed every night."

He leaned in and his lips captured hers in a soft, tender kiss. She kissed him back, her lips moving everywhere on his mouth. This right here, this man, this kiss ... she needed it like she needed oxygen or water. He dropped his hand from her hair and found her wrist.

"Come."

He helped her up from the stone wall and they walked side by side to his studio. Neither of them had to articulate where they were going. Inside, Luc set the baby monitor on the floor and she watched him search through the mass of furnishings piled up against the back wall of the studio until he pulled out a small lamp. He set it on the floor in the middle of the room and flicked it on. Incredibly, the bulb still worked and cast enough of a low-watt glow for him to rummage through the boxes he hadn't bothered to move to Pittsburgh. She heard a whispered "bon" and then he turned around, an old sketchpad and charcoal pencil in his hands.

"You want to draw me?" She knew he did, had known it the minute he pulled her up from the stone wall. This was the way Luc interacted with the world, through drawing.

He sat on the floor and crossed his legs, then patted the floor in front of him.

"I need to capture this moment. I'm sorry." He flipped open the sketchpad and turned the pages until he found a blank one.

"No apologies needed."

"I need a drawing of you the night you asked me to marry

you. Even if it's not any good." His pencil scratched on the paper, then he stopped and set down the sketchpad. "Wait. I need something else."

She watched as he hurried from the studio. What could he need? A scarf to blindfold her? She stood and walked over to the back wall. She recognized chairs and stools that she had forgotten about. Luc had moved a lot of his things to Pittsburgh, but clearly not everything.

Not his heart, she suspected.

A warm rush of nostalgia washed over her. She missed this place, his studio and home in Middleburg. Missed their lessons together. But there was no way to move back here. His business was doing well in Pittsburgh. And she had no desire to re-enter her parents' orbit, professionally. She tugged free a paint-spattered blanket and carefully spread it out on the floor. She heard Luc's footsteps coming back down the path from the house and quickly undressed down to her bra and underwear.

Luc stopped just inside the door, his eyes taking her in.

"You didn't have to do that," he said, striding toward her.

"I wanted to."

"This is just for me. For us. Our eyes only." He walked around behind her. "Close your eyes."

She did and immediately felt his fingers unhooking her bra. Then there was the whisper of something cold around her neck. A necklace. His grandmother's. Elizabeth Calhoun's. She didn't have to see it to know. His fingers finished with the clasp, then traced a line down her spine. She shivered. She knew where this evening was headed, and she welcomed it. Craved it.

"You can open your eyes."

The necklace was beautiful, even more so this close. The diamonds and emeralds sparkled in the dim light thrown off by the small lamp. When she looked up, Luc was unfolding a square of paper.

"What's that?" she asked.

"It fell out of the box the necklace was in. It was beneath the padding." He unfolded it all the way, then scanned it.

"What is it?"

"It's a letter from Elizabeth Calhoun to Alistair Smith."

"Show me."

He sat next to her on the blanket, her bare thigh touching his denim-covered leg, and together they read the letter.

My dearest love, baby James was born two days ago with a full head of dark hair (wonder where that came from) and the most beautiful blue eyes. He weighed seven pounds, nine ounces. I thought of you the entire time, A, and I am so so sorry for putting you through this. I am leaving Teddy and coming to you, bringing James with me. I love you, I love you, I love you … more than mere words can say. Ever your Elizabeth.

"But she didn't leave her husband," Marie pointed out.

"And she never sent this letter apparently."

"Oh god." Marie's words came out in a choked hiccup. "This is what she gave your grandmother. The necklace, yes, but this letter. I bet she put it in the box so she wouldn't be tempted to actually send it."

"Or maybe she was counting on my grandmother finding it and forwarding it to Alistair."

"That didn't happen either."

"No. And who knows whether my grandmother ever did find it. Maybe it's been hidden in this box all these years. Or maybe she found it and decided not to do anything about it."

"Wow."

Luc refolded the letter and carefully put it back in the box. "Do you think we should give the letter to James?"

She thought for a moment. "I don't know. Is it knowledge he would really want? That his mother wanted to leave her husband for his real father, but then didn't have the courage to act on it. It might be better to let her decision stand, instead of saddling him with a million 'what ifs.'"

"We make love so complicated, don't we?"

She touched the necklace at her throat, and immediately felt Luc's warm lips on her bare shoulder.

"The urge to draw you has passed," he murmured, his lips depositing the words across her back.

A shiver rode down her spine. "I think maybe it's just been overpowered by a stronger urge," she said.

His laugh caused his lips to bounce lightly against her skin. "And should I give into this urge here or take you to our bed?"

"Here. For old time's sake. And because I'd have to get dressed to go back outside."

He ran his finger down her spine again, and the shiver radiated out to embrace her entire torso.

"I don't mind if you draw me or paint me," she whispered. "I kind of like the idea of spending my life being drawn by you. As sad as Alistair and Elizabeth's story turned out, at least the paintings are proof that their love existed. I think it would have been sadder if there had been nothing tangible as a testament to their love."

"Mmm," Luc pulled her back against his chest, wrapped his arms around her. "I'm a Marchand though. My grand-père made hundreds of drawings of my grandmother."

She smiled. "And he was one of the level-headed Marchands. So I guess I should prepare to be immortalized in thousands of drawings."

"At least." He placed his hands over her bare breasts. "Though a few more children might take the pressure off of you."

"You have to be at the birth of the next one."

"I will. I will be there from conception to birth. And after."

Marie laughed against his chest. "Yes, I was hoping you'd be there at conception."

"I won't leave you, Marie. Never."

"If you do, I'll come looking for you."

"I believe Nishi already has that covered."

"Speaking of covered." Marie ran her hands down Luc's thighs. "Aren't you a little overdressed?"

She spun around in his arms and tugged his sweater over his shoulders and head. Her fingers fumbled with the buttons on his jeans until he took over, leaning back and pushing them down his legs. He stretched out on the blanket.

"Take me," he said. "Make love to me."

She straddled his hips and began to run her hands over his chest and arms, drinking in the sight of his body. Then she closed her eyes so she could simply feel him, his firm muscles, his warm skin, beneath her fingers and palms. She felt the rhythm of his chest quicken under her touch. She felt his desire hardening against her. His hands tugged at the underwear still clinging to her hips.

"Please. I need to feel all of you." His voice vibrated with need.

She stripped off her underwear, then his too. She ran her hands along his sides, feeling the rounded edges of his ribs, as his hands cupped her breasts and rolled her nipples between his fingers. He could stoke her desire so quickly, so effortlessly.

His hips began to push up against hers, straining to feel more of her, straining to fill her. He filled her life. Without him, there would be an empty hole in her existence, a need no one else could ever sate. She lifted her hips and took him in her hand, slowly guiding him into her. She teased him, not letting herself settle fully on him.

"Have mercy on me," he groaned in frustration.

One more tease, then she took him in all the way. His lungs emptied in a grateful rush of air, as his hands gripped her hips and began to guide her movements.

"I love you so much," he breathed.

He began to thrust into her harder and faster, pulling her body ever closer to the edge of her desire. His bedroom eyes were dark with passion and focused intently on her, as though he were seeing straight into her soul. The urge to close her own eyes, to not let him see that deeply, was strong. But she kept them open as her body plunged into the freefall of orgasm. Luc cried out as he followed her.

When they stopped falling, he kissed her. His eyes were light with happiness. He gently cupped the back of her head and pulled it down to his chest, cradled it there.

"This is where we belong. Together."

75

Marie peered out of the upstairs bedroom window. It was a beautiful afternoon in May, warm and sunny, more summer than spring. The lawn of Luc's Middleburg home had been transformed. A few dozen white chairs were lined up in rows on the grass. Soft white tulle was draped from chair to chair, creating an aisle that Marie would be walking down in a few minutes.

Her wedding. *Their* wedding.

She couldn't help but reflect on how different this wedding was from her first one to Richard Macintyre. That one had been a military wedding and more a consummation of their families' political alliance than a celebration of love.

Just beyond the rows of white chairs stood a wooden arch, blue delphinium flowers woven into its white lattice. When it came to the color theme of their wedding, blue had been the only choice. *Draw blue.*

She looked down at the flowers in her hands, a bouquet of round blue hydrangea heads. There was one place where they had deviated from the blue theme. Marie touched a finger to the base of her throat. She was wearing the diamond and emerald necklace that had once belonged to Emeline Marchand and Elizabeth Calhoun. As if on cue, she watched James Calhoun take a seat in one of the white chairs.

She felt a hand on her waist and turned her head to see Nishi. The pale blue silk of the bridesmaid's dress draped over her baby bump.

"It's almost show time," Nishi said. "I promise to keep quiet when they ask if anyone has an objection to this marriage."

Marie smiled at her friend's joke. "We deleted that part from the ceremony, just in case."

The opening notes of Pachelbel's Canon wafted up to the room.

"I think that's our cue." Nishi adjusted Marie's veil, then the two of them headed for the stairs.

"I hope I don't trip in this thing," Marie said as she lifted the hem of her gown to step gingerly onto each riser. She got to the bottom of the stairs just in time to see her parents walk outside toward the wedding aisle, followed by Luc's parents. The Marchand clan had flown over for the wedding. The rest of the wedding party waited just inside the door.

"Is Livie okay?" she asked, one last question to Nishi before the wedding party began its processional.

Livie was too young to be an official flower girl so right at that minute, she was standing with her papa at the latticed arch. The plan was for Livie to go stand with Ellie during the vows.

"She's fine. She was like a pro in the rehearsal," Nishi said. And then she was gone to join Sam, Luc's unorthodox choice for best man.

Marie's lips curved into a smile. Her maid of honor had perhaps more faith in toddlers than the mother of the toddler in question. But no matter. She and Luc had been through so much to get here, not even a toddler meltdown could diminish the joy of this day.

Luc tried to quell the nervousness brewing in his chest. He wasn't nervous about marrying Marie. On the contrary, he'd never been more certain of anything in his life. But he had waited for this day for so long—and wanted it so much—he couldn't entirely discount the idea that he might be dreaming it all right now.

He watched as Nishi and Sam began walking toward him, in the aisle between the two sets of chairs. Out of the corner of his eye, he could see his mother's jaw twitch as she turned to watch the two women. Yes, it was a little unorthodox, having a woman as his best man, but Sam was his best friend after Marie. It wasn't like she had hosted a bachelor's party for him or anything. He was too old for that. And in any case, he hadn't been a bachelor in his heart for several years now. He had belonged to Marie—and now Livie—long before this day. A wedding was simply a formality, dotting the i's and crossing the t's on a partnership that already existed.

Valerie and Denis followed a few steps behind and then after them, Jon Randall and Ellie. He and Jon had become rather good friends in recent months, not to mention business partners. Luc and Marie had moved back to Middleburg. Jon ran the Pittsburgh art school now—probably better than Luc ever could. Luc was in the process of opening a second location in Virginia.

The music's volume increased a notch as Jon and Ellie took their places. Ellie gave a tiny wave to Livie, who was standing next to Luc. He gave her tiny hand a slight squeeze. He and Marie had discovered that they could go out on dates—just the two of them—so long as Ellie was the babysitter. Livie's affection for Sam's daughter made him happy.

But nothing made him as happy as the woman who had appeared at the head of the aisle. Happy didn't even begin to do justice to his feelings.

Marie looked positively radiant. She had honored his request not to pull her hair up in some elaborate style that would remind him of "official" Marie Witherspoon. That wasn't the Marie Witherspoon he was marrying. He wanted the relaxed, unscripted, genuine Marie—the one standing at the head of the aisle, alone. She hadn't wanted her father to give her away this time. That part of the ceremony had been a little too real at her first wedding.

Marie wanted to give herself away this time. Luc had no argument with that.

So today her lovely auburn hair hung long and loose about her shoulders, the perfect foil to the emeralds in his grandmother's necklace. She had chosen an ivory gown with simple lines, strapless and with an overlay of delicate French lace on the bodice. The veil sweeping back from her head echoed the lace.

He gently squeezed Livie's hand again. Livie was also wearing an ivory lace dress with blue flowers attached to a barrette in her hair. She squeezed back.

The day couldn't be more perfect, hence his fear that he might be dreaming. The trees were in their spring bloom, budded with bright green leaves. The temperature was warm, as spring often was in the area, but not uncomfortably so. Marie had wanted to wait until June when the weather would have been more reliable, but Luc hadn't been able to wait that long. He had waited long enough. And the waiting was about to be over.

MARIE TOOK her place next to Luc. Livie hesitated a moment, but then Ellie offered her bridesmaid's bouquet to Livie and all was good.

"Flowers. We'll have to remember that," Luc murmured.

Marie's hand found his, strong and warm. Maybe it was retrograde of her, but she liked this Luc—warm, strong, sure of himself. She felt safe with him. She belonged with him.

They faced the officiant and Luc gave a small nod indicating that it was time to begin. Marie said her vows first.

"I choose you, Luc, to be my husband and lover, partner and father to my children. To stand by your side and sleep in your arms. To be joy to your heart and inspiration to your soul. To be both teacher and student as we paint our life together. I promise to laugh with you in good times and be your strength in bad. Today I pledge to love you always, in darkness and in light."

Chiaroscuro. Light and dark. They had lived through a darkness borne of fear and insecurity. There might be more darkness ahead in life, but today was about their light. Their love.

Marie slid the gold wedding band onto his ring finger. He repeated the vows they had written and then fished from his pocket her ring. His hand was steady as he slipped the small band on her finger. He pulled Marie into his arms and kissed her.

As their lips touched, he heard the officiant say, "I now pronounce you man and wife." Luc didn't need to wait for the words. He had already waited his entire life to belong to this woman. His goddess. His déesse.

Thanks for reading THE SENATOR'S WIFE!
If you're in the mood for more romantic women's fiction with take-charge heroines and sexy heroes, check out NEXT TO YOU and BACK TO US …

Go behind the scenes at Phlox Beauty, the hot beauty brand where the women are the alpha CEOs!

NEXT TO YOU...

Phlox Miller was never the pretty girl and no magic mascara or secret serum was ever going to change that—not even one manufactured by her own company. When an accident at her country home burns her face and body, she spares no expense on her recovery and plastic surgery. Now she turns heads on the street, but can't recognize herself in the mirror.

Jared Connor lost his innocence at the age of ten when his father poured gasoline around the family home and left his two young sons to die in the flames. Now an adult, he's carefully crafted a pretend life where he can hide his scars and his death row father behind the disguise of a caretaker's pickup truck and a pair of gardening shears. But when a beautiful woman with scars of her own barges into his quiet, solitary life, Jared finds it increasingly difficult to hide from what he really wants.

"Phlox and Jared have earned their space as one of my favorite fictional couples"—reader

BACK TO US …

The daughter of an actress, Zee Malisewski grew up on movie sets and in boarding schools. As an adult, she's built a life away from all that—and a successful cosmetics business with her best friend—in New York City. Men? They've come and gone. Mostly gone. She's sworn off the male species anyway, after her latest boyfriend tampers with her company's new product and nearly destroys everything she and her business partner have spent years working for. Now Zee wants a home of her own and she's done waiting for Prince Charming to show up and share it with her.

Adventure journalist Colt Buchanan grabbed his own bootstraps and yanked hard—leaving the poverty of his rural hometown behind for a scholarship to a fancy east coast college and then the bright lights of the big city. But when an assignment in the Middle East leaves his interview subject dead and Colt's memory riddled with holes you can drive a bus through, he comes back to the only place that's ever felt like home—the Manhattan apartment of a pretty Hollywood princess he never had any business wanting.

Can there be a second chance at love for a man who can't remember … and a woman determined not to forget?

ABOUT THE AUTHOR

Julia Gabriel writes contemporary romance that is smart, sexy, and emotionally-intense (grab the tissues). She lives in New England where she is a full-time mom to a teenager, as well as a sometime writing professor and obsessive quilter (is there any other kind?). If all goes well, she'll be a Parisienne in her next life. Her books have been selected as "Top Picks" by RT Book Reviews, and critics at RT Book Reviews, Kirkus, and others have called her work "nuanced," "heart-wrenching and emotional," "well-crafted contemporary romance," and "deeply moving storytelling."

Be the first to find out about new books and more by signing up for my email newsletter!

Say "hello" on social media ...

ALSO BY JULIA GABRIEL

St. Caroline Series

Hearts on Fire

Two of Hearts

Summer Again

Phlox Beauty Series

Next to You

Back to Us

Pink Diamonds (bonus scene)

Made in the USA
Middletown, DE
29 June 2019